Praise for the Morganville Vampires series

'A first-class storyteller'
Charlaine Harris, author of the True Blood series

'Thrilling, sexy, and funny! These books are addictive.
One of my very favourite vampire series'
Richelle Mead, author of the Vampire Academy series

'We'd suggest dumping Stephenie Meyer's vapid Twilight books
and replacing them with these'
SFX Magazine

'Ms Caine uses her dazzling storytelling skills to
share the darkest chapter yet . . . An engrossing read that
once begun is impossible to set down'
Darque Reviews

'A fast-paced, page-turning read packed with wonderful
characters and surprising plot twists. Rachel Caine is an
engaging writer; readers will be completely absorbed in this
chilling story, unable to put it down until the last page'
Flamingnet

'If you love to read about characters with whom you can get
deeply involved, Rachel Caine is so far a one hundred per cent
sure bet to satisfy that need'
The Eternal Night

'A rousing horror thriller that adds a new dimension
to the vampire mythos . . . An electrifying, enthralling
coming-of-age supernatural tale'
Midwest Book Review

'A solid paranormal mystery and action plot line
that will entertain adults as well as teenagers. The story line
has several twists and turns that will keep readers
of any age turning the pages'
LoveVampires

PRINCE OF SHADOWS

RACHEL CAINE

Allison & Busby Limited
12 Fitzroy Mews
London W1T 6DW
www.allisonandbusby.com

First published in Great Britain by Allison & Busby in 2014.
Published by arrangement with NAL Signet, a member of Penguin Group
(USA) LLC

A CIP catalogue record for this book is available from
the British Library.

First Edition

ISBN 978-0-7490-1513-8

Typeset in 10/15 pt Sabon by
Allison & Busby Ltd.

The paper used for this Allison & Busby publication
has been produced from trees that have been legally sourced
from well-managed and credibly certified forests.

Printed and bound by
CPI Group (UK) Ltd, Croydon, CR0 4YY

RACHEL CAINE is the author of over thirty novels, including the bestselling Morganville Vampires series. She was born at White Sands Missile Range, which people who know her say explains a lot. She has been an accountant, an insurance investigator and a professional musician, and has played with such musical legends as Henry Mancini, Peter Nero and John Williams. She and her husband, fantasy artist R. Cat Conrad, live in Texas with their iguana Pop-eye, a mali uromastyx named (appropriately) O'Malley, and a leopard tortoise named Shelley (for the poet, of course).

www.rachelcaine.com

To Tybalt, and wonderful fellow author Seanan McGuire (aka Mira Grant, also), whose tweet about him led me to think she was writing a Romeo and Juliet–related story from his POV.

That made me think about this story, but then, of course, I couldn't write it because she was already writing an alternate-viewpoint R&J story.

Luckily, it turned out she wasn't writing that story at all, Tybalt was a cat, and I got to write mine. Hence: Prince of Shadows.

Thanks, Seanan. And Tybalt. You both rock.

PROLOGUE

I stood in the dark corner of my enemy's house, and thought of murder. In his bed, Tybalt Capulet snored and drooled like a toothless old woman. I marvelled as I thought of how the women of Verona – from dewy-eyed maids to dignified ladies – fell swooning in his wake. If they could see him like this (a drunken, undignified mess in sodden linen), they'd run shrieking to the arms of their fathers and husbands.

It would make a good, vivid story to retell, but only among my closest and dearest.

I turned a dagger restlessly in my gloved hand, feeling that murderous tingle working its way through my veins, but I was no assassin. I was not here to kill. I'd come stealthily into his house, into his rooms, for a purpose.

Tybalt, the heir of Capulet, swaggered the streets of Verona and used wit like weapons; that was nothing new among our class of young cocks. He was never above offering insults, to low or high, when opportunity came. Today he'd offended my house. House Montague.

The victim was a serving girl. Insults to servants didn't call for open challenges from those of my station, but still, it pricked me, seeing the self-satisfied grin on Tybalt's face as he emerged from that rank little alcove where he'd reduced her to tears; I'd seen her run from him red-faced, holding the tattered rags of her clothes together. He'd injured the girl only to prove his contempt for my house, and that required an answer.

It required revenge, and that was something that I, Benvolio Montague, would serve him – not in the streets in open war, but here, in the dark. Tonight I was clad head to toe in disguise, and there was nothing about me to indicate my station, or my house. Tonight I was a thief – the best thief in Verona. They called me the Prince of Shadows. For three years I had stolen from my peers without being caught, and tonight . . . tonight would be no different.

Except that it *was* different. My hands felt hot and restless. So easy to drag a dagger across that hated throat, but murder spawned murder, and I didn't want to kill Tybalt. There had been enough of that between our two houses; the streets ran slick with spilt blood. No . . . I wanted to humiliate him. I wanted to knock him from his perch as the man of the hour.

I had the will, and the access. All that remained now was to choose how to hurt him best. Tybalt was the God-crowned heir of Capulet; he was rich, indulged, and careless. I needed to wound him where it counted – in the eyes of his family, and preferably in the eyes of all Verona.

Ah. I spotted a gleam as something caught the light on the floor. I crossed to the corner, where he'd dumped a tangle of clothing, and found the jewelled emblem pinned to his doublet – a gaudy piece in Capulet colours, one that would feed even a well-done by merchant family for a year. No doubt he'd underpaid for it, as well; Tybalt was more likely to terrify honest men into bargains than to pay fairly. I added the prize to my purse, and then drew Tybalt's rapier from its sheath, slowly and carefully. It came free with a soft, singing ring of steel, and I turned it in the moonlight, assessing the quality. Very fine, and engraved with his name and crest. A lovely weapon. A *personal* weapon.

He did not deserve such a beautiful thing.

I sheathed it and belted it on, opposite my own rapier. As the heir of Capulet snored, drunken and oblivious, I pulled off my black cap and bowed with perfect form, just the way I would have been honour-bound to greet him if we'd had the mischance to meet on the street. Under the breath-moistened black silk of my mask, I was smiling, but it felt more like a grimace.

'Good night, sweet prince, thou poxy son of a dog,' I whispered. Tybalt smacked his lips, mumbled drunkenly, and rolled over. In seconds he was snoring again, loud as a grinding wheel against a knife.

I slipped out of the door of his apartments, past his equally dozy servant, and considered my exit from the Capulet palace. The obvious way was to return as I'd entered, but I'd come in during the height of the busy afternoon, carrying a box of supplies from a provisioner's wagon. I'd spent the day admiring the brickwork of the Capulet cellars. Going out the same way was unlikely; the kitchen door was almost certainly locked and guarded now.

Out through the narrow gardens, then. Once I was beyond the wall's high stone barrier, I would be just another bravo on the moonlit streets, making for my bed.

I went up the stairs, taking them two at a time; my soft leather shoes made no sound on the polished marble. I'd worn grey to blend into the ever-present stone and brick of Verona; in the shadows, there was nothing better in which to disappear. Even here, inside the quiet house, it was a reasonably good disguise. I ghosted past murky squares of paintings upon the walls, and a candelabrum with two still-burning tapers (a true sign of family wealth); the tapestry at the top of the stairs was rich and very tempting to steal, but too heavy, and I had enough trophies already.

Upstairs was women's country. Lady Capulet would have the largest and most lavish quarters, to the right – the grand palace was almost a mirror of my own family's, in many ways. That meant the girls would have the smaller apartments to the left – the oldest, Rosaline, said to be studious and bookish, was probably well asleep by now. She'd have the far rooms, since she was only a cousin, not the lady's own daughter. She was Tybalt's sister, arrived in Verona only a few months before, and kept shut up hard in the palace. I'd heard a rumour she was nothing like her loathsome brother, at least; that was to her credit.

There was no servant on duty at her door, and when I tried it, I found it unlocked. A trusting lot, these Capulets, at least within their own walls. I slipped the latch and stepped quietly inside, only to find that the room wasn't as dark as I'd hoped. There was a low-burning fire crackling on the hearth, and a candle flickering on the table. It scarcely mattered if the girl had left lights burning, as the bed curtains were pulled. She'd hear and see nothing through the thick coverings. I took reasonable care not to allow the floor to creak as I crossed it, and I was almost to the window when I realised that I had erred.

Badly.

Rosaline Capulet was not in bed. She was, instead, perched in a chair on the far side of the table, reading a slim book.

I saw her before she saw me. Candlelight dusted her skin with gold, and flickered in her large, dark eyes; her neck was swan-graceful, and her slender hands cupped the spine of the volume with care. She wore a simple lawn nightgown. I could make out the shadowed curves of her body beneath the white fabric. She had put her midnight dark hair into a long braid for the night, and was thoughtfully twirling one end of it as she read.

No one had warned me she was beautiful.

She saw me in that next second, and shot to her bare feet in alarm. The book thumped down on the table, and I expected her to scream the house down around our ears; it was the usual response from a maiden surprised in her chamber by a masked stranger.

Instead, she took in a deep breath, then let it slowly out.

'What do you mean here? Who are you?' she asked. I was surprised by the steadiness of her voice. Her fists were clenched tightly, and I could see she trembled, but her gaze was clear and her chin firm. Not fearless, but brave. Very brave.

I put my finger to my masked lips in a request for a lower volume. She didn't respond, so I said softly, 'You may call me the Prince of Shadows, lady.'

That sparked interest in her expression, and a new light in her eyes. 'I've heard rumours. You exist!'

'Thus far.'

'I dismissed the tales of you as drunkard's gossip. I've heard such an array of deeds I hardly know what it is you do.'

'Thieving,' I said. 'That is what I do.'

'Why?' It might have sounded like a foolish question, but there was a sharp intelligence behind it, and I waited for the rest of it. 'You're no starving beggar. Your clothes are too fine. Your mask is silk. You've no need of stolen gold.'

She was not only brave, but unnaturally self-possessed. Mine was the upper hand, but I was beginning to wonder whether that might last only a moment. 'I enjoy taking from those who have too much,' I said. 'Those who deserve to lose for their arrogance.'

She stood very still, watching me, and then slowly inclined her head. 'Then it follows you stole from someone in this house. Whom did you make your victim this night?'

It was a test, I realised. She had her standards, and her favourites. But I refused to lie, damn any consequences. 'Tybalt,' I said. 'He's a bully and a fool. Few deserve a comedown more; don't you agree?'

The tension in her relaxed. She didn't smile, but there was a slight lift at the corners of her mouth, as if she felt tempted. 'Tybalt is my brother, and a dangerous man,' Rosaline said. 'You should take to your legs before he steals something more precious from you than you have from him.'

'I take your meaning, and it has wisdom,' I said, and gave her a bow cut even deeper than I'd given her brother, and a great deal more sincere. 'You have a kind and generous spirit.'

'Never kind, and no kin of yours, sir,' she said. She

sat down at her table again, and picked up her book, and pretended to ignore me. It was a good act, but I saw the tension crinkling the corners of her eyes. 'Go quickly. I've already forgotten you.'

I gave her another bow, and opened the shutters to her window. Beyond was a balcony, overlooking the small walled garden; it was a startlingly lush Eden set in the heart of heavy stone. A fountain played in the centre, sprinkling gentle music over the night. No bravos strolled in sight, though I knew the Capulets employed many. Tybalt hadn't been in his cups alone this murky evening.

I climbed over the balustrade, clung for a moment to the edge, and then dropped the long distance to a soft flower bed below. Luridly flowering irises snapped and pulped under my feet, and the thick, sweet aroma clung to me as I raced forward. In a heartbeat I scaled the wall, dropped into the street, shook off the dirt and manure, and began what I hoped was a calm and untroubled walk toward the Piazza delle Erbe.

I'd only just removed my mask and folded it into my purse when I heard the smack of boots on stone, and two of the city watch turned the corner ahead, dressed in the livery of the ruler of Verona, Prince Escalus. Both bore heavy arms, as they should in the dark streets, lest their wives wake to find themselves widows. The men cut a course in my direction. When the moonlight caught my face, they slowed, and bowed.

'Sir Montague,' the taller one said. 'You stand in danger here. You're in Capulet territory, and walking alone. Unwise, sir. Very unwise.'

I stumbled to a halt, as unsteady as if I'd been into

Tybalt's wine cellar instead of his apartments. 'So it would be, good fellows, save I'm not alone. Montague never walks alone.'

'Faith, he's most certainly not,' said a new voice, and I heard footsteps approaching behind me. I turned to see the familiar form of my best friend, Mercutio, who doubtless *had* been imbibing, and heavily. He slung an arm around my neck for support. 'Benvolio Montague is never alone in a fight while I draw breath! What now, you rogues, do you need a thrashing to teach you manners?'

'Sirs,' the guard said, with just a shade less patience. 'We are the city's men. A quarrel with us is a quarrel with the prince of Verona. Best you turn your steps to more congenial streets. Besides, the hour is very late.'

I let out a laugh that might well have been fuelled by raw wine. 'Did you hear that, Mercutio? The hour's late!' It was the first line of a popular – not very polite – drinking song, and he instantly joined in for a rousing chorus. Neither of us was musical. It provided great theatre as the two of us staggered in the direction of the Montague palace, drawing angry and sleepy curses from windows we passed.

The watchmen let us go with rueful shakes of their heads, well glad to be rid of us.

Mercutio dropped the song after we'd passed the piazza's beautiful statue, the *Madonna Verona,* as armed soldiers stationed in front of the overblown Palazzo Maffei watched us pass. He didn't take his arm from my neck, so he truly was drunk enough to need the support, but he had the sense to keep his voice down. 'So? How fared your venture?'

I dug the jewelled emblem of the Capulets from my purse and handed it over; he whistled sharply and turned it in the moonlight, admiring the faceted shine before slipping it into his purse. 'I have more,' I said, and drew Tybalt's rapier, which I tossed up in the air. Mercutio – even drunk – was a better swordsman than I, and he snatched it out of the sky with catlike grace. He examined the elegant blade with a delicate brush of his fingers.

'Sometimes I think your skills come from a lower place than heaven,' he said very seriously, and patted my cheek. 'The emblem we can sell, if we break it to gold and stones, but this . . .'

'It's not for sale,' I said. 'I want it.'

'For what?'

I smiled, feeling fierce and free and wild in ways that no one would ever believe of the quiet, solid, responsible Benvolio Montague. At night I could be something else than what my city, my station, and my family required. 'I don't know yet,' I said. 'But I promise you it will be the talk of the city.'

The next day, Tybalt Capulet's sword was found driven an inch deep into the heavy oak of a tavern door. Pinned to it was a ribald verse that detailed a highly entertaining story about Tybalt, a pig, and acts not generally condoned by either the Church or right-thinking sheepherders. It was a good day.

It was the beginning of the end of the good days.

QUARTO

I

Two months later

It was hot in my grandmother's rooms, as it always was, no matter the season. A fire blazed in the hearth, and from the heat it gave off it might have been kindled by the breath of Satan himself. I'd shed my half cloak before coming, but even so, sweat soaked through my hose and created damp, uncomfortable patches under the heavy velvet doublet. As I waited and suffered, a chambermaid put another log on the flames, and I felt sweat run down my face like tears.

The summons to attend my grandmother had come unexpectedly, and now I only hoped to escape quickly. There was no real chance of managing it unscathed.

She gazed at me with her most typical expression of assessment and disdain. Those of any generation younger than her own would never entirely find approval, but I, at least, escaped with only her mildest contempt. Her eyes were sharp, bitter, the faded colour of an ice-grey sky, and her face was the texture of weathered old oak. Family legend said she'd once been beautiful, but I couldn't believe it. She looked as wrinkled as an apple left too long in a dark corner of the cellar.

'I summoned you near an hour past,' she announced in her high, brittle voice, and coughed. A chambermaid rushed forward to wipe her lips with a soft linen handkerchief, then artfully folded it to hide the telltale bloodstain.

'My apologies, Grandmother,' I said, and offered her a very deep bow. 'I was with Master Silvio.' Master Silvio was our blademaster, charged with teaching the young men of Montague the skills necessary for survival in Verona. Grandmother sniffed and dismissed my excuse impatiently with a wave of her hand.

'I trust you've improved,' she said. 'There's no place for indifferent blades on the streets with Capulet's bravos always prowling for trouble.'

I smiled, just a little. 'I'm improving, I think.' Not from Master Silvio's tutelage; Mercutio had been drilling me in the finer points that Master Silvio, for all his reputation, still lacked.

'Do you think I summoned you to discuss your progress at men's silly games?' She gave me an ice-cold, stern look. 'It may interest you to hear your cousin has gone mad.'

'Which one?' Madness was always to be feared, but Grandmother's meaning had less to do with devils in one's head than her own expectations of our behaviour.

She slammed the point of her cane on the floor for emphasis. 'Who do you think, boy? The *important* one. Romeo. And I blame you, Benvolio.'

I stiffened my spine and tried to think what it was that I might have done to deserve that comment. I was often the one who ended escapades; I rarely started them. Such censure seemed unfair.

'If I've offended, I will apologise,' I said, and managed to hold her gaze stoutly, if not fearlessly. 'But I know not how I might be to blame.'

'You are the oldest of your cousins, and it is your responsibility to present a good moral example.' She said it as if she had the slightest idea of what a good moral example might be. That alone made me want to laugh, but it would be suicidal at best. The stories told of Grandmother's misspent youth were legendary. It was miraculous she'd avoided the cloister, or worse.

'I do my best.' I tried to imagine myself with a glowing halo over my head, like one of the gilded angels on a church wall, but from the snap of anger in her, I fell short.

'Are you mocking me, boy?' she asked sharply, and leant forward in her chair with a creak of old bones and older wood. Her voice dropped to a poisonous hiss. 'Do you dare mock *me*?'

'No.' I truly meant that. No one sane offered her direct insult. No one living could claim to have survived it.

She sat back with a doubting grunt and a frown. 'If not mockery, then that gleam in your callow face must be hate.'

Of course it was. I hated her. We all hated her, and we feared her, too. There was no one in our world more dangerous than my grandmother, the Iron Lady, La Signora di Ferro . . . no Capulet, no prince, no priest or bishop or pope could hope to aspire to such heights of loathing and fear.

But I'd never be stupid enough to admit it. 'I am ever devoted to you, Grandmother, as are we all.' I was a good liar. It was a requirement for living in the palace.

She snorted, little misled. 'So you should be, idiot. I

sometimes think I am the only Montague still possessed of any sense at all. Weak men and foolish women, that's what we have now.' She pierced me with that cold, alien stare again. 'Your cousin is either mad or sinfully stupid, and it is your responsibility to stop him from making a mockery of his station and this house. He is the heir, and he *must* be kept in line. Is that plainly understood?'

This was the dangerous part of the interview, I realised; the old witch might overlook polite falsehoods, but she could smell an evasion like a vulture scenting rot. 'With the greatest of respect, I am not sure such a thing is possible,' I said. 'Romeo's young. With youth comes folly; it's to be expected.'

That drew a bitter bark of a laugh from her. 'Oh, yes, you're an entire *year* older than Romeo. Such a lofty perch from which to pass judgment, young man. But you've never been foolish; I'll give you that much. You've got ice in your veins. I think you get it from your foreign mother.'

I'd have given my soul for ice in my veins just then. The overpowering heat of the room was like a hug from the devil. My doublet was soaked through, and I felt sweat running through my hair like blood. Sweet Jesu, the maid was putting another log on the fire. The room stank of hot flesh and the doggy odour of overheated wool, and the old woman's sickly perfume.

And she should not have mentioned my mother.

'Romeo is not merely foolish; nonsense I can forgive,' she said after the long silence. 'There are whispers that he writes poetry to an enemy's wench. That is the very definition of insanity, and it threatens to make our house a laughing stock, and that is not acceptable.' Her aged, claw-like fingers tightened on the arms of her chair . . . no ordinary chair, that one, with its mismatched woods and heavy backing. She'd had it made when she was still a young Lady Montague, and legend said – I believed it – that she'd caused it to be built from the broken doors of her enemies' palaces. Their villas lay empty now, inhabited only by shadows and shades, and she had made a trophy of their once-strong barricades on which to rest her backside.

We feared Grandmother for a reason.

Romeo, writing poetry. Knowing him, I could believe it, though he hadn't told me he'd done something so foolhardy. 'If such is true, he's only fevered with infatuation. It will soon pass.'

'Pass, will it?' She shivered, snapped her fingers, and a maid rushed forward to place a fur-lined cloak over her knees as the fire sizzled on, melting me in misery. 'And how if I told you that he was writing his scribbles to a *Capulet*?'

I couldn't keep the surprise from my face. 'What? Which?'

'Rosaline, I hear. The plain one.' She dismissed Rosaline with an impatient flick of her fingers; I did not. I'd met the girl that dark-drowned night months back. She was someone to be taken quite seriously. 'If he's fevered with love, his fever may well infect and sicken this entire house. I charge you to deliver him from this – you and the Ordelaffi boy, Mercutio. He's sensible enough, and ever eager for a fight should it come to blades. One thing is certain: if there have been verses exchanged, you must get them back. It won't do to have the heir of Montague made into a street joke.' She speared me with a significant, evil look. 'I know of your night-time ventures, boy, and I have allowed it because it suited me. Now you may run on my leash for a time. Get his letters from the girl. Quietly.'

Somehow, I found I was not surprised Grandmother knew of my secret career as the Prince of Shadows. 'And if I don't wish to be leashed?'

In the silence, I listened to logs sizzle and pop. The servants had all gone still and silent, their gazes fixed on me with avid interest. No one stood up to the old witch. I had no idea what had prompted me to, save the reference to my mother.

'Then, Benvolio Montague,' she said quietly, 'you may yet come to the attention of Prince Escalus's men. I hear they urgently seek a certain sneak thief.'

'You wouldn't. It would humiliate our house, and my uncle.'

She shrugged. 'Perhaps your uncle could use bringing to heel as well. But only do this for me, boy, and I'll keep your secret. Your cousin protected, your own reputation unsullied – surely you can stretch yourself to the task.'

'Surely,' I said. She had me in a trap, and short of gnawing off my own limb I couldn't hope for escape.

She took that as agreement, for which I was thankful. 'And remember, from now on, you will be responsible for Romeo and any lapses in judgment. It's been agreed.'

I did not want to be made responsible for Romeo's misadventures. This week it was forbidden love for a cousin of our greatest enemies. The next fortnight might bring something wholly new and even more addled. I had no wish to be hovering at his shoulder like Grandmother's notion of a guardian angel . . . but from the implacable look in her eyes, I had very little choice. Again.

I hoped that somewhere in the sweating shadows of this room lurked powerful angels of my very own, because disappointing La Signora di Ferro was a very dangerous game, even for a Montague of the blood. I was not the most favoured child of the house – Romeo held that honour, as principal heir. I was the older one, the sane one, the stable one. The one born of a doubtful foreign mother.

The one to whom it fell to clear up Montague's messes. Small wonder I took out my frustrations at night, in the dark, by stealing from those I hated. What other outlet could I have?

My grandmother sat back now on her throne of broken doors, and gave me what she must have fancied would be a reassuring smile. It would have made a demon shudder. 'Then that's done, and I'll hear of no more nonsense about your cousin. Now, tell me, child, what gossip bring you today? What's the talk of the square?'

My grandmother still lived for gossip, and we were all charged with providing it upon command. As a cousin, even a minor one, I had little to do but haunt the public spaces of Verona, seeing and being seen. Even though I had scant interest in market whispers, I could not help hearing them. 'I'm told that the prince has a new mistress,' I said, and her eyes turned avid. 'She's said to be quite sophisticated. From Venezia, they say.'

'Pah, Venezia! The moral cesspit of Italy,' she said, but I knew she enjoyed that titbit. 'A woman no better than a whore, and he dares parade her before decent women! Have you met the baggage?'

I'd seen the fabled mistress at a distance; she had been carried through the streets in a sedan chair to mass, where no doubt she'd confessed all her sins and been forgiven. A pity that such forgiveness never extended beyond church walls. 'No, Grandmother, I have not met her.'

'Good! It isn't healthy for a strapping young man to be

introduced to whores at your age, before you've even settled on a wife. Speaking of that, has your useless mother seen no progress on making you a match?'

My mother ignored insults aimed at her and shrugged them off, and I tried to as well, though on some very deep and quiet level I still felt the sting. I think La Signora thrust in the needle once more to see whether I would react.

I had not in years. Outwardly.

'She continues to review the candidates presented,' I said. She'd paraded several girls in front of me over the past few months, none of whom I wished to see again; the interesting ones, it seemed, were all tainted by virtue of being interesting. 'I expect I'll be married off and thoroughly bored within the year.'

'Good, good. All men's blood runs too hot, and the apostle said that it is better to marry than to burn.'

Faith, I wished she wouldn't talk of burning; the heat was killing me faster than a sword in the guts. When I bowed this time, sweat ran in a drip from my nose to the carpets underfoot. I half imagined I could hear the stone sizzling underneath as it soaked up the moisture. 'I'm expected elsewhere, Grandmother. If I may have your leave?'

'Off to carouse with your useless friends, are you? Go, then. Go keep an eye on your bibbling cousin before he does something dramatic concerning the Capulet wench. Do you think she's stupid enough to respond to him? I've heard she's odd.'

I shrugged. 'I hear she's bound for the convent – over schooled. Belike she thinks it very flattering.'

'Until her brother beats the nonsense out of her,' said my grandmother. 'Of course, if he finds the letters, he may well dispense with the beating and just wall her up in the cellars, the way old Pietro Capulet did her great-aunt Sophia.' It was a favourite bedtime story of hers . . . the gruesome horror of being bricked up in a lavishly appointed room, with only a pitcher of water and a dagger for company. Once the water had gone, Sophia most likely would have sought the dagger's point for her final comfort, but as a boy I had imagined her wasting to skin and bones as she clawed at the ice-cold walls of her prison. The dreams still haunted me.

I should not have cared if it happened to any Capulet; most of Montague would jeer and rejoice. But I remembered the brave, quiet girl Rosaline, bathed in candlelight, facing down the Prince of Shadows, and I found, to my shame, that I *did* care.

My grandmother was waiting for some response, but I gave none. She finally flicked her fingers at me in weary contempt. 'Go on, then. Be off with you.'

'Yes, Grandmother.' I knew better than to ignore an invitation to flee, and so I did, bowing deeply on my way out. I escaped through the thick, ancient doors, which boomed shut behind me as servants muscled them into place.

Freedom.

I leant against the stone wall to suck in the clean, cool air. I imagined I could see steam curling up from my sweat-soaked clothes, as if I'd escaped like Shadrach from the fire.

'Hsst!'

I looked in the direction of the low sound, and saw a shadow lurking near the conjunction of the walls. A stray bit of sunlight from a high, barred window picked out skirts too rich for a servant's, and a gleam of a jewel on a headpiece.

It seemed my fair younger sister wanted to speak with me. The day wasn't yet trying enough.

'Honest women don't hide in shadows, Veronica.' I let my head drop back hard against the stone. The ache of the impact temporarily drove away my sweaty discomfort, but not my sister . . . almost fifteen, vaguely pretty, and as deadly as a snake.

'I'm hiding from *her,* of course. She wishes to instruct me on the nature of wifely duties.' Veronica grabbed me by the collar of my doublet and pulled me around the corner, into the shadows. She let go with a sound of disgust. 'Ugh, are you poxed? You're as sweaty as a labourer!'

'Shall I go tell her that you need no instruction on wifely duties? I imagine you could write a philosopher's pamphlet on the subject already.'

'Pig!' She tried to slap me, but I caught her hand an inch from my face.

'I won't pretend you are pure as the Virgin if you won't pretend to care. If you are set on avoiding Grandmother, why come here at all?'

'Mother was concerned. She sent for you an hour ago, and bade me find you.'

'As did Grandmother. Which would you obey first?'

Ronnie snapped open a feather fan and batted it with great energy. 'Did the old witch talk about me?'

'Why would she? She's made you a fine match. You're no longer of interest.'

'She's marrying me off to an old man!'

'A wealthy old man,' I said. 'In ill health. You'll be a fortune-heavy widow before twenty, with a long future of dalliance before you.'

'Easy for you to say. You'll not be the one he'll paw in the marriage bed.' She eyed me over the fan with wicked intensity. 'Or perhaps you'd prefer that, Ben. Given the company you keep—'

I pushed her against the wall in a flash, and she hardly had time for a startled squawk before I sealed her mouth with my palm. I put my lips very close to her ear and said, 'Before you run your clever tongue about my friends, remember the boy they hanged last winter. Claiming someone a sodomite is no joking matter, Ronnie. Say it again, and I'll swear to teach you better manners.'

She shoved me back with sudden, furious strength. There were spots of red high in her cheeks, and her eyes glittered, but she lowered her voice just the same. 'It's the same penalty for me if they hear you jesting about how *expert* I am in wifely duties! Or perhaps they'll take pity on me and put me in a convent's cell, where I shall never see the sun again. Or did you forget?'

'No,' I said. 'Neither should you.'

'You are my brother! How is it that you don't protect me with as much passion as your companions? They say women may fall when there's no strength in men, you know! Perhaps my lack of moral quality is *your* fault.'

I walked away. Sister though she was, I didn't much care for Veronica; girls were raised far differently, and separately, and what I knew of her I didn't savour. The sooner she was married off, the better for us all.

I heard a rustle of fabric, and looked back to find Veronica hurrying to follow me. Her stiff skirts brushed the walls in a constant hiss. 'Wait!'

'For what? I've nothing else to say to you.'

She raised her voice to a carrying, malicious volume.

'That's not what you whispered in my ear last night, brother. Why, the things you said . . .'

I swung around on her, and she quickly danced back out of reach, eyes bright and malicious. 'Well,' she purred. 'That begged your attention, didn't it?'

'I'm warning you, Ronnie, sharpen your claws on another.' Despite the urge to strike her, I didn't. Engaging with Veronica was a hazardous business when there were no witnesses to prove my case, especially should she make some outrageous accusation. I'd seen her make malicious sport of others, to their ruin; she'd never yet done it to family, but it took little to taint a man's reputation, or a woman's, and I would not take the risk.

She was terrifying, and she was not even fifteen.

I walked away, well aware she was still scurrying after me.

I slowed as I took a sharp right turn, and the hall vaulted upward into an open atrium, with the sun pouring down to spark sparse, precious flowers into bursts of colour against the marble flagging. There was not so much risk here, as Romeo's own father, the head of Montague and most often simply known by the family's name, limped restlessly at the other end of the garden; from the look of him, his gout was bothering him yet again. I took a seat on a marble bench commemorating the death of some long-forgotten uncle or other.

Veronica drew to a stop, staring at me as her corseted breasts heaved for air. 'You lack the grace of a gentleman,' she said. 'Sprawling like a boy when a lady should be seated.'

'I would offer my place if a *lady* presented herself,' I said, but grudgingly moved over to make room for her huge skirts. She was wearing a dress too hot-tempered for the day, but my sister wished always to be noticed. Vanity before comfort. 'You'll be punished for avoiding La Signora's summons. She enjoys her little lectures on morality, and she doesn't like to be kept waiting.'

Veronica made use of her feather fan again, as if her hasty pursuit had made her faint with effort. 'I'll give a female excuse,' she said. 'She dotes on them. It makes a girl seem pleasingly fragile.'

I cut her a glance. 'You're as fragile as a barbarian's broadsword.'

She gave me a knife-sharp smile from a flutter of peacock tails. 'I've yet to see a barbarian close enough to examine his broadsword.'

I was hard-pressed not to smile. Veronica could be occasionally – *very* occasionally – amusing.

'Did Grandmother summon you about Romeo?'

I frowned at her this time. 'And if you avoided her apartments, how could you possibly know that?'

'Oh, her ladies gossip,' Veronica said. 'Romeo claims to be perishing for love of the fair Rosaline, you know.' She added to that an overdone pantomime of swooning, so realistic that I had to resist the urge to grab her to keep her from slipping from the bench. Since I *did* resist, Veronica was forced to pull herself back upright with an ungraceful flailing of arms and legs.

My annoying sister might be worth something, after all. 'You know Rosaline, do you not?'

Veronica looked cross, and the fan beat faster. 'She's a cow, that one. Fancies herself above us. She dresses as badly as a servant and pretends it to be some sort of virtue. She spends her hours *reading,* of all things. Even nuns don't *read.* It isn't decent!'

'Is she beautiful?' I knew the answer, but it was a question a man might ask who stood in ignorance. And I knew it would bait more information from my vain sister.

'I suppose she's regular enough of feature, but she doesn't bother to flatter it at all. One can't be beautiful if one works so hard at being plain. Reading gives her wrinkles, you know, around the eyes.' Veronica loved to rain scorn upon a girl's hair, or eyes, or skin, or stature, or figure . . . but seemed to have little to say about Rosaline at all. In her own terms, it was something akin to praise.

'But you'd say she's pretty enough to keep Romeo spinning.'

Veronica snapped the fan together and batted me on the shoulder with it. 'It's *Romeo*. He'd swoon over a dancing bear if it wore a skirt. If you wish to protect him, tell his father to see him safely married off before some scandal of his bursts like a boil.'

'You sound much like Grandmother,' I said, which earned me another, more forceful blow of the closed fan.

'That is very cruel, Benvolio.'

'Kind!' I responded.

'Kind as the very devil.' She rose and stalked away, skirts brushing the servants out of her way as she went like dust before a broom. A sister like Veronica, and a cousin like Romeo. What had I done to deserve so much trouble?

Romeo failed to show his face at dinner, and his absence was noted, with chill precision, by his mother, Lady Montague. She asked me, rather too loudly, whether I had news of him. I responded truthfully that I did not.

My dinner was not made any more savoury by the looks

given me by my own mother, who seemed to feel that I should leave the table and go in immediate search of my cousin.

I kept my seat. No one specifically ordered me to the search, and I was well aware it was a fool's errand. Romeo would appear if and when he wished. I'd been charged with his moral reformation only in late afternoon, after all. I could hardly be blamed if he went straying the same evening.

The nuts had been placed on the table, and my uncle Montague was well into his fourth cup of wine and loudly declaiming on politics when Romeo at last stumbled into the hall. I say *stumbled* as an accurate description; he tripped on a rug, skidded, and grabbed onto a servant to stay upright. The servant noisily dropped a tray containing the sticky remains of roast pork, and Romeo immediately pushed away, heading with speed but not precision towards the table. As always, he left damage in his wake.

'*You're* not Veronica,' he said to me as he poured himself into his usual chair. 'Ronnie usually sits there, and she's far prettier company.'

'She's out of favour with Grandmother,' I said.

'For what?'

'Ignoring her summons.'

He laughed with wine-fuelled good humour. 'Good for Ronnie. If we didn't bow and scrape so much to the old witch, life would be infinitely sweeter.' Romeo balanced his chair up on two wavering legs, and spotted Veronica sitting at the far end of the table with our youngest and most disfavoured country cousins. She looked mutinous and flushed, and Romeo gave her a drunken little wave, which she ignored with a lift of her chin.

I kicked the side of his chair, which made it wobble even

more unsteadily; Romeo thumped it back down to four legs with more alarm than grace. 'Attend me, fool. It's not just Ronnie who's in disfavour. Grandmother's not well pleased with you, either.'

'She's never well pleased with any of us, save perhaps for you, O perfect one,' he said, and waved a servant over. The servant in question had a strained, long-suffering look as he bent to listen. 'Where lurks dinner?'

'It has been served, master,' the servant said. I didn't know this one by name; he was new, I supposed, though he seemed flawlessly well trained. 'Shall I bring you soup?'

'Soup and bread. And wine—'

'Water,' I interrupted. 'Bring him water, for God's sake and his own.'

'A traitor at my side,' my cousin said. The servant left, looking relieved.

'Where were you?' I asked Romeo.

He let his head drop against the high back of the chair. We looked similar, but I was taller, broader, and not as handsome. My nose had once been just as fine and straight, but a street brawl with the Capulets had done for that decisively. At least one maid had claimed it granted me character, as did the faint scar that cut through my eyebrow, so there was some benefit to my adventures. And, of course, my eyes. My eyes always betrayed my half-foreign ancestry.

'Hmmm. Where was I?' Romeo echoed dreamily as his eyelids drooped. 'Ah, coz, I was in contemplation of peerless beauty, but it is a beauty that saddens. She is too fair, too wise, wisely too fair, since she refuses to hear my suit.'

He was *very* drunk, and coming dangerously near

declaiming his wretched poetry. 'Who inspires you to such heights of nonsense?'

'I shall not cheapen her name in such company, but in sadness, cousin, I do love a woman.'

'We've all loved women, and almost always sadly.' Well, I reflected, almost all of us had done so. But that was another subject that needed no expression here. 'We've survived the harrowing.'

Romeo, even drunk, was sensible enough to know that uttering a Capulet's name at a Montague dinner table wasn't sane. He left it to me to read between his lines. 'Not I,' he said. 'She cannot return my love; she's vowed elsewhere. I live dead, Benvolio. I am shattered and ruined with love.'

The servant returned with a bowl of hot soup, which he deposited in front of Romeo, along with a plate of fresh bread. The soup steamed gently in the cool air, and I smelt pork and onion in the mix, along with sage. Romeo picked up the bread and sopped a piece in the broth.

'I see death hasn't dimmed your appetite,' I observed. 'Do you think to change the girl's mind?'

'I must, or sicken and wither.' He said it with unlikely confidence, and took a bite of the bread. 'Already my words are in her hands tonight. They'll add to the chorus proclaiming my faithfulness. She will favour me soon.'

'Chorus . . . How many of these missives have you sent to her?'

'Six. No, seven.'

I stared at him as he spooned up the soup. I was hard-pressed to bring myself to ask the question, but I knew I must. 'And did you . . . sign them?'

'Of course,' said the idiot, and missed his mouth with

the spoon, spilling hot liquid all over his chin. 'Ouch.' He wiped at it with the back of his hand, frowned at the bowl, and raised it to his mouth to take a blistering gulp. 'I could not let her ascribe them to some other suitor. I'm not a fool, Ben; I know it was unwise, but love is often unwise. Your own father took a wife from *England*. What wisdom is that?'

I narrowly resisted the urge to cut his throat with a conveniently placed carving knife left on the tray in front of me. I took a deep breath and tried to blink away the reddish tinge across my vision. 'Leave my mother out of it,' I said. Insults from Grandmother were one thing, but Romeo using my parentage to justify his own folly . . . 'If the girl's relatives don't slaughter you in the streets, I'm certain that La Signora will order you manacled to a damp wall somewhere very deep, and have your madness exorcised with whips and hot irons. I'll wager you won't look fondly on your ladylove then.'

He was smart enough to realise that I was serious, and his drunken grin vanished, replaced by something that was much more acceptable: worry. 'She's just a girl,' he said. 'No one takes it seriously.'

'Grandmother does, and so do many others. No doubt your fairest love has whispered it about the square as well.'

He grabbed me by the arm and pulled me closer, and his voice dropped to an intense whisper. 'Ben, Rosaline wouldn't betray me! Someone else, perhaps, but not Rosaline!'

I remembered her gilded in candlelight, watching me very levelly as I stole from her brother. She could have betrayed me. Should have, perhaps.

And she hadn't.

'It doesn't matter whose tongue wags,' I said. 'She has servants paid to be sure she does nothing to dirty her family's name . . . such as accepting poems from you. If her uncle hasn't yet been told, it's only a matter of time. It's nothing to do with her. It's how the world works.' I felt a little sorry for him. I couldn't remember being that young, that ignorant of the consequences, but then, I was the son of a Montague who'd died on the end of a Capulet's sword before I'd really known him. I'd been raised knowing how seriously we played our war games of honour. 'I pray you haven't met her in secret.'

'She refused to come,' he said. 'The verses were my voice in her ear. It was safer so.'

Safer. It seemed impossible for a man to be so innocent at the age of sixteen, but Romeo had indulgent parents, and a dreamer's hazy view of responsibility.

'Your voice must go silent, then,' I said. 'I'll retrieve your love letters by any means necessary. Grandmother has given me orders.'

'But why would she send you to—' Drunk, it took a second more than necessary for the clue to dawn on him, and Romeo did a foolish imitation of shushing himself before he said, still too loudly, 'I suppose the Prince of Shadows must go after them, being so well practised in the art.'

'Oh, for the love of heaven, shut up!'

Not so far away, Montague and his wife were standing from table, as was my lady mother; we all rose to bow them off. As soon as they had achieved their exit, Romeo snapped back upright from his bow, turned to me, and took me fast by the shoulders. 'Have I put Rosaline in danger?' He seemed earnestly concerned by it, an attitude that surely would not earn him praise from any other Montague . . . except, perhaps, from me. 'Tell me true, coz; if they find my verses in her possession . . .'

'Sit,' I said, and shoved him. He collapsed into his chair

with the boneless grace of someone well the worse for drink. 'Eat your soup and clear your head. I'll send for Mercutio. If risks must be taken, it's better they're shared.'

He spooned up soup, and gave me a loose, charming smile. 'I knew you wouldn't fail me, coz.'

Mercutio was a strong ally of Montague, but much more than that: He was my best friend, and Romeo's as well. Mercutio had once refused to race off with my cousin, calling it a wild-goose chase, and Romeo had – rightly – declared that Mercutio was never there for us without also being there for the goose. In short, he was a brawler, a jester, and one other thing . . . the keeper of a great many secrets.

He kept mine, as the Prince of Shadows, and had for years, but his own secret was far more dire. He was in love, but his love, if discovered, would be more disastrous than Romeo's failed flirtation. It was not simply unwise, but reckoned unnatural by Church and law alike.

I had never met the young man Mercutio adored, and hoped I never would; secrets of such magnitude were far easier to hold in ignorance. Romeo and I regularly sent notes to Mercutio's family's villa explaining his absences, pretended to be carousing with him while he slipped away in secret to a rendezvous. Upon occasion, when Mercutio was fully in his cups, we listened to his torment in never seeing his lover's face in the light of day.

But those bouts of passionate longing were rare in him, and the Mercutio the world knew was a bright, sharp, hotly burning star of a man. He was widely admired for his willingness – nay, eagerness – to take risks others might call insane. Romeo and I knew where the roots of that dark impulse grew, but it never made us love him less.

This night, he might have knocked and cried friend at the palazzo doors and been granted an easy entry, but that was not exciting enough.

Instead, he climbed our wall.

The first I knew of his arrival was the sound of a fist pounding the shutters of my room. The noise not only made my servant Balthasar bolt to his feet in fright, it pushed me and Romeo to stand and draw swords. Romeo might be innocent, but he wasn't stupid. Assassinations were as common in Verona as brawls.

I went to the window and lifted the catch, and then gazed for a moment in silence.

Mercutio laughed breathlessly as he dangled precariously over a three-story fall to hard stone. 'Well?' he gasped out. 'Stab me or let me in, fool; I'm seconds from testing my wings!'

I held out my left hand and took his, and pulled him over the sill. He turned his slithering entrance into a tumbler's roll and bounced to his feet. There was a sense of trembling joy about Mercutio; I climbed walls purely as a matter of necessity, but he seemed to delight in tempting death. His cat-sharp face was alight, dark eyes wickedly gleaming, and he tossed his loose curls back from his face and saluted Romeo with casual elegance. 'I hear there is dire trouble afoot,' Mercutio said, and took a seat at the table with us. He held up his hand without looking, and Balthasar – well versed in the ways of my friends – placed a full wine cup into it. 'How unexpected that is!'

'How did you do that?' Romeo asked. He went to the open window and leant out, examining the sheer stone wall. 'Maybe you really can fly.'

'I had an excellent teacher,' Mercutio said, and winked at me. 'Ben, did you know your too-sly servant is plying me with your best vintage?'

'Hardly the best. He knows better than to serve the best to the worst,' I said. 'Montague has a front door; were you aware?'

He shrugged and drank deeply. 'Boring,' he said. 'Did you know that by my climbing walls in public view, half the city believes I'm the legendary Prince of Shadows? It greatly enhances my legend.' He sent me a sideways glance, acknowledging the irony. 'And besides, how am I to keep in practice for these small intrigues if I simply walk up and announce myself?'

'By all means, use my family walls at any time to hone your skills. Should the hired bravos see you, you'll also get practice in dodging arrows.'

'A benefit I will treasure. Now, whom are we here to conspire against?'

'Poetry,' I said. 'Namely, Romeo's poetry.'

'Is it *that* bad?'

'Inadvisably sent, at the least.'

'Oh, my,' Mercutio said, and smiled slowly, full of delight. 'These verses must be scandalous. Stuffed with humiliating details, I presume.'

'Worse. They're signed.'

He whistled. 'Well. I salute you, Romeo. You don't go halves when you plunge into the maelstrom. What else?'

'They're inside the Capulet palace.'

Mercutio stopped whistling at that. Stopped laughing, too. He went as quiet as he ever did, although there was still a faint vibration in him; he was never completely still. 'Surely retrieving them is not on your mind.' I'd burgled the Capulet house only a few months ago; there were unbreakable rules to my secret life, and one was to never visit the same enemy again after they'd been so badly embarrassed. Their smugness would have turned to rank suspicion. I would triple my risks.

'My grandmother says we must have them back,' Romeo said. 'If they're discovered, my name and the lady's will be filthy jokes in the square. Worse, she'll be punished. Badly punished.'

'A Capulet? Why do we vex ourselves with that? Never a Capulet born who didn't deserve to suffer; I've heard all of Montague say it often enough.'

'Not Rosaline,' said Romeo. 'She is kind, and good, and beautiful. You've seen her, Mercutio. Is she not wonderful fair?'

'Wonderful,' Mercutio said without enthusiasm. 'Her eyes are two of the brightest-shining stars in all the heavens, et cetera . . . Ben, good or bad, the girl's a Capulet, and her danger is her own affair.'

'True,' I said – also without enthusiasm. 'But there is Romeo's reputation to consider.'

'Ah, me. How many of these florid declarations did he pen?'

'Six,' I said.

'Perhaps seven,' Romeo amended. He sounded properly abashed about it, as the night wore on and his wine did not. 'It was not wise, but she is beautiful. I love her entirely.'

Mercutio gave me a look. 'Stab me and save the Capulets the trouble. Isn't Rosaline the bookish one?'

'Yes. It's possible she never even read his scrawlings, only burnt them.'

'That would have been eminently sensible,' my friend agreed. 'But I suppose we have to be sure, if your grandmother requires it.'

'If m'lord Capulet discovers them, he'll make a mockery of our family, even as he punishes his own.' I loaded the title with all the scorn it deserved. Capulet was no lord; not a drop of noble blood flowed in his veins. To be fair, none coursed through Montague veins, either . . . but in Verona, the merchants counted for more than the merely wellborn.

Mercutio traced the fine silver decoration on his goblet with a fingertip as he considered the issue. 'She *was* destined for the convent anyway. It might be enough to dispatch her there immediately before her disgrace is common market gossip.'

'Capulets are not known for their restraint. Remember the lady Sophia? Better for all if these damning letters are put to the fire. To be sure of that, we must find them.'

We fell silent. Mercutio reached for the pitcher on the table and splashed more wine into his cup.

'Her rooms face the garden,' Romeo said. 'There are two balconies. Hers is on the right, as you face it from the wall.'

We both looked at him with identical expressions of surprise, and to cover his sudden embarrassment, Romeo held up his hand for a cup. Balthasar handed him one. When I started to protest, he showed me a water jug.

Good man. I didn't need Romeo's wits wandering tonight. 'And how would you know?' I asked. 'You swore you were not alone with her.'

'I can climb as well as you.'

Mercutio batted him on the back of the head. 'A *Capulet* wall? And when did you perform this miracle?'

'Last week.'

I was sickened that Romeo had performed this little folly after my theft from the palace – which meant he'd done it in triple the danger. It had been sheerest luck he'd escaped.

'And if they'd caught you?' I drew my thumb across my throat. 'Capulets have a great many bravos employed who'd take delight in carving your skin away slowly. There'd have been a bonus for them if they delivered it as a single pelt. Capulet might have it made into a carpet, and sent it to warm our grandmother's feet.'

'I love Rosaline,' Romeo said. 'One risks anything for love.'

Mercutio gave him a disbelieving stare, then turned to me. 'You actually let this infant out in the streets, Ben? On his own?'

'He's an innocent, not a child.'

'Yes, you're right. I've known toddlers with better sense.'

Romeo's cheeks were ruddy now, but he managed to keep his tone steady. 'Are you going with us or not?'

'It's better than another evening of watching my sisters embroider.' Mercutio finished his cup and tossed it to Balthasar, who caught it out of the air with the ease of long practise. 'Well? The hour's late; any decent woman will be abed by now. The moon's in your favour tonight; since Romeo fancies himself so expert in wall scaling, he should see how the expert does it.'

Romeo had chanced on my identity as Prince of Shadows last year, after the theft of an expensive golden chalice from the vaults of the Utteri palace. It had been bad timing and worse luck that he'd been slinking back from a disreputable night, and run directly across my path as I limped through the door with a badly sprained ankle, and my prize. He'd wrapped my ankle, hidden the chalice, and lied about my late return when asked – all without a trace of shame or guilt. But he'd asked no questions, and I'd told him nothing about other adventures.

There were times – though not many – when my cousin was worth his trouble.

'Get ready,' I told Mercutio and Romeo. I'd already donned a muted dark blue tunic and hose, plain and unmarked with any family emblems; the boots I'd chosen were likewise of average quality. I could have passed for a visiting merchant easily enough, so long as no one looked too closely at my face. A muffling cloak and my silk mask would take care of that.

Mercutio had also come prepared for night-time skulking; there was no trace of his usual bright golds and greens, and he looked oddly subdued in plain brown. He pulled a cap from his pocket and pushed it down to cover his hair.

That left Romeo, who still wore Montague colours. We both gazed at him for long enough that he finally scowled. 'What?'

'We are about to do something astonishingly dangerous and quite possibly foolish,' Mercutio said. 'It might be best if they couldn't identify you from the distance of, say, the far end of a crossbow.'

Romeo fairly blushed at that, and I was reminded that he wasn't yet so much a man as still a boy – man in the eyes of the law, yes, but it would take time to teach him the responsibilities of that right. He ducked his head and nodded, then turned away to rummage in my chest for something else to wear. We weren't much of a size, but the plain shirt and vest he chose were close enough. Balthasar brought another cloak, this one of coarse black fabric, with liberal stains. It was good enough to disguise a multitude of shortcomings.

'You shouldn't do this,' Balthasar muttered to me under his breath. He wasn't much older than I, and although it was rare for master and servant to be friends, I counted him as close as Mercutio. He kept my secrets. Mercutio's, too, for that matter. 'Stealing's not a job for a group of half-drunken young fools. You know that.'

'They won't be with me,' I said. 'Mercutio and Romeo make fine distractions.'

Balthasar took in a deep breath, then slowly let it out. 'Sir, I know you're one for risks, but this – in the house of Capulet, again . . .'

'The Prince of Shadows has always stolen from the best houses in Verona,' I said. 'He's taken earrings off a sleeping duchess. What difference? It's all risk.'

'The other times were for revenge, and profit,' he said. 'This is for family. And it's different. They'll be watching for you.'

Balthasar had been in on the secret from the beginning. My first thefts had been vengeful boyish fun, nothing more – a dare, when I was only ten, from the troublemaking Mercutio. I'd stolen a pendant from one of his aunts who had beaten him for impertinence. I'd been happy to scale the wall, sneak into her rooms, make off with the pendant, and sell it in the markets. Mercutio had pocketed the money. Compensation for his humiliations.

My thieving had expanded over time to right many, many wrongs, and Balthasar had known all.

Over time, I had developed a taste for stealing. It was an art that took nerve, skill, agility, and strength; it also took instincts, good ones, to know when something was possible, and when it was not.

Now Balthasar was voicing the warning that rang in the back of my mind.

'They say things about this girl,' he told me. 'This Rosaline. She has the eye of a witch.'

'I've seen her. She's no evil eye in her.'

Balthasar snorted, which conveyed better than words what he thought of my judgment of women. 'Only witches have so much to do with irreligious books.'

I cuffed him on the back of the head, but lightly. 'Even so, you don't think I can sneak past a woman? Don't be stupid. I've done it a hundred times.'

'Not with this one,' he said. 'Not a Capulet witch. I don't like it, sir. I don't like it at all.'

In truth, I could understand, but it pricked me hard to think that any servant of mine feared a Capulet. 'Well,' I said, 'the Prince of Shadows has his tender amorous heart set on acquiring stirring love poems this evening. And possibly a jewel or two.'

He shook his head and gave me a look of disgust. 'You're going to swing one of these days,' he told me. 'If you're lucky. Maybe tonight, the Prince of Cats will get his claws around your throat instead.'

Tybalt Capulet, Prince of Cats, had been named so by Mercutio in a jest that had less to do with his grace and cruelty than it did a ribald play on words. If Tybalt caught me, my ravaged corpse would be found nailed to the same tavern door where I'd skewered his reputation.

I felt a breath of chill, and shook it off as I pulled my cloak tighter. 'Perhaps,' I said. 'He must catch me first.'

Mercutio was, of course, my partner in crime . . . He was an expert in distractions, but having the clumsy, still half-drunken Romeo along was even better. The narrow, uneven streets of Verona were dangerous in full daylight, where footpads and knock-heads lurked in shadows and blind archways. In moonlight, the villains were ever bolder, but even they hesitated to tangle with armed groups. We made sure they saw and heard us as we sauntered over the streets. It helped that Mercutio had a donkey's singing voice, and used it to bray the bawdiest drinking song he knew; Romeo and I bawled out choruses as we strode up the hill.

There was a dizzying sameness to the streets of my fair city, even to natives – all the walls were cut from the same stone, faced with marble, broken only by frescoes and the faded colours of mosaics in the half-ruined ancient walls. Verona was not a lush place; the verdant gardens of the rich were walled up from prying peasant eyes. Even from the bell tower of the basilica, it was hard to spot any sign of trees, or even bushes . . . just pale stone, marble, and clay tile roofs.

Crossing the Piazza delle Erbe, we saw another group of armed young men, these very obviously wearing the colours of Capulet, but they gave us no trouble. Had we been in Montague colours, we'd have brewed a fight, but they only shouted recommendation of the nearest wine shop and continued around the fountain. One of them bared his pockmarked backside at the placid face of the marble statue – ancient, though known as the *Madonna* because of her great beauty – until a shout from the watch guards sent them running and hooting on their way. By this time we had gone quiet, slipping like ghosts through the shadows.

A short journey brought us to the back wall of the Capulet palazzo.

Again.

There was no longer any chance of an easy entrance

to the house . . . I knew well enough that they would be checking the faces of any man entering or leaving. No, this would require extraordinary stealth and effort.

At least the wall didn't look especially difficult.

Mercutio gave me a sharp, knowing smile, and threw his arm around Romeo's shoulder to steer him down the Via Cappello. 'Go to the Via Mazzini,' I told them. 'Right past the front gates. Go buy some wine and enjoy it, loudly, in the street.'

'We who are about to drink, salute you,' Mercutio said, with a flamboyant, cloak-rippling bow. He grabbed my cousin in a headlock when Romeo tried to break free. 'You too, poet. Let's be off about our business of making trouble, and leave Benvolio to his.'

Romeo struggled, but Mercutio held him until he signalled his surrender.

'Don't hurt her,' he told me, so earnestly that I had to again hold back an impulse to cuff him for his assumptions. I was a thief, not a monster. 'Please, Ben, promise that you will do nothing but take the verses. If you must punish someone, then let it be me. She bears no guilt in this.'

He was a bit of a fool, my cousin, but he had a good heart, even while he assumed mine to be blackened. 'I will try to restrain all temptations,' I said. 'Now go. Hurry.'

Romeo nodded to me, and Mercutio led him off to a riotous drink and – very likely – trouble of their own.

I reached into my bag and took out the black silk scarf, which I settled over my head and pulled low over my eyes; I adjusted the eye holes carefully to be sure I had a full range of vision before tying it securely in place. I took a deep breath, looked up at the wall, and allowed my gaze to wander, seeking out the telltale shadows, uneven patches, cracks – everything that would allow my fingers and toes a purchase. I disliked the ivy; it wouldn't hold my weight, and no matter how careful I might be, the plants would betray marks of passage, and leave their signs on clothing.

But there was more, a subtle change to the wall itself. I'd come over it two months past, and now there was an addition, half-hidden in shadow at the top.

Knives. Blackened ones, deliberately hard to spot. If I had climbed to the top and put my hand out, the flesh would have been shredded and sliced. A dangerously clever trick, especially if, as I thought likely, they had poisoned the blades as well.

I needed another entrance – and the small gate set around the corner, in the shadows, was a perfect choice. It was meant for tradesmen and servants, and fitted with a well-oiled lock. I had packed my tools in a small padded bag, and it was the work of only a few laboured breaths to pull back the metal tongue from its groove. No dogs patrolled within – the Capulets did not favour them, fortunately – but I knew I would face the prospect of roaming guards who had absolute authority and the will to do murder.

It was probably not good that I enjoyed the challenge of that.

I slipped inside the darkened gardens; I had not noticed on my last, hurried passage here, but the bushes were fragrant now with roses, and the blooms sagged heavy and fresh. The steady hushed fountain still played its peaceful melody. I kept to the shadows and moved over the polished marble walk to the darkness below the balconies. Rosaline's was the one to my right as I faced it, and I began to study my chances.

I heard the scrape of boot on stone, and stepped back in a smooth, unhurried glide just as one of the expected roaming guards chanced to check the gardens. I credit my ability to stand stock-still to my grandmother's long and endless lecturing; however I came by it, it allowed me to become part of the shadows, and the guard passed me by without a glance. He stank of bad garlic and even worse wine, but his stride was steady, and I had no doubt he was alert enough. I waited until he'd taken a turn behind a large flowering tree before I stepped out again. I'd run out of time. His wouldn't be the only vigilant eyes here.

I leapt half my height up on the wall. The ivy was wet and slippery, but there was a hard trellis beneath, and I swarmed up it with only a slight rustling of leaves. I was grateful that the moon had buried itself in a pillow of cloud, as it made my ascent less immediately obvious. My gloves and rough clothes absorbed the splinters from the wooden framework I climbed, though I felt one or two bite deeply enough to penetrate. I paused in the shadow cast by the square edges of the balcony itself as I breathed hard, and listened.

The room was silent as the grave. This time the girl would be sleeping deeply.

I swung my legs up and over the balcony's edge, and narrowly avoided tipping over a large vase full of cut roses; the thorns caught at my cloak and made my would-have-been-smooth arrival more comical than a troupe of mimes. I dropped below the level of the balcony's lip as the moon emerged from its clouds, and carefully untangled myself before crawling through the billowing curtains and into the room.

It was reassuringly dark. The table where I'd last seen her was empty, though I smelt the smoke and hot beeswax from a candle but recently extinguished. Rosaline's bed was large, but plain; it was shrouded with heavy tapestries of scenes of women doing moral things, and they were all drawn down. No attendant slept within the chamber. Against the far wall stood an entire wall of shelves, and more books than I thought existed in the city of Verona. I stood for a moment to marvel at them – that was a great deal of expense and indulgence, for a girl   and that moment was my downfall.

I hadn't heard her move. Not at all. Yet on my next indrawn breath, I felt the ice-cold prickle of a blade on the back of my neck, and a lovely, calm, no-nonsense voice said, 'The Prince of Shadows, yet again. I let you have one visit, my prince, but two casts grave doubt upon my honour. I think this time I will summon my brother, Tybalt.'

'Don't,' I said, very quietly. 'I come peacefully enough, on a mission to aid you.'

'Aid *me*?' She seemed amused, and no little mocking. 'I've heard bravos boasting in the streets of making free with Capulet women. Have you come to prove yourself as bold?'

'It is not how I fight my battles, threatening women. Though I have heard your own house's hired killers say they would take the wall of any man or maid of Montague's. What wall do you think they meant, for the maids?'

She was silent for a moment. I thought of telling her what had started this misadventure, of Tybalt and the Montague girl in the alley, but it seemed cruel. He was a brother to her, as much as he was a vile serpent to me.

'Turn,' she said. 'Turn and face me.' A candle sparked to life in a rush of gold.

I did turn, because I wanted to see her face as well. Just to remind myself of what she was like. She was still wearing a nightgown, but this time she had donned a heavy mantle as well. A little disappointing, perhaps. I remembered how luminous she'd been, glowing through that fabric.

I bowed silently to her.

'Masked as always,' she said, and I thought she almost smiled. Almost.

'Will you ask me to remove it?' I asked.

'Perhaps. What do you want here?'

'Nothing too dear,' I said. 'Love poems.'

She was far too intelligent for her own good, because that was all I had to say: Two words, and she knew. 'From your height and shoulders, you're not Romeo; nor would you be some hired sword sent for something so indelicate. You'd be the cousin, then. Benvolio. Did you come to rob from me, or kill? Surely killing would be simpler, to ensure I didn't speak of it later.'

The mask might as well have been made of air. I felt utterly at a loss now . . . What was there to do? Beat her? Threaten her? Already, I knew that Rosaline was not a woman to be intimidated, though she was no older than I was. Killing her was out of the question. I'd not kill a woman in any case, but it was a moot point; she held the dagger. Competently.

'As a formal introduction, I suppose it must serve,' I finally said, and bowed again. 'Lady Rosaline.'

'Forgive me if I don't offer my hand to be kissed,' she said. 'Poetry? That awful drivel that Romeo has been sending me, I assume. I was hoping someone would have the sense to stop him.'

'As bad as that?'

'Your cousin reads by rote and cannot spell,' she said. 'But his enthusiasm, at least, seems genuine.'

'Then there is no cause to keep it,' I said. 'Give me the papers and I'll be on my way.'

'I burnt them,' she said, and tossed her loose dark hair over her shoulders as I frowned. 'Do you think me a blockhead? Had anyone discovered I had made such nonsense a home, I'd have been punished, and poor love-struck Romeo hunted down and cut to pieces by my brother. He doesn't deserve that. He's just a foolish boy.'

I wasn't used to women like this – unsentimental, brisk, brilliantly foresighted. I'd thought that a bookish ageing virgin would have hoarded love poems to greedily warm her in the cold, but Rosaline clearly held her own source of heat. She radiated it like a bonfire, and beside it I felt very, very cold.

I cleared my throat, because I realised that I was staring like a boy in a brothel. 'Your word on it?'

She smiled, just a little. 'I am a Capulet, sir. Why would you believe my word?'

'Why indeed, but I think I would. If you gave it.'

'Then you have it.'

'Thank you,' I said. My voice was not quite steady, but her hand on the dagger was. 'I believe our business is done, lady.'

'As done as may be,' she agreed. 'Can you exit the grounds in safety?'

'I'm the Prince of Shadows,' I said, and smiled. 'I can exit hell itself without a twitch of the devil's tail.'

'You're very close to meeting him.' She was not smiling,

not even a hint of it now. Her eyes held shadows. 'There is a racket of singing out in the street on the other side of the house. Take advantage of your distraction while you still may. The guards will be back patrolling in force soon enough, and I cannot risk myself to save you. You understand this.'

I nodded thanks to her, and slowly backed away towards the balcony window. Next to my left hand was the bookcase, and at the last instant, I pulled a book from it – the slender volume she had been reading when first I'd seen her. Rosaline gave a surprised gasp and lunged forward, but she was too late.

'Something to remember you by,' I said, and held it up as I backed onto the balcony. She might scream now, betray me to my death; I couldn't tell her intentions, and I didn't care to guess. I jammed the small volume into my doublet and swung out onto the trellis, climbing down with as much silence and speed as might be into the shadows cast by the balcony, then paused to take stock of the garden below.

Rosaline ventured onto the balcony in pursuit, and she leant over, looking directly down at me. She said nothing, and neither did I, but there was . . . something exchanged, after all.

On a sudden and probably stupid impulse, I reached up and pulled up the mask. I needed her to see my face.

And she smiled fully this time. It was wary and cool, but I felt an odd, heated jump in my veins even so.

'A fair exchange,' she whispered. 'Now you should go. Quickly.'

I could hear Mercutio and Romeo shouting drunkenly out in the street; they'd have drawn all the attention of the guards, but it wouldn't last long. I kicked away from the wall, mindful of the flower bed below, and dropped the last ten feet into the soft garden grass. Gaining my feet, I sprinted for the door through which I'd entered.

At the last moment, I spotted the guard there, examining the locks, and veered sharply away behind a bush's thorny protection. Upon her balcony, Rosaline was watching with tense interest, hands gripping the stone hard. I could almost believe she was afraid for me.

Almost.

Only one way out, then: up. I had seconds, at most, before the guard left the door and began a more aggressive search of the grounds, so I launched myself onto the wall and climbed fast. I fought for handholds as I swarmed up the wall, and achieved the sticky ivy-covered top.

Knives. I remembered at the last possible second as I reached out, and snatched my fingers back from the sharp edges. I was pinned on the wall, unable to go forward.

No, there was a way after all. The craftsmen who had embedded these deadly traps in the top of the wall had cheated the Capulets, just a little – they had left off where the ivy flourished near the corner. It was impossible to spot from the ground, but here at eye level I clearly saw the opening.

I rolled into it, gasping for breath, and balanced there as I looked back.

Rosaline was still there, watching me. I raised my hand to her, and she nodded.

And then a shadow grabbed her and dragged her back, off balance, into her room. A tall, male shadow. I saw the flash of an upraised fist, heard the smack of its landing, and her surprised cry, and then Tybalt Capulet came out to lean over the balcony's railing. He gripped the balustrade with both hands, and gazed down tensely into the garden. 'Guards!' he snapped. 'Idiots, pay attention; someone's been here! I heard my sister talking to him, and I want him found! Immediately!' He spun, slapping the curtains aside with such force they caught on an edge of the doorway, leaving me a clear view into the room.

A clear view of Tybalt advancing on Rosaline, grabbing her arm and twisting it until she cried out. 'Was it him?' he shouted, and raised his fist. 'Was it that damned thief?' She said nothing, which earned her an open-handed slap hard enough to leave a blood red imprint on her fair skin. 'I found his boot prints below your balcony last time, you jade. You helped him stain the Capulet name. What's he here to steal this time, your maidenhead? Are you fallen so low?'

She had been implicated in my last robbery. I felt stunned and stupid for not realising she would be, when I'd left such an obvious trace beneath her balcony, and I tried to tell myself that it didn't matter, that she was a Capulet by birth, and the sworn enemy of my house. The blood that ran through her veins was the same as in Tybalt's. Her father had killed mine, long ago.

It didn't sound as convincing as it should have done.

I saw her looking over Tybalt's shoulder, and her eyes grew wider as she realised I was foolishly lingering atop the wall. I could almost read the angry message in them. *Go, fool.* And she was right.

I sucked in a deep breath, tucked the book tighter into my doublet, and rolled off the edge, into the shadows.

I landed on my feet, knees flexed, and hardly paused to wince at the impact before I was running fast and light to the street that curved around the palace. I caught sight of Mercutio and Romeo running towards me, chased by a group of Capulet bravos no longer entertained by their antics, and darted the other way, slowing to allow them to catch up. Romeo, no great lover of exertion, was already out of breath, but laughing all the same in hitching gasps. 'Did you . . . get the—'

'They are destroyed,' I said tersely, saving my breath for the run. My mind was not, as I'd expected, full of triumph and elation; it was replaying the determined, grim expression on Rosaline's face. That was the look of a woman who knew pain was coming, or worse. 'I swear if you write more I will break your arm.'

He sent me a sideways look, clearly shocked; I was not joking, and he knew it. This was no lark now, no May Day jaunt that we would laugh about later. This was deadly earnest.

'Lead them away,' I ordered him and Mercutio. 'Go towards Ponte della Vittoria; you should be able to lose them and turn back towards the palace. On no account let them take Romeo.'

He nodded, grabbed Romeo's sleeve, and hauled him off in that direction.

I veered in the other. 'Where is he going?' I heard my cousin ask plaintively, though Mercutio would have little idea of my destination. I had only just decided on it, and poured on speed through darkened, narrow streets, lit here and there by glancing blows of moonlight. I could hear pursuit's baying cries behind, but it seemed Mercutio and Romeo were drawing them away. That was good. I needed time.

The avenues took on menacing edges at night, and twice I narrowly avoided the grasp of cut-throats lurking in shadows for victims; the watch did a lazy business at this time of night, and the assassins knew it. I avoided one ambling set of guards, ducked down a narrow, fetid alleyway, and came out next to the Chiesa di San Fermo, where I knew I would find a friendly ear, and a safe harbour.

I slipped through the open doors, suddenly aware of the sweat soaking my body, of the pounding of my heart, and the heavy, silken silence within the thick walls. Only a few candles glowed, painting the arches overhead as I stopped at the font to pay respects. I bent knee to the altar and hurried as fast as propriety would allow to the front of the church, where a plump, tonsured monk was praying, or perhaps pretending while resting his eyes and snoring.

I leant close to him and whispered, 'Rise up, dear friar; I call you to glory.'

His eyes flew open, blinked, and widened in what I suppose might be taken for religious ecstasy – or, more likely, horror. He scrambled awkwardly to his sandalled feet, staring at the silent altar and the crucified saviour, and then turned and saw me.

'Rogue!' he roared, and then remembered he was in the house of the Lord, and amended it to a hoarse whisper as he clapped me on the side of the head hard enough to make me see a glimpse of angels. 'Villain! Sly-tongued devil of infamy – Oh. Forgive me, sir.' He'd realised who I was, after his first outburst, and cleared his throat to try to restore himself some dignity. 'What is this, young master? You come into the house of God with such nonsense? You stand before the holy presence and—'

'Have you been into the sacramental wine again, Friar Lawrence?' I asked. He had been; it was obvious indeed from the eloquence of his breath. 'Is that not a greater sin than a shoddy trick on an old man?'

He shook a fist at me, but kept his voice to a hissing whisper. 'Old man, am I? Not so old that I cannot teach you manners again, as I did when you were just a tender child! What mean you, coming here at this hour?'

'I come in earnest,' I said. 'Forgive me, but one of your flock is in danger, and I can only think you as shepherd must rush to the rescue.'

'Flock? Have I sheep to tend now, at *this* hour when the devil stalks?'

'Rosaline Capulet,' I said. 'Her brother means to beat her, perhaps worse. If you might visit tonight, perhaps seeking after her well-being . . .'

'I have misheard,' he said, and cupped his ear towards me. 'Did you say *Capulet?* Surely not, with such worry in your tone. What would stir you to such instincts, to betray your own?'

'I betray nothing,' I said, and now there was an edge to my tone, not the worry he'd claimed. 'It's none of my affair. Should it be any of yours, a timely visit might save the girl's looks, if not her life.'

'She's bound for cloister, my boy; looks are no great asset for her.' Still, he pursed his lips, and then sighed. 'I go, then, but what shall be my excuse? How heard I her cries from here?'

'Why, good friar, surely God came to you in a dream,' I said. 'And wished you to deliver his good tidings to his would-be bride of Christ.'

'If you prove to be God, young blasphemer, I shall need a great deal more sacramental wine than exists in Verona,' he said, but nodded. 'Leave it to me, then.'

'So you may slip back into your wine-drenched prayers? No, Friar, I will come with you.'

He barked out a sharp, harsh laugh that ran around the empty church like a too-bold child. 'I scarce think a Montague would be welcome,' he said.

'Monks have no family but that of Christ,' I said, and attempted to look saintly. 'And a hooded robe conceals all else, so long as I keep my face humbly lowered.'

'Humble is not a word I think of when I consider you,' the friar said, but he was not objecting. One thing I knew of him: he liked his little intrigues. 'But you, Benvolio, you have a cold eye. Swear you will not betray yourself once we are within!'

'What profit would it be if I did?' I asked him. 'Trapped within the jaws of those who'd delight in my bloody slaughter? No. I seek only to see the thing done. I'll take no risk. See you take none either.'

The friar was only a few moments rummaging for a spare, poorly patched habit; it fit me very badly, which was all to the good, as novice monks frequently were handed the rags. Belted soundly with rope, it swaddled me in heavy, smothering folds that smelt of incense and ripened sweat.

'The sword,' Fra Lawrence said. 'You must leave it here. Even beneath the robe, it is too easily seen. You must exchange your boots for plain sandals.'

I did these things without complaint, though shedding my weapon caused me to feel more naked than removing any amount of garb. I had worn steel since I was old enough to be allowed out in a pack with my cousins to roam the streets. Tonight I was defenceless.

I am but a humble monk, I reminded myself. *God is my defence.*

That, and the reeking tent of robes I wore as disguise.

Fra Lawrence examined his handiwork and pronounced that I would do, if I remembered to keep my head decently downturned. 'And never, *never* look up,' he lectured me sternly, or as could a monk who weaved side to side from the effects of stout wine. 'You are simply there to look devout. Any hint of arrogance and I will be embarrassed, but you will be beyond any such concerns.'

I tucked my chin down, folded my hands in the voluminous sleeves, and tried to forget a lifetime of training to be a ruler of men. It was, I found, surprisingly restful.

We walked through the streets unmolested. One cutpurse slid greasily from the shadows, only to look us over in disappointment. Fra Lawrence made the sign of the cross to him with great good humour, and we padded on our way without further offence being offered. The robes seemed to weigh on me like armour, though it would undoubtedly be far less useful to turn a Capulet sword. I began to wonder whether perhaps I was being a bit *too* bold, but the chance to tweak Tybalt's nose yet again was irresistible . . . and I needed to see that Rosaline had not suffered overmuch for my failings.

Though I would not admit that, to her or – God forbid – anyone else. I could only hope that Friar Lawrence would keep his silence – which, considering that his earthly family owed mine a debt, seemed safe enough. No one wished to risk the wrath of the Montagues, and particularly

La Signora di Ferro. The thought of my grandmother descending from her chair like a decaying, shrieking devil was enough to lock anyone's throat to silence . . . even a gossiping, ever-lecturing busybody like the friar.

Or so I had to hope, for the sake of my life. My grandmother would likely hiss and remind me that even a churchman might suffer a drunken tumble down narrow stairs, for the safety of the family. I was not quite so ready to resort to such tactics. I just knew they existed.

The walk was made in hurried silence; I had managed to impress urgency upon the good friar, at least. But it still seemed to take far too long, even at the rapid pace, and by the time he had rung the bell to summon a servant, it seemed sure that we were far, far too late to be of any help at all.

Friar Lawrence's self-important godly bluster was enough to win us the courtyard, where a more senior servant confronted us with the peculiar mix of arrogance and deference that those who serve the rich always seem to have. He was hardly a hair's difference from any of ten who haunted the halls of the Montague palace, waiting for any opportunity to impress their betters and oppress their lessers. I had never before seen the sneer levelled upon me, though. It wakened anger in me, but unlike most of my friends and cousins (Romeo in particular), I was not one to draw blood. I was the peacemaker, the reasonable calm in the storm.

I would take my vengeance later, coolly and anonymously, if it rankled me, but for now, my anger was fuelled by the fact that the man was wasting our very valuable time, and I could see the temptation in Romeo's tendency to wet his steel with those standing in his way.

Friar Lawrence sent me an alarmed glance, and I quickly looked down, hiding in the shadow of the church's hood. My shoulders were stiff, and I rounded them, and folded my hands together into a penitent clasp within the sleeves.

Merciful saints, it was almost as stifling within these fragrant robes as in Grandmother's evil lair.

It seemed to take forever for the friar to persuade our entry, by virtue of invoking many visions of saints and threatening the ire of the bishop, but we were finally shown into the darkened grand hall, where an even more senior servant waited stiffly in her severe gown. She looked as if she had been born in it, and would die in it, but only after she'd destroyed the last of her enemies from sheer spite.

In short, she much resembled a younger version of my grandmother, and after a quick, cautious glance I kept my gaze fixed on the shadow-muted carpet underfoot.

'What is this?' she demanded. 'You seek to intrude on the peace of the young lady for what reason at this unchristian hour, Friar? And prate me no nonsense about visions and saintly motives; I know well the venal thoughts of men, no matter what robes they wear.'

'What unkindness you have in your heart, signora! I shall remember you in my prayers as often as possible, that you should know peace from some terrible suspicion. Why, I am a man of God! And I come on a holy errand for the Lady Rosaline, who is soon to be my sister in Christ and therefore as dear to me as any sister of my blood. Surely you do not stand in the way of angels!'

She made a very unladylike sound of derision. 'Fallen angels, belike.'

He crossed himself. Twice. 'You cut me, dear signora. Yet

I stand before you with the patience of a martyr, begging the gift of the presence of the lady—'

Friar Lawrence's indignation was cut off by a wine-harshened, familiar voice. 'Get out. You're not needed here.' I risked a quick glance upward, towards the staircase, where Tybalt Capulet was charging down towards us. His face was flushed and livid, and his dark eyes sparked with rage. 'Out, I say! If I need a lecture from the Church, we'll get it from the cathedral, not from some threadbare friar! We've had thieves here, and worse; the last we need is *you*!'

Friar Lawrence straightened, and I remembered my submissive role just as Tybalt's gaze sheared over me. 'Thieves, you say? But this is proof! My vision showed me that the Lady Rosaline needed counsel and guidance in this matter, the better to practice the holy virtues of forgiveness! Why, I felt the touch of the saints stirring me from my rest, kind sir, and one cannot argue with saints; I shall get no rest from them until I ease my mind that the lady is well and secure in her faith after such a shock.'

'Her family serves her well enough,' Tybalt replied, and I felt the prick of alarm at the wintry cast of his words. 'Begone.'

'Tybalt!' The name was said in whip-crack command, and from the corner of my eye I saw him react sharply, turning towards the balcony overlooking the hall. Since his attention was elsewhere, I too risked a glance, and found Lady Capulet herself regarding us all with annoyance and distaste. 'Such disrespect to the Church will not be tolerated. My sincerest apologies, brothers. You may address your concerns to me, and not my nephew.'

Friar Lawrence did not hesitate to exploit the opening. 'I come in haste, afire with purpose sent from heaven,' he said. 'I must urgently see the Lady Rosaline on matters of a spiritual nature. I would of course be glad of your attendance, my lady Capulet.'

She hesitated for so long that I could feel the balance shifting beneath my unsteady feet, back towards Tybalt and his simmering violence, but then she gave one single, sharp nod. 'Come with me.' Tybalt must have made to protest, because I heard her give an ice-cold hiss, and then say, 'Nothing more from *you* this eve. Your uncle will hear of your misbehaviours. Your manners are no better than those of a drudge.'

In true noble fashion, she was less concerned with the state of her soul – or anyone's – than with the appearance of rudeness to an institution more powerful on earth – never mind heaven   than the prince himself. Tybalt stood back to allow Friar Lawrence to ascend the steps, closely followed by me; I admit, I took some satisfaction in passing so near an enemy in perfect silence, hidden in plain sight. If only I'd been able to lift a trinket or two, the moment might have been perfection, but the risk was too great. Better to steal on the way out than the way in.

We followed the drifting skirts of Lady Capulet – attended now by a covey of ladies-in-waiting, including the sour-faced woman who'd first braced us – down the candlelit hall towards the room I knew to be Rosaline's. She did not bother to announce herself. One of the servants opened the way, and the party swept like a storm inside.

I did not see Rosaline right away, only heard the intake of breath from Friar Lawrence. One of the ladies gave a faint cry – distressed, but hardly surprised.

I caught sight of Lady Capulet's expression. It did not change by so much as a flicker.

I eased a few inches to the right, keeping my face as shadowed as possible as I risked a direct look at the scene ahead of us, and for a frozen moment all I could see was blood. Blood in drips and dribbles, staining the floor.

Rosaline was wedged into a cold corner, knees drawn up, nightgown bloodied from her split lip and the open cut on her forehead. It would take time for the bruises to form, but her left eye was already swollen, and the right side of her jaw distorted from the beating she'd received. She held her right arm tenderly, and I saw the bloody scrapes on her knuckles.

What sort of woman was she, to fight *back?* She'd lost, of course, and badly, but it was the sight of those wounded hands that made me feel as if I had lost my breath entirely.

That, and the fact that she recognised me.

I saw her raise her head, and she met my gaze with her own, or at least half of it, and I saw the barely perceptible reaction that ran through her. There was an emotion there I could not fully understand – fear, of course; who would not be afraid? But something more.

I thought it might – impossibly – be gratitude.

'A fortunate thing that she is to be a bride of Christ,' her aunt said, 'since His love transcends such earthly considerations as beauty. As you can see, the girl is inclined to be unbiddable at times, Friar.'

'Is such violent correction necessary?' he asked, and I heard a sharp edge to the question. 'The girl is, after all, promised to the Church.'

'And it is our duty to ensure that she reflects well upon

the house of Capulet,' her aunt said, with an imperious jut of her chin. She did not like being questioned so. 'The scriptures tell us that a disobedient child should be corrected; is that not so? I thought you were summoned to tend to her spiritual needs, not her bodily ones.'

'Sometimes one entwines with the other,' Friar Lawrence said cheerfully, and moved forward to kneel next to the girl. He took the voluminous wool of his sleeve and wiped carefully at the cut on her head. 'How fare you, my lady?'

'Well,' she whispered, and closed her eyes for a moment. 'Well enough, I thank you.'

'Well enough to understand that you have been summoned to the glorious service of Our Lord?'

'At this hour?' Lady Capulet cut in, sharp as a blade. 'Surely not. She'll need at least a week to be presentable for the journey.'

Friar Lawrence stood, pulling himself to his full height, and bulk, with his hands folded in his bloodied sleeve. 'A week, you say? To do God's bidding?'

'God's, or yours?' I risked a quick glance upward. Lady Capulet's ale-coloured eyes were far too sharp, her lips far too thin. She was suspicious of nature, and this miraculous visit had waked howls within her. It remained to be seen whether we would survive the Capulet hounds, if they had been set hard on the hunt. 'I shall send to the abbess to confirm that this . . . *vision* of yours is inspired of God, and not from some lower place. You shall hear from me within the week. If your message proves true, you may have the honour of escorting the girl to the cloister. If not, you may be sure that we will speak to the bishop and request his instruction.' The bishop, of course, was a Capulet born.

Friar Lawrence had placed himself squarely in danger for my sake, but looking at Rosaline – who had suffered for my sake, as well – I could see no alternative. Her life hung in the balance of Tybalt's temper and her aunt's indifference. I did not want to leave her here, risking more, but I caught a tiny movement from her. She had gently moved her scraped hand in a way that I knew was meant to warn me off.

So I bit my tongue hard enough to taste the metal of my blood, and kept my head bowed, my hands folded, as Friar Lawrence cooed his social graces to Lady Capulet, whose pursed mouth never loosened, and after exacting a promise that Rosaline's wounds would be tended, he led me out and down the stairs.

Tybalt still lounged there, spineless as a cat, and we were forced to edge by him towards the landing. I passed close enough to smell Rosaline's blood on him, and the heavy, angry stink of his sweat.

I felt a blind, red urge to let fly all the violence within me. My hand twisted and ached with the need to draw the concealed dagger at my waist and plunge it deep into his heart, but the cold, calm part of me reminded me that Rosaline Capulet was no kin of mine.

No kin and never kind, she'd said.

The taste in my mouth changed from blood to ashes as we left the Capulet house, and the doors slammed and bolted behind us.

I was suffocating in the folds of my disguise, and wished desperately to free myself of it, but Friar Lawrence's hand closed hard on my arm as I tugged at the ropes holding it closed. 'Not here,' he said. 'You were right to fear for her, but with God's grace we may have saved her life. Her lady aunt will not wish to have Rosaline murdered this night; they might be within their rights to so dispose of a rebellious girl-child, but they have not the liver for questions the Church might bring. She's safe enough, for now. But our pressing concern must be intercepting the message she will send on to the abbess.'

'I will see to that,' I said. At least it was something to which my skills were well suited, unlike miming a biddable young postulant. 'But what reply should we send in its place?'

'If you don't wish to damage my newly minted reputation as a prophet, I would suggest it say that I am selected to be the one to escort the Lady Rosaline to her joyous union with Christ. You might mention a saint and a vision or two, as well.'

I did not want Rosaline to be sent within the walls of a cloister, and I never to see her again, but perhaps it was the best for her; it was undoubtedly the safest. Here, in Verona, she risked her brother's wrath, which might lead to worse than we'd seen tonight.

Jesu, I wanted him dead.

But I nodded beneath the suffocating weight of the robes, rounded my shoulders in submission I did not feel, and followed Friar Lawrence across the silent, dangerous city.

FROM THE PEN OF ROSALINE CAPULET
WRITTEN AND BURNT IN THE SAME NIGHT

I have lied not only once, but many times now.

On the morning following the first visit from the strange and legendary Prince of Shadows, when he took my brother's sword, I faced the question like all who slept beneath the Capulet roof: what did we know of the robber? There is secret power in being thought weak, and a fool, as women are so often seen; when I lied, I did so without a quiver, and no one looked more closely – save my wretched brother, who found the footprints below my balcony, and the broken flowers that showed someone had jumped there.

I had managed to convince him – or so I had thought – of my innocence then, and the punishment had been vicious, but brief.

Not so last evening, when the Prince arrived, silent as a black angel, and demanded the wretched verses I had already burnt, as I will this account when I am done. I had already guessed his name, but the sight of his face, of the burning, foreign green eyes . . . of the teasing, testing look in them! I have always been practical, where my younger cousin Juliet dreams of amour; how then to explain the sudden rush of feeling to my skin, the blush in my cheek, the ice-cold fear that clutched me when I realised the risk he had taken in returning?

That last glance of Benvolio Montague had shown me too much of what feeling was within him, too. The stark, stunned horror told me that he'd seen my brother, Tybalt, come fast upon me, and that he knew what would come.

But what he could not know was how often it had come to this before. My brother was – in the parlance of our honey mouthed aunt – of a high blood, and he often drew it from others – namely, from me. Of late I had begun to fight back, since I had come into a height where it was possible – though strictly forbidden – to do so. I had scored him with my nails more than once, and even bruised him, but never did I hurt him enough to matter.

I had thought, from the look on Benvolio's face, that he might risk all to defend me, and it struck me with a deep horror, and also with a traitorous yearning. I had never known anyone to feel overmuch for me, since my father's death. I had scarce known my mother. I had been exiled from our father's home with Tybalt, passed from one uncaring set of hands to another until we had come to the chilly splendour of Verona, and this palace built of bones and memories.

I wished we had never come, and yet I am glad of it, because *he came back*. Benvolio Montague, wearing not his Prince of Shadows mask, but the robe of a postulant brother, trailing like a pet dog behind the sweaty bulk of Friar Lawrence (who is a kind man, for all his many faults). I know not what possessed the good friar to rush here to witness my shame, save that it must have been done at the urging of Benvolio.

I recognised him even before I spied those cool green eyes within the hood's shadow. I think now that I might well recognise him in any disguise he could attempt. And once again, I saw the dark, dangerous impulse in him to help me – an impulse that here in the heart of my violent and blood-soaked family could lead only to his painful death. Thank God and the Virgin that he left meekly, looking at least a little as a penitent young man should, though what might have passed between him and Tybalt, had things gone otherwise, does not bear thinking.

I write this by the well-banked light of a single candle, in haste, and the paper is smeared with my blood, for the cut in my forehead continues to seep despite the bandage provided by Juliet's old nurse; I thank the saints that Juliet did not wake to see this.

I write the words because I know I can never speak them, for my own sake and for that of the Prince of Shadows.

But I feel no good can come of any of this, however delicious it may seem to keep such a secret.

And now I burn this paper, and hope – in pagan belief, perhaps – that somehow he will know.

QUARTO
II

Romeo and Mercutio were waiting for me in my room when I regained the safety of the Montague palace. Like Mercutio, I scaled the wall, which was a good deal easier for me than it had been for him, but I had practised more, and with less wine in my belly. Still, it had been a long and exhausting evening, and I was well weary by the time I climbed over the sill and landed lightly on the carpets, not more than an arm's length from where Mercutio had sprawled himself loosely in a chair, cradling a goblet that I suspected had been filled more than once. From the angle of it now, it was well emptied.

It took him at least two breaths to recognise that I was standing at his side. Once he did, he jerked himself upright, cup falling in haste, and threw his arms around me. 'Fool!' he said, and roughly pushed me back to stare at my face. 'Tybalt did not manage to puncture that wind-bladder you call a stomach, but I may. What manner of devil has gone into you, to do such things for a woman – worse, a *Capulet*?'

I looked past him to Romeo, who had also got to his feet, but somewhat more shyly. There was an uncomfortable light of hero worship in his face. 'You survived it,' he said. '*Twice* you entered that cursed house, and escaped. You truly are blessed.'

'Lucky is not the same as blessed,' I said, and pushed Mercutio away as he opened his mouth to make some clever retort. 'I'm not in the mood for games.' I sat in the chair he had leapt from, picked up the goblet, and held it out. My manservant, ever vigilant, filled it – but only halfway. I stared at him. He added a few more drops.

'Does she live?' Romeo asked anxiously. My cousin sank down on a stool near me, looking as earnest as an owl, if considerably less sharp-witted. 'Rosaline? Is she—'

'She's alive,' I said shortly, and quaffed my wine in a choking gulp. 'Your poesy's ashes and bad memories. We'll consider this matter settled and done, and I swear to you, if I catch you spouting flowers at any other girl save the one your mother chooses—'

'But you must admit, coz, she *is* the fairest in all Verona, the sun to all the lesser moons . . .'

I hit him. It came suddenly, in a rush of hot blood that brought me from the chair. Even before I knew what I planned, my fist was clenched and in motion, and the landed blow sent knives up my arm. I might have hit him again, save that Mercutio was on me, holding me back and wrestling me to the chair. My cousin was sprawled on the floor, blood crimson on his lip and fury shimmering in his dark eyes.

'This is your fault!' I shouted at him. 'How great a fool are you, Romeo? I should—'

'Beat me bloody?' he demanded, and stood as he wiped the red from his mouth. That, more than Mercutio's hold, sent a shiver through me as I remembered Rosaline's split lip, her bloodied face, her desperately concerned gaze – concerned not for herself, but for me. 'Love survives the scorn of others, coz. Even the blows of self-righteous relatives.'

'She doesn't love you!' I blurted out, and threw off my friend's restraint to climb back to my feet. 'Mark me, Romeo: put yourself at risk again and I will do worse than beat you bloody.'

'Temper, temper, my hot blade,' Mercutio said, and patted me annoyingly on the back. 'He's a fool, yes, but an honest one. Romeo, tell your coz that you'll forget the girl and let's part friends for the night. I have a love of my own waiting for my tender attention, and beautiful as you both may be . . .'

He batted his eyelids in a way that made me think ridiculously of my sister, Veronica, and I could not help but smile, a bit. He sent me a saucy wink and a purse of his lips, and I shoved him off balance for reprisal. 'I'm not meat for your table, Mercutio.'

'But you sauce up so well,' he said, and arched his brows in comical consideration. 'Very well, I leave you to the warm fires of your familial love.'

We clapped hands. He offered the same to Romeo, and a quick embrace. 'Safe home, my friend.'

'Safe,' he said, and jumped theatrically up to the windowsill to offer us both a sweeping bow. 'But most *certainly* not to home.'

He spoilt his exit somewhat by nearly slipping as he began his descent down the wall. I watched him swarm down the stone – not quite as expertly as I, but competently – and then he was gone, a shadow in the shadows. Our lunatic friend, off on yet another risky venture.

Behind me, Romeo said, 'He'll be caught one day. You know that.' Romeo was not speaking of the dangerous wall climbing; we both knew that if Mercutio was caught at that he would talk his way out, and his madcap ways were well-known in Verona. No one would think much of it. Romeo was referring to the much deadlier rendezvous our friend was off to make.

We had known, since we were all young sprouts together, that Mercutio was made of fire and fey grace, but as we turned from boys to men expected to do the duty of our families, Romeo and I slowly realised that there was more to our friend than that. I had found it out by chance, walking in on Mercutio in close embrace with a pretty young man a bit older than either of us. I'd heard of such things, of course, but never *seen,* and I confess to a certain unsettled embarrassment that drove me from them – from Mercutio – for almost a week, before he came to see me and, with an entirely strange attitude of gravitas, asked what I intended to do. *You hold our lives in your hands,* he had told me. *You know what they would do to us. I beg you to remember that whatever you think of me, whatever sins I may commit, I am always your friend.*

And as simply as that, the matter settled for me. Mercutio was Mercutio, whomever he loved, whatever he did. Perhaps, as the Church taught, it was a cursed perversion, but I was old enough to know that many in the city practised far worse, and with far less love in their hearts. While I was not drawn to Mercutio in any way of the flesh, he would always be my spiritual brother.

I don't know how Romeo discovered the same, but soon we realised that each of us willingly lied and contrived for Mercutio, giving him excuses for absences to see his lover. I had never asked any details, and had only the one glimpse, but Romeo knew more than I, and shared it with me; Mercutio's lover these past three years was a young scholar named Tomasso, who was considering the priesthood. He was the third son of a poor merchant, hardly moving in our social class.

I would have said that Mercutio was in love with the risk, but I knew it wasn't true; he was in love with Tomasso, as purely and passionately as (if far less demonstratively than) Romeo claimed to be with Rosaline. And it worried me. Mercutio's family had already made a match for him with a girl he loathed; the wedding would be done within the next year, and I wondered what it would do to him, and to his love. I felt sorry for the girl, too. She was innocent of any wrongdoing, but she'd be punished all the same.

'He's clever,' I said, and closed and barred the window shutters. 'Mercutio will never be caught out. He fears only betrayal.'

'Not from us,' Romeo said. He cut a glance at me, and wiped a trickle of blood from his broken lip. 'I am sorry, coz. But Rosaline *is* beautiful, is she not?'

'Yes,' I said. 'She is beautiful.'

And then I retrieved my cup and demanded more wine, to wipe that admission from my mind.

I woke to a pounding head and a mouth that felt as if grape stompers had made merry in it. My manservant had somehow wrestled me out of my clothes and into a nightshirt, and I was sunk deep in my feather bed. The twitter of birds beyond the window, and the cries of merchants in the streets below, told me that I'd slept too long, and gradually I realised that the pounding was not simply inside my skull, but upon the door of my rooms.

As I stirred and groaned, rolling on my side, a yawning Balthasar rose from his low, hard mattress near the hearth and stumbled to answer the call. I knew I was in difficulty when he straightened, swept the door wide, and bowed to his fullest.

My lady mother, Elise Montague, entered in a cloud of rosewater and the soft glint of gold, and paused at the foot of my bed as Balthasar quickly hurried to the shutters and opened them to admit more light. I winced as the brightness lanced through and bounced from the red-gold chain around my mother's neck, and the dangling drops in her ears. Her hair gleamed rich as well, the colour of ripe wheat, and as always it was smooth and perfectly dressed, held in a gemmed net that framed her still-lovely face to perfection. I'd inherited my foreign green eyes from her, though my hair and skin were Italian-dark; even after so many years in the healthy climate of Verona she seemed wan and pale, and very thin in her dark, elegant gown.

She regarded me with steady, cool assessment. 'Good day to you, Mother,' I said, and sat up. 'Did I miss mass?'

'Yes,' she said. 'And your absence was noticed. Are you well?'

'I have a sickness of the stomach.'

'Ah,' she said, and snapped her fingers without glancing towards Balthasar. He quickly grabbed an armchair and moved it beneath her as she lowered herself – a trick that only the truly rich and entitled could manage, I thought, without looking either awkward or foolish. 'A disease of drink. That explains everything. Benvolio—'

'Mother, if you'll remove yourself, I'll make myself decent and call on you in your chambers,' I said. 'I'm not a child.'

'No, you're a man grown, and held to the same standard,' she said. 'Your father was little older than you when we were married.' I knew. He'd been all of nineteen, and she had been seventeen, when he'd died on the point of a Capulet dagger. She'd been heavily pregnant, but not with me; I was already a healthy boy of almost two, and had the vaguest possible memory of him; my sister, Veronica, still in the womb when he perished, would have not even that.

I groaned and rubbed my forehead. 'If you've come to aggravate my condition with talk of marriage—'

My mother turned her head and speared poor Balthasar with an utterly impersonal glance. 'Bring food for him,' she said. 'He's of no great use to anyone in this condition.' She dismissed him with a firm nod, and he scurried to do her bidding. My rooms were, I thought, one of the few places in Verona where my mother could be assured that she'd be obeyed without question; even within the Montague halls she was still the excess widow, the foreign flower dragged into the toxic hothouse of one of the richest, most ambitious families of the city. Grandmother did not approve, and God knew, what Grandmother disapproved would never find much favour within these walls, or without.

So Balthasar and I indulged my mother, and let her act the part of the aristocratic woman she would be on foreign soils.

'I need to bathe, Mother,' I said.

'I'll have it prepared,' she said with serene calm. 'But you *will* talk to me, my son. We have much to discuss.'

This did not sound at all entertaining. I sat up, pulling the covers chest-high, and tried to look less like a wayward child, though I'd always be that in her eyes. 'I am at your disposal, as always.'

A tiny hint of a smile woke a shallow dimple just by the edge of her lips, but it smoothed again almost immediately. 'Have you given thought to the girl? She comes of impeccable stock, her family's fortunes are secure, and they are eager to secure a match before she's thought too old.'

'She's fifteen,' I said. 'And boring.'

'She's appropriate, biddable, and presentable.'

'What of the Toretti girl?'

My mother gave me one of *those* looks. 'She is no longer appropriate.'

'Oh, you just made her more interesting.'

'Benvolio, do not be flippant. The girl has been . . . compromised. Her virtue is in question.'

'The interesting ones are always questioned.'

'That is why I offer you the boring ones, my son. Believe me, in the end, they will be a benefit to you, and the *interesting* ones, as you like to call them, would be a millstone on your back. You'd never live down the gossip.'

'Cruel market chatter, worth less than a goose fart,' I said. 'I care nothing for it.'

'You'd care if it came from the mouth of Tybalt Capulet,' she said, with unerring accuracy. 'I am trying to protect you, my son. If not the Scala girl, then whom? You've already rejected the best candidates I could bring you. Perhaps the Church would suit you better.'

Since one of the core tenets of our faith was 'Thou shalt not steal,' perhaps not. 'I tried on a monk's robe recently, and I didn't favour it,' I said. 'Is there no greater match to be made from another city? Or even from your mother country?'

'The last thing I would wish is to burden you with a wife so alien to you, and to this family,' she said. 'You bear enough of that stigma already, which I well know. And I wouldn't wish to exile a young girl so far from her home and family without good cause.'

'Am I not a good cause?' I asked, and I must have put some of Mercutio's charm in it, because for the first time, my mother truly smiled. It gladdened my heart. She did not often do it; the English are a serious, quiet people, and she always seemed so guarded, even with me. I could well understand why. Love and war are the same in Verona. 'I will bow to your experience, Mother, but perhaps a girl from Fiorenza, or Milan . . . ?'

'Perhaps,' she said. 'But your grandmother has already made it very clear that you will be married by the end of the year. Your friend Mercutio's banns have already been posted. She's busy matchmaking for Romeo as well. Her intent is to see the next generation of Montagues and their close allies well into the world before she quits it, you know.'

'She'll never quit this world,' I said. 'Surely a walking corpse fired by cankerous hatred can't die. From the feel of her rooms, she already burns in hell.'

Her back stiffened, and her eyes widened in alarm. 'Benvolio!'

'She's no spies here. I can say what I like. God knows there's nowhere else I'm allowed.' I felt angry and strangely exhausted, and I was glad to see Balthasar ease into the room with a tray of bread, cheese, water, fruit, and juices. He set it on the bed and withdrew to a respectful distance to stand guard at the locked door. 'Have you breakfasted?'

'Hours ago,' my mother said crisply. 'Before mass, which you should have attended. I expect you will remonstrate with your manservant for allowing you to oversleep the hour.'

'I'll strap him until he yells,' I lied, and bit into a succulent peach. A lazy wasp buzzed in the window, drawn by the sticky, sweet juice, and Balthasar sprang into action to shoo it out again. The battle between swift wings and clumsy batting hands was entertaining, at least. 'What news at the church?'

'Nothing definite,' she said. 'There's a whisper of trouble at the Capulet palazzo with one of the girls; they both pled sickness today, though Lady Capulet and her entourage came.'

'And Tybalt?'

'Present, though largely absent, if you take my meaning. He looked as ill as you. There were bruises on his hands. You did not brawl with him, did you? You know the prince has taken a dim view of public disturbances. And, of course, your grandmother would expect a more fatal outcome if you did so.'

'I did not brawl with anyone,' I said, but she cast a pointed look at my knuckles. I looked down, and was surprised to see a faint shadow of bruising there, and a small cut. 'Ah. Perhaps I did. My memory of last night is clear as . . . wine.' No, I did remember. I'd punched Romeo for his unforgivable obsession with Rosaline Capulet. In the cold light of morning, and my mother's judgmental stare, I told myself that it had been purely to defend the family honour. 'It wasn't a Capulet.'

Her gaze was far too sharp for comfort. 'The Capulet maidens were not in attendance. Might it have something to do with them?'

'No.'

'You offered them no offence?'

'Have I ever?' I raised my eyebrows and – deliberately – took another bite of my peach.

'Did you see them?'

'If I ever have, I hardly remember. I hear the elder girl is too studious, and the younger too sweet, and not even you would present them as possible brides.' I finished the peach and put the pit on the tray, then yawned. 'Are you finished disapproving for the morning? If you are, please have juice; Balthasar has brought too much.'

I didn't think she would – my mother rarely lowered her guard, even with me – but after a stiff moment she sighed and reached for one of the goblets on the tray. There was a very slight loosening of her shoulders, and now that she was not so fiercely armoured I noticed the fine lines around her eyes, and the faint shadow of weariness beneath. Life for my mother, in this house, was a lifetime of living under siege. Romeo had told me the stories he'd had of his own nurse about my mother's grief and distraction when my father died, but by the time I was old enough to note it, she had moved from tears to a resigned, chilly silence. To me, as a child, she had been as beautiful and unapproachable as the marble Madonna on her fountain – an icon of love, but not love itself.

She sipped juice for a moment in silence, then said, 'Your

sister has suggested a match for you.' There was nothing
to indicate whether she approved of the idea or not, but
any mention of Veronica woke deep feelings of alarm in me.
'The Scalas' second girl. Have you a strong opinion on the
matter?'

I considered, because – surprisingly – I did not. I knew
nothing of the girl in question, save that her name was
Giuliana, and she seemed quiet. I could not even give an
opinion as to whether she was fair; I'd scarcely noticed her
at all, the few times I'd been near. But if dear Veronica put
her forth, surely there was a snake hiding in that plain,
deceptive grass.

'I would have to inspect her,' I said.

'Something will be arranged. I will expect you to give it
your attention, Benvolio.' She replaced the emptied cup on
the tray, nodding to Balthasar, and he whisked it away.
'These are dangerous times. Very dangerous.'

'For Montague? It's always dangerous.'

'No,' she said, and her green eyes locked on mine, like
on like. 'For *us,* my son. For you and me. I have ever been
tolerated within the family, and while your grandmother
needs you, she favours your cousin over all. I understand
she set you a task.'

'I'm to keep Romeo out of trouble,' I said, and forced a
casual smile. 'Surely no more difficult than to stop the wind
from blowing. Trouble and Romeo are long wedded.'

'That is my point,' she said softly. 'It is an impossible
task she's given you, and you should know by now that the
one thing she will not forgive is failure.'

I shrugged. 'There's little enough she can really do to
hurt me,' I said. 'I am the surplus Montague; I know it;

there's no disappointment to be had for my future. I will make my own way.'

'She would not punish you,' my mother said. 'But as your mother, I can be cut off, cast out, forgotten. Even your sister stands at risk, though not as much, since she has made a good match for herself. Still, if your grandmother is angry enough, she will ruin me, and Veronica's future will be tainted as well.'

'Ruin you how?' I had forgotten my own troubles, and even my modesty; I threw back the covers and stood in my thin nightshirt, but Balthasar − good man − was there to wrap a robe around me, and bring me a folding stool on which to sit across from her.

'Mother—'

'There are a thousand ways to ruin a woman,' my mother said, with a weary shadow of a smile. 'Any hint of impropriety, any whisper of intrigue would be enough. My point is that both your sister and I are vulnerable to such things, even if you are not. So, please, my son, keep this firmly in front of you. It's not merely that you're asked to manage your feckless cousin's behaviour; it is that you are asked to protect us.'

'From our own,' I finished for her. 'From our own blood.'

'Blood has slaughtered blood since Cain killed Abel,' she said. 'No doubt even the Montagues and Capulets will one day interbreed, though it may not stop hatred from festering. It's only in stories that such happy endings are possible.'

'Peace is made, sometimes,' I said, and reached out to take her hand in mine. Her flesh was cool, pale against my darker; she even had the feel of marble, though soft and pliable it might be. 'Mother, I swear I will do all I can to protect you.'

'Will you?' It hurt me that she asked it, but I nodded, and saw a shadow of relief in her eyes. 'Then I am much heartened, Benvolio.' She withdrew her hand and stood to twitch her skirts into their correct and proper folds. 'I thank you for the promise. I will see about the Scala girl; a few discreet questions in the right ears will reassure me of her suitability before I subject you to yet another bridal inspection. But you must promise me you will consider her fairly. I' faith, I scarce know what you seek in these girls, but at some crossroads you must choose a path, for good or ill.'

She didn't wait for my response, not that I could have provided one. I didn't know what I sought in the girls presented to me, either, save that I craved . . . more. Some challenge. Some spark of intellect or spirit that would warm me in the night when the lights were dim. A comely girl was all that was required to satisfy propriety; a wife need not be more than rich and decorative, though it was useful if she had a certain political cleverness.

I could not shake the image of Rosaline Capulet, face lit gold by a single candle, reading her volume of poetry. No simple facade there, no easy match that would require nothing from me save the duties of marriage. A woman of her type would be nothing but trouble in the end, even leaving aside her impossible bloodline.

Stop, I told myself sternly. *You're as ridiculous as Romeo.* Except that I would never even consider dragging the Montague reputation through the streets for a woman. Whatever I felt, it would be kept masked, chained, and hidden away like a mad relative. Suffering was the path to Christ, I'd been told. Perhaps one day I'd be made a saint – the patron saint of fools and lovers, if those terms were not exactly the same.

My mother made polite, empty conversation for a few moments more, then swept grandly out of my room. She had a full day of intrigue and tension ahead of her, and little time to waste with her eldest – and only – male offspring.

'Will you be beating me now for letting you sleep through mass, sir?' Balthasar asked, with a helpfully bland expression. 'Shall I fetch a strap?'

I cuffed him. 'He jests at scars who never felt a wound, fool. Have I ever beaten you?'

'Perhaps it would be helpful,' he said. 'I shouldn't wish your lady mother to feel I am the devil's whisper, leading you on the path to damnation. I would never find another placement.'

'I don't need a strap to beat you.' I formed a fist, and winced; I'd forgotten the scabs on my knuckles, which stretched painfully. Balthasar raised thin eyebrows, which gave him an owl-eyed look.

'Clearly, sir,' he said. 'Will you be a peacock or a crow today?'

'Crow,' I said. 'It better suits my mood.'

My servant moved off to open cupboards and drawers, and returned with carefully folded, sandalwood-scented clothing. Smallclothes and the linen shirt, which went on quickly enough, though the short ruff, as always, chafed my neck; the padded hose did not go on so easily, but I bore it with patience. Over that came the coppice, the doublet, and as Balthasar tied on the ink black sleeves, I was already beginning to regret my choice for the day; it would be sunny and hot, and while the brighter (peacock) colours wouldn't be cooler in any practical terms, as the fabrics were just as heavy, they somehow *felt* so.

Balthasar saw the look on my face and sighed. He untied the sleeves and switched them out for robin's-egg blue with midnight slashes. The doublet remained black, but it too had the Montague blue worked in intricate patterns, needlework that must have taken the ladies a month to complete. 'I suppose, in the mood you're in, the black is the most practical,' he noted. 'It wears blood so much more nobly.'

'There will be no blood today.'

'Optimistic, sir, very optimistic. I salute you.' He adjusted the fit of a sleeve, cocked his head, and nodded approval as he went to get my shoes and the chest of jewels. I was never as gaudy as Tybalt Capulet, but I could hardly leave the house without showing the wealth of Montague in some small way. Today it was an emerald ring I wore on my undamaged left hand, and a lion brooch in gold with eyes of pale blue topaz. I stopped him when he would have decorated me further, like some feast-day statue, but I finally accepted a single earring that flashed more pale topaz. For a young man of my age, it showed almost priestly restraint.

Balthasar brought me the necessary tools of the day – a long, thin left-hand dagger, with the Montague crest worked into the hilt, and my sword. I belted them on and felt complete. The rest was necessary, but weapons, ah, those made me decently clothed.

He picked a bit of lint from my shoulder. 'Shall I accompany you, sir?'

'I'll be with Romeo,' I said. 'And with Mercutio, if he appears. No need to nursemaid me.'

'Yes, of course. I'll just get my bag.'

It was a source of bitter amusement to me that as powerful as everyone assumed a scion of Montague to be, I could not even effectively order my own servant. He was right, of course. If he allowed me to venture out alone and anything untoward happened, his head would be for the chop. Better to die with me on the point of a Capulet sword than face La Signora di Ferro.

We left my apartments and almost immediately saw Romeo, who was sitting on the same bench in the open atrium I'd shared with my sister, Veronica, earlier. He looked as dejected as a half-drowned kitten. I sat beside him. He had also chosen black for the day, relieved with only the smallest bits of colour. Anyone seeing him would believe him to be in mourning.

He had a liver-coloured bruise on his chin that gave me a savage, unchristian jolt of satisfaction when I saw it; not admirable, that impulse, and like any good cousin I choked it down and kept the smile from my face. 'You look well down,' I said. 'Last night was no small success, coz.'

'Success, you'd name it? To hear that the fairest face of the city, the fiercest heart, burnt all the words of love I wrote? To hear she had no more regard for me than for the slops tossed in the street? Perhaps it is your ideal of success, Ben, but hardly mine.' Romeo was truly sunk in the depths, and gathering up rocks to drown more efficiently. 'Still, better to have loved—'

'Shut up,' I said, pleasantly but with an edge, and he cast me a quick glare.

'You hit me,' he said. 'I won't forget.'

'Good,' I said. 'Then you'll remember the real pain and not the imaginary pleasure. There are a hundred suitable flowers blooming in the garden of Verona for you. Leave the Capulet alone.'

'A hundred, you say? And yet you seem to be unable to pick such a flower for yourself. Is it the colour of the blossoms that repels you, or the smell?'

I resisted the urge to strike him again. Balthasar, hovering nearby, had an anxious look on his face that warned me I might do well to hold my anger. 'Have a care what you say,' I said, very quietly. Perhaps it was the dark look on my face, or the tension that tightened my left hand on the hilt of my sword, that made Romeo take a step back and raise a hand in surrender.

Duels between cousins had been known to happen, even within the downy bosom of House Montague. I was rarely the first to take offence, nor to draw steel, but when I was, Mercutio had long declared me the deadliest of us three, and the least likely to see sense. Romeo was a fair hand with a blade, and witty when the mood took him, but I had a cold, green streak of poison running through my veins, and he knew it well. I had spent my entire life learning to keep it contained, lest it sicken others as well.

'I meant nothing by it, coz; you know I love you as well as my own heart,' Romeo said, in as gentle a tone as I'd ever heard him utter. 'But you wound me, and I wound you in turn. You think my love for Rosaline is a passing thing, and it grieves me you think me such a light-head.'

I took a breath and deliberately loosened my grip on the sword, but the fury inside me did not bank itself. 'Brood on, then,' I said. 'I care not. But if you even think of casting eyes on the wench again, I will do more than mar your looks. If you think La Signora will punish me, think on it again. She'd rather have a dead heir than a foolish one.'

He looked taken aback that I'd said it so directly, and more than a little afraid (of me, I think), but I did not stay to dispute with him. I stalked on, half cloak swinging, and although I did not grip my sword again, my right hand clenched tight for the need of it.

'Perhaps . . . perhaps some soothing wine, sir,' Balthasar suggested. 'Wine, shade, some pleasant company . . . ?'

'Stop your mouth,' I said, and set out instead to find trouble.

It was a frustrating thing that trouble, being so kindly invited, failed to appear. Even the usual swaggering Capulet bravos took their boasts a different way as I approached. I never got close enough to deliver any direct insult, not even to a Capulet loyalist.

In truth, I was not sure why I was so angry at the Capulets, other than Tybalt. My own cousin was the root of my fury, and I'd already bruised him for it. There was a wildness trembling inside me that begged to let fly, and let the arrows fall as random as rain. Balthasar seemed worried. Well, it was likely sensible enough; I was in no fit state for any man's company, even a servant's – especially a servant, honour-bound to cast his life ahead of mine, or futilely after. The anxious tightness of my man's face gradually cooled my anger. If I drew him into needless and fatal trouble, I would be as foolish as Romeo.

We were walking the narrow aisles around the Basilica de

San Zeno and making for the vivid, always busy Piazza delle Erbe, where the great mingled with the low, and the rich with the poor. I was a curious mixture of all . . . great in my name and my house, high and also low, in my half-English state. Rich with honour and position, and poor in purse, at least as far as my mother and grandmother knew; they tightly controlled the strings for all of us. The fact that I had a comfortable income from less honest means . . . well, that was nothing that needed to be confessed beyond the church walls.

I passed a small chapel, and on a whim paused and entered. It held a beautiful plaster Madonna and child, and small heaps of flowers – some fresh and fragrant, some wilted and dusty. I genuflected and bent a knee, with Balthasar quickly assuming a penitent stance behind me.

And then I prayed to the beloved Virgin for patience, guidance, and most of all, for my cousin to stop loving Rosaline Capulet.

Because if he did not, I genuinely thought I might go mad.

It is a signature truth of the world that when you court trouble, it tends to avoid you for sheer spite, but when you become reconciled to peace, peace behaves just the same. I left the chapel with a great deal more piety in my heart, well disposed to forgive an insult should one present itself to me . . . and naturally, upon turning the corner out of the chapel, I came faced with three louts wearing the colours of Capulet. No fine gentlemen, these; the coffers of our enemies had bought some low, dangerous men. They were decently barbered, but clearly had more experience with razors drawn across a throat than over a cheek. Their clothes were poor, and as yet clean of any fresh bloodstains, so they'd not been successful in baiting my fellow Montagues today.

Seeing me and Balthasar, alone and cut off from the support of our fellows, they clearly felt they'd been given a heaven-sent gift.

'Sir . . .' Balthasar began, but then subsided, because it was bootless. We were fish on their lines; that is to say, caught. With a resigned sigh, he began rolling his shoulders and limbering them for the fight. Being a servant, he was armed with a cudgel and a knife – a good knife, I had made very sure of that, but in a brawl with three murderers, the two of us were out armed.

I stepped forward as they arrayed around us at the points of a killing triangle. 'Peace of the day upon you,' I said, 'if you'll let us pass.'

The man I faced – the leader, it was easy enough to pick him from the pack – gave an evil leer that had little to do with a smile. He was a stout, swarthy fellow, hairy and sweaty, and he had one white, dead eye, with a scar dragged over his face to show where he'd earned it. He spit at my feet. 'Dog of a Montague,' he said. 'I'll pass you through the gates of hell, slick as you please. Unless you make it hard on me, and then I'll drag you through hot coals along the way.'

'He means,' one of his dimmer fellows said helpfully, 'to make you suffer.'

'Yes, I did get the point,' I said, and gave him a little bow. 'Most helpful.' I addressed myself to the leader of the gang. 'I have just been to prayer, and I've no desire to fall from grace quite so quickly. May we not agree to hate at a distance just now?'

'Dog,' he said, very pleasantly. 'Blue-bellied coward.' He spit at my feet again, coming nearer this time. Balthasar made an indignant huffing sound, and his hand rested on the hilt of his dagger. He was not so much offended by the insults as by the ham-fisted approach of their bearer.

'If you want to be effective, you might try something a child might not invent,' I said, still painfully pleasant. 'For instance, you may say that my breath bids fair to knock down the cathedral. Or a helpful advisory that someone has stolen half my wits, which leaves me with none. Or—'

'Mongrel son of an English bitch,' he said.

I kept my smile, but it hardened and sharpened into a cutting edge. 'Better,' I said. 'But hardly up to the standards of your patron. Tybalt at least claims to have had her.'

'I had her screaming,' the Capulet pig said, and picked his teeth at me. 'I'll have you the same, fancy boy.'

I heard steel being drawn behind me, but I did not turn. I did not need to. Balthasar's cudgel smacked with a dull thump, and I heard the muffled crack of bone. Metal clattered to stone, and one of the bravos let out a harsh yelp, before the cudgel struck again, this time with the distinctive sound of wood on skull.

The odds were now even.

'Then by all means, try and have me,' I said, still smiling. He yanked his blade free of its scabbard, and I drew my sword with an unhurried motion that brought it up into parry with a minimum of effort. I knocked his lunge out of line and continued the motion, straightening, feet settling into balance with the ease of practice. I'd been taught well, and thoroughly, since I'd been old enough to hold the sword – that was training all boys of status were given, if they were expected to survive. But more: through Mercutio's auspices, I'd been matched with brawlers, duellists, bravos with the same depraved blood instinct as these men. And, bloodied, bruised, humiliated . . . I'd learnt.

I sidestepped with a flash of my short cape, confusing the line of my movement, and drew my dagger in the same moment. As he recovered from his lunge, I struck from above with the sword, below with the dagger. The sword plunged easily just below the ridge of his collarbone, angling down as the dagger found ribs and angled up. The dagger was merely surety. The two points almost met in his heart.

He stared at me, stunned as an ox after the hammer, and then looked down on his death. I pulled steel free before he could drag me off balance, and sidestepped the gout of blood that came after. He still had his sword, and I could not take my gaze away until he was down. I'd seen dead men kill the living before, when the living failed to pay due attention.

I wish I could say that I felt horror, or sorrow, or pity, but I did not. I felt . . . cold. In the icy space of survival, the lives of my opponents meant nothing more than opportunities. I might be spurred to fight from anger, but I was never angry when I fought . . . only careful.

So I waited until the life had left the man's eyes and he fell to the cobblestones, kicked his Capulet-given sword to the side, and turned just as the second man drove Balthasar back at the point of his blade. Balthasar and I, we were old brawling companions; he knew when to engage, and when to step away, and as he did, I moved forward, sword ringing on the new opponent's blade with a sound like the devil's church bell. I stepped forward and forced the man off balance; he stumbled over a ridge in the cobblestones, and his shoulders hit the wall behind him. I held him there, *corps a corps,* and stared into his face. He looked afraid.

He ought to have been.

'Your fellows are dead,' I said. My voice was still pleasant, still calm. 'Do you want to survive them?'

He nodded shakily. He stank of garlic and the sweat that streamed down his pallid face, and suddenly I allowed myself to feel a bit of pity. He was young, only a little older than I – a little younger than Balthasar. Perhaps he'd wanted a life of adventure and swagger; perhaps he'd only been earning bread for his poor widowed mother. I couldn't know his motives, or care, but I still felt a strange kind of kinship with him in that moment.

'Rip off the filthy Capulet colours,' I said. 'Leave them in the blood where they belong. Do it now.'

I stepped back. He gulped air, staring at the crimson on my blades, and threw his sword down beside his dead comrades. Then, with trembling fingers, he tore the Capulet insignia – clumsily stitched, probably by his own hand – from his jerkin and threw it on the street.

I lowered my sword and dagger. 'A word of advice,' I said. 'Leave Verona before Tybalt hears of this, or you'll die less quickly than your friends.' I reached into my purse and retrieved a gold florin, and flipped it to him.

My manservant said, 'And tell the other Capulet bravos that they'd best avoid my master from now on, unless they want to be served the same steel.' He, I noted, had not put away the cudgel, or the dagger.

The survivor took to his heels, clutching his Montague gold, and I checked the corpses to be sure they were, indeed, dead. Balthasar discreetly lifted their purses, but left their rosaries intact.

'We should go quickly,' he said, rising and casting an uneasy glance behind us. 'Bodies on the very steps of the church . . .'

'Not by my choice,' I said.

'Would you like to explain that to the prince, sir?'

As always, my servant had an excellent point to offer, and I allowed myself to be hurried off in the opposite direction from where the Capulet exile had gone. A few turns away, Balthasar stopped me and took out a rough linen cloth, tut-tutted, and sponged spots of blood from my doublet and hands. I had already cleaned my blades, obsessive as a tradesman with his tools.

Now that the battle was past, I could no longer keep that ice-cold distance from what I'd done, and the face of the man I'd killed came back – vivid in every detail, down to the last coarse hair and the colour of his one good eye, which had been a light cinnamon brown. My hands began to shake, and I felt cold, but it was unseemly for a son of Montague to be seen to be weak.

I said, without looking at Balthasar, 'I have the need to confess.'

He betrayed nothing. I wondered how *he* felt, having felt his cudgel crunch a man's skull. 'Dangerous to go back, sir.'

'Then we go on, to the cathedral,' I said. 'Now.'

I had missed the morning mass, and was early for the noon, which was a good time to find Monsignor Giacomo in the confessional . . . but I found that it must have been a busy morning for sinning. At least ten aspired to cleanse their souls before me – four of them young ladies, accompanied by their ill-favoured escorts. One went veiled, but her dress, and that of her lady-in-waiting, signalled her house: Capulet. It might have been the lady of that house, but the veil was not rich enough for someone of her status; Juliet was a small young lady, and this one was almost of Lady Capulet's height. Therefore, it was Rosaline.

She stood patiently as she waited for confession, her no-doubt-bruised face concealed by her veil. Her hands were gloved to conceal the discoloured knuckles. I saw her head turn to regard me for what seemed like a long few seconds, and then she went back to contemplation of the Virgin's statue. Her escort left her to light a candle and pray to Saint Zeno, and Rosaline knelt in a rustle of skirts and folded her hands piously together.

'Wait here,' I whispered to Balthasar, and went to genuflect at the altar, then made my way to the niche where the Madonna waited, her marble face placid and full of peace. Her open hands offered the same, and I wanted it, badly, because the stress of taking a life tore at me, and the sight of Rosaline . . .

I knelt a few feet away from the girl and bent my head in prayer. There was a subtle, traitorous sense of comfort in being close to her, even here in sacred, peaceful space, even knowing there was no possibility of anything more between us.

'Are you all right?' Rosaline whispered, just for my ears, and I had to struggle to hold myself quiet, to not betray my surprise. *She* asked after *me?* 'You have blood on your neck.'

'It isn't mine,' I said. I felt light-headed, hot, and my heart was suddenly beating too quickly. 'I could ask you the same, my lady.'

She was so very still that she might have been marble herself, carved by the same master who'd made the holy statue. 'A nun needs no beauty.' It was calm enough, but it wrenched at my heart. 'But I will heal right enough. You must go, before you're seen.'

She said it out of concern for me, but it was her own life in jeopardy, as well I knew; I'd receive a scorching rebuke from my grandmother, at worst, but Tybalt had already punished her viciously. Any other missteps could result in one of House Capulet's famous *accidents,* so common to disobedient daughters. Easy enough to trip and fall on the steep, slick stairs, or suffer a sudden and fatal sickness. The world had no shortage of ways to die, for either of us.

'I killed two of your brother's men just now,' I said. 'They would have killed me.' Why I said it, I do not know; I simply needed to do it, and her head bowed just a little more, as if from the weight of my admission. 'It never ends, does it?'

'No,' she said softly. 'Pray God it does, someday, but it will not end today, nor likely tomorrow.'

She did not say it, but my actions had certainly rolled the cycle forward, postponing that day of peace. And, looking at it squarely, I saw it had been my own fault. If I had not been so angry at Romeo, if I had not stormed out looking for a brawl, then I would not have found one.

I crossed myself, rose, and retreated to where Balthasar was fidgeting nervously from foot to foot. He breathed a sigh of relief when I took my place beside him. He didn't say it, but I read the stiff disapproval in his body language.

I nodded to him and headed towards the exit, just as one young lady emerged from the confessional, and another took her place.

'Sir?' he asked, startled, and hurried to catch up. 'Were you not here to be shrived?'

'I've confessed as much as I need,' I said. 'The rest can wait.' In truth, in my most heretical heart, I thought there was no real forgiveness for taking a life, in this world or the next, regardless of what the priests might say.

I wished I'd been able to see her face, but I knew that witnessing the bruises and cuts again would have given me no peace, only ignited another round of fury at Tybalt. Perhaps she had known it, too. Or perhaps I only imagined the friendship between us, fragile and unspoken and as deadly to us both as a cup of poison.

Who's the foolish one now? I asked myself, and vowed that I would apologise to my cousin.

Soon.

The rest of the day went as uneventfully as most . . . Mercutio eventually appeared, looking content and tormented at the same time, and with Romeo (and supported by our own crew of hired blades, among them the fierce Abraham and slender, grim Alessandro) we went to wander the market square. It was the vital, vivid centre of the town, a place where all classes mingled, and today, as most days, it was full of colour, noise, and music. Our small band of young men – yes, swaggering, no doubt – kept together, a tight-knit group of blue and black, which in Mercutio's case was slashed with the vivid orange of his own house. I had been asked to find a new silk merchant for my mother, in a note from her to my rooms, and so I led the men on that very domestic chore, from stall to stall, looking over the goods and the honesty of the sellers.

It was at the third stall that I encountered my sister, Veronica, dressed in extravagant finery and closely attended by her pinch-mouthed nurse, who looked hard put upon. Veronica was buying – at too dear a price – a length of rich gold-and green damask. She ignored me until I was at her elbow.

'You ought to let me haggle for you,' I said. 'That's half again as much as it's worth.'

'It's for my wedding gown,' she said loftily. 'If I'm to marry the old goat, at least I will do it in the best.' She sent me a sly glance as the merchant folded the fabric and went to wrap it in a linen package. 'There's talk of dead Capulet men this day.'

'Is there?'

'Talk of a Montague who killed them,' she said. 'Might that be you, brother?'

'No.' I was in no mood to confess to my sister. She'd never met a secret she liked to keep, save her own. 'Perhaps it was footpads.'

'Footpads who made the survivor rip away his Capulet colours? No one will believe it. I hear the Prince is going to summon Montague and Capulet both, again, to put a stop to the brawling. Questions will be asked.'

I shrugged. 'You should go home,' I said. 'If Capulet blood is up, you have no business wandering alone.'

'I'm not alone,' she said. 'I'm with my attendant, as is any decent woman.'

'Tell me you're not off to an assignation.'

'Brother!'

That called for a second shrug; the outrage in her voice was far too obvious. Veronica was up to something, but what, I could not say; nor did I truly care. I'd warned her. If she insisted on putting herself in danger – or in a dalliance that could ruin her marriage, at the very least – then it was no business of mine. Though no doubt my grandmother would blame me for that, too.

On the strength of that, though, I sent two of the bravos as escorts for her and the old woman. Whatever mischief Veronica was intending, the men would keep the secret; they were well paid to do that, and they knew that my uncle took a very dark view of betrayal. She'd be as safe as might be – at least from any enemies.

From herself . . . that was another matter altogether, and one to which I was not inclined to give much worry.

Romeo was moody, and before long slipped away. I dispatched another of our followers to cover his back. Mercutio tried to talk to him, but Romeo was – as seemed to be usual for the day – unwilling to speak, and our friend came back to me shaking his head. 'He's off to brood,' he said. 'Love does some men no favours, Benvolio.'

I wondered whether he was speaking of himself for a moment, but he flashed me a broken, mad grin. 'I know where he's bound. I followed him yesterday,' he said. 'His love's a thick wine, and his mornings are hangovers . . . he climbs a tree beyond the wall and writes more poems. At least now he has the sense to tear them up when he's done.'

I wasn't much satisfied with that, but I let it pass. Hunting Romeo down wouldn't make him any less moody. He had to find that balance for himself.

I found the silk merchant for my mother, and told him that he'd be called upon soon; Mercutio fancied a pair of fine leather gloves, but they came from a stall that featured a Capulet banner, and the vendor sneered at us.

I stole them for him, a deft and quiet lift that was done in a moment as the merchant's eye roamed elsewhere. I tossed them over as we walked, and Mercutio clucked and wagged a shaming finger, but only after he'd put them on.

We purchased meat rolls from a handcart, and had free wine from a vendor hoping to supply House Montague. A street performer fresh from Fiorenza produced doves from his dirty beard, to the screaming amusement of a group of children; he had a wild-man look that made me think he put his thrown coins into the purchase of a bottle rather than food, but his hands were steady and clever enough. A mountebank sang nonsense songs and juggled while balanced on a pole, and mocked the passersby with hurled insults, all in good fun . . . until he chose to mock a Capulet who'd stopped to stare.

It was not Tybalt – it was some lesser, vacuous cousin – but he was quick enough to anger, and his shouts of, 'Capulet, to me!' quickly drew a knot of red and black around him, which ranged out to surround the jester. The jester's painted face took on an anxious look, and his eyes darted around for escape, or rescue, and found neither. Someone kicked the pole from under him, and he went tumbling, but tumbling is a mountebank's trade, and he came up unhurt – until another Capulet punched him squarely in the mouth.

'Churls,' Mercutio said. He was gripping the hilt of his sword. 'Clowns beating clowns – it's unseemly. We should take a hand, Ben.'

'No,' I said. 'Two Capulets were killed this morning, and Montague blamed. No more brawling today.'

Mercutio's sympathies were with the jester, or at least

against the Capulets now joining in the beating. 'We can't let them trounce him without an answer! We look like cowards!'

'He's no kin or oath to us,' I said. I winced, though, when I saw a boot drive deep, and the jester's head snap back. 'Balthasar, run for the city watch. Bring them.'

'Sir,' he said, and dashed away.

It took too long, but he did return with the prince's liveried men; the Capulets were warned by shouts, and melted into the thick crowds, leaving behind the huddled body of the mountebank and his broken pole. He wasn't dead, at least.

And it proved to me that the Capulets were raw-nerved today, and ready for any kind of insult to be avenged. Not a good day to be abroad in Montague colours.

I'd taken note of the Capulet cousin who'd started the trouble. Close personal note.

And so, when the bells rang to summon the faithful to mass, I said, 'Off to the chapel with us, then, you scruffy pagans. You could all do with a sermon or two.' Such a visit served two good purposes – it would ease the gossip about my missed morning mass, and it protected us from Capulet wrath for a time. In the heat of the afternoon, after mass, no one would be so eager to fight.

'Not I!' Mercutio said with such alarm he might have been the devil himself. 'I'm fresh-shrived just this morning, I assure you. I've no desire to have a double blessing.'

He winked at me, just a quick and fleeting expression that made me think his shriving was less of the spirit than the flesh . . . and had come from the hands of his Tomasso, who was studying for the priesthood. I cleared my throat in uncomfortable realisation, and nodded, and Mercutio darted off through the crowd, cheerful and mad. He made it a point to flirt with a young, comely shop girl. He often did such things, though I did not think he appreciated her beauty for anything more than what was visible. Safer for him to be thought a rake.

'The rest of you,' I said to the men, who looked sadly resigned, 'off to the church.'

Balthasar and Abraham ranged ahead, while I accepted the cordial greetings of allies and neighbours on our way through the crowds, with Alessandro and two others trailing behind. By the time I caught up to them, Balthasar and Abraham had found trouble.

Capulet trouble, in the narrow street that led off the square. As I found them, Abraham said, in a pleasant enough tone, 'Do you bite your thumb at us, sir?' A common enough insult, one that would at least occasion a challenge.

The Capulet smirked. 'I do bite my thumb, sir.'

This time, the tone was not so pleasant. 'Do you bite your thumb at us, sir?' Abraham was plainly giving him a chance to walk away, but the Capulet's smirk only widened. He shrugged and glanced at his companion in red and black. 'Is the law on our side, if I say aye?'

'No,' the other Capulet said, clearly the more cautious. His caution, though well planted, did not take root.

'No, sir,' the first said, in a hearty and mocking tone, 'I do not bite my thumb at you, sir, but I do bite my thumb.'

The second clearly gave up his attempt to make peace, and stepped forward then to brace my servants. 'Do you quarrel, sir?'

'Quarrel, sir? No, sir.' Abraham had his own blood up and

running high, and Balthasar's warning pluck at his sleeve did nothing to dissuade him. I considered calling them in, but I saw more Capulet colours pushing towards us.

And some of them worn by Tybalt.

'If you do, sir, I am for you; I serve as good a man as you,' warned the Capulet bravo.

'No better,' Abraham scoffed, well aware I was behind him.

'Well, sir—' began the first Capulet, but he was cut off.

'Say *better* – here comes one of my master's kinsmen,' the other Capulet muttered, and now that they knew Tybalt was watching, the matter was as inevitable as a falling wall's crash.

'Yes, better, sir,' the first instantly amended.

'You lie,' Abraham said.

And that was the moment when it turned from speech to action. 'Draw, if you be men,' the Capulet spat, and steel appeared, on both sides – the two Capulets, and my own men.

I had a choice then, but I knew the Capulets were wounded today, and I'd done the blooding, true enough. It would do well for Montague to yield gracefully, and in public view.

So I stepped forward and beat down their swords with my own. 'Part, fools!' I said, and shoved Abraham back. Balthasar, ever attentive, stepped back willingly. 'Put up your swords.' And it might have calmed the waters, if only Tybalt had not stepped in behind me.

His voice was silken and cold with amusement. 'What, are you drawn among these heartless hinds? Turn, Benvolio. Look upon your death.'

Balthasar was trying to signal me to withdraw, but I knew there was no way to avoid this now; it was a direct challenge from an equal, or near equal. I turned to face Tybalt, and the sight of his arrogant face made my heart race and my hands shake with the need to do for him what I'd done for his man earlier in the day.

But I did try. 'I do but keep the peace,' I said, as reasonably as I could. 'Put up your sword, or use it to part these men with me.'

He laughed. 'Drawn, and you talk of peace!' The laughter stopped, and for the rest of it, he was deathly serious. 'I hate the word, as I hate hell, all Montagues, and you,' he said, and there was such venom in it that I did not doubt him. His sword slid free, and the glint of it in the sun caught my eyes. I felt myself go into that cold space again, all concerns falling free. 'Have at you, coward!'

He was no brawler; Tybalt had been trained by the best, and he was – by many accounts – better than me, and faster. Even with all my concentration, it was difficult to follow the flicker of his movements as he thrust; I parried, but only barely, and my returning attack was beaten casually aside. I was hard-pressed, then, all my attention on his body, his eyes, the deadly grace of his blade, but I was also aware of the shouts, the riotous noise of blades clashing and cudgels clacking on one another as our men joined the fray, as did others who wanted to earn favour from one house or the other. It quickly became a street brawl, with injured men screaming and blood slicking the cobbles. Someone was giving a call to battle to strike *both* houses down and stop the fight, but it was of little note until I heard Balthasar shout a warning, and over Tybalt's shoulder I saw the tall, imperious figures of Capulet and his lady wife. Capulet – elderly and gouty – was trying to call for a sword, but she foiled him in the way that wives do; meanwhile, behind *me,* I heard a similar argument in familiar voices.

My uncle Montague was also drawn to the fight, and my aunt was hell-bent on holding him back.

Good that the women of both houses had sense, because as I managed – again, barely – to hold off Tybalt's next assault, I heard more shouts, and saw the flash of the prince's liveried men pushing through and laying about with their own cudgels. Peacemakers, clouting heads to enforce the point. Behind them came the prince of Verona himself.

Tybalt and I broke off, breathing hard, glaring hate, and I realised that just this once, my cold distance was boiling away. I wanted his blood, badly as he wanted mine. There was a grudge between us, at least in my mind . . . Rosaline, beaten and huddled in a corner, and him, wiping blood from his hands. He needed a sword in the guts to teach him better.

But it was not to happen now. There were too many witnesses, and already our men were withdrawing to safety, throwing down their weapons under the threat of angry authority. The injured were being pulled aside to make room for Prince Escalus's advance; someone hastily threw down a cloak to prevent him from staining his shoes with the blood of victims.

He spoke. I don't remember the speech, and did not attend the words even then, save that it ended in a threat to kill anyone who broke the peace again, whether Capulet or Montague.

I was busy staring down Tybalt. Neither of us had put away our swords, though a sharp word from my uncle finally made me – reluctantly – sheathe.

Another time, Tybalt mouthed to me, as he was likewise forced to stand down. He clapped hands on the shoulders of his friends, and walked away. I would have followed, but Balthasar laid a hand on my own arm and held me back, forcefully enough that I should have struck him, but I knew he had only my safety at heart.

'Calm,' he whispered to me. 'Calm, sir; you are in the presence of the prince, and he asks your attendance.'

He was right; this was no time to indulge my rages, and with an effort that shook me to the marrows, I controlled myself, then nodded to him to let loose. He did, seeming doubtful, but I turned from Tybalt and walked towards my uncle and aunt, the Capulets, and Prince Escalus. The prince, surrounded by his retainers, frowned upon all of us. He looked pointedly down at the cobbles, still stained with blood, and the moaning injured being helped away from the area.

My uncle, ever the politician, turned upon me. 'Who broached this ancient quarrel?' His words might be neutral, but his tone was accusing. 'Speak, nephew. Were you by when it began?'

I explained that it was Tybalt's fault, in a way that might have been overly witty, given the situation and the moods of those involved; Capulet scowled at me, but he did not object, which proved to me he'd seen what had transpired, at least in part. Lady Capulet was too concerned with keeping her skirts from the blood.

My aunt, however, was more concerned – of course –

with Romeo and his absence from the fight than with my own mortal danger. I was the excess elder boy; I was bred to fight Montague's battles, after all. Romeo was meant for higher things.

I tried not to resent that. I lied, a bit; I knew he'd be blamed for having been with us at the market, and there was no reason to drag him down as well. I told my aunt most of the truth – that he had gone beyond the wall, and was in the wood. To my surprise, my uncle gave the rest of the story, though I was well prepared to provide the information Mercutio had given me.

'He's been seen there many a morning,' Montague said, with a frown not for me, but for the worry he felt, though he was careful to keep his voice low, and his back turned towards the Capulets. 'Adding tears to the fresh morning dew, and adding clouds to clouds with his sighs. Black and portentous may this humour prove, unless good counsel prevails.'

I wondered how much of what my grandmother knew had reached him. 'My noble uncle, do you know the cause?'

'I neither know it, nor can learn it of him.'

I pressed him, but it was obvious Romeo's father did not know the cause of his sorrows, which was a great relief . . . until around the corner, who should come but Romeo himself, trailed by the two faithful retainers. He looked doleful, but his sorrow lessened a bit, replaced by concern, when he saw the state of the street, his father and mother, and the prince. The frowning, lingering Capulets he ignored, save a single glance.

I knew, though, that from the determined set to his chin, Romeo was bound to spout something that would be not only unwise, but dangerous, and likely having to do with the Capulets, and so I quickly turned back to his father and said, 'Please you, step aside. I'll discover his grievance.'

'Do so,' he instructed me sternly, and extended his hand to my aunt. 'Come, madam, let's away.'

The Capulets, who would not have retreated before Montague lest they seem weak, or risked his impugning them to the prince behind their backs, took a hasty goodbye as well. The prince was slower to depart, but leave he did, taking most of his men with him, save a contingent left to watch those who stayed with severe and quelling stares.

'What passed here?' Romeo asked, looking around at the remnants of chaos. 'No, let me chance a guess: a clash between two unhappy houses.'

'I have no wounds,' I said. 'Thank you for your concern.'

'You never have wounds,' he said absently. 'Was it just a little while ago I left you?'

'Just a while.'

'Sad hours seem long . . . was that my father?'

'It was.' I shook my head. 'I know I am a fool to ask, but what sadness lengthens your hours?'

'Not having that, which having, makes them short.'

I knew well where he was headed. 'In love?'

'Out.'

'Of love?' *Please,* I thought, *let it be so. Let him be mournful because he's finally reconciled to the idiocy of his suit . . .*

But no. My cousin could never be so agreeable. 'Out of her favour, where I am in love . . .'

He went on, at least sensible enough not to mention Rosaline by name, but every worshipful syllable he spoke made me ache to beat him senseless. He knew it was a sickness, knew it was impossible, yet he persisted. I answered his plaintive questions, aware that attacking my cousin in the open square would be a fool's job.

But when he finally said, 'Farewell,' and met my eyes squarely and earnestly to say, 'You cannot teach me to forget,' I almost gave in to the temptation.

And as he walked away, lost in his fog of love and madness, I said, 'I'll pay that doctrine, or die in debt.'

And I meant it, every word – I would make him forget. No matter the cost.

The aftermath of the day's riot meant that the city of Verona fell into a sullen, deceptive peace. The Capulets still walked the streets in their gang of red-clothed bravos, and our men still matched them, but on opposite streets, and at a distance. Only the women of our houses met and mingled with any kind of impunity, and although it did not look like war, it most assuredly was; I knew women well enough to understand that most of what they did, exquisitely mannered or not, was calculated to improve their own station, or that of their families. In their own ways, the girls of noble families were soldiers – merely armed with very different weapons of charm, beauty, and guile.

If the women were soldiers, my grandmother was the undisputed and widely feared mercenary captain, capable of great cruelty and unexpected generosity. My mother no longer played the game – or rather, played a different one: that of widow, one foot in her husband's grave and waiting to step the other down. Her only concern seemed to be making acceptable matches for my sister and me. Veronica had consented to the old man they'd chosen for her – no doubt the showers of pearls and gems he'd given her had swayed her opinion of him – and as for me . . .

Upon arriving home, fresh from battle, I found I would soon be combed, scrubbed, curried like a horse on parade, and put before the marriageable young girls of Verona once more.

Mercutio, stretched out on my bed with his head propped on my feather pillow, watched with great, delighted attention as Balthasar chose my clothes for the event – nothing like as subdued as I would have preferred, but a sky blue doublet with black slashes, embroidered with our crest in gold. The tie-on sleeves were more blue, worked with floral designs. I stood in injured silence, head tipped high, as Balthasar added the damned things.

'The very thing to impress the ladies,' Mercutio offered, and popped a grape in his mouth. His eyes were shining with mischief. 'Pity that outsize codpieces have gone off fashion. Now, *that* would persuade a girl to overlook your considerable flaws.'

'My master has no flaws,' Balthasar said stoutly, 'save a sometimes questionable taste in companions.'

Mercutio clutched his chest and rolled theatrically. 'A hit! A palpable hit! Ben, you must discipline this fool before something terrible happens to him in his sleep.'

Balthasar sighed. 'Finished. You look a young Adonis, sir.'

'And look how Adonis ended,' Mercutio added. 'Go on, then. Turn for us. Show the goods.' There were times when I hated Mercutio, and I silently glared at him until he sat up. 'If shopping for wives makes you so ill-tempered, perhaps you're not suited for it,' he said. It was a gentle enough intimation, but it caught me wrong-footed, and I bared teeth at him in something less than a smile.

'It isn't that I don't favour women,' I said tightly. 'You know that well enough. It's that I don't like being marketed like a prize stallion.'

'Be careful they don't check your teeth, then,' he said. 'All men must marry, lest they burn, or so says the apostle. Even I am due for the altar soon enough. Reconcile yourself, boy, and stop drawing such a face as to appeal more to gargoyles than girls.' He paused, then continued, with a grin. 'And you are not the prize stallion, you know. That falls to Romeo. There's no reason to make a gelding of yourself.'

'Your friend speaks truth, master,' Balthasar said, and brushed a bit of dust from the velvet. He clucked his tongue in disapproval and brushed more energetically, until I felt like a carpet in need of beating. 'Heaven knows, a wife would do you considerable good, sir. Perhaps you'd not feel so in need of sneaking out at night and returning with ill-got bits and bobs.'

'To be fair,' Mercutio said before I could, 'he rarely brings them back here. I sell them on his behalf. And you, dear Balthasar, get a nice income for your silence, as you'd do well to remember.'

'I do confess it every Sunday,' he said placidly. 'Your lady mother is waiting, sir. I can do no more for you.'

That was both a relief and unfortunate, since it meant proceeding from the simmering pan to the roaring fire, but I sighed – not entirely manfully – and walked towards the door with the air of the condemned to the gibbet.

'Wine, Balthasar,' Mercutio said, reclining again. 'I

feel we should toast our friend's good fortune and future marriage prospects.'

Balthasar, never loath to give away my wine, was already in motion when I swept out, walking with a steady, fateful tread through the narrow, dark halls, into the hot blaze of the atrium courtyard garden, where my aunt Montague sat embroidering beneath the orange tree while her ladies chattered like bright-coloured birds. Her sharp eyes watched me go, no doubt well aware where I was bound.

I knocked at my mother's chamber door and was admitted immediately. There were two others seated with her at her small table, and a servant was pouring cooling drinks for all. My mother, in her widow's black, nodded to me pleasantly, but her eyes had gone a little cold. I was late. She was not amused.

'Benvolio,' she said. 'My son, I present to you Lady Scala, and her daughter, the lady Giuliana.'

I spared less than a glance for the visiting noblewoman, though I gave her an elaborate bow and kissed the air above her fingers with all the best courtesy. My mother would be noting any lapses in my courtly graces, I knew, but I'd been trained well, and hard, and I knew the line of my leg and the angle of my bowed head were perfect.

Then to the girl.

This was what my mother expected of me. Giuliana was thirteen, perhaps; where Veronica was, at fifteen, a well-practised vixen, this round-faced creature looked ill at ease in her finery, like a child playing at woman. I was no old man, but the difference between seventeen and thirteen seemed dire. I felt nothing for her but a distant sort of pity that she be thrust at me like a basket of baked goods in the market. She stood, though, and, with all her concentration, performed an adequate curtsy of her own, spreading her thick, muffling skirts wide as she bobbed. She still wore a maiden's cap, but beneath it her hair was a simple, uncomplicated brown. Her eyes were the same plain colour. She gave me a tentative smile, which I returned without any sense of feeling.

I knew what was expected of me. I took up the dish of sweets and offered it to her. She took a honeyed fig with intense relief and popped it into her mouth, chewing with too much enthusiasm for courtly correctness, and an uneven blush crawled up her neck and stained her cheeks as she realised she'd betrayed both her discomfort and her childish lust for such sweet things. She refused a second and sipped her juice, gaze furious and fixed on the table before her.

I did feel sorry for her, at least a little; she was a pawn in this game, and I at least had the status of some higher piece, perhaps a knight, perhaps even a castle. I'd be sacrificed in the end, but I could more likely achieve my ends than she.

'Do you play chess?' I asked her on impulse. Her gaze flew up to mine, wide and surprised, as if she'd never expected to actually have to *speak* to me. She glanced quickly at her lady mother, who gave her an encouraging smile.

'Y-yes,' she said. 'On occasion.'

'Would you like to play?'

'If – if my lady mother—'

'Of course,' Lady Scala said warmly. 'My daughter is most clever with such things. And with singing, and the lute. She's been well and classically trained.'

My mother's chess set was a large, baroque thing; it had

belonged to my father, I knew, and many was the time I had sat as a very young boy, struggling to learn the rules of the game. By eight I had been decent enough to outmanoeuvre my mother; by ten, I'd bested the chess master employed by her to test me.

Giuliana took her place across from me and studied the board. She picked up one of the pieces and studied it curiously. Her fingers, I noted, were still chubby, still child-length. She had growing left to do. 'I've never seen one like it,' she said. 'It's very beautiful.'

'My mother brought it from England,' I said. 'It was a gift for my father.' The pieces were minutely carved ivory and ebony, truly masterworks. She put the king carefully back in his place and, after a few seconds of contemplation, opened with her pawn. I countered. She moved. I countered. It went on so for several silent minutes before I began to see her pattern forming, and felt an unexpected surge of admiration.

Giuliana looked up at me, recognising that I'd appreciated her strategy, and smiled. The shyness was gone now, replaced with confidence. 'I studied under Master Traverna,' she said.

'And you do him credit,' I said, and moved out my knight. 'But I studied under Master Scagliotti, who defeated him twice.'

'*Only* twice,' she said, and moved her castle. 'Check.'

I glared at her, then down at the board. She was correct. I'd completely overlooked her trap. I quickly moved out of danger, and set up an attack of my own, which she defeated. Before long, we'd quite forgotten that we were expected to be potential mates, dancing politely around each other, and were trading wicked barbs as the pieces fell between us.

She was merciless, the tiny Lady Giuliana. I won, but it was a close thing, and if we'd been facing each other on the battlefield, the cost would have been high on both sides.

The colour was bright in her cheeks for another reason, at the end – true pleasure, I thought, and I was glad to see it, because I'd not had such a challenging and entertaining game in some time. I rose from the chair as she tipped her king, and took her hand in mine. She rose, suddenly awkward again, and the blush deepened as I bent over her knuckles and brushed my lips lightly over the skin. I kept my gaze on her as I did it, and saw the response in her. It frightened her, I saw; she might never have felt such a thing before.

All in all, not as much of a disaster as it might have been, and when the lady and her daughter took their leave, my mother turned to me with a radiant, completely delighted smile. 'My son, you conquered her heart completely! I had no idea you could be so charming.'

I shrugged. 'The girl's clever,' I said. 'Far cleverer than she looks, or than her mother wishes her to be.'

'I know such things appeal to you,' my mother said. 'But, Benvolio, remember one thing: A clever wife can be an asset or a burden. She'll require close watching, that one.'

'I thought you wished me married, Mother!'

'As I do, my son.' She touched my hair gently, and kissed my cheek with paper-dry lips. 'I also wish you happy. That is a selfish failing, but I cannot help it. Do you wish me to offer for her hand?'

I closed my eyes and sighed. Giuliana's baby-fat face, lit with a shy smile, appeared before me, but beside it was another face, older and leaner, framed by falling waves of night-dark hair.

Another clever girl, one whose spell I could not break no matter how much logic argued I must. When I shut my eyes I saw her glimmering in candlelight, her body a delicious shadow beneath the nightgown, her full lips rapt and parted as she read her poetry.

I opened my eyes then, and said, 'Not as yet. But I do not say no outright.'

My mother, in that moment, looked as transcendently happy as I could ever imagine. She gripped my shoulders and kissed me effusively – both cheeks, then the mouth. She framed my face with her thin hands and gazed on me with true joy.

'I am so glad you are seeing sense,' she said. 'This would be a good match, Benvolio. The girl comes with a good dowry, and her family has ties to the pope himself, as well as several dukes. I could not hope for better.'

Neither could I, I thought. There were certain things that would remain beyond my reach, and one of them, always, would be Rosaline Capulet. Best I resign myself to that now, and find what joy I might. Giuliana was, as yet, no great beauty, but she had a sweetness of spirit and a sharpness of wit that would do well enough to complement me.

But I felt a sense of loss, of failure, so great that I could not bear to be in the glare of my mother's happiness. I took my leave quickly, pleading affairs to conclude, but I had no refuge back in my own rooms; Mercutio was there, waiting for an account of my gruesome failure, and to admit some partial success in my marriage hunt would be unsettling and humiliating. I did not know how I felt. I did not want to explain it to him, for fear he might suss out the grief I felt at losing a girl I'd never had.

Instead, I went to see Master Silvio, the blademaster.

He was at work with one of the distant cousins – Pietro, this one, up from the country and fumble-footed. I leant against the wall of the large, empty room and watched as Master Silvio – dressed as always in a doublet, hose, street shoes, and half cape – drove the boy back at sword's point out of the marked square. 'No,' he said, and lowered his point as the boy struggled to find his balance again. 'No, this won't do, my boy. You wield that blade as if you plan to reap wheat with it. Elegance, young master. Precision. These are the foundations of the art of the sword – Ah. Young Master Benvolio. Did we have a lesson today?'

'No,' I said. 'I need a bout to cool my blood.'

Silvio's thin eyebrows arched. He was a tall man, spidery, with long greying hair that was always queued back to prevent it from obscuring his vision. His eyes were a startling cool grey, and according to the talk of the streets, Master Silvio had been responsible for the deaths of at least a dozen men in his life of duelling, if not more. He had not a visible scar on him.

Duelling with the master was something few wanted to do for recreation.

Young Pietro passed me and whispered, 'Thank you,' as he collapsed on a stool in the corner, breathing hard. His clothes were soaked with sweat. I chose a rapier and dagger from the collection neatly hung on the whitewashed wall, and turned to Master Silvio.

'You're wearing your finest,' he said. 'Perhaps it might be wise to—'

I attacked in a leaping lunge, and he glided out of the way of the blade in a fade so graceful he might as well have been a ghost. He had none of the brawler's technique so valuable in a street fight, but in a noble duel, there was no one better. He was right: I ought to have at least removed the hanging, annoying sleeves, but I had a black fire burning, and I needed to put it out.

'You always tell us to be ready to fight in what we wear,' I said. 'An enemy may not wait for me to remove my finery.'

He smiled. It was a meaningless expression with Master Silvio, merely a polite movement of the lips that affected the eyes not at all. 'I do say that,' he said. 'Very well, Benvolio. Have at me.'

I did, using all my concentration – I had a good reach, a sound balance, near-flawless control of my blade. It did me no good at all. Master Silvio, fighting at his true level, disarmed me in ten exchanges, swirling his blade up mine to corkscrew it out of my grip and into the air. I dropped, rolled like a tumbler, and came up to grab it before it hit the ground, but that left me fighting in an awkward crouch, unable to fully rise. 'Not bad,' he told me, as he threatened me with a slow and agonising death at the point of his blade in my guts. 'But not quite fast enough. You should never try that unless you can make it to your feet again before your opponent can reach you.'

I threw all my strength into knocking his sword back and gained the space to straighten, then retreated two steps to firm footing. 'Should I content myself with being dead, or take the risk?'

'There are never only two choices, Benvolio.' I used a trick Mercutio had taught me, coming in close and forcing Silvio's hand to an awkward angle, but the man danced easily away, sidestepping the foot I placed to trip him, and then I was exposed and extended, and his sword was at my throat, the point just stinging me. His grey eyes were very, very cold.

I dropped my sword and dagger in surrender. For a long moment, he did not move his point, but then he suddenly whipped it up and took several long strides back. I'd waked some instinct in him that was best not stirred, I realised. For one moment, he'd actually wanted to kill. Considered it, in the cold, animal way that a hungry beast considers prey.

'You're a fool,' he said. 'And you've ruined your doublet. Your mother will be most unhappy.'

I looked down. There was a vivid slash across my chest, one I'd not even felt. It had gone deep, all the way through the padded velvet, cut the linen shirt beneath, and there was a thin line of blood on my skin. Now that I'd seen it, it stung like a swarm of bees. The sight of the blood made me feel light and watery.

'Satisfied?' he asked me tightly. 'Did I exorcise your demons, young master? Do you imagine that's what your uncle pays me to do, indulge the whims of spoilt young men? I am here to teach you, and from the look of it, you've learnt nothing of any significance. Were I in earnest, you would be choking on my sword just now, and your mother doubly grieved. The blade is no game.'

'I know,' I said. I felt remarkably still, all the black rage gone as if it had fled through the cut in my chest. 'I killed a man yesterday with a sword and dagger to his heart. I don't even know his name.'

Silvio turned to regard me, and the chill slowly faded out of his gaze, replaced by something like regret. He came back to put a firm hand on my shoulder. 'Best you don't,' he said. 'I recall how it felt, to pass such judgment the first time. Sending a man to God is a heavy thing, young master. Little wonder you feel burdened.'

It wasn't the killing, though, or at least not in whole. It was so many things, all impossible to explain. For Master Silvio, who lived for his art, there would be no understanding of this awful feeling of loss for what I'd never owned. And he was not wrong in what he said; the dead man's face, with its deep scar and blind white eye, haunted me. He was an enemy, and he had earned what he was paid, but I still felt that there was a debt owed.

Master Silvio watched me for a long moment, then nodded. 'I see there are still demons in you to be exorcised. Take up your sword and we will do drills. There is nothing like drills to drive the thoughts from your head. Sweat is better than wine for emptying the soul.'

He was right in that. The ritual of thrust, parry, retreat – of the eight parries and the eight thrusts – of the steps of the deadly dance – all that drove the candlelight from my mind, and even the shadow of her smile dimmed.

Dead men did not haunt me so much as Rosaline's smile.

Better to marry than to burn.

The apostle had it very right.

FROM THE PEN OF ROMEO MONTAGUE DISCOVERED BY HIS SERVANTS AND GIVEN TO LA SIGNORA DI FERRO

She hath, and in that sparing makes huge waste,
For beauty starved with her severity
Cuts beauty off from all posterity.
She is too fair, too wise, wisely too fair,
To merit bliss by making me despair:
She hath forsworn to love, and in that vow
Do I live dead that live to tell it now.

I had spent the last week collecting the various accounts of insults offered to House Montague, and they were gratifyingly legion: a poet who'd refused to take a birthday commission from my lady aunt, on the grounds that he was already sworn to write an ode for Capulet; a goldsmith who'd delivered a shoddy piece of work to my uncle; the feckless cousin who'd caused the beating of the jester in the marketplace; and an aspiring ally of Capulet who'd made rude jests in my hearing regarding my lady mother.

That one, I put at the top of my list.

'A man bound for marriage ought not take such risks,' Balthasar complained as he chose my grey clothing, soft boots, and silk mask from the locked chest.

'I am not bound for marriage. I said only I would not refuse her yet.'

'If you are caught on one of these dark nights, you will be hanged, and your station won't save you.'

'You fret like an old woman,' I said. 'And I do not mean my grandmother.'

'She'd be the first to consign you to the scaffold.'

Balthasar wasn't wrong in that. What he didn't say, and wouldn't, was that I would not go alone; he might escape hanging, but Mercutio, caught with the stolen goods, might well perish. Balthasar himself would certainly be turned out penniless, reduced to working as a sell-sword, a footpad, or worse. I would be the ruin not just of myself, but of my friends.

And still, I had to go. I do not know why; perhaps, as Mercutio had once suggested, I had a devil in me that no amount of holy water could exorcise. Or perhaps it was the last rebellion I was allowed before I was led to the altar, to marriage, to all that was laid out for me through my life. I was a Montague, after all. I had responsibilities.

As Prince of Shadows, I had no such burdens. I had only liberties – liberties not given, but taken. Wearing the mask, I was finally, irrevocably in my own control, and no one else's.

'You're risking your neck for little gain,' Balthasar grumbled as I tucked the mask away.

'I risk my neck every day in the streets for no gain at all but my family's name,' I said, and buckled on my sword and dagger. 'I am a soldier in a war that never ends. Why not risk all for myself instead?'

He shook his head, as if he didn't understand – and likely he couldn't fathom why I did these things. Balthasar was doggedly loyal, and clever . . . things one wanted in a servant. But he had no . . . no *spark*.

I had met few indeed who did.

And one of them had glowed golden in the candlelight, twirling her braid around a finger as she read of a love she would never know . . . Rosaline's spark was set to be hidden away, if not extinguished entire. And I could not – *could not* – think of her again, for the sake of my own soul.

Instead, I ducked out the window, down, and into the streets.

Unlike most evenings on which I ventured out, I hadn't asked Romeo or Mercutio to join . . . I wanted to be alone, to test my edge against the whetstone of the city guards and the security of my target's walls. It was late enough that the God-fearing had taken to their beds, and the rest were deep in their cups or embarked on more sinister business than mine. I had made enquiries, and I knew where the man who'd insulted my mother lodged; it was a surprisingly respectable district, and a quiet, well-kept building, though not utterly without the usual drama of the city. As I stalked beneath it in the shadows, I heard the familiar notes of voices rising in a sleepy quarrel from the second story, and a babe's thin wail from the third's open window. It was a hot, still night, and all the shutters had been thrown wide to admit whatever breeze might visit.

My target lived on the less favoured top floor, four stories up in the cramped space beneath the roof. From his open window, no lamps glowed; no voices echoed. Either – likely – he was out drinking and boasting and courting loose women, or – less likely – he was abed and deep asleep. I did not much care, either way, save that I would have to be more careful in the second case.

I used the staircase, cat-footing lightly past tight-shut doors. On the third-floor landing, the neat-kept building began showing signs of neglect and hard use . . . battered walls, a broken-off bracket where a lamp had once burnt. It was ink-dark, but I did not mind that. I found the lock by

touch and tried it gently; it was fixed fast. That called for
the lock picks. I prided myself on this skill, in particular; I
had practised for months blindfolded or sealed in pitch-black
rooms until I needed nothing but touch and sound to break
any lock I had ever met.

This one was no different. Cautious exploration told me
he'd left the key in the hole on the other side of the door, so
he was home, and abed; I smiled a little, inwardly, and took
out a piece of sheepskin I carried rolled up in my bag. That,
laid flat, slid easily under the door's gap, and I pushed the
lock picks in and heard the dull thump of the key falling on
the cushion on the other side.

It was not even technically lock picking if he'd made it
so easy.

I used his own key and came inside, shutting the door with
care behind me and locking it again. I could hear him now,
snoring lightly. He was facedown and loose-limbed . . . but I
had not reckoned on the girl.

Because there was a girl.

She was lying next to him – wide awake, staring at me
with saucer eyes. As she opened her mouth, I put a finger
to mine, and pulled out two gold coins from my purse. She
paused, blinking, and I mimed locking my own lips as I held
the coins out. She mimed back a throat cutting, then looked
at her bed companion. I admit, by that time I had begun to
realise that the sheet did not by any means cover all of her,
and though the darkness made it more of a suggestion of
assets than the true sight of them, the room was suddenly a
good deal too warm, and my clothing too tightly sewn.

I shook my head. No throat cutting for her snoring
friend.

She silently held out her hand for the coins, and I dropped them in, careful not to make them chime, and I closed her fingers over them before lifting her hand to drop a kiss on the rough skin of her knuckles. She drew in a sharp breath, and I almost thought she might scream, but then she sat up and . . .

Kissed me.

It was surprising, and I should have pulled away for many reasons, not the least of which was my own self-preservation, but there was something darkly wonderful about the danger of it. She was only a bit older than I, and warm and round and womanly, and willing, and for a moment I entertained a feral thought that perhaps he *might* not wake . . .

I didn't pull away. It was not a sweet kiss; it was wet and wanton and very pointed about what the girl wanted of me, and until her man grunted and rolled on his side, I was almost, almost tempted.

I stepped back, breathing hard, and saw her dizzying pale skin shining in the faint moonlight coming in the window. I smiled at her and waggled a chiding finger at her. *No.*

She shrugged and, clutching the gold, subsided back into the bed. Her paramour rolled over, flung a heavy arm across her, and went back to buzzing like a beehive.

It was a beehive I did not want to overturn, and so I worked quickly, ransacking the few items of furniture in his room. Nothing of any value; even his sword was of only middling quality. He did, however, have a fine Capulet dagger half-hidden beneath a mess of filthy smallclothes, and I tucked that away before turning my attention to his locked chest. It was not large, but it was of better construction than anything else he owned, and it was a bit more of a challenge to open than the average – half a minute, perhaps, which seemed an eternity when considering that the saucy trollop might at any minute decide to keep my gold and betray me anyway. But she kept her part of the bargain, and I eased open the casket, and within . . .

. . . within was all that remained of his family's honour. I took out a tattered old parchment, heavy with seals that gleamed with gold leaf in the moon's glow; that, I stowed away. There were a few heavy chains, a few gems, and, at the bottom, a weapon that was racehorse to the nag he carried for his daily wear. My enemy, one Giuliano Roggocio, had once come from a prominent family, one fallen to low times; I knew the name Roggocio from family tales. My grandmother's backside rested on wood taken from one of their household doors. She had seen the death of that clan, and likely had been its cause, and they had been wealthy beyond dreams.

The man had reason to hate my house, but none to blacken the name of my mother, and for that, he would have to pay the rest of his family's fortune.

I took the chains and jewels, and the sword, and I left him the parchment, with its seals of nobility. Let him rejoice in his bloodline as much as I rejoiced in mine.

I locked the chest again, blew a kiss to the girl, and climbed into the window. The night was hot and still; a cart rumbled noisily over cobbles somewhere to my left, but from the sound of it, it was several streets over. A baker, most like, starting the cycle of bread for the day. I faced back into the room, balancing on the sill, and gauged my target.

I heard the snoring buzz of Roggocio's slumber suddenly break into a snort, and I looked down to see his eyes coming open, and staring straight at me.

'Dog!' he shouted. 'Thief! Stop!' He vaulted naked from his bed and launched himself at me. I was caught wrong-footed, balanced on a thin sill, and I knew that if he dragged me into the room I'd have no choice but to kill to stop him. Him, and perhaps the girl.

That, I would not do. I was a thief, yes. But no assassin.

Roggocio did not make it easy for me. He grabbed for me, and his scrabbling fingers ripped at my mask and pulled it loose.

With the moon at my back, I could only hope he did not see my face.

I leapt up, caught the edge of the roof, swung my legs into the room, and hit him squarely in the chest, sending him flying back onto the bed and the alarmed, now-screaming girl. I reversed the momentum to take me the other direction, over the lip of the roof and onto its slick clay tiles. A difficult trick, but one a good sneak thief must know to survive. I regularly dosed my soft boot soles with resin to make them grip, but the hardest part was to catch my balance, which I did, spreading my arms wide to shed momentum. Even then, it was a near thing. The pitch of the roof was steeper than I'd thought, and one of the tiles broke free and began to slide. I knew better than to flail; if one tile was loose, the others were no better. I dropped flat, catching myself on both hands, and swarmed up to the peak of the roof, where I pulled myself upright again and ran lightly down the centre seam, leaving the sound of alarms and cries behind. I surprised a sleeping cat, which bounded off with a yowl of protest, and then I gathered speed to make the leap to the next, lower roof. From there, I dropped into the iron basket of a balcony, and then down to the cobbles.

A near miss. Very near. But still, a success. I told myself

that he could not have seen me, and even if he had glimpsed some part of my face, he could never have associated those features with those of Benvolio Montague.

With my bag full of treasure, I sought out Mercutio.

He was not asleep. I'd thought to catch him still abed, but he was up, dressed, and prowling his rooms restlessly. When I climbed in his window he jumped like the cat I'd startled, sword half drawn, and sheathed it irritably at the sight of me. 'Where have you been? I've been waiting for word of your corpse! Don't you know better than to do this alone?'

For answer, I held out the bag. He swore at the heaviness of it, and dumped the treasure out onto the bed. It was better than I'd expected. In the dim room where I'd pilfered it, I hadn't been able to assess quality, but these were fine indeed, the last vestiges of a once-wealthy family. He whistled as he held up a ruby as large as a robin's egg. It had a heart of fire in it that made me shiver, and suddenly I felt that I'd made a mistake, a large one. These were jewels that would be difficult to dispose of safely – too recognisable, like the sword.

'This could be cut down,' Mercutio said, examining the ruby, 'though it would be a pity to ruin such a thing. Look you, how the light catches in it, like blood.'

'Exactly like blood,' I said. 'We need to be rid of these things quickly.'

'And this?' He held up the sword, admiring the watered steel. 'I could have a goldsmith mount another hilt on it. Shame to waste such a beautiful blade.'

'Make sure the goldsmith keeps his mouth well closed,' I said. 'There's a rope in this for us if he doesn't.'

'Isn't there always?' Mercutio opened a secret door in the wall of his room and put the things within, locked it back, and hung the key on a chain around his neck. 'It will take time, you know. Not even I can work miracles. I'm not the Christ of crime.'

'Heathen,' I said. He pursed his lips and blew me a kiss. 'Were you truly dressed out of worry for me? It seems unlikely, I think.' He sank into a deep armchair, one long-fingered hand pressed to his forehead to hide his eyes. I did not need to see them to read the dejection in his body. 'Trouble in your sinful paradise, my brother?'

'What would you know of sin?' he shot back. 'You've cold milk in your veins when it comes to love; I know it.'

I thought, unwillingly, of Rosaline, but I said, 'I had a naked woman kiss me tonight while I was rifling for these little trinkets.'

That surprised him enough that he took his hand away from his face. 'Naked.'

'As sinful Eve,' I said. 'And quite a willing mouth on her, too.'

'And?'

I shrugged. 'Best to get on with the job, I thought.' Though there had been a drunken moment when I'd considered something much different, in wild and exotic detail.

'Disappointing.' He put the hand back in place again. 'We'll teach you how to use a woman yet. Granted, I have only a little experience in that way, but more than you, I'd wager.' He laughed a little, but it sounded like gallows laughter to me. 'I'm to get more, it seems.'

I sat down opposite him, suddenly worried that this was not merely Mercutio's usual dark moods. 'Tell me,' I bade him.

'My dear and sainted father has decreed that I soar too high to remain free, and so I am to be caged,' he said. The bitter taint in his voice chilled me. 'Caged and hooded, jessed and trained to the perfumed hand of a lady. But no matter how you tame a falcon, still they will hunt, will they not? Hunt, or die.'

'What's this talk of death, my friend? Of cages?' Surely his father, whatever he suspected, would not put his own son to a public trial for the crime of sodomy; that would forever tarnish his own name. Were they discovered, my own offences would be puffballs and nonsense beside it.

'I put it to you plainly: I am to be swiftly married off,' he said. 'Married and buried, wed and dead. 'Tis no accident the words rhyme so well.'

I let out a sigh of relief. 'And 'tis no surprise, as they'd published the banns – what brings on this dark—'

'Dark and lark, love and dove, hawk and handsaw, I am not fit for this, Benvolio; *I am not fit* – do you not see it?' He was weeping, I realised with a start; he angrily swept tears from his cheeks and glared at me as if I were the cause of all his suffering. 'I will hurt her, this soft bride of mine; I cannot help it – I am all the wrong shape, you see? I may be forced, as she may be forced, but both of us will bleed for it . . . but blood is all that families require, marriage blood, maiden blood, proof of cruel love . . . She is too young; she cannot understand what I am, what I feel, what I know of myself. I am to hurt her, and she is to hurt me. And it comes on us fast as plague.'

It was clear to me then. 'There is a date set.'

'Two months hence,' he said miserably. 'Two months. And Tomasso weeps and will not see me, and there is naught I can do to make any of it less vile. We have been wed in heart for five years, from the moment we first clapped eyes on each other, and now it is broken, broken as my heart. I know I will hurt this girl, in revenge. It is not a pretty thing, but the thought of her sickens me, and I cannot . . . I cannot—'

'Run,' I said, and leant forward to lock gazes with my friend. 'Take the money you've been paid for the gold and jewels thus far, pay for passage to some friendlier place, and take Tomasso away. There is a way out, Mercutio. You must take it.'

'Now you thieve for me, instead of your whims and honours?' He laughed softly, and shook his head. 'I might steal away, but Tomasso – he is too afraid, I think. Verona is all he knows, all he loves besides me. I have begged him to go; we could be pilgrims on the road to perdition, but he will not have it. You have a generous heart. I love you for it, but my own heart is bound here, too.'

'Then refuse,' I said. 'Refuse the girl. Refuse the wedding.'

'I would ruin her more by doing that than if I blooded her,' he said, 'and you know it. A marriage promise broken stains the girl, not the man who refuses her. She would be doomed. It would destroy her, and her father's honour.'

He was right. We lived in a world that lived and breathed honour, and a promise was a bond that we broke only with dire consequences. A lesser man than my friend would not care a fig for the girl, or her family, but Mercutio wasn't so shallow. The world was a bundle of spikes and razors, and any move he made would cut deep. Better to sacrifice Tomasso, and a love that could never be acknowledged, than to make the innocent suffer.

That did not make it any less painful.

'If you change your mind,' I said, 'my gold is yours. You know this.'

'I know,' he said, and clapped hands with me, then embraced. 'I know.'

I kept company with him until just before dawn, then slipped away in the grey. I came home to a bed well warmed with hot bricks, and a sleepy servant who put it about that I was abed with a summer's ague, to buy me the morning to rest.

I slept ill, and dreamt of blood and a woman's wet kiss, and candlelight gleaming on skin and shadow. Dark eyes that challenged as much as they welcomed.

Rosaline.

The next day brought fate, and doom, and death with the dawning.

The first I knew of the trouble was a hammering on my door. I'd slept a bare two hours, perhaps, and Balthasar even less; he went yawning and red eyed to admit Romeo.

'Sir, your cousin is not well—' Balthasar tried to stop his onward rush, but Romeo simply swept him aside.

'It's Mercutio,' he blurted, and threw the covers back on my bed. 'He left me in the market after mass, and I saw him being followed, and I think the servant was from his own family's house. Get up, Ben. *Get up!*'

I did, grabbing for whatever clothing came to hand – a wrinkled linen shirt, hose that had seen better days. I did not bother with a doublet, only threw on a leather jerkin and loose calf-length trousers like a labourer. 'Change,' I ordered him. 'No Montague colours. Balthasar, get him something less noticeable. Do it quickly.'

Balthasar scurried off to the chests to find something as Romeo began to unbuckle and untie his Montague doublet. The hose would do, being dark. I took away his too-recognisable dagger and sword and substituted a good but plain set from my stores. We dressed quickly, in charged silence, all too aware

that we might be too late. If Mercutio was being stalked, it
would be better if it were a straightforward enemy who wished
to plant a sword's point in his chest . . . but if someone from the
Ordelaffi household was on his trail, something darker was
brewing. He never allowed a servant to trail him, hadn't since
his childhood; he'd allied himself with us both from nature
and from necessity, to avoid his family saddling him with such
a hindrance. It was new, and worrying, that they felt the need
to eye his comings and goings.

We dashed down the hallway, past startled servants, and
at the door we came face-to-face with my sister, Veronica,
and her giggling cadre of scheming, vicious friends, who
were arriving fresh from the market. One of them, I noticed,
was one of the Ordelaffi girls, a cousin of Mercutio's.

Veronica stepped back and fanned herself, and her
friends goggled at us with a fresh wave of muffled laughter.
'Well,' she said. 'It seems too early by far for a costumed
ball, and why you would go as *peasants* . . .'

Romeo pushed her out of the way, and Veronica gave a
shrill squeak of alarm as he darted past. She turned on me,
furious at the slight, and her eyes narrowed. 'Going to find
your dear friend?' she asked. The giggling of the girls with her
stopped as if it had been severed by a blade. 'His family seeks
him, too. Wherever could he be, do you think? What might he
be doing so early in the morning, hidden in the trees?'

I looked from her to the Ordelaffi girl, sharp faced and
fox-like, with the cruel gleam in her eyes of someone with a
grudge. I gripped my sister hard by the shoulders and shook
her until the jewelled pins in her hair began to slip free.
'What did you do?' I asked Veronica. 'What did you say?'

'It's a sin,' she said, 'what he does. And you know it. You

have sometimes been cruel to me, brother. Measure for measure, that's how we play, is it not?'

'You'd kill a man for your wounded pride?'

'I'm a Montague,' she said. Her colour was high, and her eyes bright and vulpine. 'I do not suffer slights. Not even from *you.*'

I should have hit her, but I did not have time. She had wasted enough of it already.

I dashed out after Romeo, caught up, and said, 'He's in the trees.' We both knew the place; it was a trysting spot that we'd seen Mercutio go before, to meet Tomasso.

I prayed God he was not meeting him this morning.

God does answer all prayers, but sometimes, he answers with a cold and remorseless denial . . . and I knew, as I came through the gates and started running down the path, that there would be no miracle for us today. There was a knot of men already there, most in Ordelaffi colours, though a few onlookers had already gathered to see whatever show was being staged for their benefit . . . and then I saw Tomasso.

The young man was thin and serious, as befitted a would-be religious man, and he still wore the sort of postulant robes that I'd swathed myself in when I'd gone out with Friar Lawrence. His hood was thrown back, and his face was set and pale, but tranquil as a martyr's.

He was on his knees, with his hands bound roughly behind his back, and a circle of armed men surrounded him.

They were having a good deal more trouble with Mercutio. I heard the ring of steel, and saw him darting between the trees, graceful and full of fury as he tried to win the way to his prisoned lover.

He failed, but not from any lack of skill; he gave up on his own accord when Lord Ordelaffi, burly and crimson faced, shoved aside the soldiers and stalked up to his son bare-handed. Even enraged, Mercutio could not wound his father. He dropped the point of his sword, and his father took it from him and flung it viciously away, then followed that with a closed-fisted blow so mighty it laid Mercutio in the dirt.

Romeo lunged forward. I grabbed him and held him still. My grip was too tight, and would leave bruises, but I could not care about that just now. I burnt, as Romeo did, to go to the help of our friend, but there was no help now.

We could do nothing but stand and watch.

The beating his father gave Mercutio was brutal, and it went on a long time. It was not quite the death of him. He was breathing yet, and capable of lifting his head from the ground of his own accord, though I was not sure that he could see through the torrents of blood that obscured his face. His father made sure of clear vision, though, by having servants wipe the crimson from his eyes and hold him in a wavering, kneeling position for the rest that came.

Lord Ordelaffi left him there and turned towards his men. 'Finish it,' he said in a rough, disgusted voice. 'Quickly. Let us be done with this unpleasant business.'

I had never spoken to Tomasso. The only knowledge I had of him was from Mercutio's lips, who'd spoken of his kindness, his warmth, his intelligence, his passion for God and learning. He did not struggle when they pulled him roughly to his feet, nor when they fitted the noose around his neck.

Mercutio tried to save him. I could not hear the words, but I knew he was telling his father anything, *everything* to spare the boy's life, trying with all his skill and wit and charm; when he started to raise his voice, to beg whether others might hear, his father ordered a belt passed around his throat, and had him choked just enough to silence him. Romeo was weeping to see it, and it was all I could do to hold him back. And myself, God help me.

Mercutio could not even scream as they hauled on the rope and pulled Tomasso from his knees, and then his feet.

It was not a large tree they hanged the boy from. I don't know why that bothered me so, that it was so small, so *pathetic,* because the branch was sturdy enough to bear his slight weight when they pulled him up, and though his toes kicked just a few inches above the ground, it was enough; it would serve as well as a mighty height.

It took a horribly long time to be finished, and Romeo wavered as if he might be sick, until I hissed in his ear, 'If they see you flinch, they'll turn on us, too.' The mood of the onlookers was gleeful, not solemn; they cheered when Tomasso swung, and threw stones at him as he twisted and died. I wanted desperately to kill them, kill them *all,* but I hung on to my cousin in grim fury and let none of that show. *You've cold milk in your veins,* Mercutio had accused me, but I was all fire and ash now, and hardly holding it in. No one had yet recognised me, or Romeo, and if they did our station might not save us; we were Mercutio's close companions, and in the heat of this awful frenzy, that would be enough to see us beaten or killed. It would destroy the Ordelaffi family, but likely politics was not on their minds just now.

I thought they might hang Mercutio after, but instead they left him weeping and bloody on the dirt, fingers plunged deep in the soil as if he wished to bury himself in it.

Lord Ordelaffi said a few words to his chief servant,

then stalked off with most of his attendants, heading for the walls. He wiped his son's blood from his hands with a silk cloth, and left it lying soiled at the side of the road. One of the peasants scurried over to retrieve it. The blood would wash out, and silk was precious.

The servant had a good voice for speaking, deep and authoritative, and he told those of us still lingering that the filthy sodomite who'd been justly hanged had waylaid the heir of Ordelaffi, but that Mercutio had resisted him and vengeance had been exacted for the crime, and everyone must attest that justice had been done.

It was a thin enough fiction, but it would be accepted. Blood had been spilt, and all Christians knew that blood washed away sin. Mercutio's reputation would be forever tarnished, and I knew that they'd marry him off quickly to his unwanted bride, to still any rumours.

But they'd have to wait until he was healed enough to stand on his own.

It took three of the servants to haul Mercutio up and force him on his way, but not because of resistance; all the fight was out of him, and only heavy despair remained. There were too many between us and him, and there was nothing we could do for him now. But it was a sickening, bitter horror to watch him dragged away, knowing how alone he would be.

The Ordelaffi made it clear that all should leave, and left Tomasso's body to swing and twist in the morning breeze. I drew Romeo with me uphill to the gates, and took him to the side until the last of the family's retainers were gone.

'We should cut him down,' Romeo said, wiping the tears from his face. 'Mercutio wouldn't leave him.'

'Mercutio has no say in it,' I said, 'and they'll be watching to see who dares come next. If we go ourselves, it'll be the end of us. Go get Friar Lawrence. They can't argue with the Church claiming the dead.'

He left, then, glad of something physical to do with his anger and grief. I sank down to a crouching position against the wall and breathed, just breathed, until some of my sick fury began to subside into something more manageable.

I thought I'd known the depths of cruelty men hid, but this . . . this was another thing entire. I'd known all our lives that we were fragile, easily punctured flesh, but seeing the boy choke on that noose, seeing the laughter and jeers from those who'd killed him . . . hearing the thumps as rocks pelted his dying body . . . that had shattered something within me, something I did not know was so precious.

I hadn't known I had innocence left in me until I'd felt it die.

I ached, suddenly and wearily, to see Rosaline, to take comfort in her warm smile, her dark eyes. But I knew that she would ask me the hardest question of all: *Why did you not help?*

I hated myself, as much as I hated any of the men on that rope.

Because I was just as much to blame.

Friar Lawrence came at a hustling pace, with Romeo chivvying him along like a dog driving a wayward sheep, and when he saw me sitting by the gate he frowned and slowed. 'Benvolio?' He offered me his hand. I stared at it uncomprehendingly for a moment, then nodded and wearily got to my feet. 'Come.'

'We dare not,' I said. It tasted foul in my mouth, and worse when I swallowed. 'If we're recognised—'

'Ah, of course,' he said, and nodded. 'I understand. I'll

care for the poor wretch. Go home. Take your cousin. I trust you know better than to try to see Mercutio just now.'

I did. I was not sure of Romeo, truly, but I nodded. I held the friar's hand, looked into his eyes, and said, 'Be gentle with Tomasso. He died bravely.'

'He died a sinner,' Friar Lawrence said, but it was not an accusation, only a sorrow expressed. 'But even a sinner may be brave. I will see him shrived and buried; fear not. I will not mark his grave, though. There are those who would defile it, even inside the church's precincts.'

He spoke as if he knew, and he likely did.

I put my arm around Romeo's shoulders when he tried to follow the friar out of the gates. We watched as he walked down the hill, paused in front of Tomasso's hanging body for a moment, prayed silently, and then lifted the boy to loosen the noose from his throat.

The way he carried the body, held close to his chest like a sleeping child, made my throat feel tight enough to shatter.

I turned Romeo towards home, and made him walk. 'I swear,' he said in a raw, naked voice, 'I swear I will find who betrayed him. Someone did, Ben. You know someone did.'

'I know,' I said. My own tone sounded flat and lifeless. And I did.

But I could not tell Romeo that it was my own sister, his own cousin, who had done it. On my life, I could not.

In the end, we spent the day silently, together, playing chess. Neither of us drank, because we knew well that once we'd begun we would not stop until we drowned ourselves, for sheer misery. From time to time, Romeo would say something, always painful: 'We should have stopped it,' perhaps, or, 'They would not even let him mourn.' I scarce noted it, except as the punctuation to the roaring silence that filled the space between us.

When Balthasar finally said, very tentatively, 'Shall I bring food?' it occurred to me that our family would soon be down to dinner, and our absences would be very strongly, ominously noted. I could not bring myself to care overmuch, but it was Romeo who – surprisingly – did.

'No,' he said, and stood up. 'Bring us water to wash off the dust. We'll dress and go down.'

'Will we?' I asked him without looking away from the flickering light of the candle on the table. I'd been staring at it since it had been lit, and now it was a guttering nub. 'Why?'

'For the same reason you forced us from that place,' Romeo said. 'Because Mercutio is our friend, and Mercutio's friends had best show themselves to be good and well-mannered sons. The family will protect us, but they'd best hold no doubts of our innocence in private.'

I was being shown a fool by my own younger, less responsible cousin. Without him, I might have remained immured in my apartments, hiding and brooding, and that would have occasioned comments – if not in public from the family, then in private amongst the servants, who would rattle their gossip about the town. And soon I'd be suspect as well. My own extended bachelorhood would be dragged out as proof.

Romeo was right. We had to show our clean, well-scrubbed faces and, when the music was played for us, dance most sweetly.

I could not forget Mercutio's wild mood before dawn. *Married and buried, wed and dead.* Would they still wed him? Or would his family lock him away in some monastery, sworn against his will to holy orders – no, they dared not; he was their eldest son and must be made to run to heel. They'd marry him, and he was right: He'd hurt the girl, more now than ever before. Her family had been willing to sell her for position, as all girls of means were sold or bartered; they'd simply seek a better bargain now that Mercutio's reputation lay in tatters, but marry her they would, and as quickly as possible. His father would demand it, to shore up the Ordelaffi name. I did not like to think on that unhappy wedding night. If it was consummated at all, it would be done coldly and ruthlessly. Mercutio had nothing in his heart now but ashes and gall, and that would make a bad marriage, a poisonously cruel one.

The certainty of seeing my sister at dinner made me feel sick with the desire to close my hands around her plump neck, but I rose, allowed Balthasar to dress me in appropriate clothes, and met Romeo in the hall, newly washed and berobed himself. He looked at me sombrely, nodded, and the two of us strode into the dining hall together.

Conversation dimmed upon our entry, but we looked neither right nor left, heading steadily and calmly for our seats. They sat empty, awaiting us, and as we took our places servants quickly sprang into action to bring us wine and soup. I know not what flavour they placed in front of me, though certainly the cooks had laboured for hours on the preparation. The wine and the soup and the napkin would, at the moment, all have the same inedible texture.

I ate mechanically, smiled when the occasion seemed to call for it, and made conversation with my mother, who watched me with unnerving focus. She was worried, I thought.

I did not look at nor speak with Veronica, who sat only a few places away. She, for her part, was busily whispering with our younger cousin Isabella. Their hushed giggles scraped raw on my nerves, but I resisted all the violent impulses that tried to move me, and smiled, and smiled, and smiled.

At last, someone spoke plainly, and it was my uncle. 'Benvolio,' he said. He was several cups into the wine, and leaning on his elbow as he tasted the next, then nodded for it to be filled to the brim.

'Sir?'

'This business today with young Mercutio,' he said. 'I trust there is no truth to the rumours of his behaviour?'

'Rumours, sir?' I stared at him, blank faced, daring him to speak of such things at the table.

He was not quite that drunk. 'No matter, no matter. I was only concerned for the safety of my nephew and my son, who have spent so much time with the boy. Nothing untoward occurred, then?'

I laughed, and it sounded surprisingly carefree to my ears. 'We have always been the soul of propriety, I assure you, Uncle. I know not what rumours are being passed, but you know that our enemies often try to blacken reputations in unsavoury ways.'

'For cert, yes, but this comes not from an enemy,' Montague said. A pin would have made a sound of thunder had it dropped; somewhere far down the table, a fork clattered noisily as it fell on a plate, and there was a hiss of disapproval like a pit of snakes disturbed. 'This comes from his own household.'

I shrugged. 'Mercutio and his father have been at odds

lately, as you know; it comes of having a strong-willed heir, as you do yourself, sir.'

He laughed, casting a proud and indulgent look on Romeo, who seemed dangerously silent. 'Of course, of course. A high-spirited boy is a credit to any father,' he said. 'But you should be more cautious with your friend. I do not wish to think ill of him, but your own reputations may suffer should these rumours persist.'

'They won't,' I said. 'It's air and nonsense. Why, Mercutio's to be married soon.'

Montague was more acute than the wine would indicate, because while he still smiled at me, he cut his eyes towards his son and said, 'Romeo? 'Tis true, what Benvolio says?'

'Has my cousin ever been a liar?' Romeo asked. 'You wound my brother, and in wounding him, I bleed.'

'Come now, fond as I am of you both, you are not brothers.' No, because if I had been born of his loins, I would be the heir, a fact that made Montague justifiably unnerved. Heirs had died at the hands of their cousins before, many times, to make new heirs.

'As good as,' Romeo countered defiantly. 'Raised as brothers, and brothers in affection and in temperament. Call you him a liar, sir, you call me one also.'

'Smooth your rough tongue, my son, I asked only out of love,' Montague said. Romeo attacked his game bird with such single-minded ferocity I could only think that he wanted to pull something apart with his bare hands, and dinner was the least dangerous choice he might have. 'Well, then, that's clear enough. My dear? Shall we retire and leave our children to their amusements?'

He stood, and Lady Capulet stood obediently to leave

with him; it was her place to go, whether she was hungry or not, sated or not. I wondered whether she had always been so content with that lot, so biddable. Surely not. Surely once, she had been young and afire with her own potential. Even girls dreamt of what they might do, did they not? I had no idea what they dreamt about, but I did not think it was a lifetime of being ordered, of walking behind, or enduring whatever was allotted to them without complaint.

Some women created their own worlds, like my grandmother. Some, like my mother, were trapped like flies in amber by their choices and lives. I had never been sure which of those extremes described my aunt.

We finished the dinner, Romeo and I, in apparent good spirits, dissembling as if our lives depended on it, which might have been the case. I had left stolen goods at Mercutio's apartments. If he was of a mood to turn on me, it would be a simple thing – he had seen us there by the wood; I knew it. He knew we had watched Tomasso die, and done nothing.

I could not imagine that he did not hate us.

Try as I might, we did not, as it happened, avoid Veronica in the end. She and the insipid younger cousin trailed us back from the dining hall – it seemed a deliberate strategy – and I heard part of a whisper with Mercutio's name, and that shrill, muffled giggle, and it broke the fragile hold I had on my own fury.

I rounded on her.

My sister, concentrating on her gossip, did not see me until it was too late to dodge. I grabbed her by the back of the neck and dragged her squealing around the corner, into a darkened alcove, while Romeo forced the cousin along down to the hall with a firm arm over her shoulders. 'Enough,' I told Veronica in a voice that ought to have made her grateful she still breathed. 'If I hear you say his name again—'

'You'll *what*?' She struck my hand away from her, colour burning hot in her cheeks. 'Hit me, as you did Romeo? Beat me, as Mercutio's father did him? Do you imagine anyone will *allow* you to touch me? I am an *asset*. You — what are you? An extra Montague, of little value. They can't even sell you for a dowry.'

'They hanged the boy today, while Mercutio was forced to watch,' I said, keeping my voice low and vicious and intimate between us. 'Someone dropped a whisper in the wrong ears, and I know it was you, Veronica. I *know*.'

'Oh, do you?' A smirk danced at the corners of her full mouth now, and she fussed with the lace around her collar, fluffing it into just the right shape. 'As I hear it, the first complaint came from someone who chanced to see the two of them in carnal embrace behind the church itself. Someone you would never suspect, I'll wager.'

I had no idea what she was talking about, and I tightened my grip on her shoulders. I saw a flash of panic in her eyes before the arrogance returned. 'Make yourself plain,' I said. 'I've no time for this, and you *know* I am out of temper.'

'A Capulet,' Veronica said. 'A Capulet girl was the one who complained of their unnatural embrace to the bishop himself. Or so it's said.'

'*Which* Capulet girl?' I did not believe her. I did not *want* to believe her, truth be told, and I saw the vinegar-bitter flash of victory in her eyes.

'The one Romeo is always bleating about,' Veronica said. 'The plain one bound for the convent. Rosaline. And so, we are revenged upon her, too.'

I let her go and stepped back as if she'd caught fire. I

wanted to believe she was lying; I did not want to believe that Rosaline, of all people, had been the one to do such a cruel and heartless thing. *But she is devout,* I thought. *She plans for a life in the Church. She does not know Mercutio. All she would see is something ugly and venal and perverse, conducted in the dark. Small wonder she would be offended.*

But it felt wrong to me. Very wrong.

'You're lying,' I said. 'You soul-rotted little villain, you *lie.* You're the one who bent the bishop's ear and blamed the Capulets for it.'

Her lips curled into a perfect bow of satisfaction. My clever, evil little sister, so good at twisting her words. 'Your *companion* was a liability to the house of Montague with his behaviour,' she said. 'Bound to be caught eventually. Now he hates the Capulet wench for betraying him, when before he might have seen our quarrel with them as some game of chess, bloodless and adventuresome. I did you a favour, brother, binding him closer to us. I did *him* a favour. Don't think Grandmother wouldn't approve. It was her own idea.'

It had the breathtaking cruelty of something the old witch would order . . . betray Mercutio's secret love, use the Capulets as scapegoat to bind the bitter, wounded boy closer to the Montagues. Politics at its most brutal.

'La Signora might have given the order,' I said in a voice just above a whisper, a voice I could hardly hear over the mad thudding of my pulse and the red rush of blood in my ears. 'But she used you as her puppet, sister.'

Veronica lifted her hands in a gesture of utter indifference. 'I am a woman. I must get used to being used.'

'You're not a *woman.* You're a child playing at things you don't understand.'

'I'm as much a woman as you are a man, Benvolio! I've my blood for a year now! And soon I'll be wed and bedded, and breed more allies for this house. What use are you, then? Another excess *boy*?' She shoved past me and rejoined her silly little cousin, and the two girls swept down the hall in a hiss of silk and a cloud of floral perfume.

That evil should smell so sweet . . .

'What quarrel was that?' Romeo asked, once I'd come back to him. 'To do with Mercutio?'

'Malice,' I said. 'And one day, she'll feel the scorpion's sting of it on her own back.' My tone was so dark that he gave me a sidelong look of concern. 'I'll go in secret tonight, to see that Mercutio's well cared for.'

'Then I come, too,' Romeo said.

I did not have the heart to tell him no.

Slipping into Mercutio's rooms was an old established routine for me, but teaching Romeo my methods was less simple, and the Ordelaffi household was on edge, to complicate matters. We did manage, but it was a near thing, and on clambering sweaty and trembling through the window we found Mercutio's rooms dark and silent. No lamps lit. No sign of life at all.

'They've sent him away,' Romeo said in a harsh voice. 'Ben, they sent him away!'

'Or worse,' I said. I found a candle striker and lit one of the half-melted tapers on the wall sconce. The light was thin and feeble, but it served . . . and I found Mercutio's bloody clothes in a heap nearby, piled in a way that meant a servant had not been allowed to attend him. There were drops drying on the floor. Romeo took the candle and followed me, holding it high enough for me to suss out the thinning trail, and it led us past the undisturbed bed, to the pallet where Mercutio's manservant would have laid his head, in better days.

But tonight, huddled on it was our friend.

He'd had no care – not even the rudest. He lay in his smallclothes, smeared with blood, face swollen and near unrecognisable. Romeo and I said nothing for a long moment, and then I looked at my cousin, and he nodded and lit a second candle from the first. He left me with that light, and moved off. When he returned, he held a basin of water and a cloth. The water was clean, at least, as was the rag. Mercutio groaned when we helped him sit against the wall, but he did not try to resist as I sponged the worst of the crusted blood from his eyes, nose, and mouth.

Once cleaned, he did not look much improved at all. His eyes were swollen shut, his nose clearly bent, and while he had by some miracle not lost teeth, one had gone loose. Two fingers were broken, and Romeo reset them and helped me bind them fast for healing.

When Mercutio finally spoke, it came slow and slurred and dull. 'Did they leave him there? In the tree?'

'Rest easy,' I said. 'Friar Lawrence has seen him decently laid to rest.'

'He was brave,' my friend said. It was as if he were on a far distant shore, the words coming but dimly. 'You saw, Benvolio. He was brave when they took him.'

'He was,' I agreed. It was suddenly hard to speak, and I had to look away, into the shadows, and not at his beaten face. Grotesque as it was, I knew it was only a small reflection of the pain within. 'Most brave.'

'I would have died with him, you know.'

'I know,' Romeo said, when I did not. 'You fought for him, Mercutio.'

'And I will never stop fighting for him,' he said, still in that cool, impartial, dull tone. It was not defeat in his voice – it was the opposite: a conviction so overwhelming that it was simply fact, requiring no passion to vindicate it. 'I will find who betrayed him. I will have my vengeance, come the devil himself between us.'

I felt a chill crawl my spine, listening to him, because I knew he meant it. He would dig like a terrier until he found his rat, and crushed it.

But the rat was my sister, and beyond her, my grandmother. His enemy was *Montague*.

There was a doom coming on us, and I could feel it as strongly as the prickling of the air before a storm. *Better his father had sent him away,* I thought, and it was a terrible thing, a traitorous thing, but true.

'Come,' Romeo said, and shouldered Mercutio's sagging weight to help him rise. 'A hot cup of wine, and your bed, and cold compresses for your bruising.'

'What a little mother you are, Romeo,' Mercutio said, and laughed. It was an awful sound, empty as a pebble rattling in a cup, but it died as soon as he sank down wearily into his bed. I fetched the wine, and Romeo the compresses. As I fed the wine into my friend's swollen mouth, he caught my wrist in his broken hand and squeezed. He did not even wince at the pain he inflicted on himself. 'I beg you, Benvolio, do not leave me tonight, else I may find a dagger a better friend than you.'

'You've often said my wits were sharp as any dagger,' I said, and forced a smile, though I did not think he could see it through those swollen eyes. 'There's no need for a poor substitute.'

'We will not stir from your side,' Romeo said quickly. 'You have my word, as Montague.' He said it with pure sincerity, and I had to bite back a wince. What value did our words have, as Montagues, now? 'I am sorrowed for you, Mercutio.'

'Sorrow,' Mercutio repeated, and let out a slow, weary sigh. 'There will be sorrow enough soon, so that every mouth in Verona can chew a rancid feast of tears and bile and hate.'

'Think on that tomorrow,' Romeo said. He sounded unnerved now, just as I felt. 'Tonight, you must rest and heal.'

'Tomorrow, and all the days after,' Mercutio agreed. He let out another sigh, as if giving up his ghost, and made a pathetically small whimper as Romeo pressed a cool compress over his swollen eyes. 'Tomorrow, for my enemies. Tomorrow, for blood. Tomorrow, for the wretched living. Tonight is for the sainted dead.'

I got him to drink some wine then, and his shivering slowed as the feather bedding crowded close around him. When he finally slept, Romeo looked at me and said, soft enough not to wake him, 'Was it the Capulets who struck at him so, do you think?'

He had not heard Veronica's confession, nor guessed at it; he knew only that we'd quarrelled.

'I think whoever did will soon regret it,' I said. I hated my sister, and I feared the selfish, cold chit, but she was still blood, still family. I should lie for her. I should lie to protect the Montague family and Romeo from his own better nature . . . and yet, I could not bring myself to it. 'The truth, like blood, will out.'

I took the key from Mercutio's neck. I tested the door and found his apartments locked from the outside. That was good; it meant Mercutio's lord father had decreed his son be abandoned to his wounds and demons at least for the night; not even the most loyal of Mercutio's servants had dared sneak back to his side. I left Romeo at the bed and opened the secret compartment where Mercutio had taken possession of the jewels, gold, and sword I had stolen the night before; those I put into a leather bag.

'Where are you going?' Romeo asked in a charged whisper, as I swung up into the window and checked the street below. It was the dregs of the night now, when even criminals stole off to their straw beds. 'You promised him you'd not go!'

'I'll come back,' I said. I lifted the bag. 'If they search his rooms and find this, he'll swing like Tomasso, and so may we. I'll take it to a safer place. If he wakes, say I'm gone to the jakes. It'll be true enough.'

I slipped out before he could object, swarmed down the wall, and went at a quick, light pace through the warren of streets to the public jakes located near the river. It was a foul place, and no matter how carefully I stepped, the ground was soft and wet and stank of effluence and rot, but that was all to the good.

I held my breath as I came to the bog house, with its wooden seats over the pits; I tied a thin silken rope, one of several I had hidden on me, to the buckles of the bag, and lowered it into the filthy liquid, then tied it to a rusty hook below the seat. I'd hidden things here before, and disposed of others. No sane man searched a waste-filled midden for treasure. It would be safe enough until I retrieved it – or not. I did not greatly care now, as long as it was not found in Mercutio's possession, nor mine.

I came back to the Ordelaffi house before the blush of dawn rose, and slipped back in with more ease than I'd had when dragging Romeo along. I found my cousin asleep with his head pillowed on the bed next to Mercutio, whose face was still hidden under compresses. I kicked off my filthy boots and left them by the ruined, bloody clothes, and found a pair that fit me well enough from my friend's closet. Then I changed out the compresses and drank wine and fought off my own exhaustion until I heard the rattle of a key in the door.

'Hsst!' I said, and slapped Romeo's head sharply. He jerked upright, eyes wild and wide. 'Under the bed. Hurry!'

He pushed the chair back and slid beneath the wooden frame, and I scooted in from the other side and pulled the hangings down to conceal us, just as the door opened and heavy footsteps crossed wood, aiming towards us. No servant walked thus, with such assurance. I lifted the draperies just enough to spot the expensive leather of the shoes, and the gleam of gold buckles.

Lord Ordelaffi looked down on his son for a long moment, and then dragged a chair close – the same one Romeo had pushed away – to sit. Dust sifted into my face as Mercutio moved in the bed, and I closed my eyes against it; it crawled into my nose, and I had the horrible fear I might sneeze, or Romeo might, but we both stayed dead silent, somehow.

And Lord Ordelaffi finally said, 'You live to see the dawn, then. It is a sign from God that even He does not want you.'

Mercutio's voice came thready and weak, muffled by the swelling of his nose and mouth. 'And no credit to the love of my father.'

'You brought this horror on yourself, with your filthy ways. But I pray you to take the instruction it offers: Give up your sinful perversions, and embrace a life of piety and duty to your family. You will not be offered this pardon again.'

'Pardon? Why, sir, I beg *your* pardon, for if that was pardon, then fists are love and nooses are kisses. You speak of duty? Duty is the rope that strangles me. Piety is a bed of broken glass. And *family* is the company of hateful demons.' His voice was half-mad. The bed shifted, as if Mercutio had rolled on his side, away from his father. 'I want none of it.'

'You beg another beating!'

'I do not *beg*. Even if you hate me, I am your son and only heir. Kill me, kill your own name.'

'What matters a legacy when it will breed none of its own?' Lord Ordelaffi shoved the chair back and paced with sharp agitation. I watched the shadow move beneath the draping curtains. 'You *will* marry the girl when you are presentable enough, and you *will* get her with child. Past that, I care not of you, or for you. You are no son of mine, save in necessity. We will never speak again.'

He left then, and slammed the door behind him. I heard the metal scrape of the lock.

Romeo and I slithered out from under the bed, and I wiped pale dust from my face and coughed. Mercutio had taken off the compresses. His face was not as swollen, but the bruises had flowered dark, and he scarce looked human.

But he did look . . . different. No longer the fast-witted, silver-tongued jester I had known all my life. There was something older in the hard-to-see glint of his eyes, and the tension in his puffy chin.

'You stayed,' he said. He sounded less distant today, but

no less flat. 'I love you well for it, but if you're found in my company here, you'll be named as sodomites for certain. I am a pestilent friend; I poison all I touch. I beg you, go, and don't return. Once I am safely married and lashed to the family plough, I can see you again. Not until then.'

'Mercutio—' Romeo looked at him with real worry on his earnest, handsome face. 'You spoke of daggers as friends last night. Say you do not mean it, for the love we bear you.'

'A dagger is the only friend I cannot corrupt. Even my blood cannot defile good steel.' But Mercutio carefully shook his head, which must have hurt. 'Fear not; I will not give him satisfaction in seeing me safely buried. No, I will gadfly him a while longer, the wretched man who frowns on perversion while he capers at murder. I will bring down the guilty; see if I do not. *All* the guilty, even should I pull down the temple on my head, like Samson.'

I wanted to be glad for him, to wish him success in that, but I was all too aware that the temple that he would be pulling down would be the palace of the Montagues. My sister and my grandmother had set this tragedy in motion, and the coming waves were sure to wash us to far distant shores.

It might be up to me to be sure those waves did not drown us all.

FROM THE DIARY OF MERCUTIO
HIDDEN BY HIS HAND

In only a week's time, how quickly Tomasso has disappeared from the world. His body has not yet completed a feast for the worms, and yet no one remembers him. I am presentable enough to dine in the hall now. My father ignores me; he will keep his silence towards me to his dying day; I know that. No one remarks on my face, or my newly crooked nose. No one asks whether I am well. I am a ghost at the table, as dead to them as the boy they helped murder.

None of them knows his name.

None of them cares.

Damn all of them to hell.

It has been almost a month. The bruises are gone from my face, and the mirror shows me a new man – a stranger, with shadows in my eyes and a cruel tilt to my mouth. My father took the heart from me, and what remains is a cavern of roaring blood, and no pity left.

My servant Elias has brought me whispers and pieces of rumour, and I turn them over greedily, as once I turned over the treasure the Prince of Shadows brought to me. I have wealth secreted away, clean coin from the sale of my friend's ill-gotten loot. I had meant it to take us away, into a new and likely impossible life together, but with Tomasso gone the gold means nothing, save a tool to loosen tongues and buy my vengeance.

Today Elias has told me a Capulet betrayed us. I' faith, I almost hate the Montagues as much; I know in my head that Romeo and Benvolio could do nothing for me, or Tomasso, yet knowing they saw his death, saw my humiliation, goes hard. Hearing of Capulet guilt makes me think had I not been such fast friends with Montague it would not have happened.

My fault, again.

I pray every night for forgiveness. I pray that Tomasso will intercede for me, but I do not pray for salvation; that is beyond me now, and I know it.

All that is left is vengeance, and I will have that, at least, if nothing else. I will contrive a revenge yet.

The worst is upon me. I am wed.

She sickens me, though I should have pity on her; she is as trapped in this web as I, but she is a symbol of all I have lost of myself. And I loathe her. It is a bitter bed we make, and after, she weeps herself to sleep. I tell her that once she bears a living heir she can be shut of me, and I know she is well content with that. We both cling to the promise of loneliness. Men say that love is cruel, but it is the lack of it in the act that is cruellest.

I saw my Prince of Shadows in the market today, but I avoided him. I think he would have followed me, but I fell in with some drunken fellows instead; he prefers his sobriety, my serious young friend. I wonder if he is still stealing, and if so, where he hides his loot. (Even here, I will not inscribe his name. I owe him that much.)

Today Elias brought me a priest. He was to hear my confession, but I confessed him, instead; I heard from his own lips how Rosaline Capulet, that convent-bound bitch, had pointed the finger at us and roused my father's ire. It is proof enough.

My wife's maidservant came to me with reports that my wife sneaks away to visit a witch, one who doses her with potions to make her more fertile. She desires a babe as badly as I, and for the same reasons – it is our salvation from this fleshy purgatory we inhabit.

I forced the wench to tell me where the witch lives, and tomorrow I will pay her a visit.

The witch must have been in terror that I would betray her; the penalty for such unholy acts as she commits is death, but I will not betray anyone with a secret. I threw gold on the table, a mountain of it, and told her to continue to dose my wife with whatever herbs might induce her to conceive, but to make for me a curse, a great and terrible curse.

Imagine my surprise to discover that this young slip of a witch once had a cousin, a cousin I so tenderly cherished. She had come to Verona to discover the reason for Tomasso's death. Once she learnt who I was, she was cheerful in her help to me.

I had long considered carefully how to achieve my vengeance. One blade alone might cut a few throats, but not enough, and not the right ones. No, I needed to destroy the Capulets, root and branch, before turning the vengeance upon my own father and his varlets.

A curse for love, cast in my own hand and faith and flesh. A curse of love, on the house of the guilty.

Let them feast on love, as crows feast on the dead.

Perhaps I am, after all, mad.

I have made me a poem of my madness, and it concerns Queen Mab. In part, it reads:

Sometime she driveth o'er a soldier's neck,
And then dreams he of cutting foreign throats,
Of breaches, ambuscadoes, Spanish blades,
Of healths five-fathom deep; and then anon
Drums in his ear, at which he starts and wakes,
And being thus frighted swears a prayer or two
And sleeps again. This is that very Mab
That plats the manes of horses in the night,
And bakes the elflocks in foul sluttish hairs,
Which once untangled, much misfortune bodes:
This is the hag, when maids lie on their backs,
That presses them and learns them first to bear,
Making them women of good carriage.

I think Mab has made me mad. I no longer care.

I have consorted with the witch to make this curse,

and there are three parts to my vengeance: flesh, mind, and spirit. Let me then speak my mind, here:

CURSED BE THE CAPULETS.

CURSED BE THE HOUSE WHO BETRAYED US.

Let Queen Mab visit her madness upon us all.

QUARTO

III

One would believe that Tomasso had never existed, save for the new twist in Mercutio's once-straight nose; the bruises had faded, and if our friend's humour had taken a turn for the bizarre and bitter, I could scarce blame him. He had been wed, with all the necessary pomp, to a blushing young girl; Romeo and I had helped put Mercutio to bed with her according to custom, a strange and horrible business knowing what we did, but we'd been spared the awkward business of listening to any consummation behind the curtains, though some servant would have done so.

Instead, I had been forced to listen, *still,* to Romeo's half-drunken rambling paeans to the beauty of a woman he would not name, but who must have been Rosaline Capulet. She was not, of course, in attendance at the wedding; the Capulets would not set foot where Montagues entertained. Yet her shadow loomed large over all.

Romeo had brought home the rumour that Rosaline had been the hot tongue who'd betrayed Mercutio's secret;

he mourned, but he forgave her this feminine weakness, which undoubtedly did not run true to my grandmother's plans. I kept him from writing poetry, or going anywhere near her, but it seemed to me that he would never lose his infatuation. Romeo had never been so constant in love, and it worried me to think that he might have truly set his heart on something so massively unwise.

I stole.

I suppose I could claim that the pressure of knowing of my sister's cruel betrayal, and Mercutio's misaimed bitterness, was to blame for the Prince of Shadows' thieving rampage in Verona; I made a list, sitting in the stillness of my rooms, and in the evenings, almost every evening, I escaped the claustrophobic pull of my guilt to bring misery to someone who deserved it more.

I stole the diary of the wife of the Ordelaffi servant, in which she confessed her horror of her husband's fondness for unnatural acts, and – more damningly – the pilfering he'd done from his master's coffers. The diary found its way into the chambers of the Ordelaffis' busybody cook, who soon presented it to Lord Ordelaffi.

The servant was driven out into the streets, stripped and beaten. I watched from the safety of a nearby wine shop. It was a sour sort of victory, because with him went his innocent wife and children, now reduced to beggars.

I remedied my wrong by visiting the jakes late the next evening, and retrieving the stinking bag of gold and jewels that I'd hidden there. The jewels and the sword were too easily known, but the gold I transferred to a clean cloth bag. I found the sad little family huddled in a sour alley, shivering in the chill; the father, already weak, seemed likely to die. I could not bring myself to care overmuch. But the haunted terror of the wife, and the children . . .

I knew they could not see my face in the shadow of the grey hood, and even if they did make it out, the silk mask would tell them to seek no more.

'Sir,' the wife said, staring up at me from where she knelt on the cobbles beside a very meagre little brazier, cooking what seemed to be a skinned rat for her frightened family. 'Sir, I beg you, in God's name, leave us be . . .'

I threw the bag down on the cobbles beside her. It broke open, and coins scattered like dreams over her dirty skirts. She gasped and pulled back, as if the coins might turn to serpents . . . but when they did not, she looked up again, still open-mouthed. Tears glittered in her widened eyes.

'Not for him,' I said. 'He deserves his fate for what he's done. Take your children and flee.'

She shook her head, but I knew, as she clawed the coins back into the bag and tied it shut, that she would do as I said. Her husband was dying. She might linger long enough to see him gone, but I'd read her diary; there was no love between them, and his death would free her.

Widows had more power than wives.

As far as the other villains, Tybalt Capulet still swaggered, cock o' the walk, through the streets, ever more arrogant and overweening, and I badly itched to take him down, this time hard enough to leave scars, if not a corpse. My sister, Veronica's, wedding drew near, a happy event that meant we would be shut of her forever, and I'd rarely have to spy her cruel, smiling face again. I wanted to avenge Tomasso's death upon her, but her blood, if not her sex, protected her from my rage.

Fortunate for her.

As for Romeo, he was hopelessly entangled in family politics. I doubted he even bothered to learn whom it was they intended for him to wed. It would hardly matter what he thought about it, and so he plunged himself headlong into his empty worship of Rosaline, a girl he'd never so much as met, an impossible match that was a safe indulgence of his lovesick notions.

We were each gone mad, in our ways.

I continued to steal, relentlessly. I came near to getting caught several nights, as the prince's men had become furious at my success and doubled their patrols; my likely targets also made it more difficult for me, and on two occasions I had been trapped in the house, hiding, until the stir had died and I'd been able to creep away with my ill-gotten goods. And a curious lot of things they were: the treasured riding whip from Lord Ordelaffi, with which he'd often lashed his son; the hoarded savings of two of the Ordelaffi men who'd pulled on the rope; the jewelled ring of the bishop himself, who had written a sermon praising the moral outrage of the people of Verona over the sinful perversions of sodomites, adulterers, and witches.

He'd delivered it at Mercutio's wedding. A very pointed commentary indeed.

In my own small way, I continued to exact vengeance, though I knew the sin really flowered from the root of my own house.

I knew I should confess all these things, but I did not trust the slick, bland-faced priest who often occupied the booth in the cathedral; I knew he was an ambitious man, political, and it would be well within his interests to drop a word to the bishop I'd relieved of his precious ring. Better to let my sins fester in my heart and damn me in heaven's eyes, rather than Verona's.

My real confession came at an odd time, and in an odd way.

It was inevitable that my obsession would see me caught, sooner or later; I was a great thief, but not invisible, nor invincible. It was a very late Thursday eve when I burgled a fat purse of jewels from the shop of a Capulet goldsmith who beat his apprentices, and who'd blinded one with hot metals; all well and good, but I'd been surprised by a vicious dog, and as I limped away with ill-got goods weighing me down, I also left a bright red trail of blood from my badly bitten leg. It was not a graceful escape, nor an effective one, as the goldsmith roused his household and guards and sent them beating after me, with the vicious dog howling on its leash.

I had just enough time to make it to the small, shop-worn chapel, where Friar Lawrence dozed near the altar in an untidy heap. He woke with a snort, glared at me, and then saw the blood trail I'd tracked inside. 'What's this?' he said, and started to his feet to waddle his way to me. 'You cannot be here!'

'Trouble,' I said in a gasp. I'd doffed the mask – no point in straining our friendship – and I showed him the bloody gouge in my calf beneath the ripped hose. 'They're after me, Friar.'

'For what crime?'

'Being tasty to their pet?' I said, but my heart was not in the humour. 'Later, later – for now, I stand well set to be hanged if you do nothing. I beg you for sanctuary.'

He frowned. 'You must touch the altar for that.'

I limped forward, gritting my teeth against the burn,

and laid my palm flat on the velvet-covered marble. The suffering Christ looked down on me with a severe expression, and I quickly crossed myself. 'In all humility, I ask for sanctuary from those who would see me killed,' I said. 'And best if they know not who they're really hunting, Friar.'

He spied the bag I held in the other hand, and nodded towards it. 'What carry you there?'

I tossed it to him. 'A gift, for the Church,' I said. 'Imagine the poor that might be fed from such a beneficence.'

He gazed at me for a moment, then opened the bag and made a gulping sound. 'Stolen goods!' he thundered. I could hear the howling of the dog drawing nearer. 'How dare you, boy!'

'I keep none of it,' I said. 'I give it freely to the Church. May Christ himself witness my sincerity.'

Friar Lawrence was caught in a dilemma, and if the situation had been less dire it might have been amusing. He considered for far too long before he said, 'Quickly, go behind the altar.' He tossed the heavy bag behind with me, tore the cloak from my shoulders, and used it to mop up the spots of blood, all the way to the door of the chapel, and then out to the street to confuse the trail. 'Stay here and be quiet, for the love of God and your mortal flesh!'

I eased back against the wall and took the respite to pull pieces from my linen shirt to bind up the wound tightly. The bleeding had slowed, which was lucky, but the limp would be difficult to conceal, and a nasty betrayal should anyone put out word to look for such to the guard. *One problem at a time,* I told myself. *First, you must get home alive.*

I heard the dog come nearer . . . nearer . . . and the

shouts of the men, with the high-pitched, anxious tone of the goldsmith riding over all.

Then it all swept past, without a pause.

I collapsed in sweet relief for a few moments, and was about to rise when I heard the chapel door swing open. I thought it would be the friar returning, but instead, it was someone else. I heard the light tread, the quick, nervous breathing, and the rustle of stiff fabrics as someone knelt before the altar. I risked a quick glance over and saw a hooded figure – but not the figure of a monk, or a man.

Those were the skirts of a woman.

She began to raise her head, and I quickly ducked down again, silently swearing at the ill luck. 'Friar?' Her voice was low, and a little uncertain. I heard her rise to her feet. 'Friar Lawrence? Are you here? I've come at the appointed time . . .'

All was clear, then; the friar's vows of chastity were well lapsed, and this was some girl come for an assignation. I'd ruined the holy man's night in many ways, it seemed – but then the chapel door opened and closed again, and I heard the hasty slap of sandals and the heavy, laboured breaths of the monk. 'My lady,' he said, 'I am sorry; please sit. It's been a . . . surprising night. I've another wayward lamb to tend, so if you would not mind—'

'Another . . .' She gasped. 'There's someone here! I knew it! I could hear him move!'

'Another with as little reason to be known as you, my lady, so please console yourself. He will not see your face, nor you his. Wait here, in the shadows, while I fetch him to the confessional.'

He appeared a moment later, frowning down at me. I gave him an innocent look and held out the bag, which he snatched away with righteous haste. 'Up, you sinner,' he said. 'And keep your mouth well shut on the lady's presence here, mark me.'

I hobbled up. 'I swear,' I said, 'your amorous trysts are safe with me.'

I heard her gasp again, but this time it sounded less fear than fury, and though she had her hood up and face turned down, she could not resist an angry glare in my direction.

And the candlelight showed me just a small glimpse of sweetly familiar lines and flashing dark eyes, and I knew who she was, just as from the same glimpse she marked my face, and her lips parted in shock.

Rosaline Capulet rose, threw back her hood, and hastened to my side. 'You're hurt!' she said. I could not take my gaze from her. The beating's effects had long passed, and though there was a thin scar near her hairline where she'd been cut, she looked as lovely as ever. I'd never thought to see her again, nor to be so close if I did, and the smell of pressed roses and oranges washed through me like warm rain.

And then she touched me, gentle fingers on my arm, and in flinching I almost fell. 'Your face,' I said stupidly. I couldn't stop drinking in the sight, the miracle of it. I controlled myself with an effort of sheer will. 'I am glad you're well healed.'

'You are not!'

'I'm well enough,' I said. Her presence was too overwhelming, and the implications were beyond me. 'Why are you here, at such an hour, without escort?'

She looked quickly past me, at Friar Lawrence, who firmly took hold of my shoulders and steered me towards the confessional. 'Now, now, sir, you've spoilt my efforts to keep fire and fuel apart, by which I mean Montague and Capulet, but you *must* mind your own affairs. The lady's are none of yours.'

'But—' Surely she was not here for an assignation with this fat old man. The thought burnt holes in me. 'She should have taken her vows by now!'

'I delayed,' she said from behind me. 'I dissembled. I pretended illness. But now my mummery's come to an end. I am to be sent to a convent, where my faults will be . . . corrected,' she said from behind me, and I resisted the friar's grip and turned to look straight at her. She was straight and tall now, hands clasped low, and the candlelight caressed the curve of her face like a lover's hand. 'Next week. The friar has promised me that he will send me tonight to a friendlier order, where I may at least be granted leave to read and study. My brother's wish is that my spirit be broken, but I will thwart him in this. If I must be God's, I will be God's on my own terms, and not Tybalt's.'

'Tonight,' I said. It felt like a blow, though there was no reason for that. 'You go tonight.'

'Aye, boy, she's risked much to steal away for this chance, and you'll not ruin it from familial spite!' Friar Lawrence pushed me into one side of the confessional and tried to slam the door, but I caught it on both palms and shoved back. Rosaline had not moved.

'He's not forgiven you, has he?' I asked. 'For letting me go?'

She did not answer, but then, she did not have to; I knew the truth well enough. I was the reason her brother threatened her with the loss of the one thing she feared – her study. He'd see her sent to an order that held to the belief that women should be dumb beasts, content to parrot the responses given them and mortify their sinful flesh . . . and it would kill her; I could see it in her eyes. All that was precious in her would die.

My fault again.

'There are rumours about that you betrayed Mercutio and his lover,' I said, and saw her flinch. 'I know you did not. It was said to put him against your family, not out of any truth.'

She let out a slow breath and nodded. 'I heard of the boy's murder,' she said. 'I would never have betrayed them, even had I known. I believe God loves all, sinners and saints, and judgment is His business, not mine. But I'm grieved to be another excuse for hatred between our houses.'

I did not know what else to say to her. *I've thought of you* was true, but ridiculously wrong . . . I was a Montague, and unlike Romeo, I knew my path. I finally said, 'I am glad you're well, lady.'

Her sharp gaze took in the blood on my dark clothing, and the bite beneath the ripped fabric. 'I am glad the dog was slow,' she said, and smiled a little. 'Though that limp will betray you tomorrow.'

'I know.'

'Stage a fall down the steps of your house,' she said, 'in the early morning, before witnesses. Be sure the injury is well wrapped before you do; you'd not want blood to betray you, but you can feign a wrenched ankle then and none can disprove it.'

It was good, practical advice, and I nodded to her. I no longer trusted my voice; it wanted to soften, to warm, to say things I could not allow. It came to me with a horrible sense of sorrow that she would know these things from all her sad experience of concealing and explaining away her own injuries, suffered at the hands of her brother.

I let the friar shut the door, and sank down on the confessional seat with a feverish feeling of . . . what? Loss? I did not want to examine the feeling so closely; it felt too big, like a storm caged in the bone of my chest. She'd been alarmed for me. Worried. She'd touched me so gently, and the shape of her fingers burnt and tingled still.

And tonight, she was leaving to fade away into a convent, never to be seen again. She'd have her books, her study. I should be happy that she was safe from her family's ambition, from her brother's fury.

But I could not be happy.

I waited in the cold, lonely confessional with my ears pricked for any words from her, any sounds; even the whisper of her skirts against the floor tantalised my senses. The smell of roses and oranges lingered on me, though I could not say why it clung so closely; she'd scarcely touched me at all (though it burnt still on my skin). I ought to have been ordering my thoughts around salvation, around repentance, but all I truly repented was that I would never see her again. I gently bounced my head upon the hard wood behind me, trying to disrupt the thought. The chair was uncomfortable, the space narrow and close, and as the imaginary, intoxicating smell rising from Rosaline's skin faded, the reality of stale incense and sweat descended around me. I heard Friar Lawrence whispering to her, his voice low and urgent, and her own replies carried some hints of reluctance. I thought she might wish to say something to me, some sort of goodbye . . . but perhaps it was only fear of change, of trusting to her fate.

I put my hand flat against the door, a silent valediction, a goodbye, a wish . . . and I waited, in silence, as I heard the groan of the chapel's outer door open.

I slowly lowered my hand to my lap. I suppose it would have been appropriate to spend the time in prayer, but all I could think was that God had just taken away my only light in a dark, comfortless future – however distant and dim it might have been, still, it had been *hope*.

And now it was gone. No, I had to be honest with myself: Now *she* was gone.

I heard a sudden sharp cry, and a flurry of footsteps. I heard Friar Lawrence make a frustrated, deep-throated growl, and then the door of the confessional flung open.

Framed in the light from behind, with her cloak spreading wide with her motion, she looked an angel – more an angel than I was ever like to see. She stared at me with wide eyes, and I thought she had no more idea what to say than I, in that moment. We did not need words, I think, though fantasies tumbled through my mind in blurring bursts of colour – her hair unbound and heavy as silk in my hands, her lips soft against mine, her breath whispering secrets.

And then I knew, with the fatal misery of a doomed man, that I wanted her, a Capulet, in ways that I had never wanted a woman before – not a hasty, impersonal fumbling in the dark, not the duty of a cold husband with an unfamiliar wife . . . something else, for the sake of passion, and fire, and challenge.

'Go,' I said. 'I pray you will be safe.' My voice came out low and gentle, and I had the gift of her smile, for just a moment.

'Go with God, Benvolio,' she said. 'Be careful.'

And then Friar Lawrence stepped between us, shook a finger at me in stern remonstrance, and slammed the door on me.

I did not mind. I closed my eyes in the dark and heard her say my name, again and again: *Benvolio*.

I had never realised how little happiness I had in life until she had shown me distant flickers of what it might appear.

I clung to one foolishly optimistic thought . . .

She had not said goodbye.

'Bless me, Father, for I have sinned,' I said to Friar Lawrence. He cleared his throat and leant forward on the other side of the screen. He smelt like garlic and wine, and he needed a bath, but probably found them unholy.

'I've told you already, I am not a priest; I may not grant you any forgiveness,' he said. 'And by sitting here and pretending to holy orders, I have sins of my own to confess!'

'Be quiet and listen,' I said. 'I expect no absolution. I want only a friendly ear.'

'Well, then, you may have it, and right gladly,' he said. 'Is it true, then? Are you this legendary Prince of Shadows?'

'Who told you so?'

'The girl, though hardly in so many words. I think she was sad to leave, when she had been light-hearted enough before . . . Did you take her virtue, boy?'

'What? No!'

'You creep in the windows of the innocents,' he said sternly. 'By her own admission, you came a-calling at the Capulet palace in the dark of night. I remember a certain evening when you importuned me to rush to her defence when her brother was angry. I thought it might be a case of lost family honour.'

'Rosaline's honour is not her family's,' I said. 'And I did not take it, in any case.'

'Well, then. Continue, if you wish to confess.'

'I confess that I steal from the arrogant and the venal,' I said. 'I steal to punish them for their insolence and their cruel pride. And I have no shame in that.'

'A straightforward nobleman would simply take it out in challenge,' he said. 'And I hear you are no novice at the blade, and have a hot temper when pushed. Why this cold, dark-of-night pursuit?'

'Duelling is a death offence, by the prince's own command,' I said. 'And it takes skill to become a good thief. Skill, and nerve.'

'Very well, then. You steal. What else?'

'I've killed,' I said, more quietly. 'Two Capulet men who cornered us in a narrow place, if I might answer for my servant's sins as well.'

'A fair match?'

'Fair enough, and outnumbered.'

'Then you've no guilt for that, beyond that of any decent man. What else?'

I hesitated, and then said, 'I let a boy be hanged, and I did not try to stop it.'

That brought a long silence from the monk, followed by a heavy, soul-deep sigh. 'Aye, you are far from alone in that,' he said. 'No doubt your cousin Romeo flinches from that memory as well. But to act on your own against a mob would have been foolish and useless. Your friend Mercutio courted his disaster, and the boy's life was the price. You have sin, perhaps, but not in as great a part as he, who had not the courage to turn away from his lover, nor to defy his family. I knew Tomasso. He was a sweet young man, but weak willed and too much in love. It was never to end well; may God have mercy upon his soul.'

Now, to the hardest. 'It was not the Capulets responsible for betraying Mercutio to his father,' I said. 'It was my sister. Veronica. I know common talk blames Rosaline for it. That was Veronica's malice.'

'It matters little now, and Veronica's sins are not yours,' Friar Lawrence said, and I saw the shadow on the other side of the confessional screen shake its tonsured head. 'The boy's gone to God; Rosaline is safely on her way to the convent. The trouble between the Capulets and Montagues can get no worse.'

'It can if Mercutio takes it in his head to seek vengeance.'

'The boy was rashly angry, true, but he's calmed now; he's well married, and rumours say there will be a babe on the way soon. His grudge against the Capulets may well stand, but what of it? You have as good a reason, or better.'

He meant my father's death. But my father had been born into the feud; the Ordelaffi family had typically been allies, but only on the outskirts of the conflict. Mercutio might have cheerfully accepted his own death at the hands of a Capulet, but not his lover's, by intrigue and at the end of a rope his own father had carried. There was no honour in it.

I judged it would not gain much to argue, so I let the point pass. 'I have had lustful thoughts,' I said.

'So have all men, my son.'

'Forgive me, Friar, should you not upbraid me for my shortcomings, and make me promise to do better to earn my forgiveness?'

'Oh, yes, I see your point. Very well, then. Think on the girl no more; she's lost to the world now. And I know you are sensible enough to know you'd never have had her in any case.'

I did not want to answer that, so I let silence answer for me, until Friar Lawrence's shadow gave a sad sigh. 'Ten Our Fathers and a donation to the poor for the part you played, however small, in Tomasso's death. Ten Hail Marys for your lustful thoughts.'

'And my thieving?'

I heard him rattle the heavy bag I'd pressed into his hands. 'I think this would buy you a dispensation even in the court of the pope, my son. Fear not; I will not waste it on sinful pursuits. I will commission a new saint for the chapel. Perhaps Saint Nicholas.' There was mischief in that. Saint Nicholas was commonly held to be the patron saint of thieves. In a sly way, it was a dedication to the Prince of Shadows as a generous donor.

'You'll need to sell them far away,' I warned him. 'Della Varda will recognise his own handiwork easily enough.'

'I will sell them in Fiorenza,' Friar Lawrence said placidly. 'I was bound there soon in any case. And even should he track them to my door, what guilt has a holy brother for accepting a generous, and anonymous, donation? The bishop will never let him have it back. What's given to Christ is always Christ's.'

The friar had a streak of larceny in him, I thought, and I wondered what his occupation had been in the days before he'd shaved his pate. Something a good deal less holy, I thought. 'I wish you luck, Friar.'

'And I you,' he said, with more concern in his voice. 'Stay

a moment, and hark me well. This stealing you do has less of greed in it than grief, and it will bring you more. You see it as an adventure, sir, and so the poets would name it, stealing grandly about in the moon and avenging your honour in secret. But I tell you, it will bring you nothing but pain in the end. I beg you, and I instruct you, to give it up and follow a straight path. Make me a promise, then, and receive your forgiveness with your God.'

I thought for a moment, and then said, reluctantly, 'I cannot promise, Friar, for it's worse to break a promise to God than to continue to sin, and seek forgiveness later.'

'Boy . . .' He sounded aggrieved, but the friar knew me better than to deliver another speech. 'I cannot grant you absolution for what you do not regret.'

'You said you could not grant me absolution at all,' I reminded him, and opened the door of the confessional. 'Thank you for listening, Friar. Be careful with your new donation.'

'God be with you,' he said.

But I felt, as I left the chapel and limped homeward, that I walked alone. More alone than ever.

Romeo was still an utter fool. I found this out nearly by chance, as I sought him out in the predawn morning. He was not abed, as he ought to have been. Instead, he was sitting at a table, bathed in candlelight, scribbling furiously with pen to paper. His handwriting, I saw when I leant over his shoulder, had far too many ornate flourishes to be addressed to a merchant or banker.

No, this was to a girl. And so I did what any near-brother would do: I snatched it away from him and held it up to the candle's glow to read it while he argued and tried to grab it back.

It was written, by name, to *my Lady Rosaline,* and it was all the things he had been warned not to do, not to say, not to think or feel. It was a death sentence for him, should it ever see eyes beyond my own, and I cursed under my breath, stalked to the fireplace where the embers were banked low, and threw the thing in. I brought the blaze back to a brisk roar with a poker before my cousin attacked me with his full strength, knocking me almost into the inferno myself. I kept hold of the poker, more to prevent him from using it than out of any murderous impulse, though his stupidity was reason enough to bash him senseless.

I threw him back, but in the process my bad leg gave way, and I overbalanced with him, crashed over an inconveniently placed trunk, and ended up on the losing end of the battle, with my furious cousin sitting on my chest, fists clenched and ready to batter. 'You puking dog!' he spat. 'You vile, insolent—'

'You disobeyed me,' I said. I sounded calm, though I felt none of that. I still held the poker in my hand, and I could have brained him with it, but I did not. 'We agreed you'd write no more to her.'

'I wasn't!' His fury was already sliding past, his fists loosening. Romeo was still a child in many ways – he was quick to temper, and quick to forgive. He'd grow slower in both before long; the world would beat the gentleness from him, the way it had me. 'I write not to her. I write for my own . . . my own amusement. I would have burnt them when I was finished!'

'Then I just hastened it along,' I said, and winced as his

weight came down harshly on my wounded leg. 'Off with you; you're as clumsy as a jackass on cartwheels.'

Even after he rose, I was slow to follow, and had to grasp a wall sconce for help in finding my balance. He frowned at me, my critique of his poetry already fading. 'What's the matter with your leg?'

'A dog,' I said. 'He found me tasty. Worry not; it's been well looked after; I'm not likely to burst and bleed.'

'A dog,' Romeo repeated, and his frown deepened. 'A guard dog? Were you seen?'

'Espied,' I said. 'And pursued. It's been seen to, I tell you. All's well.'

'Not if it's known you were injured! Can you walk without betraying yourself?'

'I've a plan for that,' I said. *Rosaline's plan.* 'Tomorrow morning, you and several servants will be witness to my falling down the steps. So long as the wound is well wrapped, it can be passed off as a wrenched ankle.'

'And if they make you show them?'

'The day some common merchant's street thugs can force a Montague to strip will be a dark day for our house,' I said. 'You know it will never happen. All I need do is stand on the family's honour and face them down. If not with bravado, at sword's point.'

He nodded slowly, gravely. My cousin had acquired new gravity these past few months, especially since Mercutio had been removed from our presence. We had both felt heavier, I think. More tethered to our duties and responsibilities. Would that it were not so . . .

'Come,' I said, and clapped him on the shoulder. 'No more moping over women. Love is a pain that both of us can well do without. Off to our beds, and dream of nothing but sleep itself.'

He gave me a weary, crooked smile. 'I dream only of red lips and sweet kisses,' he said. 'If I did not know her destined for holy orders, I would think her a demon, to haunt me so.'

He loved an idea, I thought, and not the girl herself; to him, Rosaline was a perfect, unobtainable jewel, more icon than flesh. I did not, in that moment, hate him; instead, I rather pitied him. My cousin was in love with love, and it would never be requited.

At least I had seen the woman behind the pretty fog of words, seen the flash of temper and sweetness in her, known her for a wholly unique and engrossing puzzle. That puzzle would never be solved by me, nor by Romeo, and I had to be content with that.

I ruffled his hair, which made him give me an ungentle shove, which I returned, and the play went on until I cried for mercy with my poor, dog-chewed leg aching. Then I limped off to my bed, leaving Romeo to seek his.

And his poetry sizzled into ashes in the fire.

The morning brought my mummery of a fall – so well acted, in fact, that I knocked my head and was half a day dazed, aching, and bruised. That it had been done not only in front of servants and Romeo, but before my august uncle and aunt, was a great benefit. I was much fussed over, my aching ankle wrapped tight, and told very sternly to rest and allow it to heal. Content in the knowledge that my fall would be the talk of the day at the market, I hobbled back to bed, where I stayed for another two days until the dog bite had mended, and the aches and pains faded. I wore the bruise on my forehead as a badge of honour.

The next morning I rose, and Romeo and I strolled slowly
through the market square, talking with the high and the low,
bargaining for a list of things my mother had given, trailed by
retainers and would-be friends. Without much warning, we
spotted a familiar face in the crowd: Mercutio. Romeo saw him
first, and gripped me tight by the arm – by happenstance, his
thumb closed hard on a bruise, and I was for a moment silent
as I resisted the urge to curse him roundly.

'Look you,' he said, and pointed. 'Our hound has left his
dog-house. And much changed he seems.'

He did. Mercutio seemed to stand taller, walk with a
more confident and aggressive stride, though instead of
the vibrant colours he had so recently affected, he wore
black – a deep shade of night, slashed through with thin
lines of orange. It suited him, and yet I felt a misgiving on
seeing him. There was a certain bleakness to him, but also
a sharper edge, like a knife whetted to its breaking point.

Yet, upon seeing us, his old familiar smile burst into
glorious warmth, and he rushed upon us to throw arms
around us both. 'You familiar devils! How could you still
live without me, fair-weather friends?' He shoved Romeo,
and playfully batted at me, and we scuffled like happy
schoolboys, laughing.

Romeo ruined it by blurting, 'Marriage seems to agree
with you, Mercutio!'

I saw it all in a blinding flash, sudden as a lightning
strike: Mercutio's eyes widened and darkened, and there
was violence in him, hatred, fury, self-loathing . . . there,
and then immediately gone, vanished beneath a smiling
facade. If he shoved Romeo too hard then, if his smile was a
bit too wild and harsh, well, then, who but me would know?

Not Romeo, who had seen only what he wished.

'You should try it yourself, to settle your wild spirits,' Mercutio said. 'Or are you still writing poor phrases to that cold-hearted bitch?'

I put a hand on Romeo's shoulder to prevent him from spitting out a reply; it was surprising to me how violent my own reaction was to hear such fury from my own friend. I did understand it. The anger, the pain, the self-loathing, all that I could grasp; he felt he had betrayed not just his dead lover, but his own true self. And he blamed Rosaline for it all.

'He's well quit of his affliction,' I said, and Romeo – wiser than I'd feared – kept his silence, though anger smouldered in the tense lines of his face and shoulders. 'We're well pleased to see you out about the town, my friend. We have missed your cutting wit.'

It was a prime opportunity for him to respond with a play on words, a jest that would have made a brothel keeper blush, but he only smiled that slightly unsettling smile, regarding me with eyes I could not easily read.

'Well, then,' he said, and put his arms around our shoulders, 'the first thing we must do is to drown your wits in wine to make mine seem all the more clever. Especially yours, Benvolio. You've a thirsty look to you. Come, a cup of wine and tell me your troubles, then, for I'm a married and respectable gentleman now, and my wisdom has of course increased tenfold.'

The words held a mocking edge that discomforted me, but I went, and Romeo went, where Mercutio bade us – which was to an unsavoury and ill-smelling hole of a tavern known to harbour the roughest of criminals. I pulled away as he turned us towards the door. 'No,' I said, and tried to make it a joke. 'Your wisdom may have increased tenfold, but my courage has not; let's find someplace more congenial, my friend; this is only seeking a needless quarrel—'

'What?' Mercutio turned with a grandly opulent gesture, cape swirling like black fog, and fixed that strange smile upon me. 'I'm the one dragged to the altar, and everyone knows marriage cools the blood. Yours should be hot still, and thirsty for Capulet swords.'

This was not a wholly new Mercutio, but it was my friend in his worst and blackest moods, and it worried me that instead of creeping out slyly in private, his distemper burst out of him in defiant daylight, while half the street gazed on it.

But still, I tried. 'Mercutio, surely a Capulet loyalist lurks in that sinkhole. Kill a Capulet, and it's our lives forfeited, and for what?'

'Worse,' Romeo said gloomily, retreating to stand next to me. 'We might lose.'

'Then you'd be dead,' Mercutio said. 'And beyond any shame.'

'You've met our grandmother,' said Romeo. 'She'd pursue us well beyond the grave, that one.'

'I don't do the bidding of an old woman,' Mercutio said. 'Come, now, boys, I do not look to fight. I only give the fight the chance to look at me.'

'Why?' I grabbed his arm and held him back from entering, sure that if he did I'd never see him alive again. 'Why do you do this?'

His eerie smile faded, and for a moment he regarded me with sober intensity before he said, 'Grief cuts deeper than

Capulets,' and shook off my restraint. 'Go or stay. I care not.'

Then he walked inside the tavern, and Romeo and I were left to stare at each other. Balthasar, greatly daring, leant forward to whisper, 'Sir, for the sake of my children, I beg you, walk on.'

'You have no children, Balthasar.'

'I could have, someday. But not if you bid me stand at your back in there! We'll all of us end the day face down in a hasty grave, sir, if you follow him!'

'Are we then to let him die alone?' Romeo responded hotly, and plunged inside, after Mercutio.

'Well.' Balthasar sighed. 'I suppose it's as good a day as any to meet God, sir.'

And he, with Romeo's retainer and three of our best bravos, followed me into the lion's den.

As it happened, the Capulets were not in force within the confines of the tavern at present, though a few of their more ragged followers lurked in the the corners; rather, we were presented with a wall of sweat and muscles who had no use for the more refined folk at all, save as a source for ready profit. Seeing the three of us, they must have thought the lambs had walked calmly into the butcher shop, ready to make a fine dinner.

They hadn't reckoned on Mercutio, who strode in with a catlike grace, gave the room a wild, sharp smile, and bowed most mockingly. 'Greetings, you fine fellows,' he said, and kept his hand provocatively on the hilt of his sword as he swaggered to the rough, stained wooden counter that served as a bar. 'I'll have wine for me and my good companions.' He winked and bounced a gold florin from the bar – a hundred times what any foul pressing available in this place was worth. The haggard woman standing behind the plank reflexively snatched the coin from the air, opened her hand, and gaped as if she'd never seen such a thing . . . and likely she hadn't. Her grubby fist clenched hard around it, and she glared at the rough men staring in her direction to warn them off. They shrugged and turned their attention back towards Mercutio. Surely, if there was one gold florin, there were more.

'We should go,' I said quietly. 'Whatever demon has possessed you, this is madness.'

'Love is that demon,' he said. The woman – a nightmare collection of beetled brows, moles, and wildly growing chin hairs – slapped down wine cups that were no cleaner than her hands. 'If love be rough with you, be rough with love . . . It is a disease, and this the very cure of it. Drink, my friends, drink and be merry; fine wine and cheerful company, what could be—'

A massive man, stinking of garlic and wine and wearing a dirty Capulet band on his arm, shoved Mercutio hard into the bar, sending the wine cups tumbling and flooding. The barkeep leapt away from the sudden crimson flow, both hands clutching her precious florin, and took to her heels behind a sagging curtain. She'd not be calling for the watch, that much was certain, and there were ten men between our outnumbered party and the dim door.

Mercutio calmly righted a cup, saving half the wine therein, and quaffed it in a convulsive, thirsty gulp. He then turned belly-to-belly with the man who'd shoved him. 'Clumsy churl,' he said. 'You owe us drinks.'

I shouted a wordless warning as the man yanked a dagger free from his belt, but it wasn't needed; Mercutio, still smiling, slammed the chipped pottery cup into the man's face, and as the mountain stumbled backward, roaring, Mercutio pulled his own dagger and stabbed down cleanly, pinning the man's wrist to the bar. The man swung at him, still shouting, and Mercutio sank just enough to avoid the blow, came up with a second dagger in his hand and glittering murder in his eyes.

And that smile, oh, that *smile,* it chilled me even as I pulled my own dagger, and felt Romeo beside me doing the same. Balthasar had already drawn his cudgel and was laying about with it in an attempt to clear space around us. One of his fellows – Romeo's man – had already fallen. The crowd of men around us churned like a stormy sea of flexed muscles, anger-darkened faces, and then it was just a fight for our lives, no sense to it, no strategy. There was no room for swords, only the sweaty, desperate work of daggers and clubs. If Balthasar had not been at my back, and Romeo at my side, we three would have been immediately overwhelmed, but we acquitted ourselves well enough. Mercutio fought alone.

I had always known he had a dark, furious side in him, something fey and feckless, and now it had taken him over like a black spirit as he spun, stabbed, dispatched foes with elegant thrusts and clever twists of his body. He looked . . . alive. He looked disquietingly happy.

I had seen a caged tiger once, a beast brought by ship from India and destined for some grand palace; the thing's brilliant beauty had impressed me, and so had its utter savagery. No mercy in those glowing, furious eyes, those bared fangs. To face it was to face death.

Mercutio was just such a tiger, alive with the desire to destroy everything in his path, for the sheer bloody sake of his own pain. I was afraid for all our lives, but I was most afraid *of* him, in that moment; there was something merciless and blind in him, something that required blood.

And oh, he claimed his due in that filthy tavern. I know not if he killed men, but if they were spared it was only God's hand at work; by the time the crowd had fallen back from us, he was spattered with fresh red blood, and his dagger ran with it, and the floor was thick with writhing, groaning men. We had lost two of our own, fallen senseless, and I had two minor wounds; Balthasar limped from a cut on his thigh.

'Mercutio!' I shouted to him as we achieved the blessed sanctuary of the doorway. I could scarce believe we'd survived at all. 'Mercutio, *away,* now!'

I watched him raise the dagger to his lips and kiss its bloody steel, sketch a mocking salute, and then jump lightly over the fallen foes to join us. In the brilliant sunlight, we were wine-stained, cut, bruised, and my heart still pounded from a sickening mix of exaltation and terror. I wiped my dagger roughly clean and sheathed it, then grabbed Mercutio by the shoulders. I felt the fine vibration of his body through the hard grip of my hands.

He was still smiling, but there was something entirely wrong in it.

'Do you *wish* death?' I said to him, and shook him hard. 'You court it like a lover!'

He said nothing. Nothing at all. And I shoved him backward, threw a look at Romeo, who shook his head and wiped spots of blood from his cheek. 'We must away,' Romeo said. 'Now, coz. There are dead men to answer for, and best we not be here when the questions are asked.'

'I'm still thirsty,' Mercutio said. 'And you never had your wine. We should go back.'

I cuffed him hard across the face, and for a moment I saw real confusion in his countenance, as if I'd woken him from a deep dream, but then he raised a hand to touch the raw spot where I'd hit him, and shook his head.

'What a sad thing,' he said, 'when the sons of Montague have milk and water running in their veins.'

'Better water than *that* wine,' Romeo said. 'Come, Mercutio, you've drunk too deeply already, for only that could explain what you've done. I beg you, let us see you safe home.'

'Home? To my *wife*?' Mercutio's tone was so dark that I feared suddenly for that misfortunate girl's safety. The friend I had known before his lover swung on the tree . . . that Mercutio could be as cruel as a gadfly, but it was all vinegar wit, no spite behind it. The venom in him now was new, and boded ill indeed. 'After so long apart, do you long to see me gone so soon from your company, my friends? I thought you loved me well.'

'We do love you well, Mercutio, and you know that I would gladly die by your side, but this – this is black folly. Come away; come and have a quiet cup of wine in a congenial place. Will you?'

Romeo spoke so gently, so earnestly, that perhaps even Mercutio's much-scarred heart was moved a bit . . . He reached out and clapped a hand on Romeo's shoulder. 'Well, then,' Mercutio said. 'Well, then, perhaps the loss of a florin is not so great a thing. But you, dear one, will buy the drinks.'

'One,' Romeo immediately replied. 'One drink. And then safe conduct home.'

Whatever madness had taken hold of Mercutio seemed to pass, then; we wiped away what blood and stains we could, and found a quiet shaded corner. One drink turned to three before it was done, and Mercutio seemed in fine enough spirit – fine enough that when interlopers approached within a few feet of us on the other side of the screen, he bade us hush and listen. It was no mere underling, lurking near; it was the sour Capulet himself, walking attended by a dim-witted servant and Count Paris, a cousin of Mercutio's and a relative of the prince himself. An earnest man, older than us, and in need of a wife, it would seem; rumour ran that he sought Capulet's daughter's hand in marriage. I heard only random moments of their conclave; Count Paris claimed that younger maids than Juliet had made happy mothers – a claim her father disputed, sagely, with the observation that those wed and bedded too soon were often marred by it. Eventually, they closed their business – apparently something of marriage, to do with the young Juliet – and moved on.

It was nothing to me, until Romeo said, 'We need diversion, cousin.'

I looked at him, frowning, but not yet alarmed. We'd all had, perhaps, too much wine on too hot a day. Romeo lunged to his feet and hurried off, with Mercutio only a step behind. When I joined them, I saw Capulet and Count Paris walking off together, well satisfied, and the dim-witted servant was left struggling with a paper he had been given.

Before I could stop him, Romeo fell into step with the fellow, looking over his shoulder at the paper he was scrying.

'God-den, good fellow,' Romeo said, and clasped his hands behind his back, the very picture of a polite young gentleman of Verona.

'God gi' god-den,' the servant said, and thrust the paper out. 'I pray, sir, can you read?'

'Ay, my own fortune is my misery,' Romeo said, and after some banter, he took the paper and read it. I hurried to join them, as he began to recite names . . . Count Anselme, the widow of Vitravio, Signor Placentio, Mercutio. Rosaline was on the list, though I well knew she was gone; so was Tybalt, and I assumed, though I had not caught their mention, that the Capulet household entire would be included.

'A fair assembly,' Romeo noted. 'Whither should they come?'

'Up,' the servant said.

Romeo sent me an amused look and put a conspiratorial arm around the man's neck. 'Whither, again?'

'To supper,' the servant said. 'To our house.'

'To whose house?'

'To my master's.'

The man was duller than a bucket of pitch. Romeo almost laughed, but managed to contain it. 'Indeed,' he said, 'I should have asked you before.'

'My master is the great rich Capulet,' the servant said proudly, and puffed out his chest, as if absorbing the gold and status merely by attachment. 'If you be not of the house of Montague, I pray, come and crush a cup of wine. Rest you merry!'

He darted on, intent on delivering his message, though

I doubted he would remember half the names Romeo had recited to him.

Romeo stared after him thoughtfully, and I felt the first inkling of disquiet. 'What, coz?' I asked him.

'Rosaline,' he said softly.

'She's gone,' I said. 'Gone to safety, far away. She'll not be there.'

'And if she is?'

I threw an arm around his shoulders and walked him back toward where Mercutio waited. My thoughts whirled furiously, shouting in the dark cavern of my skull, but above all was the clear, bitter voice of my grandmother, reminding me astringently of my duty, and the consequences.

'I will go,' he declared. 'It is a masked feast, I heard it said. I will go in secret. If she is there . . .'

'Coz, I said she would not be.'

'You could be *wrong*,' he said, and there was no levity in it now, only a calm certainty. 'I will go, Benvolio. If she has been spirited off to the convent, then my love for her must fade, as God wills. But I will go, to see for myself that she is gone.'

'You risk your life for nothing.'

'No,' he said. 'I risk it for an angel come to earth. And so would you, if you were not made of ice.'

He had no idea how much I burnt within at that, hot as the devil's breath; he had no right to take this risk. No right to love her so diligently.

No right to put me so far at risk, because I could not let him go alone, unguarded, into that pit of vipers.

Some of the anger came out in my voice as I said, 'Then let us go to this masked feast. All the beauties of Verona will be assembled there. Look upon their faces, and you'll think your swan a crow.'

I said this, but I did not mean it; there was no woman in Verona, however fair, who held the power of Rosaline, I thought – though Romeo had an appetite for beauty, and he'd have plenty to dine on at this Capulet party.

Mercutio, watching us with bright, malicious eyes, finished off his wine and dashed the cup onto the cobbles, where it shattered. When the merchant shouted, he threw a coin to him without looking. 'What mischief are you proposing?' he asked, and flung his arms over our necks, more to sustain himself than to embrace us. 'What amusements? And mention not any woman's name, or I shall choke it from your wretched throat.'

'A fine amusement,' Romeo said. 'But you must promise to be on your best behaviour, Mercutio. If you hold your temper, it will be a great adventure, and a trick for the ages.'

I had never meant him to involve Mercutio in this folly. I was sickly aware that in doing so, he had raised the stakes of this game from merely dangerous to catastrophic.

'A trick?' Mercutio echoed, and gave us a slow, delighted grin. 'You have only to lead me to it.'

Romeo and Mercutio had the bit between their teeth, and whatever misgivings I had mattered not. I gave up trying to persuade them, and instead hoped only to help them survive this adventure. Misadventure, more like.

That night, cleaned and dressed in nondescript finery, we stole out of the Montague palace without any colours to mark us, and took only a few servants, in case we had to take to our heels quickly. My mask was of an owl; Romeo's was a cat, likely in mockery of Tybalt. As for Mercutio, he wore a fanciful gold thing, bright as the rising sun, but then he was – of all of us – the only one who had an excuse to be at the feast. 'Being a distant cousin to the prince has its privileges,' he told us, as he tied on the gaudy thing. 'Even the Capulets fear to slight my family, though they disapprove of my . . . friendships.' I wondered whether he referred to the one with us, or the one his family had tried so hard to erase. Poor Tomasso – he had vanished entirely from the memory of Verona, except in whispers. No one dared remember him.

No one except Mercutio, of course, though if that was who he was thinking of at that moment, I knew not. He seemed back to his usual merry self, full of mischief and sauce.

We were but moments from escaping cleanly when there was an imperative rap on my chamber door, and we all went still and quiet. *Ignore it,* Mercutio mouthed, but I shook my head, removed my mask, and went to answer the summons.

It was not a summons, however; it was a visitation. The knock had not come from knuckles, however bony; it had been the hard wooden top of my grandmother's cane, and the old witch herself stood there, layered in black and swaddled in shawls. I'd rarely seen her standing, and never, *never* had she darkened my door. She was not alone, of course; no fewer than four attendants shuffled around her in the narrow spaces, hovering anxiously lest she drop suddenly under the strain. They were under the delusion that she was a frail elderly woman, but what I saw in her face was volcanic fury, and no weakness at all.

She stamped her cane on the flaggings with such force

the echo silenced all other sounds, and glared at me under thick grey brows. 'Well?' she demanded. 'Do you mean to keep me waiting inhospitably on the step, like a rude churl? Or must I have your manners beaten into you?'

I stepped back and gave her a profound bow, and my grandmother doddered over the threshold, each stab of her cane an emphatic pounding, like coffin nails being driven deep. Her retinue followed, all in the same dreary black, even the footman, who by rights should have been liveried in Montague colours. The old woman detested bright things as much as she detested everything else.

The footman shut the door behind her party and stood against it with the obvious intention of keeping all inside. I did not protest. I was curious – too curious, perhaps – at what had winkled my grandmother from her blazing hearth.

She glared at us each in turn. 'Take off those foolish masks,' she snapped at Romeo and Mercutio. Even Mercutio moved quickly to obey, and stood eyes cast down, clearly wishing not to be the reason for her appearance

He was not. She turned that dragon's gaze upon me, instead. 'I *warned you*,' she said, and stabbed an age-crooked finger towards my chest. 'I warned you there would be consequences for misbehaviour. Someone's tongue wagged, boy. The three of you, in a tavern only a little better than a midden! Blows exchanged, and men sore wounded! Did you think the prince would not hear of it and summon your uncle – and you, fool Mercutio, your father! – to his presence? You've shamed us, and raised Capulet in his estimation, and that cannot be allowed.' Her watery eyes narrowed, and her lips tightened with it. 'Montague must be seen to be of greater wit than mere tavern brawlers. If you would risk your skins on foolish games, then play one that favours us in the end! I hear you've taken it into your empty heads to sneak into the bosom of House Capulet. Then do so. Find a way to embarrass them in their own home. Perhaps seduce that less-favoured girl cousin—'

'Rosaline?' Romeo asked, coming to alert like a greyhound spotting a rabbit to chase. 'Did she not enter a convent?'

'Gossip says she never reached it,' Grandmother said, and a thin smile cut her lips. 'Her brother Tybalt rode out to bring her back, since she ran to a convent of her own choosing rather than the one her family chose. She's been kept close, but whispers say the Capulets wish to present happy families at their feast tonight, so she will be on display, and likely dancing. You wished to ruin the girl once, Romeo. This is the perfect time.'

'Ruin her?' He was taken aback, the innocent soul. 'I never—'

'Men ruin women,' she interrupted him, 'and that is all they do, never mind all the amatory nonsense. All you need do is lead her off alone. Surely that is no great challenge for your too-tender conscience. Now, go and goad the Capulets until they rise to the attack, and mark me well: if one of you is cut for it, I will not weep. A few scars are what's needed to make you men instead of feckless boys!'

I could not stop myself. I said, 'And if we are killed?'

'Then you are a martyr for your family's honour, and there's no better end for you,' she snapped back, and emphasised it with a crack of her cane on stone. 'Go and humiliate the Capulets *without* spilling their blood in their home. I cannot count on your uncle to salvage our honour this night if you fail.'

She turned, and then, without any warning, lashed out with her cane and caught Mercutio on the thigh, hard enough to leave a bruise. His jaw tightened, but he said nothing. Grandmother glared at him with real menace. 'And you,' she said, in a low and harsh voice. 'You, pot stirrer, unnatural creature, redeem your reputation with either a sword or an heir of your blood, and do it quickly. Lead any of mine to your perversions and I'll see you dead where your weak-willed father won't. Keep your sword *sheathed!*'

Mercutio said nothing, but there was something glowing in his eyes that almost matched La Signora's bile. He bowed his head, but neither she nor we were under any delusion that it was surrender. His gaze followed her as she hobbled her way to the door, and out, followed by her attendants.

Then he donned his mask again, and the malice was almost hidden behind it.

'If I heard rightly, your matriarch has given us orders to embarrass House Capulet,' he said. 'And I intend to obey. What of you, Benvolio? Romeo?'

Romeo nodded, but the light in his eyes came not from mischief but hope. The only word he could hear from all that Grandmother said was a name. *Rosaline.* I had a foolish boy and a man ridden by a demon as companions, and sad to say, Rosaline's mention had affected me as well. Something within me had quickened, something I thought I had successfully rooted out.

Hope.

This was gravely unwise. I could feel it now, a deep and uneasy tide within me that warned me we were embarking on a road that would lead only one way: down, into the dark. Grandmother would not weep at our scars, nor our deaths; Mercutio was bent on proving himself as violent a man as any in Verona. Romeo, my kind cousin, would be as easily led into trouble as he was into love.

And I, the responsible one, I knew I ought to put a stop to it, take whatever fury came roaring from the dragon's mouth . . . but instead, a traitorous whisper in my mind said Rosaline's name once more, and I knew that whatever doom was to come, I would go, and willingly.

We did not steal off in darkness, as was my usual habit; instead, we went to the Capulets' feast in full view, masked and escorted, with torches lighting our way and warning off all footpads who might have tried us. Three young noblemen, eager for the feast and dancing. As fast as Romeo and Mercutio strode, I still led them. My heart pounded, but not from exertion; I had not thought to ever set eyes on Rosaline again, and if I had not I would have been well content that she was safe. If she was God's bride, I could not be jealous of that, but now she was here, alive and real, and Romeo was extolling her beauty to a bored and restless Mercutio.

'I tell you, she has the fairest skin of any I've seen,' Romeo said, a little breathless from the pace I'd set as we walked the Via Mazzini. We saw other torches burning, other parties making their way to the Capulets' stronghold; from the look of things, our arrival would be little noted. Some of those I spied, in the colours of the Scala, were ten strong or more, bringing along wives, daughters, sons, and distant cousins to share in the feast – perhaps even my possibly affianced, Giuliana. Capulet would spend coin on this, to be sure, but so he should to impress Paris with his daughter's social prominence. A count of Paris's status needed a wife he could present proudly.

'I will seek out Rosaline,' Romeo said eagerly, as we came closer to the street, and all the lurid lines of torches began to converge. 'I know she will come away with me. All you need do is lure Tybalt, and ensure her ladies are likewise occupied – perhaps in dancing—'

Mercutio ruffled his hair. 'So eager to deflower the girl?' he said, and jumped lithely away as Romeo rounded on him. ''Tis the job your grandmother set you, or missed you her message? Humiliate Capulet by showing that their precious convent-bound virgin is a trull. Unless you'd rather I do it for you.'

Romeo shoved him away. I could not see his expression behind his mask, but I imagined his scowl resembled the one that twisted my own face. 'Enough,' I said sharply. 'I am the eldest Montague, and there's no reason for Romeo to risk his life for this. If Tybalt wants to wet his blade, better I be the pincushion than Montague's heir.'

'Don't,' Romeo said, and grabbed my elbow. 'Ben, don't. Grandmother may win her wars this way, but we should not.'

'Women's wars are the bloodiest of all,' Mercutio said, and laughed bitterly. 'A Capulet woman betrayed Tomasso to hang, and well I know it. I care not for their honour, nor for their safety. Your grandmother is right. To the wall with the Capulet wench, and let her maiden's blood be the price they pay for what she's done.'

I shook free of Romeo and faced Mercutio instead. 'What demon infected you?' I said. 'Suffering for suffering, is that to be our lives? Blood for blood? Blow for blow?'

'Measure for measure,' Mercutio said. 'It's ever been our lives, brother Ben, and if you did not always know it, then you are a bigger fool than I ever knew, and it's well your cousin is heir and not you. Weak English stock has watered your good Veronese blood.'

He turned his back on me, and I made a convulsive move for my sword, but reason stopped me – reason, and the knowledge that Mercutio would say anything, anything at all, to goad those near him. Even his friends.

'It is a demon riding you,' I said, 'and the demon's name is grief. But push me again and I will push back, Mercutio. Mark me.'

He held up a languid hand. 'I care nothing for it,' he said. 'Come if you are coming. If you do not, I'll seek out this Rosaline myself and prove her false to her faith and family before the bells next ring.'

What could we do, then? Romeo and I each had our reasons for moving with him to the officious Capulet servant at the door ticking names from his invitation sheet. Mercutio gave his own, and waved at the two of us and named us country cousins. The servant frowned, but passed us in; Mercutio was a distant cousin of the Prince as well as Count Paris, after all, and no one wanted to be accused of slighting the potential bridegroom's relatives.

Within the low-ceilinged hall, torches blazed, throwing a cheerful glow over groaning tables of food and drink pushed far against the walls. I'd not ventured into this space before, during my explorations of the enemy's household, and my eye was caught by the grand silk Capulet banner fluttering on the wall, embroidered with the family's crest and motto: *We repay all.* It was a clever enough turn of phrase, and it meant they paid debts and swore vengeance with equal vigour.

I was busily thinking of all the ways I might use that arrogant flag against them. I might steal it and use it to drape a donkey – yes, a donkey carrying a drunkard dressed in Capulet colours through the town square. The image made me smile, and I marked it down for later use. The ridicule would madden them, and Tybalt in particular.

My smile faded, because in the middle of the bright whirl of masked and anonymous strangers, I saw a girl's straight back, high-held chin, and the graceful rise of her neck. She was too tall for common fashion, and her mask was plain white with only a small sparkling of red crystals to brighten it. She did not need much ornamentation, I thought. The dress she wore was also plain, and demure – it would not have been wrong gracing a dowager, and was well suited to a girl destined for the nunnery.

But despite its best efforts, her costume did not make her plain.

Rosaline stood against a pillar near the edges of the room, smiling politely and refusing all offers to join in the dancing; she held a small cup of wine, but I did not think she was drinking.

I was not the first to spot her. Mercutio was. He swept towards her without hesitation, sketched an elaborate bow, and kissed her hand with perfect gentility – and did not release it. He bent close, and I saw his lips move beneath the mask. I saw Rosaline seem to draw back against the pillar; whatever he had said, it had repelled her.

Romeo stood next to me, sighing. 'I wish I had not come,' he said. 'You have dancing shoes with nimble soles; I have a soul of lead that stakes me to the ground so I cannot move. I cannot see her.'

I realised, with a jolt of surprise, that he had looked right over Rosaline, the very girl he idolised so . . . and surveyed the crowd with all the joy of a mourner at the grave.

Mercutio had still not released Rosaline's hand, and I could see the paleness of her knuckles as she struggled to pull free. His lips were moving near her ear, but as I watched, she finally tore her hand from his and edged past, disappearing into the crowd in a whirling flutter of skirts.

I felt unaccountably hot and flushed beneath the mask, and my fists had clenched tight. But I held myself still as Mercutio came back to us, still eyeing the crowd with a glitter I did not like. 'Come, gentle Romeo, we must have you dance,' he said, and pushed my cousin a little. 'You are a lover; borrow Cupid's wings and soar with them above a common bound.' Another push. Romeo pushed back.

'I am too sore pierced with his shaft to soar with his feathers,' he said, and whatever else he said I lost, because I saw Rosaline again through the crowd. She was turned towards us, staring not at me, I thought, but at Mercutio. I could not read her expression past the mask, but she seemed to me disturbed.

Romeo and Mercutio continued to quarrel behind me – or rather, Romeo to insist he was done with love, and Mercutio to mock him with long-winded talk of dreams. I edged away from them, moving slowly so as not to attract their interest, and entered the dance that swirled in the centre of the room. The older men and some of the women sat and watched the merrymaking, and I nodded and offered my hand to a passing young girl masked as a deer; we made our steps, and I handed her off to another man in rich Capulet colours, with a mask of blood red and gold. Tybalt. I recognised the arrogant set of his jaw, and looked away in the hope he did not likewise know me. He did not seem to, and the dance passed on, steps and claps, turns and hands briefly clasped as the musicians sawed and brayed on . . .

. . . and then, suddenly, my hand was on Rosaline's palm, and we were turning slowly, like petals in a lazy wind, and our gazes met and locked. Her lips parted, but she did not speak. So neither did I. When the measure was danced, rather than release her, I pulled her to the side, and she came, most willing.

'You should not be here,' she whispered. Her voice was low and urgent, her eyes fierce behind their covering. 'If my brother spies you—'

'Do not let anyone lead you off alone,' I told her. 'Promise me that you will not.'

'Mercutio already tried,' she said, and studied me with what I thought might be a frown. 'I am no fool, to be so lightly ruined. What's planned for me?'

'Nothing good,' I said. 'Capulet seeks retribution for its losses today, and Montague will try to strike first – why are you *here*?' It came out more passionately than I had meant for it to, and more vexed.

'No fault of mine,' she said. 'I was safely in the convent when Tybalt came to remove me; the abbess would have refused him, but he threatened to do great violence if deprived, so I agreed to return. They'll send me on to their own choice of holy order soon. I only am put up here to provide a plain ground for Juliet's brilliance.'

She did not sound bitter, I thought, only resigned. Like

Mercutio, I was holding to her hand, but she did not try to pull free. If anything, her fingers tightened on mine, to the point of pain.

'Can you not try again?' I said. 'Slip away, find a place they will not look . . . ?'

She shook her head slowly, never looking away. 'The arm of my family is long, and there is no hole into which they will not reach. Best if I do not risk others for my own selfish purpose. Whatever comes, I will bear it.' She blinked, then, and glanced away. I followed the look to Mercutio, who had his head bent to listen to another young girl – a more distant relation, but still Capulet blood. 'Your friend . . . I know he has been sorely tried, but he seems so greatly changed from what I remember.'

'What did he say to you?' I was aware of the dance moving behind us, of sharp glances from some of the older guests towards us; we could not be seen to linger. 'Did he —'

'Look after him,' she said, and slipped her hand free of mine. 'There's a darkness in him that will spill out, if it has not already. Another reason I should withdraw to the peace of my rooms, and thence to the convent. This is my cousin Juliet's triumph, after all. I would not wish to draw from it.'

'Rosaline . . .' I said her name, and heard the gentleness in my own voice; I saw the answering flash in her eyes, and heard the intake of her breath. I took another step to bring us closer, but I did not touch her. Not again. 'God be with you, if I cannot.'

'And with you,' she said. I saw a quick, silver shine of tears over her eyes, quickly blinked away. 'And with you.'

Then she turned and was gone, weaving her way out of the heady crowd.

I felt cold, suddenly, as if the only source of heat in the room had gone with her, and the hair on the back of my neck prickled with sudden alarm, for I saw Mercutio had disappeared as well . . . gone into the shadows with the tender young Capulet cousin. Mercutio nursed a wicked and sincere hatred, and there was little he would not do to avenge his lost lover.

Then I saw Romeo.

Juliet Capulet ought, by all rights, to have been on the arm of her suitor Paris, but the count had gone to greet his more powerful relative, the prince of Verona, who had arrived with much flourish in the hall. The disruption had broken apart the dancers, and all eyes were trained towards the prince and his party, not towards the blushing, inconsequential girl in whose nominal honour this feast had been devised.

And the girl, small and sweet and looking more child than woman in her gown and mask, was staring up into my cousin's face. His *unmasked* face, for he'd pushed the covering up, and she had likewise displaced her own, and I saw the expressions on them both: rapt. An almost religious ecstasy, something beyond mere attraction. It verged into the profane.

Romeo had ever been a follower of Venus, but *this* . . . There was something new in his face, his eyes, in the bend of his shoulders toward hers, and the clasp of their hands. I saw it mirrored in her, blinding and beautiful but also dangerously fanatical.

Worse: I saw Tybalt had seen it, too. I was close enough by to hear him mutter to Capulet, 'Uncle, this is a Montague, our foe – a villain come in spite to scorn us.'

Capulet was no fool; he spied my cousin immediately and said, 'Young Romeo, is it?'

''Tis he, that villain Romeo,' Tybalt spat, and pushed forward with his hand on his dagger. I tensed and felt for the familiar hilt of mine; it was worthless to start a brawl here, but I couldn't let a Capulet murder my cousin without any attempt to foil him.

I did not need to put myself on the point of Tybalt's knife, for his uncle drew him back sharply. 'No,' he said. 'Verona brags of him as a virtuous, well-governed youth, and I would not for the wealth of all the town do him harm here.' His words were honey, but his expression vinegar; he was thinking of the politics of the matter, and of the prince's royal presence in the very room. 'Be patient and take no note of him.' Tybalt made a rough, low sound of protest, and tried to pull free, but his uncle's grip tightened to steel. 'It is *my will*. Show a fair presence and put off these frowns. It ill becomes a feast.'

'It fits when such a villain is a guest; I'll not endure him!' Tybalt said.

'He *shall* be endured!' Capulet said, and twisted the young man's arm. '*I* say he shall. Am I the master here, or you?'

'You,' Tybalt gritted out from between his teeth, though his red-faced fury was plain beneath the mask. ''Tis a shame.'

'For shame, I'll make you quiet,' his uncle replied, and the threat was plain in his voice. 'Go to, and cheerfully.'

It was a dismissal, and Tybalt took it as such, though he looked straight murder upon my cousin Romeo, and I knew very well that this would not end with the eldest son of Capulet being sent away without his supper. He pushed his way through the crowd, leaving in the same direction as his sister but with a good deal less grace.

I watched, in outright horror, as Romeo drew the Capulet girl off behind the shadow of a pillar, and their hands entwined in love knots, and their lips met first softly, then more strongly. A Capulet girl would be well ruined tonight, without doubt, but I had not looked to find it here, and from the earnest hands of my cousin.

I was obscurely relieved to see the fat old nurse of the Capulets waddle over to spoil the moment, sending Juliet off to attend her mother, and staying a moment to answer eager questions from my cousin before shaking him off like dust.

I made my way to him, and marked well the pallor of his face, the dark and shocked look of his eyes.

'She is a Capulet,' he said; I do not think he said it to me, more to himself. 'My life is my foe's debt.'

'We must begone,' I said, and grasped his elbow to lead him out. 'The sport is over.' If sport it had ever really been. I searched the room for Mercutio, and saw him emerging from an alcove. He spied us, and arrowed our direction, pausing to deliver mocking bows to Capulets along the way.

Capulet himself rose to block us from the exit. His eyes were bitter and black, but his tone had a honeyed, poisoned sweetness. 'Gentlemen, do not prepare to be gone just yet; will you not have food from our feast?'

'We've had our fill, gentle Capulet,' Mercutio said, and gave him his very deepest, most mocking bow. 'Our thanks to you.'

Capulet's smile curdled like sour milk, and he nodded. 'I

thank you all; I thank you, *honest gentlemen*. Good night.' He called for torches to see us home, and as if our departure were a signal, many others began to offer their goodbyes as well.

Romeo, like Lot's wife, could not but stare back with pure and aching fascination while I drew him onward, and when I glanced as well I saw the Capulet girl Juliet straining to follow us, against all sense and decorum, and her nurse firmly anchoring her in place.

I felt the same irresistible pull through my cousin's flesh, trying to draw him back to her. It was more than infatuation, more than love.

It was something darker than that, and with a darker end.

'I must turn back,' he said, as soon as we had him outside in the street. The chill of the night bit hard after the overheated gaiety of the feast, and I wrapped my cloak tighter around my shoulders as I fought to keep hold of him. 'Benvolio, I must go *back!*'

Mercutio threw his own arm over Romeo's shoulders and steered him firmly away from the Capulet palace, and towards our own safer territory. 'Madness,' he said, and laughed to rub knuckles over Romeo's curls. 'Give him a taste of his fair Rosaline and he's hungry all over again. There's nothing so fair about that wench, or any.'

Romeo began to hotly fire back, but then withheld his choler, and I realised why almost at the same moment: Mercutio, it seemed, had missed Romeo's encounter with Juliet, and therefore thought his longing was for his obsession of this morning. But no man who'd gazed so hotly on a girl as Romeo had on Juliet could still harbour feelings for another; he'd forgotten Rosaline in the second he'd fixed eyes on her younger cousin.

For some obscure reason, I did not wish to tell Mercutio of it, and I could see that Romeo was likewise reluctant.

'Mayhap you're right,' I said, drawing the focus from Romeo's sudden silence. 'Home with us, then. We've scored a coup this night; Capulet had to swallow their pride and allow us to put our feet beneath their table. Grandmother will be well pleased with that.'

'I put my feet beneath more than their table,' Mercutio said, and gave me a wild, sharp grin like the edge of a dagger. 'She'll be better pleased than you know.'

I felt a surge of anger, of dislike, and looked away from him. He was not, I thought, the friend I had known for so long. He was whole without, and ruined within, twisted and burnt and blackened, and I mourned for him, because the Mercutio I had loved died on a rope months ago.

'Home,' I said, under my breath. 'Home and safe.'

Though I had the disquieting notion that what had just occurred would follow us no matter how far we ran, and that safety would never again be ours.

FROM THE DIARY OF VERONICA MONTAGUE, BURNT UPON ORDERS OF LADY MONTAGUE

My brother, Ben, has done everything possible to avoid me these past months, since the death of the pervert outside the city wall; God wills that these vile, unnatural sinners be condemned and cast out, and whatever Benvolio believes (heretic that he is), I believe that I did God's business in whispering of the assignation – still, best the blame fall on the Capulet whore, for safety's sake, for Mercutio makes a bad enemy. I had thought he would swing alongside, but his father was too merciful, and now I must beware constantly of his wrath. 'Tis lucky I thought to swing the guilt towards our enemies when I did.

Benvolio knows the truth, and hates me as much as a brother might hate a sister, but I do not think he would break ranks to betray me to his friend. I keep a watchful eye, nonetheless.

The banns have been cried, and my marriage day

approaches! Would that I could marry a young and virile man, but Lord Enfeebled is still rich, and I will have wealth and position enough to move among the finest company. God grant that he expires soon, or I will have to visit that witch they whisper of in town to procure something to speed him on his way. My old nurse says that many a gouty old goat of a husband has been hurried to paradise; I think it more likely they have been shown the straight path to the devil's own bedchamber.

When I am wedded, for safety's sake, I will put it about that Benvolio and Mercutio are . . . more than friends. It will be easily believed, and this time, both with pay with their lives; even the soft-hearted prince will see that it must be done. All that I need do is purchase some commoner witnesses to swear they glimpsed such unnatural practices, and any risk from my brother will be finished.

But first, the wedding. I have insisted upon the finest quality for the feast, as befits a woman with such a well-endowed purse, and I am inviting the better half of Verona to celebrate with me. My mother is pinch-faced about the expense, but she's ever treated me as her lesser child; I will see she pays me some due before I leave her maternal embrace.

'Tis a pity that men run the world. I was born to be a prince.

I suppose I will settle for marrying one, when this old fool is dead.

Weeks passed.

The mood between our houses turned ever darker. Hatred grew on hatred, quickly and violently, for slights both real and imagined. No edict from the prince could stop it from coming to blood. First, a distant Capulet cousin was knifed in the street by someone not even allied to our house, yet it was cried about on Montague; next, a Montague servant was set upon and beaten to death while on an errand for my aunt, and this was – possibly unfairly – set at the Capulets' door.

And as untimely as ever, my sister's wedding approached at the speed of a runaway horse, and with as much decorum; Veronica had turned shrill and moody, and nothing was good enough, not even the fit or fabric of the gown. My mother was tight-lipped on the subject, but my uncle was not so circumspect; he complained, loudly and often, of the lavish expense in ridding himself of the unwanted burden of a niece. Whatever he had cheated from her bridegroom would hardly cover the cost, though we all secretly rejoiced that she would soon be gone.

I came around the corner from my apartments on a bright Thursday morning, with the Angelus bell's chime still hanging in the air, and found Veronica weeping on a bench in the garden. She was sitting uncovered in the sun, which was strange to see – she always claimed that sun ruined a woman's skin, and yet here she was, bathed in the glow, dishevelled and red eyed, with a single maid hovering anxiously nearby to catch the wet kerchiefs as Veronica finished with them. The maid had not escaped my sister's ill temper, I saw; there was a red mark on her cheek in the shape of a plump small hand. Perhaps she'd not brought enough kerchiefs to soak up Veronica's tears.

I tried to move past without incident, but Veronica looked up and in a choked, watery voice, whispered, 'Benvolio? Please . . .'

I could not remember a time she had ever used such a word, and so I paused, to gaze down at her. I did not feel any sympathy. Whatever troubles she suffered, she had more than earned them, and I had not forgotten our filthy family secret. The blood that was on her dainty hands had rubbed off on mine, and I would never forgive her for that.

'What?' I asked. It sounded abrupt, but I did not care, not at all.

She burst into tears again, this time (I was sure) feigning grief. I was tempted to walk on, but the maid sent me a beseeching look, and since I pitied her mightily for her role in soothing Veronica, I sighed and sank down on the bench next to my sister. 'What?' I asked again, more gently.

'Nothing's as I thought it would be,' she said, and muffled

her words against the kerchief. 'The dress is wretched, Benvolio, our uncle has imposed such a restraint on it that it won't flatter me, and the feast – why, there's hardly a feast at all! It's the one day when I can show my quality to the women of Verona, and he's making me hardly better than a common fishwife . . . How can I rise in esteem with such a beginning?'

Not so much a female complaint as a problem of ambition meeting its limits, then. 'It's of no matter,' I said. 'You bring the family blood of Montague, and your husband is rich enough. Society will embrace you as a woman of quality, Veronica.' God help society, but what I said was true. 'Now stop your tears. It ill becomes a woman grown to weep like a spoilt child.'

She sent me a murderous glare through swollen lids, but she wiped her eyes, blew her nose, and threw the soiled kerchief to her attendant. Then she stood up, smoothed her skirts and patted her hair (none of which made any difference to the red mottling on her tearstained face), and took in a deep, trembling breath. 'You are acid and vinegar, brother dear, but at least you are bracing. Tell me, then, how fares your friend Mercutio?'

I sensed a barb under the honey, and was instantly wary. 'Happily espoused. I see him little now. He has new responsibilities.'

'Espoused,' she agreed. 'But happily? It stretches the word's meaning to say so.' She leant closer, and dropped her voice to a low whisper. 'I hear that he saw a witch. Perhaps to cure himself of his . . . appetites?'

I shoved her away. 'Peddle your gossip somewhere else,' I said. 'Witches! What next, then? Furies and dragons? Will the old Roman gods come down from Olympus?'

She shuddered and crossed herself. 'I pray not. But you should not mock, brother. Witches exist; all the churchmen say it. It takes a dire cause to drive him to one.'

'Then go be pious and pray for Mercutio's immortal soul,' I said, and stood up. 'Pray for mine, while you're at it. I'm sure I have sins to be forgiven.'

'Many,' she agreed with false sweetness, and snapped open a fan. 'I should leave this dreadful sunshine. It won't do to go to my wedding with spots!'

I wished her a plague of them, as disfiguring as possible, but I said nothing, only stepped aside as she swept past me, heading indoors. Her servant followed with a handful of soiled kerchiefs she'd have to wash and iron and have ready for the next ill-tempered tempest, which might come any moment. She, at least, had my genuine sympathy.

Two more days passed, each another twist of the strangling cord of tension that gripped our household; I kept within the precincts of the palazzo, and so did most of us. Veronica threw more fits, but I observed them only at a hearty distance. My grandmother demanded my attendance once, to interrogate me on Romeo's behaviour and express her pleasure at what had occurred at the Capulet feast; it seemed rumour had run riot in the streets that we had trespassed with impunity, and that one of the minor Capulet girls had been sent, in haste, from the city. Mercutio's doing, but the old witch was eager to take the credit for Montague.

As to Romeo, he seemed quiet. Subdued, in fact. I saw no more poesies from his pen lauding Rosaline's beauty, at least, so perhaps the visit to the Capulet feast had yielded some positive result after all.

By the end of that time, the tension and suppressed violence of the household drove me out into the dark once more. I crawled rooftops, dropped silent into bedchambers, and took away the adornments and prizes and secrets our enemies cherished. It was a busy few nights, seeking out Capulet allies and discovering their vices; some were expensive but not sinful, like the man who had an entire room filled with brocades and silks – not for his wife or daughters, apparently, since there were also finished (and never worn) doublets and cloaks made to his measure. I took the richest selection of fabrics and had them sent to my mother and aunt as a gift from a friendly merchant willing to conceal the silk's origins in order to draw their business towards him.

But there were far darker secrets, and less cheerful prizes. I found a heavy, locked chest in the home of a count, and instead of gems discovered inside the body of a young servant girl; this I left in place, as it was too unwieldy to move, but posted an accusing letter on the church door, along with the bloody silk banner in which she'd been wrapped. I doubted he would ever pay for the crime, but the girl's pitiful, huddled end had deserved that much effort.

On a moonless night, carefully chosen for cover, I crept into Capulet's feasting hall, removed the banner, and stole the most doleful-seeming donkey I could find; it bore the indignity of being tarted up with the florid silk banner, and the all-too-drunken Capulet adherent I'd paid to ride it through the streets as a tribute. Unfortunately for the fool, he ran afoul of a nest of his own. It did not end well for him.

I missed having Mercutio at my back. I was taking risks, I knew – ones that might destroy me. But it was as hard to stop stealing as others found it to give up drinking. *Perhaps I'll give it up for Lent,* I thought as I crouched in the shadows atop a roof, watching the moon rise. It was only a quarter full, and was the colour of rich cream. So many stars above, and as I stared upward, I spotted a vivid shooting star that burnt as red as Lucifer's horns. It was gone in a few seconds.

I heard someone passing below on the street, and flattened myself; in the dark, I would be just another decorative corner to the roof, but the moon illuminated the passerby clearly. He was alone, and anonymous in a worn cloak too big for him, but when a stray gust of wind caught the edges and sent them flying, I spotted the familiar, deadly line of a rapier. No commoner, though he had left off his finery save for the sword.

I was curious. The hour was very late, and I was very bored, waiting for my latest target to douse lights; I made a decision, lowered myself to the iron of a balcony, and then from there to the cobbles, where I quickly stepped to the shadows as he turned. I'd made no noise; this was a man on business just as illicit as mine, clearly.

I followed him down the winding streets. He turned in the shadow of the cathedral, and from there we were in less friendly territory – for me, at any rate, since it was Capulet controlled, and patrolled by their men. I took to higher ground again – rooftops – and watched the brave (or foolish) wanderer. He had sense enough to hide when Capulet guards ambled by, arrogant and loud, spoiling for a fight; as soon as they'd sauntered on, he hurried around the corner.

I dropped down to the street, following in the shadows,

and was on the point of avoiding a man asleep in a doorway, cradling a wine-skin, when my dark-adapted eyes picked out the familiar sigil of the Ordelaffi on the drunkard's doublet, and the changeable, cloud-draped moonlight limned the sharp lines of his face.

Mercutio. He was drunk and asleep – muddy and filthy in a doorway that, unless my nose had numbed itself, had been used as a privy more than once.

My casual curiosity about the wayward traveller I'd been tracking vanished, and I glanced about to be sure no one was watching. I still held doubts about Mercutio – we'd avoided his company since the last ordeal of the Capulet feast – but for the love I had once borne him, I could not leave him lying dirty in the street, an object of mockery and a target for thieves and murderers.

I tossed the wine aside, which woke a sleepy murmur from him, and pulled him up to a sitting position. He was as boneless as a corpse, if considerably more mobile, since he shoved at me with ineffective, drunken fury and then flopped back flat on the dirty cobbles.

'I should leave you here, fool,' I said to him in a low, fierce voice, but in truth, my guts ached for him; this was no simple indulgence, coming here into enemy territory. He'd made himself a true foe of the Capulets at the feast by bringing us under his invitation, and for him to be lingering here, helpless . . . it smelt of a desperate desire to meet his God.

I got him on his feet, with great effort, and held him there with his arm around my shoulders. We had stumbled on for several steps before he seemed to realise that he was upright, and several more before he said, tentatively, 'Benvolio?'

'Aye,' I said. 'Hush, fool; know you not where we are?'

'In the lion's den, my Daniel,' Mercutio said, and laughed, raw with wine and a barely suppressed wildness. 'Hear them roar? Raaaaaar!' He swiped at me with a claw-crooked hand, which I slapped aside. He giggled and nearly slipped to the ground again, but I bolstered him up. 'Have you any shiny trinkets tonight? No? What good are you, then, for a thief?'

'Quiet!' This, I realised, had been a mistake, however good-hearted my intentions. Whatever demon drove my friend to drink himself senseless within the easy grasp of his foes would also push him to betray us both. 'For the love of God, man, even if you court your own death, don't court mine!'

He giggled again and shushed himself – noisily – as we stumbled along. If we ran into a Capulet watch, all would be lost; I was anonymously dressed, but Mercutio wore Ordelaffi colours. I stripped off my long cloak and threw it over his shoulders, shrouding the betraying crest.

As we turned the corner, I spotted the single, stealthy traveller I'd started out to follow. He was staring up at a wall, and as I watched, he sprang up and began to climb it. I knew that clumsy scramble, especially when his hood fell back and moonlight exposed his face, angelic and determined beneath a riot of black curls.

My cousin Romeo.

I bit back the impulse to call to him, warn him; the wall, I well remembered, was trapped at the top, and he was ill prepared to deal with such things . . . but I had underestimated him, and as he scrambled up, he balanced carefully above the sharp points, and vaulted over with more grace than I'd have credited. Perhaps my cousin had learnt something from me after all.

'Romeo!' Mercutio suddenly brayed, and I almost dropped him in my surprise.

'Hush, man; he's leapt the orchard wall—'

'Nay, he's stolen off to bed, but *whose* bed?' Mercutio thumped me painfully in the chest with an outstretched finger. 'I'll conjure him, like that mad old witch – no, hush; we speak not of witches . . . Romeo! Humours! Madman! Passion! Lover!'

He was too loud, far too loud, and I shoved him onward, desperate to get him away. He dragged his heels, and would not quieten, rambling nonsense that I only half heard. 'The ape is dead, and I must conjure him . . . I conjure you by Rosaline's bright eyes, by her high forehead and her scarlet lips, by her fine foot, straight leg, and quivering thigh, and the domains that there adjacent lie—'

'Be still!' I whispered furiously, and shoved him to the wall hard enough to bang his head on stone. 'For the love of *God*—'

'That in your likeness you appear to us! *Romeo!*' Mercutio's eyes were acid-bright, his face almost exalted with feverish intensity, as if he believed his childish nonsense was real spellcraft, as if he believed in witches and curses, devils and furies. 'I conjure thee *appear!*'

I had no choice, because I could hear the fast-approaching footsteps of Capulet guards. I hit him hard, twice, to daze him into silence broken only with incoherent moans. As the guards turned the corner, swords drawn, I drove a fist hard into Mercutio's stomach, and he bent over and promptly vomited up most of the wine he'd downed, all over my boots.

I supported him as he sagged, and stayed in the

shadows; the hood covering his face would do well enough, but I was too recognisable to Capulet eyes. 'Pardon,' I said, and slurred the word hard. 'My fiend – my *friend* is worse for wine; your pardon, excellencies, most surely pardon—'

'Fool,' the taller of the three guards said, and kicked Mercutio's leg so he staggered and fell in his own mess. 'Wine-soaked idiots! Take your stinking hides home or I'll carve them for you!'

'Pardon, lord, pardon, most sincere—' I grovelled, cringed, and dragged Mercutio with me until he could find his feet again. The Capulets threw stones at us, and one hit with enough force to leave a fist-size bruise on my back; I was lucky he did not hold more ill will, or I'd have a broken rib. Mercutio stayed silent, panting and groaning, until we were well around the corner; then he shoved me hard away.

'You beat me,' he said – moping, like a child.

'I saved your life,' I snapped back. 'Move; we must be gone quickly, before they follow.'

'Let them!' He pushed me again when I tried to take hold of him. 'You think Romeo would be angry at my conjure? It would anger him to raise a spirit in his mistress's circle of some stranger, to let it stand until she laid it down. That would be *spite*. My invocation was fair and honest, in his mistress's name . . .'

He was still fevered, I thought; all this talk of witchcraft, of conjuring and invocations gave me chills. Veronica had spoken of witches, and said that Mercutio had sought one out. What madness was this? A dangerous one.

A fatal one.

That, and the thought of Romeo beyond the Capulets' garden wall, chilled me. Was he seeking Rosaline yet again? Had he misled me after all? No, not chills . . . the cold turned hot, flamed into anger.

Anger that he *dared* put her at risk.

I tried again to move Mercutio, but he shook me off. 'Go, then,' I said. 'Be off home.'

'I seek Romeo!'

'You seek him in vain, to seek him here where he means not to be found. Go.'

Changeable, like all drunkards, he suddenly threw his hot, sweated arm around my neck and gave me a sloppy smile. 'Come with me,' he said, 'my good friend. I am alone and lonely, and I need the comfort of my friends. What have I left but friends?'

'Go home,' I told him. 'The cloak will hide you. I know not what you'll say to your lady wife, but . . .'

His smile curdled, and he looked murder at me for a few seconds before he pulled away, settling the cloak heavily around his shoulders. 'The brave Prince of Shadows,' he said, and acid dripped from the words. He sketched a bow that nearly ended with him collapsed on the street. 'Prince of thieves, prince of liars, prince of idiots. Why have you killed no Capulets for me, Benvolio? Is there not death between them and me, for the sake of the one I don't dare name under penalty of the same? You creep, you steal, you take your revenge in secret. I crave more; do you hear? I desire *blood*!'

'You desire your own ending,' I said to him, and it was brutally honest, and said in love and fear. 'Please, my friend. There is blood between Capulets and Montagues, it is true – a lake of it large enough to row on at our leisure. But you can still escape the crimson stain. Let it be done.

Look forward, to your future. Find your way, I beg you, before you're lost to yourself, and to all of us.'

He grabbed me behind the neck and pulled me close, pressed our foreheads together, and said, 'I'm already lost, my dear Ben. But I'll drag those who've killed me to hell alongside me.' It was a broken whisper, full of the anguish I knew boiled within him, but in the next second he pushed away and staggered on, one hand trailing the wall for support.

I let him go. Mercutio trailed fate like a cold black cloud, and for a moment I could almost see the sinister shape of it in the cloak that rose and flapped in the night breeze.

Death, I thought. *Death stalks behind him.*

I should have gone with him, but fear for Romeo, and my family responsibility, held me there after he'd stumbled around the corner, heading vaguely in the direction of the Ordelaffi palazzo.

I looked up, found a handhold, and climbed to the roof of the two-floored shop building. As I passed the open shutters I heard the twin snores of the shopkeeper and his wife; his were low and rumbling, hers thin and halting, though from the lumps wrapped in sheets she was twice his size and half the volume. I scrambled up, balanced on the roof tiles, and ran lightly along to the far end, which overlooked the Capulets' garden wall – from which I saw, in pantomime, the love-struck Romeo kneeling among the flowers, and the young Juliet bending towards him from her balcony. *Well,* a part of me thought, *at least it is not Rosaline again.* Though, in truth, I was not sure this was any better for Montague, and it might be a good deal worse. The yearning between them seemed almost a visible shimmer, like heat upon stones, and she went in and came out, went in and came out, as if she could not bear to be parted from him. Finally, though, in she went, and her doors shuttered to him, and Romeo, dejected and melancholy, climbed the garden wall to leave.

He looked up, then, and saw me perched there watching, and the guilt and horror that flashed across his face were, at least, a little gratifying.

But I forgot it, and nearly forgot him, as another set of windows opened, another set of curtains billowed, and another girl stepped onto her balcony. Taller, stronger, older, more richly beautiful to my eyes. She did not look towards us, but up, to the eastern horizon.

Rosaline looked sad. So very sad, and so very alone.

Romeo dropped down into the street and put elbows on his hips, looking up at me. 'You spy on me, coz? You dare to—'

I hushed him with an outstretched hand, still staring at Rosaline, whose gaze had sharpened now, and fixed on me exposed and visible across the way. She saw me – I knew she did, for her eyes widened and her hands tightened on the railing – but she said nothing, and raised no alarm.

I nodded towards her. She slowly nodded back. It lit a burning fire within me that drove away all the chills. That one single gesture told me more than all the flowery speeches that must have passed between my cousin and his new love.

She will be leaving soon, sent away to her tomb in the convent. You'll never see her again, the solemn, practical part of me advised. And so I looked on her, with honest hunger, for as long as I dared. She was so beautiful in the soft glow, all her curves caressed by the dim light; her hair was a glossy dark fall with hints of blue, like a raven's wing. The wind played with it, and I could imagine the heavy weight of it in my hands, warm and soft, scented of flowers.

Her lips parted, as if she would speak. I did not give her the chance, because I could not bear it.

I slid down the tile roof, took hold of the edge, and dropped lightly down into the street in front of my foolish cousin. 'Come on,' I said, and dragged him homeward.

My cousin was not himself, in ways I could not begin to explain, nor to fathom. He had always been headstrong and blind to the consequences of his actions, but he was never completely insane . . . poetry to a Capulet girl had been ill-advised, an embarrassment, but he had known full well the limits even as he wallowed in the hazy cloud of passion.

He well knew that there was no chance of any dalliance with the soon-to-be-wed Juliet, apple of Capulet's eye. Or he *should* have understood. His infatuation with Rosaline had been a boy's love, one that imagined an angel where a flesh-and-blood woman lived, and never expected to so much as brush his fingertips on the hem of her garment.

Yet that night, in the safety of his rooms, he said, 'I shall have her, Benvolio. She shall be mine, only mine. I cannot live any other life than with her. I knew the instant I saw her, but the touch of her fingers, the taste of her lips . . .' He was not caught up in a fancy; I could see that. He was utterly serious, as serious as any man twice his age. It was only that it was a subject he dared not take seriously, on his life. 'I know you think me foolish to go to her, but I could do nothing else. I could not sleep nor eat without seeing her smile again, and now that I have sated that hunger it only grows more fierce. I must marry her, Ben. Marry or die.'

'I think you mean marry *and* die,' I said, 'because you know you cannot have her. Her family and ours will never stomach it.'

He shook his head in impatient disregard, and stalked the room restlessly. He'd dismissed his servants, and I'd left Balthasar behind, so there were no potentially prying eyes to carry tales back to our grandmother, but still I felt the hot breath of her presence on my neck. *He is your responsibility,* she had told me, and given me that devil's look that meant I had best not disappoint her, and she would know – oh, yes, somehow, the ancient crone would know what was brewing here.

But more than my fear of her was my dread of the blind look in my cousin's eyes. That was more than mere love. It was a martyr's exaltation. And it was unnatural.

It raised chills along my spine.

'You can't understand,' he told me, with the fever of a true fanatic. His eyes glowed with passion, and his face was alight with it. 'Benvolio, you've never felt such joy as grips me even at the mention of her name: Juliet, *Juliet.* Was there ever a more beautiful sound since God first spoke? You can't understand; you have not seen her. She is . . . she is perfection; she is the most perfect woman ever formed . . . She is made of light and love . . .'

'She's a child,' I told him flatly, and stood up to block his path. He stopped, but did not back away, and the madness did not dim in his eyes. 'She's a Capulet daughter – no, *the* Capulet daughter, on whom they pin all their hopes – and she is all but married to Count Paris—'

'He cannot have her,' Romeo said, and the exaltation

turned dark, then, and violent, and his right hand gripped the dagger at his side. 'She is a precious flower; she cannot be so rudely plucked by such as him; I will not bear the thought of him pawing her—'

'Cousin, think! He is the prince's own close friend and relative! You will not only humiliate your uncle; you will earn us the prince's enmity for all time. You will destroy Montague, and for what? A girl, a girl barely of an age to bleed, much less know what she—'

He struck me. It was not a love tap, either; it was a full blow, delivered fast and strong and without any warning at all, and I was rocked back a step, but only a step . . . but as I brought up my own fist, he pulled his dagger, and the needle point aimed straight for my throat.

I stopped short, balanced on the balls of my feet with my neck a bare inch from the tip of the blade. There was a very dark, antic look in my young cousin's eyes, something that I thought was eerily akin to Mercutio's black moods; I was far from sure that he would not spike me straight through if I dared move. It would mean his life, but I was beginning to think, considering what I had seen this night, that Romeo no longer cared a fig for his life, or mine, or anyone's, save this Capulet girl's. I slowly took a step back, and some sanity came into him; he looked a bit ashamed as he lowered the dagger, though he did not sheathe it. 'I warn you: do not speak of her so,' he said. 'I love you well, Ben, but I love her more than any creature on this earth. If it were not blasphemous, I would say I love her more than God and man alike. No, I may say that. I must say it, and if God must damn me, then let it be done.'

I winced, because even the boldest man did not tempt

God so. 'You don't know what you say. I beg you, Romeo, for your life's sake—'

'Beg away,' he said, and finally sheathed steel as he turned his back on me. 'I should kill you, you know. I should at least cut out your tongue so that you can't betray us before we can be wed in the sight of God.'

'Wed,' I repeated. He meant to climb it, then, this ultimate pinnacle of madness. I felt numbed. He had not threatened me so much as simply expressed aloud his logic, but in it was no room for the love we had always borne each other as brothers. I was simply a barrier to his desires now, one to be minimised, or destroyed if necessary. 'You really mean to wed her.'

'Juliet,' he said, and turned back towards me. He held my gaze with that wild martyr's look and beatific smile. No saint had ever seemed so exalted, nor so bent on self-destruction for the sake of his ecstasy. There was nothing sane in it, and nothing that could be reasoned to. 'Her name is Juliet.'

'Romeo . . .' I said it gently, the way a man will address a strangely feral dog, and held up my hand in a gesture of peace. 'Coz, I know you love her; it is plain to the blindest eyes. But I beg you think what you are doing to yourself—'

'I care not.'

It was a bitter pill, but I swallowed it, and said, 'Then to her. Do you imagine for a moment her family will stand for such an insult? They'll murder you, and the girl – at best, Juliet will be disgraced, spoilt, unmarriageable. And if you believe that Count Paris will not avenge the wrong done to him—'

'I don't care,' he said. 'Christ forgive me, Benvolio, but there is nothing in the world for me but her, and nothing for her but me, and if I cannot have her, better I am dead, better we are both dead, better the *world* is dead and our dreams with it. Do you understand?' He wanted me to, desperately, but all I saw was a man in a sweated fever who was making no sense. 'I can let nothing stand between us. Nothing, and no one.' He pulled in a breath. 'I don't wish to do it, but if you think to betray me, I will betray you first. The prince would do anything for a man willing to identify the Prince of Shadows.'

I did not believe it. He was my cousin, my brother, a bond as unbreakable as my heart to my chest . . . but I read the intention in his face, the determination and anguish in his eyes. He could not mean it, and yet he did.

I stared at Romeo in silence for a long, long moment, and then said, 'You're mad.'

He gave me a twitch of a smile, but it did not alter the truth of what was in his face. 'If this is madness, then I would rather die mad than live sane.'

I backed away from him then, in defeat, and went back to my own apartments. I felt sickened and cold, and there was a bitter metal taste in my mouth. When Balthasar began helping me remove my clothes I realised I had sweated them through. He clucked his tongue as he took them. 'It's a wonder you've not caught your death of ague,' he said. 'Terrible vapours out in the night.' He took a closer look at my face and frowned. 'Master?'

I shook my head, and he found a heavy robe to drape around me. I still felt chilled inside it. 'I need to take a message out,' I said. 'I cannot go myself. Will you see it delivered?'

'Have I ever failed you?'

'Never,' I said, and sat down at the writing table to draw out paper and ink. I wrote quickly, sanded it, folded it, and sealed it with wax – but without the Montague marks – before handing it to him.

He glanced down at it, then up at me, eyebrows raised. I had written no names – neither inside nor out.

'Rosaline Capulet,' I said, very quietly. His eyebrows climbed higher, but he said nothing, only nodded. 'Be most extremely careful.'

'Leave it to me,' he said. 'Will you expect an answer?'

'I hope,' I said, and sat back, frowning. 'I hope that I do.'

FROM THE HAND OF BENVOLIO
MONTAGUE TAKEN BY BALTHASAR, HIS
MANSERVANT, TO FRIAR LAWRENCE BEFORE
MATINS AND THENCE DELIVERED BY THE
FRIAR TO ROSALINE CAPULET

From your brother in Christ,
I am deeply concerned for the soul of your fair cousin,
whose devotion to her most dear Lord is wavering; I
believe she may be tempted by one who means to lead
her astray. I pray you, watch for her safety and lead her
to the paths of righteousness. I will likewise guide my
wandering brother back to the fold.
Go with God's love, and my own.

FROM THE HAND OF ROSALINE CAPULET
DIRECTED TO BENVOLIO MONTAGUE,
CONFISCATED FROM HER SERVANT BY
TYBALT CAPULET
NOT DELIVERED

From your sister in Christ,
Alas, your warning has come too late, for I find that my
innocent cousin's true faith has been corrupted, and in its
place a dangerous heresy has taken vital root. No words
of mine will be sufficient to sway her from this false
doctrine, though she knows she risks her immortal soul.
I urge you, do all you can to prevent this false prophet
from further corrupting her sweet and trusting soul. I
dare not entrust this to the friar's delivery; he intrigues
too closely with my cousin for my comfort, and may not
bring this to you. I beg you, act swiftly to prevent what
may be tragedy. I can do nothing but pray you succeed.
Walk carefully, and with God, beloved brother in Christ.

If only I had thought to write a letter also to Friar Lawrence, explaining in bare words the risk, all might have proceeded quite differently . . . but that is my sin of overbearing caution, and no one else's. Romeo barred me from his rooms all the next day, but I thought him penned up inside; his manservant swore it was the case. It wasn't until my grandmother summoned me to her chambers that I knew something had gone wrong. Badly wrong.

Into the smouldering, sweltering furnace I went, where my grandmother sat mounded in blankets and warmed by the blazing hearth. I was surprised to find that my mother was with her as well – not only my mother; beside her, looking fevered and mutinously angry, sat my sister, Veronica. She was all but married, and I had hoped to be spared any further contact with her until then.

At least she was sweating through her clothes as well, though she strove to look composed and elegant – a difficult thing when one's hair clings in damp threads to one's face, and sweat runs like a widow's tears.

My mother did not sweat, though there was a faint glistening on her brow. She sat quietly, hands folded in her lap, and gazed at me with steady warning.

I bowed to her, to my grandmother, and threw Veronica a barely perceptible nod.

'Stand up,' my grandmother said. She looked pale and chill and half-dead, but her eyes gleamed with virile power. 'Where is your cousin?'

'In his rooms,' I said, and was assaulted quickly by the conviction that I was wrong. I left it at that, because showing weakness would be like running from a lion. Sweat already beaded on my brow, and I could feel the damp patches soaking beneath my arms. *Jesu,* it was like the bowels of the devil in here.

She let me stew in silence for a full minute, and then snapped her fingers. A serving woman stepped forward out of the corner, eyes downcast, visibly terrified. She kept her shaking hands knotted in her apron.

'Tell him,' my grandmother said. The woman darted a quick look at my mother, who nodded encouragement.

She licked her lips, and her voice came softly, and faltering. 'Begging your pardon, sir, but I empty chamber pots, and . . . and when I came to fetch it, young Master Romeo was not there.'

'His manservant swears he's within. You just didn't see him.'

'No, sir, I . . .' She licked her lips again, and took in a deep breath, for courage. 'Nobody marks my comings and goings. His chamber pot was under the bed, like always. I had to go all the way through. He wasn't there.'

'Was his chamber pot used?' my grandmother asked. 'Come on, girl; speak up. My ears are old!'

'Some part used,' the girl stammered. Her rough-scrubbed hands were white where they were pressed in on themselves. 'As if he was there in the morning but no longer.'

My grandmother shoved her back in the shadows with a flick of her hand, and the girl was grateful for it. Then all the attention came back to me.

'He is not within these walls,' Grandmother said. 'Do you know where he is?'

'No,' I said. Better to admit it. A lie would only make it look worse.

'Your cousin has been out many times recently without you. Were you aware of *that*?'

'Some of it,' I said. My own voice had tightened up, and I tried to ease my tone, and the tension that had taken hold of my shoulders. The heat, the intense heat was making me feel light-headed, and sweat dripped uncomfortably down my face. 'I will find him.'

'Best you do, before something worse happens. Is he still on about that Rosaline girl?'

'No,' I said, which was the perfect truth. 'He sees the wisdom of leaving Rosaline alone now.'

'Good,' Veronica said primly. 'Loose-tongued viper that she is, she'd betray poor Romeo in a second. Look what came of her last gossip.'

My grandmother glanced her way, and Veronica shut her mouth, quick enough for her teeth to click together. 'Did I seek your opinions, girl?' Veronica, I thought, had best watch herself. The temporary diversion did not last, because Grandmother's attention turned back to me with the force of a shove. 'Is it some other girl, then?'

I risked a lie. 'I don't know.'

'Pray God it is, and someone suitable,' she said. 'You've been little use to me in the matter of Romeo, Benvolio. I am most displeased. Tell me, what do you believe your future is in this house?'

'Why, Grandmother,' I said, 'I believe that it is whatever you decree it will be. But you have need of someone to avenge your wrongs and be your strong right hand.'

'Is that what you are, then? My strong right hand? The scriptures tell us, "If thy hand offend thee, cut it off." I warn you, boy: bring your cousin to heel and make him comport himself as befits the true heir of Montague, or there will be consequences. Grave consequences.'

My mother was uncharacteristically worried; I could see it in her normally unreadable face. She feared for me, and that meant more than Grandmother's threats.

I bowed my head. 'I will find him,' I said. 'May I have your leave to—'

'Go,' my grandmother said, and pointed her cane at me with an unsteady hand. 'Find the boy. Tybalt Capulet sent a much distempered letter here complaining of Romeo's behaviour at the feast, and I think he means to scrape a duel if he can. Prevent that at all costs. We cannot lose Romeo.'

She burst into wet, red coughs, and I escaped quickly. But I was not the only one. My mother rose and followed, and so did Veronica.

'Bide a moment,' my mother said, once we were without the doors. She took a dainty linen square from her sleeve and dabbed at her forehead. 'I am sorry, my son, but she is in earnest in her anger. Romeo's betrothal will be announced soon, and his behaviour must be seen as above reproach. His promised bride is of excellent family, and far wealthier than we are. You understand the politics of this.'

I did. Children of such houses were bought and sold for favours and profits, all under the cloak of the Church and tradition. Romeo and Mercutio, my sister . . . all affianced without consent, and I dangled on the precipice, fighting the drop. Rosaline alone had escaped that customary fate, but she was soon to wed Christ. *Maybe that's your escape,* part of me whispered. *Take on that suffocating robe for good. Priests may claim celibacy, but it's the exception, not the rule.* Yet taking the cloth would not free me from the family; far from it. They would expect preferment, and push me from priest to monsignor to bishop to pope, if they could. At least Rosaline could look to a future of prayer and study, if lucky.

'I understand,' I said. 'But the old woman will be on her deathbed soon, at the rate she coughs up her blood.'

'She'll die in that chair, ordering us about,' my sister said sourly. 'Doubt that not. And she's got venom enough to poison us all if she's roused to bite. So be quick about your work, Ben. I have only a few days until I'm free of all this. Don't spoil it for me!'

'What motive could I have for that?' I asked her, in too-honeyed tones, and she frowned. She knew all too well what motive I harboured. And what hatred I concealed under the smile. 'Mother.' I bowed to her, ignored Veronica, and walked away with fast, hard hits of my heel on the floor. My uncle was walking the other way across the atrium, head bent as he listened to one of the five or six rich men gaggled around him; he looked gravely interested in what they were saying, though I doubted he was. The masks that duty pressed upon us . . . He seemed not to note my passage at all, and I hastened my pace, went quickly up the stairs and into my rooms, where Balthasar nearly stumbled into me in hurrying to open the door.

I said nothing at all to him, changing to clothes that would best reflect the might and power of Montague; besides, the ones I had worn were stinking already, and I wanted the smell of the old woman's room off of me. Balthasar silently presented me with sword and dagger, which I added, and donned his own before topping it with a half cloak, and then the two of us slipped away, out through the hallways and a little-used door that creaked when we opened it onto the back garden. It was a pleasant enough day, sunny and mild, and the flowers rioted in their colours among the sharply trimmed topiary trees. Like the Capulets, we had bravos in our pay, and some loitered in the sunny space; Balthasar summoned two of them, and we left through the side gate.

'Dare I ask?' he said then, as we walked through the square with pigeons exploding upward from our path. A child's choir was singing near the fountain, and we avoided a loose chicken being chased by a red-faced servant. The market was still busy up ahead, full of movement and colour, though it was late in the day to be buying anything but livestock or dry goods. I headed for the market, not knowing where else to stop; we could enquire among the stall merchants and malingering wealthy and see whether Romeo had been spotted. Someone would have seen him, most certainly. No one could hide for long in Verona.

I gave courteous, though brief, greetings to acquaintances as we entered the outskirts of the market, and sent Balthasar to ask after Romeo at various merchants friendly to the Montagues – they sometimes wrapped our house's colour into their shades, or flew it in a banner, though that was a risky venture in a city so polarised as ours was becoming. Capulet colours were also in evidence, in approximately the same numbers. I saw a few of their paid men sauntering through, but they seemed at ease, and one even escorted a plump woman I took to be his wife, trailed by two small children. Well, then, even the Capulet adherents were human.

I was not happy to know it, since it made hating them more difficult.

A stall haunted by a sinister-looking old woman proffering vials of oils and concoctions made me slow my steps, and Balthasar sent me a curious look. 'Master? Are we not seeking Master Romeo? I don't think you'll find him in this old witch's quarters.'

'Not this old witch,' I said, and turned on him. 'There's word of a witch doing business in Verona. Mercutio is said to have sought her out. What know you?'

'Little,' he said, and looked away at a grubby child running past carrying a struggling, squawking chicken, with a butcher wielding a cleaver in wrathful pursuit. 'She's said to be new to the city. Purveyor of potions and charms, telling of fortunes, the usual thing.'

'Why would Mercutio seek her out?'

'Perhaps his wife has been to see her. A husband's well advised to see what a wife's been up to, visiting those old hags. They're known for their poisons.'

I hadn't thought of it, but poison was a common weapon among all the classes in Verona – rich and poor, high and low. It was more often used by women than men, but politics was a dirty business, and poison a tool of the trade.

But not Mercutio, surely. As much as he hated those he saw as enemies, he would kill with close, personal violence. Not some subtle and cold design.

But if he did, some evil angel whispered, *if he did, whom would he choose?*

Not me, even if he blamed me. Not Romeo, for similar reasons . . . he loved us enough to kill us quick and clean, face to honest face.

But the Capulets . . . perhaps. A poisoned drink for a poisoned tongue. I went cold considering how easily Rosaline might be touched by such a thing . . . an innocent, struck down by one who was avenging an innocent. He might also be turning that cold hate on his own father, a thing that would surely damn his soul to eternal flames.

'Find her for me,' I told Balthasar. 'Do it quietly.'

He looked gravely doubtful, now. 'Your grandmother will take it ill if you make visits to such heretical company . . .'

'I care not,' I said irritably, although of course I did care, and his warning was well-spoken. 'It will not be Benvolio Montague who visits her, be assured. Find her; our secret friend will go in my place.'

'Ah,' he said, and looked much cheered. 'You might tell our secret friend that these evil creatures are well used to threats. They generally require silver to loosen their tongues.'

'He is in funds.' Actually, the Prince of Shadows had been bent too much on revenge recently, and not enough upon profit; I would need to begin to remedy it soon. The thought of the remaining loot dangling below the jakes was tempting, but all that was left were pieces that would be easily recognised if traded in Verona; I needed to find a jeweller I could trust to cut the rubies that I'd stolen, and a trustworthy sword maker to refit the very fine blade to a new handle. But I had enough to bribe some low witch, certainly.

'Sir,' Balthasar said, and jerked his chin in the direction he wished me to look. I turned towards the cathedral and saw that Count Paris – accompanied, of course, by half an army of hangers-on – was making his leisurely way through the square in our direction. It was slow progress, because he paused every few steps to exchange politenesses, bow to ladies, inspect vendors' wares. He spotted us, and corrected his wandering course to move in our direction.

Ever the dutiful servant of my family, I pasted on a smile and sketched a bow to him as he approached. 'My lord Paris,' I said, and waited until he granted me a gracious, minimal gesture of his hand to straighten. 'I trust this day finds you in fine health.'

'Tolerable, Benvolio. I hear your sister's wedding day approaches. I anticipate the day.'

'As do I,' I said, with much feeling. The faster Veronica's shadow left my door, the better life would seem. 'My congratulations on your own recent match.'

'Ah, yes, young Juliet.' Count Paris was a handsome man, and, like all who'd survived the cut-throat world of Veronese nobility, no fool at all. He gave me a carefully measured smile. 'A pity we could not arrange such a match with Montague, but alas, your fair sister's hand was already promised.'

Your good fortune, I wanted to say, but I smiled back, with equal false sincerity. 'I wish both bride and groom the happiest of lives,' I said. 'Good sir, have you seen my cousin Romeo about today?'

'I have,' he said. 'He seemed in a great hurry. I wish you luck in catching him. Fair day, Benvolio.'

'And to you.'

We bowed again, I much deeper than he, and his parade swept by us. Behind me, Balthasar let out a gusty sigh. 'He'll soon regret having Tybalt as a relation,' my man said.

'Anyone would,' I agreed. 'Now be off with you, to find this witch woman.' I sent him a nod as a dismissal.

He did not go. 'I shall not leave you alone and unattended,' he said. "Twould not be right, sir.'

'Don't be foolish. I can well care for myself.'

'All the same, it's my head in your grandmother's wine press if you tumble onto the point of a Capulet sword and I'm not dead before you to prove my loyalty. No, master, I'll not leave your side unless you are with better company.'

He was maddeningly stubborn, but he was also right. It was dangerous to be left alone, wearing bold Montague livery, in a crowd that could, at any moment, erupt with partisan violence. I looked around for succour, and spotted a familiar face.

'Oh, no, sir,' Balthasar said in a low, disapproving tone. Because the familiar face was that of Mercutio, lounging like a lazy cat in the sun on the central fountain's low ledge. He nursed an empty cup, and looked vaguely into the crowd with dull disinterest . . . until he spotted me.

'Well met, Benvolio!' he called as he lurched to his feet, and the sad relief in him was too much to deny. He was brokenly lonely, and I had not the heart to turn him away. 'How fare you this fine day?'

Balthasar was giving me a disapproving shake of his head, and I grabbed him close to whisper, 'As long as he clings to me, he cannot interfere with you and your mission. Go. Now.'

'Master—'

I shoved him hard away, and he stumbled off into a run, still frowning with unsettled worry.

My servant had ever had better sense than me, or any of my kinsmen.

I turned to Mercutio, and flung an arm around his shoulders in friendship. 'I do well enough, though I lack for pleasant company,' I said. 'I seek Romeo; have you seen him?'

'What, lost again? I thought he was never to be separated from your skirts, nursemaid!' He clapped an arm around my neck and squeezed, but not hard enough that I needed a defence. 'I've not seen the villain, but shall we winkle him out of his hiding place? Surely you don't think him still licking the cobbles behind that Capulet wench.'

I thought for a moment that he knew of my cousin's new, mad obsession, but he was not, in fact, thinking of Juliet; I knew that from the bitter, angry expression that twisted his face from angel to devil. He was thinking of innocent Rosaline, into whose cipher he had poured all his grief, loathing, and hatred. I feared for her again, thinking of what he would do – or might have already done.

If he had resorted to poisons, I could not save an enemy's daughter at the cost of my broken, wronged friend, and it might come to such a choice. But neither could I stomach sheltering Mercutio if he murdered the innocent, Capulet or no.

Mercutio was well drunken, even by the early hour; from the smell and state of his clothes, he'd not bothered to visit home, nor change his linen. His smell had a metallic edge of sweat and anger, sweetened with too much wine. But there was no peaceful looseness to his muscles, as there should have been; beneath my arm, his shoulders were bunched hard as a hangman's rope. When a passing servant in Capulet livery gave us a wide berth, he lunged at him, clashing his teeth, and laughed as the youth blanched and scurried away.

'You'd best be off home, Mercutio,' I told him. 'A bath would serve you.'

'Many things would serve me,' he said. 'But none so well as a Capulet on the point of my blade.'

'Too hot for that, and the mood hotter still,' I told him. 'If you will not go home, then will you not come with me? Balthasar is on errands, but I'll order a bath for you, and a bed. You can sleep in peace under our roof.'

'Can I?' he asked, and drew in a sudden, wrenching breath. 'I would much desire the peace of a dreamless rest, but, Ben, I will confess to you as I cannot to those hard-mouthed priests: I cannot sleep, in peace or out of it. I shut my eyes and Tomasso's face is before me, or worse . . . he is not dead, and I cannot release him to his rightful rest.' He ran a hand over his face, wiping sweat, and I noted how it trembled. 'He haunts me. He lies beside me, and will not speak; we are parted but not parted enough. How then may I sleep, unless wine weighs me down into the dark?'

He sounded as broken as I knew he was, and it made me

cringe; weakness in our world drew wolves. 'Come, then,' I said, and clapped him firmly on the back to brace him. 'A bath, and a safe and solitary bed in a place where your ghosts cannot find you.'

'Your grandmother will take it ill.'

'My grandmother may take it as she likes.' Brave words, but he was right: She *would* resent that I sheltered Mercutio under her roof. Even decently married, and with a rumoured babe on the way, he would never be beyond gossip. 'It's too bright a day for trouble.'

We might have escaped that trouble, save that in that last moment, Mercutio spied Romeo.

My cousin rounded the corner from the cathedral, walking with brisk, purposeful steps. I spotted him in the same instant, and noted the vivid, almost religious ecstasy of his smile; he was bestowing it upon the low and high alike, and making no effort to cast a careful eye upon his surroundings. My cousin, the strutting young peacock, was kitted in his finest, and he glowed and glimmered in the warm light like some hero of legend.

It was not a day to be making himself so obvious a target. He'd not even bothered with a single retainer to follow behind and keep the knives from his back. If my grandmother was right, Capulets would be sharpening their blades for just such an opportunity.

Mercutio saw none of that. He saw only a chance for rough play, and before I could stay him he lurched forward, shouting too loudly, 'Signor Romeo, *bonjour!* That's a French salutation to match the French cut of your breeches, sir, and where hid *you* last night?'

Romeo's ecstatic smile faded. He did most ardently want

to avoid the scene, but could not, so he pasted on false cheer and came towards Mercutio, with me following behind like a reluctant old uncle. 'Good morning to you both. What do you mean, hid?'

'You gave us the slip, sir, the slip,' Mercutio said, and waggled his finger. 'Your cousin's been eaten with worry.'

'Pardon, good Mercutio.' Romeo bowed. 'My business was great, and in such a case as mine, a man may strain courtesy.'

Mercutio laughed and likened courtesy to curtsies, and lifted invisible skirts to deliver a mincing little illustration of it. 'I am the very pink of courtesy,' he said, and got in my cousin's way as he tried to bow his way onward.

'Pink for flowers?' Romeo's smile fixed, and was growing cold. This was a turn I did not much like; it was a taunt, a very pointed one. That earned us a murmur of disapproval and a scorching look from a passing old dowager and her entourage.

It also earned Romeo Mercutio's shove. 'Just so!'

'*My* pump is well flowered,' Romeo said. It was the sort of jest a gentleman might make only among close company, not on the streets in full hearing of passersby. It was also cruel, harkening as it did to Mercutio's enforced marriage – a subject with which our friend was as much anguished as angry.

I stepped forward, but I might have as easily stepped between two men bent on duel. They ignored my intervention.

Mercutio laughed, and snapped teeth. 'I will bite you by the ear for that.' He threw a heavy arm around Romeo's neck, snake-quick, and locked him in embrace. 'Come, is not this better than groaning for love? Now you are sociable; now you are Romeo. This drivelling *love* of yours is like an idiot that runs up and down, the better to hide his toy in a hole.'

That earned us *more* angry glares, for it was too close to vulgarity for the public, and Romeo caught the hint quickly. 'Stop – stop there.'

Mercutio tried to go on, and I was sure he would plunge us into real trouble, but then a fat nurse separated from the oncoming crowd, attended by a servant, and headed towards us with purpose. I nearly remembered her swollen, heat-pinked face; she huffed as she approached, and whisked the air vigorously with her fan. *What now?* I wondered, because I saw Romeo freeze in place like a schoolboy caught with a stolen apple. He writhed free of Mercutio's headlock and shoved us both away.

'Go home,' Romeo said to me. 'I'll follow anon.'

I placed her, then, this overstuffed woman; she was Capulet, the nurse who sometimes hovered near young Juliet when the girl was allowed the freedom of the air. I had seen her quaffing large wine cups at the feast. 'Coz . . .' I took Romeo by the arm, and he shook me off. The servant walking behind the nurse – a Capulet, though without the identifying colours – half drew his dagger as he looked at me, and I released my hold. 'Come with us.'

'I said I will *follow*,' he said, and turned back to the nurse.

Perhaps, if I'd been alone, I'd have dared force the issue, but Mercutio was already offering more insult, in form of an offensive goodbye to the fat old nurse, and I could see her face purpling with outrage. Two of the city guard turned towards us and headed in our direction, and all I could do was grip Mercutio's elbow to draw him away, and leave Romeo to his intrigues.

'Fool!' I said, and pushed Mercutio as soon as we were far enough away to pull no more attention. 'What do you mean to do, humiliate him? He is your friend!'

'And your cousin,' Mercutio said, 'yet I see you're no more fond of him just now than I. All that bleating over the girl, the girl, the *girl*. I've my own female, and they're not of much use, Benvolio, not of much use at all.'

'Save for heirs,' I said. 'And once you have them, surely you will be free to do as you please . . .'

'Will I? Here, in this city of righteous, upstanding deceivers, heretics, monsters, and murderers?' He laughed, but there was wildness in it, and despair. 'There is no freedom, Benvolio; you should give up that folly now. This city is made of stone, and the stones will press us down, and down, cutting off all light and hope until dark is the only light you will ever see; do you understand me?' He gripped me by my arms, searching my face intently. 'Dark is the only light.'

I nodded, because in that moment his intensity made me both wary and sad. My friend suffered, most intensely, and I knew there was nothing I could do to take it away. 'I cannot leave Romeo on his own,' I said. 'He's . . . not himself.'

'Who is?' Mercutio barked a bitter laugh, and wiped sweat from his brow with his forearm. 'Are you his fretting wet nurse now, and he a mewling infant? Has it come to such a pass?'

'Yes,' I said. 'It's come to that.'

He shook his head, still smiling that odd, intense smile,

and shrugged. 'Very well,' he said. 'A pity, a great pity, that you have no backbone to stand straight to an old woman. A sick one, at that. You've disappointed me, Benvolio. I thought you more of a man.'

'A man keeps his vows,' I said. It was difficult to say it calmly, but I managed. 'And you're no stranger to quaking in fear before that old woman. You said it yourself: she'd humble Hercules and affright Hector.'

'True,' he said. 'Well, then, keep to your useless vows. I'm to the tavern to find merrier companions. Your face could curdle vinegar today.' He took a few steps, then turned back towards me, sudden devilish pleasure lighting his face. 'Did you hear? There's rumour of displeasure between Count Paris and Capulet. Something about his affianced's behaviour. Perhaps someone succeeded in ruining the girl after all. It wasn't me; was it you?'

'No,' I said. My throat felt tight, my brow suddenly sweated. A crowd of boisterous lads had pushed between us and the shadowed corner where Romeo was huddled in private whispers with the nurse. The *Capulet* nurse. I broke away from Mercutio, ignoring him as he called my name, and pressed through the bodies.

When I broke through to the cleared space next to the wall, I saw the fat haunches of the nurse, flanked by her thin servant, waddling away down the street. A tight knot of Capulet bravos lingered at that end, glaring towards me; going that direction, chasing their servants, would earn me a useless confrontation and accomplish nothing. She'd never talk to me.

And Romeo was gone.

I heard a sharp, musical whistle, and looked up. On the

low roof of the overhanging building, I saw my cousin's face looming over the edge. He gave me a mad smile and mocking wave, and disappeared from view.

I cursed the Montague colours I wore; there were too many eyes on me now to follow him to the heights without exciting notice. I could not afford to put it in common minds that I had such criminal abilities, and he knew it.

'Oh, no, coz,' I muttered. 'Not so easily as that.' I looked down, then, to the crouched, motionless beggars who ever huddled in shadows and rags, begging mutely with outstretched hands. Anonymous beneath filth and matted hair – men, women, children, all rendered invisible, save when they had the temerity to pluck at the garments of the rich. Then they were beaten.

I made my way to where they dwelt in misery, and sank down into a crouch, eye level with half a dozen glittering pairs of eyes. I took out my purse and counted out silver, which I deliberately laid in outstretched, shaking palms. 'A gold florin to anyone who finds my cousin Romeo Montague before the next hour is sounded. Go quickly.'

Palsied and starving they might have been, but they moved, melting away in scurries and leaps.

If I could not find my cousin by stealth, I would follow him with hired, hungry eyes.

Let him hide from *that*.

I sent a runner back to Montague for the loan of a brace of bravos; I would need them soon, I thought. While I awaited arrival of the bravos, my servant Balthasar reappeared. He made his way through the square and sank down upon the lip of the fountain next to me, cupping water thirstily. I bought an orange from a passing fruit seller, and he peeled and ate it like a starving man.

'Well?' I asked him then, as he seemed in no hurry to report.

Between juicy mouthfuls, he nodded. 'I found her out,' he said. 'She'll meet you, but she's wary, that one. And frightened.'

There was, I sensed, something my faithful servant was neglecting to tell me, but I allowed it; he would never put me into deliberate danger, so the detail would be a harmless one, something that might bruise me but never cut. 'Where?'

'A place near the river,' he said. 'Two hours hence, no sooner.'

I nodded, thinking fast; I'd promised my spies rewards, and this witch would require gold as well, to loosen her tongue. 'I've rogues out hunting for my cousin. Stay here, and should any find him, send one of the Montague men to track the clue before you part with a florin,' I said, my gaze following a fat old nobleman with an overstuffed doublet, and a downcast child of a wife trailing behind. His purse was as overstuffed as his shirt, and he wore it as arrogantly as his codpiece – an accessory now fading from fashion, but still prominent on his generation's loins.

I rose to follow.

'Master, where are you—Oh.' He had spotted the man, too. Balthasar knew me all too well.

'I go fishing,' I said, and set off after my fat, well-fed trout.

Taking the merchant's purse was a challenging affair, but gratifying, and the florins that spilt out when I counted them in a darkened alcove even more so. I now had funds to fuel my search for Romeo, who – considering the reports we began to receive – was ever more determined to evade me.

Beggars turned up, oh, yes, eager for florins, but the men sent to confirm came back with discouraging news – either the fools had identified the wrong young man, or Romeo, if he had actually been spotted, had quickly slipped away. One reported him near the cathedral, another near the river. Another still had sworn my cousin had been drinking and weeping in a wine shop half the city away.

It was not until the fourth of these beggars came looking for payment that I caught Romeo's game. It was a fine one, and under different circumstances I might have enjoyed my cousin's rhetorical response. Not today.

As the man stammered out his story of my cousin sighted in an unlikely spot, he not only avoided my gaze, as might be expected, but he patted at the stained, flat purse knotted to his rope belt. I listened to his story with half a mind, watching his fingers. They twitched, they patted, they stroked . . . and I knew.

I drew my dagger, eliciting a surprised intake of breath from Balthasar, and struck fast and accurately. Not for blood, but for money. I sliced open his purse, and out tumbled and rolled a bright gold florin.

'Did you pay him, Balthasar?' I asked, as the shocked beggar began scrambling after the coin, desperate to retrieve it.

'Why, no, sir, I would not. Not without proof of your cousin's whereabouts.'

'Someone did.' As the beggar grabbed the coin in his shaking fingers, slapping away idle hands of passersby seeking to scoop it up, I took hold of a handful of his greasy curls and yanked him upright on his hams. 'My cousin paid you, didn't he? He knew what I'd do. He poured florins out and had you peddle me falsehoods.'

'Please, sir, please, I'm just a poor man; on my life, I meant no harm; I was only doing as I was bid—' He cowered, clutching the coin in death-grim fingers, and though I wanted to kick him, I shoved him away and wiped my hand in disgust. I just hoped his lice had not jumped onto me.

'As you were bribed, you mean,' I said. 'Go, then, tell your fellows that they'll get no more from us. Take your gold and spend it, but expect nothing else from House Montague, lout.' I aimed a kick at him this time, but he dodged it – well used to that activity – and, clutching his bounty, he escaped into the crowd.

I had the taste of dust and metal in my mouth, and I could feel my skin going tight and cold. Balthasar, next to me, said quietly, 'Master? What do we do?'

'Keep looking,' I said. 'If you catch word of him, find me at the Lamberti Tower.'

'Sir—'

I shook my head and walked away. I scarce noticed the walk, though I avoided the worst of the street filth as I strode along. Balthasar must have dispatched a guard to follow – he'd scarce have allowed me to wander so – but I paid no attention to that, either. I turned the winding streets through the airless, hot afternoon. The red brick and tufa and grey stone caught flame in the light, making it seem I was walking through fire, and my only instinct was to get *away*. To find a perch above, and see the world as small and harmless. There was a darkness closing in; I knew it. I felt it all around me, like dagger points pressing my skin.

The Lamberti Tower was the highest point in Verona, set in the middle of the Piazza delle Erbe, and I knew it intimately; the narrow stairs were familiar to me, and it was well that I'd chosen a time when the massive bell was silent, or I'd have been forced to wait for the peals to die. It remained quiet, and I raced up the winding steps as if I might leave my troubles behind. The narrow tower had a curious smell – new mortar and ancient dust. They'd but recently built it to its present height. There was yet discussion of building it higher, though so far the prince had rejected such talk as irreligious and harkening back to the Tower of Babel; it wasn't wise to risk God's wrath.

Irreligious or not, I wished the tower had been built even twice as high. Lofty as this perch was, it was still too close to the streets, the teeming people in the square. To my own looming defeat.

I leant my head against the bricks and let the cooler breeze fan my face and dry the sweat from my hair. I felt a surge of hot frustration, and a traitorous bit of admiration. My cousin had learnt well, it seemed; he'd mastered just enough of the arts of stealth and misdirection to evade me. I'd have been proud, if not for the cause of it . . . the girl. The Capulet girl. *Juliet.*

I knew my cousin. I could believe him so bent on passion that he would sacrifice his own life, but what of the life of the one he supposedly loved? Romeo would never sacrifice her so lightly, if it was a true passion. Likewise, he'd never butcher his family's honour so openly.

But perhaps it was just, as they'd always said, that I

misunderstood true passion, that my veins were full of cold, thin water. My mother had always told us that courtly love was a poet's invention, designed to make the process of arranged marriage a more pleasant one; my sister and I had never been under any illusions of our place in the great order of things, or that our happiness should come before our duty.

How then was it my cousin, the heir, who forgot those same lessons to drown in the gaze of an enemy's daughter?

Being at a height slowed my pulse and calmed my agitation, and here, away from the noise and stench and bustle of the piazza, I could finally order my thoughts. The reports that had come to us were useless, paid lies, but my eyes focused on each of the places in turn, and in my mind, I blacked them out as possibilities. Four reports. Four sections of town where he would *not* be, unless he was more twisty-clever than I'd ever imagined.

I noticed a curious thing. At this lofty vantage, the false trails formed a pattern, a very visible pattern . . . and in the centre of it . . .

In the centre of it stood the Chiesa di San Fermo, that unprepossessing little religious sanctuary in which I'd once hidden, and in which Friar Lawrence regularly laid his head when avoiding his monastery. If Romeo was – however impossibly – serious in his quest to join his course with Juliet's, then they would need a churchman's blessing, though doubtless her family would immediately seek annulment once it was known. But the damage would be done. Her marriage to Paris, and to most any noble of good birth or merchant of good coffers, would be finished. She'd be damaged goods, a burden and a shame to the Capulets.

Was this Romeo's plan? Was it all an elaborate charade to entrap and ruin the girl, for the shame of her family? I might believe it of Mercutio, in his current black and bitter moods, but my cousin had ever been good-hearted and sincere in his affections, even when they were wrongheaded. He lacked the coldness of a schemer.

His behaviour smacked of something else . . . some dark purpose moving pieces in a game I could not yet fathom, not even when viewed from such a height.

I had to find my cousin – if not before the vows were exchanged, then before he could ruin Juliet's prospects. If she remained a virgin, the rest could be smoothed over with Capulet gold and influence, but once her maidenhead was breached, it was not so simple; her cousin Tybalt was not the forgiving sort, and she would likely meet with a convenient accident, or worse. They'd be rid of her, one way or the other. I cared not, except that the consequences of it would rebound on another, less-favoured girl: Rosaline would be their only marriageable asset, however flawed they saw her. They'd sell her like a second-prize cow at market, for the hastiest of prices.

It should not have bothered me, but I could not deny that it did.

My cousin might have outsmarted me, but the fact that he had directed us away from the chapel said ominous things to me, and it told me we had little time to lose.

I descended the tower's staircase, and ran into Balthasar, who was panting and sweating from his run in the hot streets. 'Master,' he said, and braced himself on the stonework as he whooped in jagged breaths. 'We should withdraw to home.'

'Why?'

'The streets are abuzz with the rumour that Tybalt Capulet beat a servant girl and sent her running from his door for her life.'

'No news there,' I said. 'He's a heavy hand with his own sister.'

'There's more,' my servant said. 'It's said that he beat her for carrying secret love notes.'

'Romeo,' I said, and felt the doom sink deeper. 'To Juliet.'

'No, sir,' Balthasar said. ''Tis said it was a note from his sister Rosaline to *you,* master. Tybalt was apoplectic with rage. He called you a whoreson coward, to be making peace in the streets and sullying their honour behind his back. The rumours say he declares that if Montague will make war on Capulet women, he will make war on ours! And, sir, it was not only him; his ally Paolo Mazzanti was with him.'

That chilled me to the core, even as the oppressive heat of the day closed around me like a boiling blanket. I needed to see to the safety of my mother, and my sister, and even Lady Capulet. Tybalt's fury was clearly beyond control.

And I could not help but wonder: if Tybalt had near killed a serving woman for carrying the note, then what had he done to its author? 'And the Lady Rosaline?' I asked, and did not meet Balthasar's wounded gaze. 'What news of her?'

'Locked up, it's said.' He knew. Yes, he knew. 'O sir, 'tis most unwise—'

'I know it is unwise; I am no infant,' I snapped. 'Mind your place.' I'd rarely said it to him, and never with such a cutting edge of warning. 'It was no love note, whatever Tybalt says.' She'd replied to the note I'd sent, I thought, the one warning her to have a care for her cousin. Rosaline might be sheltered, but for all that, she had a streak of hard practicality that mirrored my own; it would have been a careful missive, cloaked in the most obscure language.

It was only that it was directed to me, and not to Friar Lawrence, the safe intermediary, that alarmed me so deeply. What had she found so urgent that she abandoned caution, and was now caught for it?

Juliet, and Romeo. The friar conspiring with them, misled and dazzled by their passions. He had a soft heart, our friar; he had been sheltered from the raw realities of our lives, and did not reckon on the outcomes.

My heartbeat had sped fast, and I felt my muscles tightening; all my instincts bade me to rush to Rosaline and see for myself that she bided safely, but I forced myself from it. Disaster loomed on every corner now; it was Romeo I needed to stop if this was not to become a bloody farce. *War upon women.* Like all of our wars, it would be one of stealth, of assassins, of sudden and unpredictable violence. My sister Veronica's wedding approached, and in the procession we would all be in the open, exposed, ready to be picked off at will by Capulet and Mazzanti, allied together. Yet the wedding could be neither delayed nor avoided; if our family did not appear, it would be an unforgivable insult to her noble bridegroom and his house.

'We must go within our walls,' Balthasar urged me, with great good sense. 'Sir, Tybalt seeks blood for the insult to his house, now more than before. You cannot be caught out.'

I knew that, and yet I also knew that I was the only one with a slim chance of preventing much worse. 'I will go,' I said. 'But first, I will stop my fool cousin from marrying Juliet.'

If I'd shocked him by sending supposed love notes to Rosaline, this made him a gaping, wide mouthed fool fit for a cap and bells. 'Sir! It cannot be so.'

'We must make it not be so,' I said. 'Now.'

I arrived at the church and flung the doors wide, only to shock three wisened old women who had been on their knees in prayer. They did not rise – likely they could not, so easily as all that – but they cringed back from me as I strode inside. 'Friar Lawrence!' I shouted, loud enough to ring from the walls. I swept aside the coverings on the confessional, but he was not there.

He was nowhere in the church, not even dozing on his narrow mat behind the curtain. The old women gaped at me as I searched, and finally one said, timidly, 'Young sir, he has not been here for more than an hour.'

'What?' I rounded on her, scowling, and she flinched back into her companion, so alike in their wrinkles they might have been twinned. 'Where did he go?'

'I know not; he did not say—'

'Which way?' I was grasping at straws now, but one by one, they all shook their heads. They had been deep in prayers, they said. He'd spoken kindly to them, but said nothing of his destination, only that he would return soon.

I would not give up. I *could not.* I left the church and looked up and down the street; a few houses down was an open shop of some kind, and from the smell it was selling baked goods. I paid three times the amount for an order of gingerbread the cooks of Montague most likely did not need, and purchased myself the news that Friar Lawrence had indeed passed by only an hour before. I followed the man's pointing finger to another spot where the friar might have changed directions, and bribed another shopkeeper. In this way, I mapped the way to a small hovel near the river . . . an anchorite monk's dwelling, as much a cell as any monastery room. There was little inside save a narrow bed, a few jugs of wine, half a loaf of stale bread, a half round of cheese, a table, and a chest of smallclothes and trinkets, none of any note or value. The crucifix on his wall was crude, but reverent.

He was nowhere to be seen . . . but something caught my eye as I made for the door again. Through the light spilling in the window, I saw something shining, as alien to the dull room as a flower in a field of ash. I plucked it up, and held it in the light.

It was a pearl, one that had been drilled through and sewn to a garment; it retained the loose thread that had been pulled loose. It was small, befitting something a modest young woman might have sewn to her dress, or an ornament for her hair. It was little enough, just a simple lost pearl, and it might have sparked a thousand theories for its presence.

But I had only one, as I turned its smooth, warm shape in my fingers.

Juliet Capulet had been here, in this monk's cell. And if she had been here, so might have been my cousin Romeo. I was too late.

'Sir,' Balthasar said from behind me. He sounded strained and grave. 'The friar comes.'

I nodded, my face set and hard, and he put his back to the wall. His hand was on his cudgel, and he looked frightened, but ready to go where I led.

He was no doubt praying it would not take him to damnation for striking a holy man, but in this moment, in the white-hot burn of my fury, I cared not for my soul, nor for his.

I cared only to stop our unsafe little world from flying apart around us.

Friar Lawrence saw me, and his plump face went still for a moment, then took on an expression of resignation as he closed the door behind him. 'Master Benvolio,' he said. 'What brings you?'

I held out my palm and let the pearl roll from one side to the other. The guilt was plain to see in him, but he assumed a brave martyr's stance, with his hands folded together in his sleeves.

'Don't you know what will come of this?' I asked. My tone was tight and dangerous, and he took note, but he did not back down.

'Peace, if you will allow it,' he said. 'Montague and Capulet have too long let their blood flow down these streets; your own father died for—'

'You betrayed us.'

'I am on no one's side but God's, my son. Their love was so strong that if I had refused to bless it, it would have been done without God's seal; there is no doubt of it. Would you have me step aside and allow the sin instead?'

'You've said the words, but I may yet stop them from this folly. Where are they?'

'I'll not say.'

'Where?' I gripped him by the shoulders and stared hard into his eyes, and he flinched. 'He is my cousin, close as a brother, and I won't see him dead on Tybalt's sword. Now tell me where they plan to make their bower, and do it quickly!'

The look he gave me was oddly sad, as if he pitied me in that moment – and also knew that I might do him harm. 'The passion between them is too great, Benvolio; I've never seen the like. A madness, you understand, a thirst slaked only by love's drink, or death. Which would you have?'

This time I shoved him against the wall, and with my right hand I drew my dagger. I did not put it to his throat, but he knew that was where it would be bound if he delayed me again.

Friar Lawrence squeezed his eyes closed a moment, and his lips moved as if he prayed. Whatever God instructed, he did not seem happy with it, but he finally said, 'They will do it by night, in secret. You need not seek them out now; they will wait. I made them vow it under the eyes of God. There is time to separate them, but I warn you: what pulls them together is nothing a mortal man may battle; it is a holy fire, I tell you, a most holy fire that burns in them.'

'The devil can stoke a fire as well as ever God could,' I shot back, but I sheathed my dagger. 'You swear on the cross that they parted from each other?'

'Yes,' he said. 'Juliet's nurse has taken her home, and Romeo has gone as well. I swear it upon the cross.'

'If you see Romeo, tell him I know,' I said. 'Tell him this is done. It goes no further.'

Friar Lawrence gave me a sad look, and poured himself a cup of wine, which he downed in a great, messy gulp. 'I remember a boy swaddling in a robe and playing a monk one evening, for the love of a girl,' he said. 'Have you no pity in your heart for your cousin's strong desire?'

'No more than I will have pity for you, should this go badly,' I said, and drew the dagger. I sank it into the table to a depth that would have reached his heart. 'Mark me, Friar. I speak not for myself, but for Montague.'

Balthasar shut the friar's door behind us, heaving a sigh of relief that he had not been forced to crack the friar's skull for me. I was not feeling lighter – the damage was still great, most certainly, and the marriage would have to be undone by the Capulet and Montague elders alike, but it could be fixed in secret, with careful diplomacy.

Romeo would be punished; Juliet would be hastily married off. But all could still end well enough. So I wished to believe.

I had frankly forgotten my appointment with Mercutio's witch until Balthasar reminded me, skipping close to murmur it in my ear as we passed out of the cloister's walls. We were not so very far from the river; the muddy, rotting stench of it hung heavily in the air, churned but not dispelled by surly gusts of wind. I was eager to make straight home and beard my cousin in his chambers . . . or beat him, as Tybalt had thrashed the servant. Perhaps pain would bring him to his senses. Failing that, my grandmother's towering wrath certainly would.

But even so, I shifted course and followed Balthasar's lead down narrowing, noisome alleys, stepping over drunkards and beggars and keeping a close eye out for villains. I was a richly dressed man in hostile quarters, and not all thirsty blades belonged to Capulet hands. Some merely wanted my purse. Ironic that it was full of fresh-stolen florins. But I was in no fit mood, and my scowl must have warned off any who might have accosted us; we arrived at the docks, where fishermen unloaded their cargoes, and costermongers loaded carts to trundle them to a late market. It was too hot, and the air was slick with the thick scent of rotten oceans.

'There,' Balthasar said, and pointed me in the direction of a cloaked form in the shadows.

He had kept a detail from me, indeed; I'd expected some broken old woman, with moles and an evil cast to her eye. As the woman pushed back her hood, I saw before me a lovely, pointed face, clever and calm, framed by thick brown curls only barely managed by carved wooden combs. She looked a little older than I, but not by more than a thin handful of years, and she might have been a modestly placed merchant's wife or daughter. Her clothing was not fine, but it was well fitted, and clean. She carried a nosegay of herbs to ward off the stench of the docks.

She was hardly the crone I had expected to find. That, then, had been Balthasar's juicy, withheld titbit of information.

I was clearly not what she had expected to find *either*, because she cast a near-panicked, betrayed look towards my servant, and dropped into a quick curtsy. 'Sir,' she said. 'I little expected to see someone of your quality. I apologise for the condition of our meeting.'

'You're the witch?' I had little patience for niceties, even given the pleasant surprise. 'Mercutio has visited you?' I kept my voice low, but she still blanched, and cast anxious looks about us. No one noticed, in the clamour of the dock.

'I cannot tell you, sir, with great respect—'

'Is he planning to do harm?' I asked her bluntly. 'Have you given him poison?'

'No!' she blurted, and put out a hand that showed she was no stranger to hard work. 'No, sir. Please, I beg you, do not say so; I sell only helpful herbs . . .'

'Then why does he seek you out?' I leant in on her, threatening, and she shrank back against the wall. I put out an arm against the stones to block her escape, and Balthasar took up a post to hold her on the other side. 'Confess. Now. I have no time for games.'

She looked pallid and terrified, and miserable. 'Sir, it is only that your friend and I have a grief shared; his friend Tomasso was my cousin, and my dearest friend. I will confess that I hate those who took his life, and that also I share with Mercutio, but I have provided no poisons, I swear. Only—' She had babbled on too far, and I saw the realisation of it cross her face in horror. If she could have breathed the words back in, she would have.

'If not poisons, then what?' I snapped, and grabbed her chin in my hand to raise her eyes to mine. She was frankly terrified, and she was right to be. I was in a killing mood. 'Confess to me, and you might escape death. Defy me . . .'

'I only helped him,' she whispered. Tears shone wetly, and spilt down her cheeks; I felt the quiver in her flesh where I held her still. 'I swear, my lord, the guilt is not mine; it is not—'

'*Tell me!*'

'I showed him how to cast a curse,' she whispered. 'The sin is upon him, sir, not me; I swear, not me! Please, sir, let me go. Please!'

I would have dragged her to Prince Escalus in my fury, but Balthasar cried urgently, 'Sir!' and instinct screamed at the same moment, and I released the girl and spun, drawing my sword and getting it free of its scabbard just in time to block a deadly blow aimed for my heart.

I did not know the man who faced me, snarling, until he said, 'Dog of a thief! I know who you are!'

It was Roggocio, the fool I'd robbed on a night that seemed so far distant now, the one who'd ripped away my mask. He'd glimpsed my face indeed, though until this moment he had not known my name.

Shock ran through me, cold and hot, and as I settled into the chill silence of the fight, I knew that I could not let him walk from this. He knew too much, enough to betray me, enough to add even more chaos to the already brewing pot of poison.

That, and of course he intended to see me dead.

Balthasar cried another warning, and I heard his cudgel smack flesh; Roggocio had at least one friend willing to come to his aid. I trusted Balthasar to hold my back, and focused upon the blade in Roggocio's hand. He was well practised, as would be expected if he'd survived so long as a hired bravo; he wielded a plain but quality blade, well suited to his hand and height. I concentrated not on his eyes, nor on his hands, but on the whole of him: the tiny betraying flickers that would tell me where he'd strike.

It took two passes and clashes of steel, and then he showed his intentions too soon. I parried just enough to move the line of his blade past my chest, turned with it, and struck hard and low, aiming for finding the vulnerability of his inner thigh. My blade slipped easily in, through, and I cut sideways to open the vessels. Blood gouted like a fountain, sheeting gory down his hose, and he let out a short, sharp cry as he fell to his uninjured knee. It was a killing wound, and he knew it instantly. He'd be bled white in only a moment.

As deaths by the sword came, it was a quick and almost painless ending. But he fought it, trying to rise, failing, collapsing back to the cobbles. His sword continued to stab the air, trying to reach me, until his hand lost its grip.

He looked past me then, and I glanced back to see his compatriot rising dizzy from where Balthasar had struck him down. He was in no fighting condition, but he retrieved his fallen sword and sheathed it to show his peaceful intention.

And then Roggocio, with his fading last breaths, said, 'Tell Tybalt that my murderer is the Prince of Shadows.'

It seemed as if the world stopped.

Few were close enough to hear or understand his ragged words, but I did, and Balthasar, and so did Roggocio's companion. I looked to him, and his eyes met mine, and widened. Then he took to his heels, running.

'Get him!' I snapped to Balthasar. I'd forgotten the witch in the press of events, but now I saw her running as well, darting between fish carts and making for her own safety.

I had to let her go.

Tybalt could not learn the truth, or I was a dead man.

Balthasar was dogged, but while he was loyal and solid, he was no runner; Roggocio's friend was as fast and lean as a greyhound set on deer, and as nimble. He used the crowds, carts, and obstructions to slow us, and within only a short distance I'd caught my servant and passed him, yet had not gained a step on the man running ahead.

The throng in the street was slowing me too much.

'Keep after!' I shouted to Balthasar, and turned sharply towards a stack of wooden crates beside a wine seller's shop. I no longer feared excited comments on my acrobatic skills. There was far worse to be risked. I leapt and made the top of the first crate, then vaulted up to the next. From there, it was a leap to grasp the ledge of the roof, and I scrambled up, heedless of the birds that flapped in agitation at my boldness. Once on the low, flat roof, I raced without opposition.

The next building was built close, but still separated, and I sped faster and leapt the distance, risking a glance to the side as I did to see that Balthasar had fallen farther back, and the man we pursued still had half the street on us. He seemed to know where he was bound, which was worrying; I did not, and it was hard to form a strategy without a clear objective, except to catch and kill.

The next rooftop was more treacherous, littered with bottles left by someone who did their drinking in secret, and probably by moonlight; I managed to avoid them, and when I made the next leap, to a pitched tile roof, I saw that I'd gained on my target.

If I'd been thinking of my danger, I might have hesitated at the next jump, which was wider and to a higher point, but now I was fiercely committed, and I had forgotten caution. I could see that only half the next building's length separated me from my quarry now. He'd run into a funeral procession, and though he was pressing through, to the outraged cries of mourners, he had lost his lead on me.

I put all I had into the dash to the edge, and launched myself into the gap, aiming for the next roof. I missed.

The rise was higher than I'd thought, and the gap farther,

and as I realised I'd miss the roof itself, I saw that I would instead fall inside a small stone balcony with a closed door. There was no real choice to make; I braced myself, landed hard, and threw myself forward with my shoulder as lead.

The balcony door slammed back, and I stumbled into a bedchamber. No one was inside save an old woman embroidering by an open window; she blinked at me as if I were a phantom, and I did not wait to see what she might do, but moved out and into the hallway. It ran straight the length of the house to another balcony, the mirror of the one I'd landed on.

I burst out into the sunlight, put both hands on the hot stonework, and vaulted over and down. I landed hard, rolled, and ignored the aches and bruises, because only a few feet ahead was the bravo I'd been chasing.

He glanced back and saw me. His eyes went wide, and he dodged to the right, down another street and away from the choking crowds. I raced after, but I tangled with a fat old priest and went down hard enough to leave me bruised and dazed.

I shook the impact away, scrambled up, and dashed in pursuit.

He was just throwing himself through the doors of a laundry when I spotted him at the corner, and I ran after. My breath was coming in fast pumps now, sweat soaking my Montague finery; I smelt the strong soaps and lye of the vats, and saw him as he shoved aside a burly washerwoman and ducked behind some hanging wet bedsheets.

I yanked them aside. Another door. I plunged through and had just enough time to see that he'd decided to make a stand; he'd hoped to catch me surprised, and he almost did, but I knocked his blade up with my elbow as I spun, and drew a dagger with my left hand. He was fast, faster than I, and he avoided the slash and turned to run on.

I aimed and threw the dagger, but he veered and it missed its mark, merely slicing a wound in his arm and then ending its course in the wood of a barrel. I snatched it free as I ran after him.

Our pursuit burst out into the open streets surrounding the Piazza delle Erbe, to shouts and cries and flocks of pigeons making for the skies, and as I dodged the fountain, I felt a hand grab at my shoulder.

I spun, blindly striking with the dagger, and it was a lucky thing that Mercutio was just as quick, or I'd have opened his throat. That earned me an instant response as he stepped back and put a hand on the hilt of his sword. There was unreasoning black murder in his eyes. 'That was ill considered,' he said. 'What game have you flushed?'

'A quick and deadly fox,' I said, and pushed into a run as I shouted back, 'If you're going with me, keep your head!'

I did not think he would do it – he was more drunken now than he had been before, when he'd left me in disgust – but he laughed, and easily caught up and paced me. 'You're like one of those fellows who enters a tavern, claps his sword upon the table, and says, "God send me no need of thee . . ." and by the second cup, you'll draw it for no reason!'

I had little breath for it, but I grinned and said, 'Oh, am I such a fellow?'

'You're as hot a Jack in your moods as any in Italy, and as soon moved to be moody,' he said, and dodged a squawking rooster that fluttered in his path. 'And as soon moody to be moved!'

He went on, firing quick and razor-edged barbs at me, and he was not wrong in most of what he said. I had a bad temper, a black one when it moved over me. I *had* quarrelled with a man once for coughing in the street, and with a tailor – but not for wearing his new Easter suit before Easter. I could not remember the quarrel rightly, in this blood-hot moment.

But he was right: I was a dangerous man when put into this evil mood.

Roggocio's compatriot was ahead of us, but not far ahead, and he was tiring, as greyhounds do when the sprint bids fair to become a longer footrace. Mercutio whooped and passed me, vivid with the joy of taking unthinking action.

And then I saw where the bravo was taking us.

Tybalt, his cousin Petruchio, and many more of his adherents than I cared to number, all lounging like a pride of lions in the shade of a portico. Tybalt spotted the running Capulet bravo and came to his feet, sinuous and graceful, and around him his fellows roused.

They descended the steps to meet the man I'd chased, who pushed through to Tybalt's side.

'Stop,' I said, and pulled on Mercutio's shoulder. 'The odds are against us.'

'Well against,' he said. 'But I thought you were on a hunt. Will you let your quarry slip away so easily?'

'By my head, the Capulets will have us if we are not careful.'

'By my heel, I care not,' he said, and bared his teeth in a fierce grin. 'Come, Benvolio, you led me a merry chase. "Tis a shame to end it with a coward's retreat.'

He spoke to my anger, my fury, my fear. My blood was

up, and though I knew it was wrong, though I knew it was disastrous, I let him draw me onward at a walk.

Even then, it might have been avoided; we might all have passed like wary ships on the sea, all our gun ports opened and glares all around. But then Tybalt stepped into our path and said, 'Gentlemen, good evening. A word with one of you.' The speech was courteous enough, but his hand was already on his rapier, and there was fury in his face. The sight of him made the skin tighten on my back – not in fear, oh, no, but in utter fury. I could not see him without thinking of Rosaline, and bruises, and threats.

And Roggocio's companion was urgently whispering in his ear. I knew what he was telling him. I knew it from the way his expression shifted from casual malice to something more intent – no longer a lazy cat toying with mice, but a lion on a wounded, limping deer.

He knew who I was, what I was.

And now it remained only what hay he would make of it.

Mercutio, ignorant of the undercurrents, said, 'But only one word, with one of us? Couple it with something; at least make it a word and a blow.' Sweetly said, with a poisonous sting in its tail. He meant to provoke, and Tybalt scarce needed it . . . but he spared a second from his pleasurable contemplation of my doom to send Mercutio a scorching, dismissive look.

'You'll find me apt enough to it, sir, if you will give me occasion,' he said.

I felt the darkness come on the day, despite the sweltering sun, and put a warning hand on Mercutio's shoulder. He shook it free, and his tone took on a sharp, angry edge. 'Could you not take some occasion without giving?'

Tybalt pointed at me. 'You, I shall save for a later feast, for the insult to my house and to my sister. I've weapons enough to wound you when I wish.' He altered his aim towards Mercutio. 'You consort with Romeo.'

'*Consort?* What does that make us, minstrels? If you would make minstrels of us, you may expect nothing but discord.' Mercutio tipped the still-sheathed hilt of his rapier forward, the better to drive home his insults. 'Here's my fiddlestick, then. Here's what will make you dance.'

We'd already attracted a crowd of onlookers – idlers and fools, but a few well-to-do and even here and there a noble, surrounded by their own attendants, all bearing witness to this folly. Not even a folly – a farce; Tybalt knew he held the winning ground, and his gaze upon me said as much. These were merely the first steps in a deadly serious dance.

We could not win, and I knew it. It was madness, but Mercutio was in the grip of a long-burning fever, and he gazed at Tybalt as if he held the cure for his distemper.

'We're in the most public of eyes,' I said to them both. 'Let us take this to some private place, or else keep a cool head and go. Mercutio—'

He shook me off, and stepped forward to Tybalt. A more blatant challenge I could not imagine, and Tybalt did not back away – nor did he answer it, not yet.

'Men's eyes were made to look,' Mercutio said, and swept his own gaze up Tybalt, and down, in a lazy and insulting appraisal. 'Let them gaze. I will not budge for any man's pleasure.'

Tybalt laughed, a flash of white teeth like the glint of a blade. 'Marriage has changed you, then. I wonder how much. Can a woman make a man of you?'

Mercutio let out a sound that was as much growl as curse, and tried to draw. I held him back, even though my own blood beat hard at my temples, urging me to draw, strike, end him and the smirking bravo next to him. End the threat to my close-held secret.

I saw a distinctive flash of Montague colours, and for a bare second I allowed myself a surge of relief. I thought that Balthasar had arrived to back us – but no. Not Balthasar, and no bravos pushing towards us, nor allies rushing to our backs.

Romeo alone had joined us.

My wandering cousin had chosen the wrong moment to show himself, but having done so, he did not back away; after a hesitation, he came forward, hands outstretched and empty, a calm and almost angelic light on his face.

Well, I'd meant to find him. And I had. But a worse place of discovery I could not imagine.

'Well,' Tybalt said, and stepped off from Mercutio. 'Peace be with you, sir; here comes my man.'

'I'll be hanged, sir, if he wears your livery. If you run, he'll chase you; perhaps that makes him your man . . .' Mercutio was still trying to bait the Capulet heir, but Tybalt had eyes only for Romeo. If there had been fury in him before, now it was nothing but rage, absolute and tipping towards insanity.

'Romeo,' Tybalt said, and closed the distance between them quickly. My cousin should have reached for his sword, but he did not. His hands remained empty and open. 'The love I feel for you demands no better term than this: you are a villain.'

Romeo spread his hands even wider, and his smile did

not falter. 'The reason I have to love you excuses such a greeting. I am no villain, and therefore, I'll say farewell. You know me not.'

He tried to pass and come to us, but Tybalt was having none of peace now; he lunged and shoved my cousin back in an explosion of violence as sudden as it was inevitable. 'This does not excuse the injuries you've done me and my house. Turn and draw!'

'I never injured you. I love you better than you can know, until you know the reasons.' Romeo's face was . . . exalted, like that of a saint going to the cross. I felt sick at the sight of it, the unreasoning and unwavering purpose of it. 'Good Capulet – a name I love as dearly as my own – be satisfied with that.'

He tried to *embrace* Tybalt Capulet, who backed away as if my addled cousin bore some plague. It was more shocking, in its way, than Tybalt's assault had been, and while I blurted out Romeo's name in warning, Mercutio drew his sword, and *that* sound, the sound of blade clearing scabbard, was the only thing in the world that rang in my ears – that, and the indrawn breath of the crowd around us.

Tybalt turned towards Mercutio, towards the real danger.

'That was dishonourable, Romeo,' Mercutio said. 'A vile submission, to make peace. Come, Tybalt, rat catcher, will you draw?'

The crowd was pressed closer now, avid, and I could smell the sweat and fear and excitement like lightning in the hot, still air. I did not draw, not yet. The chance that we could still make away from here, and kill Tybalt at a less public time, stayed my hand.

So perhaps the rest was, in the end, my fault for the hesitation.

'Why, Mercutio, what would you have with me?' Tybalt asked, and made a rude gesture a man would give to entice a whore, so that there was no mistaking his meaning. The onlookers laughed, and Mercutio's face turned a dead, awful white, while his dark eyes blazed with the flames of hell.

'Good King of Cats, I'll have nothing but one of your nine lives, and if I do not like your behaviour, I'll beat out the rest of the eight. Will you draw, sir? Make haste, lest mine is at your ears before it's out.'

Tybalt's mimicry ended, and in a cold voice he said, 'I am for you, then.' And he drew his sword.

It started slowly, with a tap of blades, humble as spoons clanking, but the two of them circled, measuring, and I saw that Tybalt moved like the cat we'd always named him . . . lithe and quick and deadly. Mercutio was a fine swordsman, precise and strong, but he'd had drink, and there was emotion in him now, fuelling a too-hot fire, while Tybalt seemed cold as a man three days dead. Tybalt glided right; Mercutio stumbled to counter. It was clear who would win, if it came to a real fight.

Romeo saw it, too, and he stepped forward again. 'Good Mercutio, put up your sword.' But neither of them heeded, nor even *could* heed, so focused were they on each other. I felt a terrible surge of hopeless anger – at Romeo, for stumbling upon this; at Mercutio, for setting himself on this black and futile course; at myself, for failing to prevent it.

Tybalt flung himself forward in a deadly fast attack, a simple and elegant thrust headed straight for Mercutio's breast. Whether slowed or not by the wine, Mercutio still beat it aside, and riposted towards Tybalt's bent thigh, a cut that would have opened a vein and left him bled as white in the gutter as Roggocio, had it landed.

But it did not. Tybalt, Prince of Cats, leapt free of it, growled, circled, and came back for him while Mercutio was off-footed, and scored a shallow cut along my friend's right arm. Not much, just a thin red line to dampen the white linen sleeve, but it was enough to show that death was coming, and coming fast.

Romeo shoved me aside, and pulled his own rapier free. 'Draw, Benvolio! We can beat down their weapons; we must stop them . . . Tybalt, Mercutio – the prince has expressly forbidden this in the streets – *Hold*, Tybalt! Mercutio!'

I drew then, but it was too late, too late, too late. Mercutio attacked, and, drunken or not, blinded by his demons or not, he would have killed Tybalt with that blow had it landed, but it failed . . . only because Tybalt's heel slipped on some wet mess in the street, and he was not where he ought to have been when the steel slid past.

Romeo, seeing that it was about to come to real blood, lunged in between them and spread his arms to face Tybalt. What he meant to do, I do not know; maybe he meant to take Mercutio's place in the duel, or perhaps only to stop the fight. But it did not matter. Tybalt had already begun his answering lunge, and I felt frozen in place as I saw the steel glide forward, point and edge, towards Romeo's breast. But Romeo twisted, and the lunge slid on, grazing his ribs as it went . . .

To bury half the rapier's length in Mercutio's chest.

Mercutio's lips parted, and he gave a little cry of surprise as his rapier fell from his hand to rattle in the street. Tybalt seemed equally shocked as he recovered, and yanked his blade free of my friend's ribs. It slid out with a terrible sound, steel grating bone, and the blood that gouted out was the exact shade of Capulet livery, the same that Tybalt wore on his doublet and his cap, the same slashed into Petruchio's sleeves and particolored hose as he rushed forward to pull Tybalt away. I did not hear what the Capulets said; my ears seemed tuned only to the sound of Mercutio's tortured, hitching breaths, and the pulse of his blood flowing to the stones. I was there with him without feeling myself move or ordering my body to make the effort; he was falling, and I was there to catch him.

And with me, Romeo, pallid Romeo, his face blank with shock that his peacemaking had gone so terribly wrong.

Mercutio's blood was foaming pink on his lips, but he was still talking. If a grimace counted as a smile, he smiled. 'Benvolio, I'm hurt,' he said. He sounded surprised. 'May a plague curse both your families...both...your...families...' With the repetition, it took on the edge of horror. His eyes rolled wildly, and his weight went heavy in my arms. 'I'm finished . . . Is he gone? Escaped?'

'It's nothing,' I said. My breath was coming too fast, the lights were all too bright around us, and my heart pounded in my temples like a drum. I tasted sweat, or tears, or both. 'You will be fine.'

He flashed bloodied teeth in something too fierce, too painful to be a smile. 'Aye, aye, a scratch, but 'tis enough. Where is my page?'

He had no one, as ever he'd had no one . . . none but two of us, kneeling in his blood, holding him up. Romeo grabbed a gawking boy and twisted his ear until he yelped.

'Go, fetch a surgeon!' Then he tried to smile for Mercutio. 'Courage, man. The hurt cannot be so much.'

'Not so deep as a well, nor so wide as a church door, but 'tis enough; 'twill serve,' Mercutio said. He gave a bubbling, wet laugh that sounded too much like a death rattle. His breath smelt of blood. 'Ask for me tomorrow, and you shall find me a grave man. I am not long for this world, my friends—' Pain struck him deep, and his body arched against us, fists clenching and trembling as if he fought off death like an enemy. His face screwed up under the agony, and suddenly his eyes opened wide, and he grabbed for my collar and pulled me close – close enough to feel his hot, fevered breath on my face. 'A plague on both your houses; mark me, Benvolio; I am sorry . . .' But whatever he meant, it skittered away from him under a new wave of pain, and when he collapsed again, loose in our arms, he had wandered into black humour. 'A dog, a rat, a mouse, a cat to scratch a man to death . . . a braggart, a rogue, a villain that fights by the numbers . . . Why the devil did you come between us?' His voice went suddenly and unexpectedly childish and petulant, as he caught Romeo's stricken gaze. 'I was hurt under your arm!'

'I . . . I . . . was trying to help,' Romeo whispered. 'I thought it for the best . . .'

'Help me into some house, Benvolio; I feel faint – a plague on both your houses, they have made worm's meat of me . . . your houses . . .' He gripped my collar so tightly I thought he meant to strangle me. 'Your houses, do you understand? It is a curse . . . Oh God, take me in . . .'

I would not let him die here in the street, stared at and remarked upon by the common folk; Romeo seemed too stunned to act, so I stood, gathered Mercutio's body up in my arms, and walked through the square. If he was heavy – and he must have been – I did not feel it. I felt little except a burning wish that he not die there on the ground, or in my arms, before we had reached some comfort.

'Benvolio?' Mercutio asked. He sounded thin and weak and far away, and I could not bring myself to look down at him.

'Hush,' I said. 'I'm taking you home. Your father will call for a surgeon.'

'No surgeon, and I have no father,' he whispered. Though I did not stare down at him, I could see from the corner of my eye the pale, bloodless colour of his skin, and the brilliant red still flowing over his doublet, soaking it hot and wet against my chest. 'The surgeon's already had me with his sharpest knife. Did you think Tybalt was such a deft hand with a blade? One thrust, clean . . .' He seemed, at this moment, to admire it. 'I always mocked him, but he has proved his point on me.'

'Quiet. Save your strength.'

'I have none to save,' he said, and then, as if in surprise, 'You carry me.'

'Aye.' I was gasping for breath, I realised, and staggering from effort. There must have been men and women in the way, but they'd drawn back like waves from Moses himself, save that the red sea was trailing behind me. Mercutio's blood dripped from the points of my elbows and from the edges of my sleeves. I was carmine with it. Made Capulet.

My shoulder found a wall, and I leant there a moment, just a moment, to clear the blurring from my eyes. My head and heart pounded together in a deafening chorus, and it came to me with sudden icy clarity that I might collapse well before I carried him the rest of the way to either his house or mine.

'Listen,' Mercutio whispered. His hand tugged hard at my collar. 'Listen, I must make a confession; be my confessor, dear friend—'

'No,' I said. 'No, you will not die.'

'*Listen*, I sinned. I sinned most gravely against you; I meant only for it to attach to the one who betrayed us, but I see now; I see I was wrong—'

'Quiet, for the love of God!' I was on the hottest verge of grief. Mercutio's mind was wandering, and I could not listen; I could not.

Still, he talked on. '. . . not Capulet, not Capulet guilt at all, but Montague as well, enemies upon enemies, and poison to one is poison to all, and I am sorry—'

'Hsst! Young master! Here, bring him here!'

I lifted my head, and blinked. There was a young woman standing in a doorway ahead; I did not recognise her, except as someone who was willing to help in this most extreme darkness. I took in a deep breath and pushed off the wall, staggering the last ten feet and into the shadow of her lintel.

The inside was cool and dark, and smelt sweetly of herbs. It was no noble bed I laid Mercutio upon, only a narrow mattress stuffed with lumpy straw, but he sighed in relief just the same. The girl came behind us, carrying a steaming pot full of water, some rags, and some foul-smelling unguent in yet another pot, and then it came to me in a rush that I knew her. The witch.

Her gaze was troubled as she stared down at my friend, and she shook her head as if she knew well what the outcome of this would be . . . but she said, 'Help me take this off him,' and reached for the ties of his doublet. I caught her hand, staring at her, but she shook her head. 'I mean to help, sir, only help.'

I heard nothing but regret and grief, and so I released her. I'd take help from the devil himself, if he'd appeared in a puff of smoke and promised to ease Mercutio's pain.

Together we folded back the thick padded velvet; it was stabbed through, and sopping with blood. The linen shirt beneath was as red as any Capulet's cloth. She bit her lip and rolled Mercutio on his side, saw the open bloody lips of the wound on his back, and let out a little resigned sigh before she wadded up pads of cloth and bade me press against the wound in his chest. As I did, I felt the stammering beat of his heart. I knew that if he lived, rot would carry him off in agony; a wound such as this would almost certainly fester, and no surgeon could stitch together what had been cut apart within him.

'We can buy him a little time,' she said in a low voice, 'but the blade went too deep, and too true.'

Something arrested my attention then – beneath the thick red blood, there were dark stains on Mercutio's chest. No, not stains – inked letters I did not recognise, with an odd and ancient slant to them. I rubbed at them, but they did not smear.

'Leave it,' the girl said. 'He needs to save his strength.'

I knew she meant he would never regain it again, and nodded to tell her. Mercutio's eyes had closed, and the lids looked translucently pale, all his healthy colour fled. His lips were the colour of cold seas.

I did not think he would ever open those eyes again,

but he did, and lunged up to grab my arm with unnatural strength. 'A plague on both your houses,' he blurted. 'I never meant it so, Benvolio; I am sorry – break it . . . break it before it consumes . . . promise . . .'

And then his eyes rolled back into his head, and his mouth lolled open, and he fell back into the hands of the young witch who'd given her bed to soothe him.

'He is not yet dead,' she whispered, and eased him down again. She had packed the wound in his back, and now she smeared the cloth with thick white unguent. She motioned for me to do the same, and I fumbled my own handful of cloth in place, and anointed it. Then I held him up as she wrapped the bandage tight around his chest, from armpit to waist, covering the wound and the eldritch writing I'd seen upon him. Before she was through, though, a flower of red had bloomed on his chest, spreading its sinister petals in a slow, inevitable growth.

But still he breathed a little. It seemed a miracle, and one I was willing to embrace. 'I thank you,' I said. 'You did not have to help, after my rough treatment of you.'

She shook her head. 'I could not do otherwise,' she said. 'I grieve, but Mercutio knew the price he would pay for his revenge. I warned him.'

'You spoke of a curse—' I would have questioned her, but Mercutio opened his eyes just then, and the vague fear in them chilled me. 'Hush, friend, I am here.' I gripped his bloody hand in mine and sank down next to him on the narrow space. He coughed, and blood leaked from the corner of his mouth. His face was ashy grey, the pallor of death already on him.

'Did I do wrong?' he asked me, and the childlike worry

in his voice broke me within. 'Ah, Ben, for love, I did it for love, and for justice; please, I never meant – I never meant it to harm you or Romeo . . . forgive me.'

'I forgive you,' I said. I thought it was confusion, as he wandered in the dark fogs closer to his end. 'I would forgive you anything, Mercutio, my brother.'

Of a sudden, his eyes were bright and eerily clear, and he gripped my hand very hard as he said, 'I will hold you to that, for I have done you dire wrongs. Love is the curse, Ben. *Love is the curse.* Do you understand?'

He was shaking, every muscle gone rigid, and I knew this was the last. He was clinging tight to that frayed and breaking rope, and I held his gaze, hard though it was. His grief for Tomasso had driven him to this. No wonder he loathed love so much. And thinking bitterly on Romeo, on his folly with Juliet Capulet, I thought Mercutio must be right.

I held his grip, though it bade fair to break my bones, and said, 'I do. I understand.'

He searched my face most earnestly, and then closed his eyes. It looked like defeat. 'No,' he said. 'No, you do not. Ben—'

But whatever he might have said next was lost in a terrible bout of coughing, as he struggled for breath and drowned in his own blood, and though his lips moved, I heard not another word.

I felt the exact moment his spirit departed. It was only then that I realised I had let him die unshriven, here in this dark hut full of witch's charms and herbs. Mercutio's hand went slack in mine, and the tension in his face fell away. His eyes looked into eternity, and for a long moment I could not move for fear of breaking, but then I reached over and folded his hands on his shattered, bloody breast, and closed his eyes. I put two gold coins on his lids, and then turned to look at the girl cowering in the corner, now terrified.

She shook her head so violently curls came free from beneath her neat kerchief, and pressed her trembling hands to her mouth. Her eyes were bright with tears and terror. 'Please,' she whispered. 'Please, sir, I know you think me evil, but I only wanted to help him—'

'I care not,' I said, and handed her another coin. 'Fetch Friar Lawrence here. Tell him Mercutio Ordelaffi needs last rites. It is the least I can do for him now.'

She looked wary, but she snatched the coin away, wrapped it in a fold of her skirt, and darted out into the street. I went to the door and breathed in the hot, still air, and gradually became aware of the shouting and furor coming from the piazza. A well-dressed merchant scurried past, trailing harried attendants; I stopped one with an outstretched hand – one well reddened with blood. Well, it made for a useful warning. 'What proceeds?' I asked him. He flinched away from me. 'What is that noise?'

'Romeo Montague,' he said. 'Romeo is bent on dying on Tybalt Capulet's sword, it seems, for grief!'

I thought that I could not feel anything, but suddenly fear blazed back up within me, real and immediate. 'Wait, does Romeo live?'

'I know not!' he shouted back, and broke into a run. 'If so, not for long!'

I cast a tormented look back at my friend, but there was naught I could do for him now. If my cousin would recklessly throw himself onto Tybalt's sword now . . .

This might not be the only death I could regret today.

'I'm sorry,' I said to Mercutio. I bent and pressed my lips to his pale forehead, and then I ran for the piazza.

Tybalt had fled the place of Mercutio's murder when I'd carried my friend away; he'd since returned, though his adherents urged him to flee. He stood still in the street, surrounded by his fellows, and his sword was out. He stalked restlessly back and forth, black gaze fixed on my cousin.

Romeo had likewise not put up his sword. Finally, some Montague cousins and bravos had arrived to back him, which was all, I thought, that had held the peace thus far – that, and the fact that they had waited to hear the news – bad news, I realised, that I was bringing. But it was too late to turn away; I had already been remarked, as I pushed through the crowd damp with Mercutio's dying blood. Romeo's gaze had fallen on me, and now Tybalt's did as well. A hush went through the crowd in a rippling wave.

'How fares Mercutio?' Romeo asked me. He knew. Any man could see, from the evidence soaking my clothes. But still he asked, so that the answer would be clear to those watching.

'Mercutio is dead,' I said. It felt like fiction, though I knew it for fact.

Romeo nodded. He looked older than his years in this moment, older than I; he looked every inch the heir of House Montague, weighed down with the responsibilities of that office.

Tybalt, perhaps ten feet away, had gone very still in watching us. He could have put up his sword, and by all reasonable measures ought to have done so; his blade had already broken the peace, already claimed a life, but perhaps knowing that, he cared not for the future. I could smell the violence on him, and the rage. He was in the grip of a blood fever that only our two deaths would break.

'And here stands the furious Tybalt,' I said. I put my hand on my sword's hilt. If the peace was broken, let it be well shattered and done. Mercutio's death had been stupid, meaningless, and in part it was laid at my own door; if I hadn't met with the witch, if Roggocio's companion had not escaped to Tybalt's side, then none of this would have happened.

'Alive in triumph, and Mercutio slain,' Romeo agreed. His voice rose, and hardened. 'My forgiveness has gone to heaven with him. Now, Tybalt, call me villain again – Mercutio's soul is but a little way above our heads, staying for you to keep him company, and either you or I will join him!'

'You consorted with him here, and will go with him there!' Tybalt answered.

Romeo lunged forward, all restraint fled. Tybalt met him in a clash of steel, both of them slipping in Mercutio's spilt blood on the stones. One of the Capulet bravos drew his blade, and I lunged for him with a shout of fury, because, like my cousin, I needed to avenge my friend's terrible, useless fate. I was aware of the striving of Tybalt and Romeo, but I duelled my own enemy – the bravo I'd chased through the city, who'd led me to this field of slaughter. He was as quick and deadly as any I'd faced. His blade slithered over mine in a lunge, and tore a bloody strip from my shoulder; we parted, circled, and I feinted high and lunged low, aiming for his thigh and the vulnerable vein there. He parried, and pinked me again, but he slipped on the cobbles and his point wavered, and I riposted hard and fast and ripped a thick red line on his cheek. He dropped his sword and staggered back, clapping a hand to the wound.

I stabbed him in the throat and ended him.

Not soon enough, since he'd told Tybalt what he knew of my secrets. I had to silence Tybalt before he could accuse me in public . . . and before he learnt of Romeo's ill-advised marriage vows with his cousin. Silence, but not kill so openly in the street, under a Capulet's blade; this situation required quick, silent assassination away from prying eyes, if I was to save my house.

It was vital that Romeo not be seen, in public, to bring about his death.

I spun towards the other battle, intending to wound Tybalt enough to render him unable to speak – a blow to the throat would do – just as Romeo, down on the cobbles where Tybalt had toppled him, rolled and slashed, catching the Capulet – more by luck than skill – on his unprotected vitals.

Tybalt staggered back, eyes wide. For an instant, the cut looked small, but then it parted, and the blood, oh, the blood. He fell into the arms of his adherents, thrashing in his death agonies, and I scrambled forward and dragged my bloodied, hard-breathing cousin to his feet. His eyes were fiery with the fight, and his lips parted in a feral grimace.

It was all done, then. All hope gone. My problem had been solved, but Romeo's, Montague's, was only just begun.

I shook him, hard. 'Romeo! Be gone from here. Tybalt's slain, and the prince will see you dead if you're taken; do you hear me? *Be gone!*

The exaltation suddenly faltered in him, driven out by my words, and by something else, something much greater, and worse. He looked horrified well beyond what he ought to have done. 'Oh, I am fortune's fool!' he whispered, and clung to me for balance. 'Benvolio—'

The Capulets were turning on us, screaming in their fury. 'Why do you stay?' I shouted at him, and shoved him. 'Go! Run!'

He did, the bloody sword still in his hand. Mine also was blooded, though not on Tybalt, but I quickly wiped it and put it away, because there was a loud shout from the piazza behind us. The city's watch had finally arrived, and with them, summoned no doubt by breathless messengers, came the prince of Verona, my own aunt and uncle, and the Capulets as well. Mercutio's father was not in the group, and I thanked God for it; I might have added him to the tally of corpses for the day, from pure bitterness.

My uncle looked at me with bewilderment, and a good deal of fear, and I understood in a moment – here I stood, in the centre of the bloody scene, drenched in red, while Tybalt gasped his last among his cousins.

'Where are the vile beginners of this fray?' Prince Escalus snapped, as he stepped forward out of the watch's protection. He looked every inch the city's ruler, iron faced, tempered hard by his years. Even his grey hair had the glint of steel in the lingering sun.

His eyes swept the scene, and came to rest upon me.

I bowed low, and found the words to explain, sticking close to truth, since there were too many witnesses to Romeo's act for any hope of clemency. Lady Capulet let out a bloodcurdling wail, and broke free of her husband's hand to throw herself down beside Tybalt's twitching corpse.

'Tybalt, my nephew, my brother's child – Oh, my prince, my cousin, my husband, look, his blood is spilt! My prince, if you are true to your word, blood of ours was shed by Montague, and Montague blood must answer it!' She gathered Tybalt's limp form in her arms, and though I knew there was more politics than grief to her emotion, still it raised a sympathetic murmur in the crowd.

The prince noted it, but he was not like to be moved by theatrics. 'Benvolio, who began this bloody fray?'

'Tybalt,' I said without equivocation, and gave him the tale, ending, 'Romeo came between them, beating down their blades, but Tybalt struck under his arm, and hit the life of Mercutio, then fled.'

'Fled?' The prince cast a significant look on the dead boy gathered in Lady Capulet's arms. 'Here he lies.'

I bowed my head. 'He came back to have at Romeo, who was much aggrieved; he entertained revenge, and who could blame him? They went like lightning, and so was Tybalt slain.'

'And Romeo?'

'Fled, my prince. This is the truth, on my life.'

Lady Capulet gave me a bitter, hateful stare, and said, 'A kinsman of the Montague! Affection makes him false, and he lies! Some twenty of them must have fought my Tybalt, to bring him down. I beg for justice, my prince, and you must give it. By his own cousin's words, Romeo slew Tybalt. Romeo must not live!'

'Romeo slew him,' the prince agreed. 'And Tybalt slew Mercutio. Who now owes the price of my kinsman's dear blood?'

My uncle stepped forward then. 'Not Romeo, Prince. He was Mercutio's friend. His fault concludes but what the law should have ended: the life of Tybalt.'

'Whose word have we that Benvolio Montague did not kill my cousin himself!' Lady Capulet spat. 'Look, you, he is drenched in red blood that cries for vengeance!'

'Mercutio's blood,' I said. 'My friend lies in a hovel not far from here, if you wish to water him with your tears. And his blood *did* cry out for vengeance, and you hold that vengeance in your arms.'

She gave a raw shriek of fury, and let Tybalt's body thump back to the street as she rose. 'Will no one kill this Montague?' she demanded, and turned that basilisk's gaze on her own bravos, who quailed. 'Tybalt's death demands it!'

No one stirred hand or foot. The watch's armed presence ensured it, and so did the prince's moody, cold stare.

As the silence fell, the prince said, 'It is fair that Capulet have a measure of vengeance, and so, Romeo—'

My aunt gripped her husband's arm hard.

'Romeo,' the prince continued doggedly, 'is immediately exiled hence from Verona, never to return. I have an interest in your grief; my blood also for your rude brawls lies bleeding. But I'll punish you not with death, but with so strong a fine that you shall all repent the loss of Mercutio. Nay, Lady Montague, I am deaf to pleadings and excuses, and tears and prayers shall not purchase out your son's abuses, so give me none. Let Romeo go in haste, or when he's found, that hour will be his last. Go now, take Tybalt's body and attend our will.'

The Capulets were pleased, I thought; if they had lost

the ever-raging Tybalt, then it was public justice to them that Romeo had been taken from the Montagues, if not in body, then in fact. He would no longer be the heir on whom we rested our family's future. He was disgraced, cast out, and exiled. The enormity of it had only begun to strike me. My cousin, feckless and reckless as he was, had been unquestionably the hope of Montague, and now, in an instant, in a lucky strike in the heat of a battle he had not invited, he had lost everything. Exiled from our family, our city, from everything and everyone he knew and loved. From his own love.

If there was anything, anything at all, that could be gleaned as silvery hope from the ashes of this disaster, it was that at least that Romeo would now be forced to give up his mad pursuit of Juliet. His life would be forfeit if he lingered inside the city beyond this hour, and Friar Lawrence had told me that though vows had been spoken, no marriage bed had been made. Even in the eyes of God, it was still no marriage at all.

Still, Mercutio's cry upon being mortally struck haunted me, as I joined my family for the uncomfortable journey back to our palazzo. *A plague on both your houses!*

Surely his dying warning was already coming true.

I took my leave of my aunt and uncle and went to my rooms, where Balthasar had already arrived; who had found and informed him of the day's dark events, I did not know, but he had arranged for a tub of hot water, and took away my bloody clothes. Whether they were to be cleaned or burnt, I did not care. I sank into the steaming bath with an almost pitiful sense of gratitude, and washed death's leavings away.

I stayed in the tub, easing stiffened muscles, until Balthasar came back with a bath sheet to dry me. As he scrubbed me down with rough, efficient motions, I felt I was a toddling boy again, and a strange lassitude washed over me. I wanted to take to my bed and be coddled until the fever passed, but this fever was cold, not hot, and I feared it might not be banished so easily.

Inside me was a wild, howling emptiness where all my certainties had once lived. I had lost Mercutio, burning bright in both anger and love; I had as much as lost Romeo, just as hot-spurred but with a sweetness to his temper that Mercutio had never dreamt. My brothers in spirit, if not in blood, and both gone, blown away on an ill wind.

I had never felt more alone.

Balthasar wisely said nothing to me, only brought me warm wine and sat me in a chair near the window, where I might look down on the streets below. After a moment, I rose and closed the shutters. The cobbles outside were stained with a sunset Mercutio would never see, and it put me too much in mind of the blood I'd washed away in the tub. The sight of grey Verona's stones reminded me of his pallid face and slackened lips.

I closed my eyes awhile, and when I opened them, my mother was there.

Balthasar must have brought her a chair, for she sat straight-backed and proper across from me, dressed in her habitual mourning black with glints of gold at her throat and cuffs. In the privacy of our house, she had taken off the wimple; her hair was pinned up in a complex series of braids and knots that must have taken her lady's maid hours to achieve. As always, she seemed almost blank of expression, but I thought there might have been a flicker of concern, at least a passing one.

'Benvolio,' she said.

'Mother.' My tone did not invite discussion.

She ignored the dismissal. 'I am sorry for Mercutio,' she said. 'He was a loyal friend, if sometimes a loose one.' I waited. She had not come to see me to give me her regrets. After a moment's silence, she came to it. 'Your cousin Romeo is ruined in Verona. No one faults him; he was right to kill the Capulet villain for Mercutio's death. But without him, Montague has no male heir to take hold of its fortunes. Your uncle must name you, Benvolio.'

'Me?' I said. It was fool's work to be surprised, but yet I was. I had not thought of it, and now that I had, it disgusted me. I had never wanted such a role, and never at the cost of Romeo's future and fortune. 'My uncle does not favour me, Mother. He never has.' I did not say, *Because I am a half-blood*. The English in me was a matter of constant suspicion, however much I looked or acted the part of a true Veronese. I would always be seen as an alien, either here or in my mother's home of London.

'Needs must he favour you now,' she said, and looked down to fuss with a fold of her skirts. 'Have you seen your poor cousin since the brawl?'

'Not since he fled, as I urged him to do,' I said. 'Should I seek him out?'

'Under no account should you be seen to involve yourself in his troubles. He has done Montague a good turn, there is no doubt of it, but be careful, my son, lest you share his fate.'

The phrasing, I realised, was deliberate; I should not be *seen* to involve myself; she meant I should be careful. It was a masterful piece of misdirection. My mother gave nothing away in either her posture or her voice, but there was a slight tightening around her eyes that told me she was worried — worried to be sending me this message, which doubtless had not come from her. She was only the helpless messenger.

I sensed my grandmother's palsied, iron-strong grip was behind it.

I nodded to show I understood, and my mother rose to go. She took a step, then stopped, and without turning said, 'Do you grieve, my son?'

'Does it matter?' I asked.

She shook her head silently, and a little colour burnt in her cheeks. 'I liked the boy,' she said. 'He had a love of life, and a careless grace that was good for you, I think. I hope he taught you some of that joy.'

'You taught me to be cautious,' I told her. 'And that lesson, at least, I've learnt well.'

She turned and looked at me, and her light green eyes met my darker ones. She was still lovely, my mother, though her beauty had faded like a painting kept too long in the sun. I wondered what hopes she had once held for her life, and what dreams. She was far too practical to harbour anything so useless now. 'Then be practical now. Guard yourself,' she said. 'There's a fey darkness in the air. I fear the bloodshed is not done, and as Montague's heir, you will be at even more risk.'

'Is that my grandmother's sentiment, or yours?'

That woke a flash of temper from her, after all. 'I am still your mother, Benvolio. I am allowed some concern for my own child!'

'That doesn't answer.'

She gave me a long, measured look that reminded me that buried very deep within that calm exterior lay the same fiery temper I carried burning like a coal within my breast. 'I lost your father to this age-old quarrel, and now your cousin has fallen prey to it, and your friend. If I do not fear for your safety, then I am naught but a fool.'

I smiled a little then. 'I don't think you a fool, Mother.'

'Only a cold schemer, like your grandmother?' Her own lips twitched in what might almost have been a smile then. 'I come from warmer stock. Your sister has taken well after the Montague example, though.'

Veronica. Ah, yes, my dear, sweet sister, on whose plump shoulders so much of this must rest . . . She had, for sheer malice's sake, betrayed Mercutio and Tomasso, and turned Mercutio's rage against the Capulets. Her invisible hand had pushed the blade that had taken him, and Romeo's that had killed Tybalt. Perhaps she was a worthy heir to the old crone, after all.

'Your uncle has asked her bridegroom to delay the wedding to next week, for the sake of propriety, but the old goat won't have it,' my mother continued. 'He says we have no sons to mourn, and the Capulets would not attend in any case, so why delay? He means to bed Veronica with unseemly haste, it seems.'

Perhaps, I thought, he had caught a whisper of my sister's unmaidenly behaviour . . . or he was simply randy and feared he might die unsatisfied. I might have pitied her the fate, if she were not such a cold-hearted schemer and like to earn more from it than she paid.

But my mother's point was not to bring my sympathy, but to warn, and I followed her there only a moment later. 'At the wedding, we will be exposed,' I said. 'All of Montague, defenceless in the cathedral for the ceremony. But surely even the Capulets would not attack us there, on sacred ground . . .'

'Sacred ground did little to sway the assassins of the Medici,' she said, rightly; the story of the long-ago attack on Lorenzo the Magnificent was legend. They had failed to kill him in the cathedral, but they had bloodied the holy floors with his brother's gore instead. Assassins struck in church all too often, where God seemed to take little interest in enforcing peace. 'We must be tightly on our guard, my son. Always, but most especially, in the house of our Lord.'

It was a grim message, but I knew she was right; if I was to be made heir of Montague, I would be the first and most vital target for Capulet revenge. And revenge they would have for Tybalt's death; that much was sure.

She nodded to me, and then left, proud and unbowed by all that fate had heaped upon her. There was something to admire in my mother, something more than her carefully lived life. She knew tragedy with an intimacy that was almost obscene, and yet it had left her unbroken.

I stood up and threw off the sheet. Balthasar caught it deftly and folded it, and said, 'No house colours, then, sir?'

'No house colours,' I agreed. 'It's time to keep to the shadows.'

I scouted the night as the Prince of Shadows, all in grey, blending with the stones and shades. I thought to find evidence of Romeo's departure, but instead, and disquietingly, I heard tavern tales of my cousin being seen in the streets of Verona after his hour had passed — not riding hard for the city gates, either, nor buying supplies for his departure. He'd been seen moving with stealth in streets that I knew bordered the Capulet house — a way I knew well, as I'd watched him run it not so long ago, in darkness.

It came to me then, with a cold slap, that he was not intending to leave Verona at all. He meant to finish his marriage vows, tonight, with Juliet Capulet.

In her bed. Within Capulet's walls.

That made cold sense; she was a prisoner there, rarely seen without the palazzo, and it had been a miracle she'd been allowed out to make her confession to Friar Lawrence today — even if it had been no confession at all, but a marriage. Romeo must go to her, if he wished to have his marriage rights.

But to do such a thing tonight, with his head in the noose — it defied all belief. Was this love, to betray one's family, and to defy certain death? To risk the life of the one you adored? It seemed less love to me than a fever, a sickness burning away caution and good sense.

But perhaps I'd never really loved at all.

The heat had finally broken with a sharp snap, and clouds boiled the skies overhead. Winds stirred the torrents of darkness, and lightning seared and thunder rumbled. It covered any sound of my light-footed passage over roof tiles as I took to the heights, but the risk for me was worse. I felt the sizzling fury in the air, and any fool knew that lightning struck down those who stood tallest in its way. That was dangerous enough, but with the wind came the fat, still-hot drops of rain . . . a patter first, and then a torrent, making slick the tiles and bidding fair to send me tumbling. I lost my balance twice, and caught onto the leaded roof peaks in time to stop my slide. Once, as I neared the Capulets' quarter, a white-hot bolt of God's purest fury hit the top of the Lamberti Tower, and rattled the tiles under my feet. I heard the muffled cries and prayers of those in the house on whose roof I stood; someone clapped shut a window's wooden doors.

Only a few rain-drenched beggars and disheartened curs watched my slow, cautious progress, and then only in the brief flashes of lightning. The murky dark was my friend, at least; if the watch dared to be about, they'd not easily spot me. My grey, cloaked figure was easily mistaken for a chimney pot, in the flash of a second.

The Capulet garden was silent. No fair maids haunted their balconies this evening; they would be sensibly tucked away from the storms. I paused on the wall, staring at the dark, shut doors of Rosaline's room; she would still be within, sealed up on Tybalt's orders, awaiting her quick dismissal to the convent. Perhaps –

No. I had more frightening business tonight. She was in no more danger from her brother, at least.

The Capulet household was silent without, but when I found an open window in the servants' attic the room was empty. No servants were abed, which meant that the Capulets were still well awake themselves. I found an extra set of livery that fit me well enough, and left my wet clothes behind; my hair was dry, as it had been concealed beneath the hood. I could do little about my hose, or my shoes, but I hoped no one would look closely. The Capulets kept a large household, and I quickly gathered up a heaping armload of linens, the better to conceal my face. The servants' stairs were narrow and hot, large enough for only one, and as I descended, a fat, red-faced wench waited impatiently at the bottom for her turn. 'Be off with you!' she snapped, and shoved my shoulder as I edged past. 'No dawdling tonight, you fool; they're in shorter temper than ever, what with that young beast dead!'

I mumbled something from behind my laundry and hurried on. Clearly, Tybalt had no mourners among the servants, if she could speak so freely – and with such contempt and relief. I descended stairs to the next floor, where the rough, cramped confines changed to the fine stone, wood, and carpet of the family portion of the palazzo. My damp shoes were silent on the covered floors, and I paused to take my bearings. From the direction of the wide staircase at the end I heard the hum of voices, and low cries and sobs, no doubt from Lady Capulet and her attendants. Here, all was quiet. I tested the door on my left and found it locked; when I bent to peer through the lock, I saw a glint of candles on the other side. The key had been used and taken away.

Rosaline was locked within, as much a nun now as when she would be taken to her holy cell in mere days.

I could sense her lively, restless presence beyond that door, and I felt an impulse to speak with her, tell her what had occurred, ask her what might be done. As I stood indecisive, I realised that another had come upon me, footsteps also muffled by the carpets – the stout red-faced woman who'd braced me upstairs.

'Fool!' she hissed, and elbowed me aside from the door. 'You should have asked me to come with you. You'll not have a key for the lady's rooms, and mind you, in and out; no conversing with her. Those were Master Tybalt's orders, but I'd not ignore them just yet, for my life.' She twisted a key from her ring and unlocked the door, and stiff-armed it open. 'Hurry, then; deliver your sheets. I must lock it after.'

Inside, Rosaline started up to her feet. She was fully dressed, I saw, in a rich black velvet gown; her hair was up in a style too severe for her face. She was pallid, and her eyes were red, but as her gaze fell on me, she grew even paler. For an instant I had a sick, terrible conviction she would betray me, but she finally pointed at a table close to her curtained bed. 'Put them there,' she said. I carried the tray over and settled it there. 'Bide a moment; I have things for you.' She quickly set a plate, a glass, and a bowl upon another tray on the table where the candle burnt – dinner things, still crusted with uneaten food.

'Mistress, the boy has duties,' the servant at the door called. 'I'll send another to fetch those.'

I quickly grabbed the tray and bent closer to Rosaline. 'I need your help,' I whispered. I made a show of fumbling things, while I waited for her response.

It did not come. She gazed at me for too long, and then finally whispered back, 'Why should I help a Montague? This night, of all nights?'

'For your cousin,' I said.

I had no chance for anything else. The servant at the door was clearing her throat impatiently. Rosaline had said nothing in reply, and I could not be certain of her, not at all. My position here became more dangerous with every heartbeat.

I bowed and backed towards the door with the tray. As I did, I managed to tilt an uneaten piece of bread towards the edge, catch it between two fingers, and knead out a thick ball of the soft interior. As I backed through the door, I fumbled the tray again, the better to give the senior servant something to criticise, as with my other hand I pressed the dough in place to block the tongue of the lock.

'You'll not last in this house, you clouted, beetle-headed dotard!' My shrewish superior followed that with a blow of her open hand to the back of my head, and this time the tray threatened to tumble free of its own accord. She pulled the door closed with a bare curtsy to Rosaline, turned the key, and put it back on her ring.

I quickly raised the tray to distract her from my face, but she ignored me as thoroughly as her noble masters would have done. I was far below her own social station. 'Drop that and I'll see you whipped, boy. I don't need Lady Capulet boxing my ears for your incompetence—' She would have continued berating me, but suddenly she paled. Coming up the steps was a pinch-faced matron in better clothes – still not one of the Capulets, but a high order of servant, and, from the look she gave us, one in charge of our worthless hides. My tormentor quickly curtsied, and I bowed over the tray.

'You,' the newcomer said, fixing her beady dark eyes on the large woman next to me. 'Downstairs to the kitchen. There are dishes to wash.' She glanced at me, still bent over the tray. 'Take those with you, Maria. You, boy. Chamber pots. Quickly.'

She did not wait to see that she was obeyed; she only swept past us with majestic, eerie quiet, and in her wake, my companion – Maria – irritably snatched the tray from my hands. 'Well?' She probably would have cuffed me again, if her hands had been idle. 'Go about it, then! And *quietly!*'

I bowed again, as clumsily as I could, and she hurried towards the back steps with the tray.

I stepped back against Rosaline's door. The dough had done its work, and the lock had not closed. It slid open, and I stepped through and swung it closed after me.

When I turned, Rosaline was standing not two feet from me, and she had a shining dagger pointed at my throat.

'You dare,' she said softly. 'You *dare* come here, with my brother's blood on your hands.'

'I had Mercutio's blood on them, not Tybalt's,' I said. 'A man your brother killed without cause. My friend.' My hand flashed out and gripped her wrist, but I did not try to take away the knife. I focused instead on her face, her eyes, the fragile strength and grief in her. 'You know I did not love your brother. For your sake, I am sorry, but for your sake, I also hated him. For every blow he gave you, I hated him, Rosaline.'

She caught her breath, and I saw her bite her lip; tears started in her eyes, and I would not have seen her cry, not for my life. 'He was my brother.' Her voice broke on the word.

'Brother or not, he had no right. I cannot forgive him.' What was my treacherous hand doing? It had moved from her wrist, glided up her arm, and now it touched her cheek. The skin there was warm and silken, and suddenly I was aware of the scent of her, roses and spice and candle wax and tears, and the danger of the dagger in her hand meant nothing, nothing at all. I felt drugged with the tingles of pleasure of my skin on hers, even in so small a measure. My fingers trailed down, traced the tight line of her jaw, and I felt the fast beat of her pulse. She raised her chin, but did not step back. The point of the knife wavered a bare thread from my throat. It was good it was there, I thought absently, because the pull to go closer to her had the pulse and depth of the ocean.

She suddenly pulled in a trembling breath and saved me from courting my own murder by stepping away. She dropped the dagger as if it had burnt her hand, then wrapped her arms around her body, bent her head, and turned away. A curl of dark hair shook loose and fell against the graceful curve of her neck, and I ached to ease it back . . . no, to take out the pins that held her hair, see it tumble loose and silky around her white shoulders.

'Why are you here?' she whispered. '*Jesu*, Benvolio, do you not know they will cut you to pieces?'

I snapped back to my purpose, but it was an effort; I had gone a great distance away, it seemed, and what I'd come to do had faded in proportion. I turned away from her, stared hard at a candle's flame, and tried to clear my mind. 'Your cousin,' I said. 'She slipped her escorts this afternoon. She's exchanged vows with Romeo.'

'What?' Rosaline whirled. 'How? How could she – What folly is that? Does he not know my family would destroy them both?'

'Mine too,' I said. 'My grandmother would sooner see them dead.'

'But . . . married? Oh, this is a disaster! I thought it only a flattery, a fantasy to sustain her before the reality of her coming wedding; I never thought . . . I thought she might act improperly, never with such recklessness!'

'We can still stop it,' I said. 'But I need your help.'

'How?'

'I think Romeo is here,' I said, and I saw her press her hands to her mouth in horror. 'In her room. Perhaps readying to be in her bed. I dare not go in; she'll shriek the house down, and Romeo and I would both be food for the dogs. If you interrupt them . . .'

'Then I am only the concerned convent-bound cousin, shocked to find them contemplating such sin,' she finished, and flashed me a shaking smile. 'Yes. I will go.'

It was a risk, even so; she was supposed to be locked in, though I supposed that they would see that as a minor enough rebellion if she was caught. I doubted Juliet would care.

'Make him leave quietly,' I cautioned her. 'Any betrayal would cost him his life. Please.'

That woke a silvery flash in her eyes, and I knew she was remembering that Romeo's sword had taken her brother's life this day. It would be so simple, so easy to gain the revenge her family desired so much. Nothing but a raised voice, a shocked cry . . . and it would cost her nothing but my own regard.

I caught her hand as she moved past me, and for just a moment, our fingers curled in on one another, sealed in pain and urgency . . . and then she opened the door of her room, and was gone.

Fool, I told myself in a sudden, ice-cold fury. *She'll betray you; she must betray you; she is a Capulet born and bred, sister to Tybalt, dead by Montague hands . . . and you've trusted her with the life of Tybalt's killer, on the day of his death.* Yet I could not help but trust her. It was a faith that had no basis in fact, but what faith ever does?

I took the bar from the door and blew out the candle, then waited by the new-opened exit intense silence. I heard nothing – no outcry, not even a muffled argument. What if instead she had gone down the stairs, warned her aunt and uncle? What if even now Capulet guards massed at my back and below in the garden? I could scramble up to the roof, but the Capulet palazzo was too removed from its neighbours. Not even I, with all my practice, could make such a leap, and not from rain-slicked tiles. I'd tumble to broken bones, at the very least, and capture, and a slow death.

I heard the creak of the door behind me, soft and stealthy, and drew my sword without turning.

I closed my eyes in sweet relief as Rosaline's hands closed on my shoulders, and she leant forward to whisper, 'I would not betray you, Prince of Shadows. Not even today.'

I put up the sword, closed the balcony doors on the pounding silver curtain of rain, and braced them again with the wooden beam. When I turned back, she had sparked tinder to light the candle anew, and in its glow I saw there was high colour in her cheeks, and a strange look in her eyes. She placed the light upon the table and sat, hands folded together. After a moment of hesitation, I did the same.

'Was he within?' I asked her, and saw the blush in her cheeks grow brighter.

'You might say it so,' she said, and avoided my gaze by fixing her own upon her hands. 'Even if my uncle discovers this treachery and voids the vows they exchanged, Juliet will not go virgin to Paris's marriage bed.'

I imagined her stumbling upon so intimate a scene, and silently removing herself without giving an alarm – because an alarm would do no good. The act of love brought the marriage vows to life, and Romeo's sin was now made holy. It did not mean the Capulets would not see it undone, but Juliet would never marry highly, or marry at all, even if they cut Romeo down in the streets and hid the secret. The roles of the two girls had now been switched. Juliet was bound, at best, for the convent if they prevented her from escaping with Romeo; Rosaline, the untouched maiden, would be Capulet's asset to spend now.

Perhaps Paris would take her. Or some other, richer man. But not me. Never me.

I felt a wild, furious urge to fling sense to the winds, to do what Romeo had done with his Juliet; my grandmother had ordered it. *Ruin the girls, ruin the family;* that had been her message, but it had been a hateful one, and one I could not believe had any place in Romeo's heart.

'Benvolio,' she said, and her voice pulled me out of a dark contemplation – would she resist me if I took hold of her, kissed her, bore her back to that curtained mattress? Would she cry out for help, or would she sigh my name, rise to meet me, crave the same senseless release I did? 'Benvolio, Juliet knows well that this is a fool's course. Why has she done such a thing?'

'For love,' I said. My voice had dropped lower in my throat, and I could not stop gazing at her, not to save my soul.

She took in a deep breath and slowly let it out, but

she did not meet my eyes. 'Juliet is a child, but she is no fantastic. She has been raised knowing her duty to this house, and she has been at peace with it all her life. One chance meeting with a boy – the sworn enemy of her own family – would never overcome it. She might engage in flirtation, but this . . . Benvolio, this *cannot* simply be love. It borders on sorcery.'

She was right, I thought, and with a chill, I thought of the witch, of her talk of curses. Of Mercutio's last words. 'Madness or love, done is done, and this is very thoroughly done. Whatever passes now is beyond our ability to change.'

'Have you given thought to how it changes us?' Now, finally, she looked on me, and the colour stayed high in her cheeks. Her fingers were restless, fretting at the wood of the table. 'When this is known – and it must be known; she cannot be so foolish as to damn her soul with a bigamous marriage to Count Paris; nor would Friar Lawrence allow it   then Juliet will no longer be my uncle's to give away.'

'You will be,' I said.

'I know.' It impressed me how quickly she'd reasoned it out, even given the rapid shocks of the day. 'I think you may no longer fear imprisonment in the convent, at least.'

'Perhaps not, but now I dread the other outcome. Unlike Juliet, I was never resigned to that duty, to marriage to a man I did not know, bearing children for the sake of family honour. I do not know . . . I do not know how I can manage it.' She was immediately ashamed of this confession, I saw, and turned the blade of it on me. 'At least your station increases from this.'

'Ah, me, yes, I become the target of every Capulet assassin and ham-fisted fool seeking their favour,' I said. 'Tell me again how great my good fortune might be, Rosaline. I fail to properly appreciate it.'

She laughed a little, and covered her mouth with one hand, as if afraid someone might hear her inappropriate merriment. She ought to be in mourning, I thought; she must feel guilt for that, too, for knowing relief that her brother would never torment her again. 'I am sorry,' she said. 'I should have guessed such a rose came with thorns.'

'Poisoned thorns, and poisoned wine and poisoned meat. I shall have no peace from my great fortune, I promise you.' I hesitated, then said, 'And it is the last time the Prince of Shadows may walk the night. From now on, I will be only Benvolio Montague.'

'*Only?*' Her voice was unexpectedly warm now. 'That is a great deal, you know.'

'A half-breed heir is hardly what my uncle dreamt of,' I said. 'It is not so much as you think. The colour of my eyes never lets them forget what I am.'

That startled her, as if she had never considered such a thing, and I liked her for it. 'Your eyes are beautiful,' she said, and it was an honest and unconsidered thought, one she immediately regretted, from the way she looked away. 'I mean to say, they do you credit, and—'

I stood up. She did, too, in reflexive defence, and her gaze darted to the dagger discarded near the bed.

'No,' I said. 'I will not hurt you.'

'Will you not?' She licked her lips. I wished she had not; I wished I could stop admiring the shine of them in the flickering light. 'It is what men do, hurt women.'

'Not all is pain,' I said. This was not how I had meant to bend the conversation, but it seemed to travel so on its own.

'Did you see pain when you peeked in the curtains of your cousin's bed?'

She looked away, colour rising in her cheeks. 'I do not think so.'

'Then what is it you fear?'

'Drowning. Losing myself. Being . . . being controlled.'

'Both may surrender in this battle,' I said, and somehow I had moved closer to her, fatally close. 'And both may win. I know this.'

'From experience.'

I smiled a little. 'I'm no child,' I said. 'And men are expected to know a few things.'

Her lips parted, and her eyes widened, and I wanted . . . I wanted so badly just then to kiss her, to taste the sweet darkness of her, but to do it would be to drown, as Romeo drowned. I was not *quite* ready to trade my soul for it.

But oh, so very nearly.

I pulled away from it, and her, and I saw a flash of guilty relief in her eyes as she likewise stepped back. 'I will trust your word,' she said, and she meant more than seemed obvious by it. 'How do you mean to leave here?'

'Perhaps like Cleopatra, wrapped in a carpet?'

'I regret I have no carpet large enough to wrap your thick head.' We were back on even footing now, and she even summoned a smile for it. 'The garden is too wet; you will leave tracks to betray your presence.'

'I will go out the servants' door, as I came in,' I said, and reached beneath her bed to fetch the covered blue-glazed pot. She gasped, this time in dismayed amusement. 'I was ordered to empty chamber pots, after all. Fear not. I'll leave it there for your attendant to find for you.'

'You can't—' I held up the chamber pot, and she bit her lip on a laugh. 'You are mad, you know.'

'Though it is madness, there is method in it,' I said, and bowed a little. 'Your servant, my lady.'

'I would give you a blow, were you not holding that thing.'

I put it aside on the floor. 'Come, then. Give me the blow. I deserve it.'

She came forward and raised her hand, but when it fell, the slap was nothing but a gentle contact, and she leant in, and then . . . And then I was lost.

I had kissed her before, but lightly, gently, and this was no gentle thing; it was all the pent-up grief and loss and compromise we knew would be our lives from this moment onward; it was all that we would have been, could have been, and never would. It was madness, and magic, and in that moment I understood with fatal clarity how my cousin could have thrown away his life, and all our lives, for love. If this was sorcery, then I had learnt to love it.

Rosaline Capulet tasted like all I had ever wanted in my life, and now I knew that for truth.

I do not know how she found the strength, but she stepped away from me. I saw how pale she was, how unsteady, how flushed and oddly awkward; I saw her hands curl into shaking fists, as if she would pummel herself for her sins. I could not speak at all.

'You must go,' she whispered. 'Dear God, what is happening to us? How is this possible? We are not fools; we understand the world . . . This cannot be us. It cannot be.'

I shook my head. The wood of the door was at my back, and I used it for bracing until my legs had found their strength again. Then Rosaline backed away and took up the dagger from the carpet. She wedged herself into a corner as if terrified of her own passions.

'We cannot do this,' she said, and tears sparkled like stars in her eyes. 'Please go away from me. Please.'

I picked up the chamber pot, opened the door, and escaped into the hall. I had the presence of mind to scrape loose the bread dough, and heard the lock click shut between us.

I was as hot as if poison coursed through my veins. *Pick the lock,* something in me cried. *Pick the lock; forget all this; lose yourself in her. Let the future fall. Let houses burn, as long as you are together. Nothing else matters but love.*

I thanked God for the sobering weight of the blue pot in my hands, and escaped down the back steps to the servants' door; a bored guard gave me a glance and opened it. I walked to the jakes and dumped the thing, carried it back to the steps of the house, and left it there for someone else to discover.

Escaping into the rain cooled my hot blood, at least, and I spent an hour walking in it, staring up at the clouds, letting the water wash away thought and impulse and desire until I could, finally, get the strength to journey home.

I would have to tell them the truth about Romeo's marriage to Juliet, but not yet.

Not until morning.

FROM THE HAND OF ROSALINE CAPULET TO FRIAR LAWRENCE

My faithful brother in Christ,

Today my lady aunt, the most kind Lady Capulet, has announced to me that as hasty as my brother's burial might be, so must be her daughter Juliet's marriage to Count Paris, who has most eagerly sought her hand. She believes that only thus will the tragedy of our family be healed.

We know why this must not happen.

Good friar, I beg you to come with all haste, as she is much distraught, and I am sure you know that her heart will admit no new love whatever comes.

I know that you are attending to the needs of House Montague, with the exile of the murderer Romeo, but I beg you come to our aid quickly, before terrible events overtake us all. You, good friar, must find a way to ensure Juliet's happiness.

Your sister in Christ,
most faithfully,
Rosaline Capulet

FROM THE DIARY OF FRIAR LAWRENCE

I pray God will forgive me all the grievous sins that mount almost hourly before me. I thought that I abetted only a little sin, that of disobedience, for the sake of love, but now I find I am party to so much more, and so much worse.

First did I, against the laws of Verona and the express wishes of our prince, give aid and comfort to young Romeo, whom I hid against his exile from the city, though he was guilty of shedding Tybalt's blood; and then, fearing Juliet's despair would lead her to a greater sin of self-murder, God forgive me but I sent the boy to her bed. I meant only to sanctify the marriage they so greatly desired. I had no thought of the other consequences.

Now, with Romeo safely on his way to Mantua, Juliet is forced to marry Paris and forswear her lawful marriage. She speaks of daggers, and the great and terrible sin of self-murder lest her bridal bed be also her bed of adultery. I know not what to do. I will pray upon it, and let God lead me to His will.

Ah, the bells begin their sad tolling – for a wedding for Veronica Montague, and after, for the twin funerals of Mercutio and Tybalt. I must to the Lord's duties, though my heart is ashes.

God forgive all I have done.

God forgive what I must do next.

QUARTO
IV

The next morning was the solemn mockery of a marriage for my sister, Veronica.

I had slept not at all; my body ached dully, my eyes felt rubbed in sand, and I was of short temper as Balthasar dressed me in my finest clothes for the wedding. Well, at least someone would be happy today, I thought, even if it was Veronica's aged bridegroom; Veronica would be happy after the night's work of pleasing him, because she would have shed House Montague and become mistress of her own estate, with her own funds to begin her social conquest of Verona. After today, I'd have little to do with the girl, and of that, I too could be glad.

'Balthasar,' I said, as he straightened the hang of my sleeves, 'I would have you take a journey for me.'

'A journey, sir?' He brushed dust from my shoulder. I could not tell from his expression what he felt.

'To Mantua,' I said. 'My cousin will have need of a servant, even in exile. Would you go, to watch after him?

He is still in danger. Capulet's reach is long, and it carries a dagger.'

'I would be most pleased to be of service, but I would hate to leave you,' he said.

I opened up the chest kept locked by my bed, and took out a bag of gold coin. 'This is the last of the Prince of Shadow's profits,' I said. 'There'll be no more of it. Take it, with my thanks. I shall see you once the clouds have lifted, and Romeo is back in the prince's favour.'

'Do you think such will happen, sir?'

'I pray it will. The alternative is that I remain Montague's heir for life, and how do I deserve such a punishment?'

'I cannot think of a reason, sir,' he said, and the gold disappeared, tucked within his doublet. 'Shall I take a message?'

'Only that he should keep himself out of trouble,' I said, and allowed myself a frustrated smile. 'Though history proves that seems impossible. I should tell you that he's newly wedded, before he blurts it out in drunken sorrow.'

'Wedded, sir?'

'To Juliet Capulet.'

It was the sign of what an excellent servant he was that Balthasar hesitated only a little before saying, without any surprise, 'I see, sir; that is a complicated matter indeed. I take it your grandmother does not know?'

'She knows,' I said. 'I told her.'

'That must have been . . . eventful.'

'In truth.'

He asked no questions, and I offered no details; the ferocious old harpy had all but accused me of collusion in Romeo's folly, and I bore the mark of her cane in forming bruises on my back. Only the fact that she was so ancient had spared me from far worse. But she'd not tell my uncle; I knew that; my defeat was also hers. She had no cause to spread the word of our humiliation.

Only to dole such misery out to me.

Balthasar pinned a Montague badge to my chest and said, 'You look very well, sir. I trust you will take care in the confines of the church, and along the way? I worry that I won't be there to watch after you.'

'I will have to look out for myself.' I clapped my hand to his shoulder, and he looked away. 'You've been a good servant and a better friend.'

He nodded without speaking, and slipped a jewelled dagger in its sheath at my side. Though decorative, it had a keen edge, and so did my rapier, which he belted on as well. It might give offence to the bridegroom, but I cared little what the greedy old man thought of me.

I cared about living through the morning.

Balthasar took his leave, and I joined my mother in the hall; my aunt and uncle descended the stairs a moment later, dressed in heavy velvets. Montague, too, was armed, but only with a dagger. I did not doubt the ladies were likewise encumbered, but those blades were concealed in sleeves, boots, or bodices. My mother seemed cool and distant, and she held a rosary that she had brought with her from England; I recognised the well-worn beads.

Veronica came last, and in a cloud of cooing attendants. My sister wore her wealth stitched densely on the gold-chased fabric of her bridal gown – pearls and sapphires, with the flash of rubies and diamonds at her throat and ears. She seemed much satisfied with herself, I thought, and I fell in at the front of the party with Montague swords before my uncle dragged me back by his side, to a safer position. Of course. I was now his heir, though he liked that fact as little as I.

The procession to the cathedral was made under the hot sun, and two days' rain had become a miserably humid morning; the cobbles steamed, and so did I, inside my fine clothes. Veronica's face turned pink from the heat, a fact that displeased her enough to demand fans and shade from her attendants as we walked in a block down the narrow streets. Gawkers had turned out, of course. Some wished us well, and tossed flowers; some only stared, and some spit and made curse signs when they thought they could do it unobserved. Near the piazza – busy as always – I spotted Capulet bullies massed in a clot of red, and they broke loose and pushed through towards us.

'Beware,' I said to my uncle, and pointed at the oncoming men.

'Walk on,' he ordered. 'We are bound for the church. Let nothing stop us, certainly not some weak-bellied Capulets!'

And so we went on, and the guard tightened around us until I had to watch close to not tread heels upon those nearest . . . and just as we came close to the shadow of the cathedral, the Capulets, allied with others, sprang their trap. More poured from the street adjoining, and still more closed in behind, and then with a roar they sprang on us, knives and cudgels and swords, and the melee was on.

Veronica screamed in frustration and fear as she was buffeted by brawlers on either side; the guards around us were hard-pressed to defend us. I drew my sword and lunged over a guard's shoulder, burying the point cleanly in a Capulet soldier's chest. They had roused all their allies against us, and hired more bravos; they had opened the treasury in order to hurt us, and hurt us they had. So far, none of their blades had reached beyond our guards, but the cobbles were already wet with blood, and bodies fell to my left under a strong assault. I pivoted in that direction, drew my dagger, and slashed with it to parry the attack of a hired man. He grinned with the excitement of hot blood, and of all that there was to notice, I was oddly struck by how good his teeth were . . . and then I beat tempo on his rapier, one, two, three, and then a pivot and riposte in quarto, and my sword slid between his ribs and out his heart, and he was down, grimacing now.

But the next attacker caught me in the side – a glancing blow that gouged off flesh and hit rib, but a hit nonetheless, and the tenor of the brawl had changed around me as Montagues rallied and fought for their very lives. Women were screaming, and I saw blood on Veronica's dress; I had the fleeting thought that she would be *very* cross, but then two Capulets came at me, and I sorely missed the quick blade of Mercutio, and Romeo and Balthasar on my right hand. Alone, I was vulnerable, and I felt it never so much as in that moment, with blood running hot from my side, and every lunge, thrust, and parry seeming to take more strength than the last.

There was renewed shouting, alarms being beaten, and just as I was forced back and knew I was overmatched, the watch's men crashed into the lines of Capulet bravos and sent them running. The Capulets themselves were not so fainthearted, and a few stayed to fight, but only one tried for me. I beat him back until the watch could take hold.

In the aftermath, I leant against a cool stone wall and caught my breath in gasps. My body shook with effort, and now that I had the leisure, I felt the wound's sharp ache. But the blood, though free-flowing, was nothing fatal, and I turned to look at my family.

My mother was safe, still ringed by guards; with her huddled her maids and my aunt's party. But my mother was fighting to be free of the restraints, and for a moment I did not understand, until I saw Veronica standing alone, facing a lissome Capulet boy no older than she. He was mayhap a minor cousin, a page to his illustrious uncle, or perhaps he had even served Tybalt at table.

I did not know his name. All I knew of him was that he had my sister's right hand in his – a hand that held a small jewelled dagger – and that, as she collapsed against him, he cradled her as if he were surprised by her sudden drop.

I do not remember leaving the shadow of the wall, nor pulling the young boy away from her; I remember only my mother kneeling beside her, and Veronica's bewildered eyes peering up into mine as her hands restlessly travelled over and over the Capulet dagger that lay buried in her breast.

I turned on the boy, hauled him upright, and shoved him hard against the wall with my dagger aimed for his eye. 'Why?' I shouted. He looked as smooth skinned as my sister; surely he was even younger than she, hardly allowed out of his schoolroom. His Capulet colours fit him badly, as if he had not had time to be measured for them. *We pull children from their nurses to fight our battles,* I thought, and it was eerily clear and cold in my mind. The boy was afraid, and so he should have been.

'I did not mean . . .' He licked pale lips. There were tears in his eyes. 'Sir, please, I did not mean to hurt her, but she stabbed at me . . .'

I did not move. *Kill him,* my grandmother's voice shouted in the back of my mind. *Why do you hesitate? Your sister's blood is on his hands, struck down before the church on her wedding day! No one will judge you wrong!*

I lowered the dagger, though I kept hold of his throat. 'No more,' I said. 'Tybalt is dead. Romeo is gone. My young sister lies dying. It is *enough.* Go and tell your war-making uncle that before I write it in your own blood.'

His eyes widened. 'You . . . you mean to let me go?'

'Swear to lay down arms against my family, and go free.'

Suddenly his young, pale face twisted into a wolf's smile. 'Coward,' he spat. 'Unnatural brother, who loves his sister so little. I spit on your family, and I spit on your coward's oaths!' He was still afraid, but he knew there were Capulets watching, Capulets who would carry tales of him back. Like me, he was trapped by Verona itself, in the web of our ancient hates.

But I let him loose, and pushed him into the arms of the captain of the watch. He frowned beneath his shining helmet, and said, 'You give him to me?'

'For hanging,' I said. 'For murder of my sister. I stand witness, and so is my mother and all these here. Let Capulets be seen for the villains they are.'

'Coward!' the boy cried. His voice cracked, though, and his eyes were wild now. 'You will not even avenge her! *Coward!*'

I raised my blade to eye level. 'This crimson stain on me is Capulet blood,' I said. 'Blood of honest and brave men, though they be enemies. I would not sully it with yours, boy.'

He shrieked as they led him off. There was no doubt of his guilt, and though the Capulets roared in protest, and would hasten to the prince for appeal, the boy would swing, and justice would be done.

I did not care.

Veronica still lived, by some evil miracle; my mother's trembling hands touched the hilt of the dagger in her breast, then drew back, then touched again. Around us, voices cried for surgeons, but no surgeon could physick her back to life. She was dead, yet still suffering.

'Benvolio,' she said, and her voice was weak and small and lost. 'Benvolio, my dress, my dress is stained—'

I took her hand in mine and knelt beside her. 'Hush now; it will be cleaned. 'Tis not so bad as that.' I put gentle fingers on her cheek. She wept, though I am not sure she knew of it. It made her look so much like a frightened child. 'Rest awhile now. The surgeon is coming.'

'That boy,' she said, and squeezed my hand tightly for a moment. 'Wretched Capulet boy, did you see him? I only meant to frighten him away; I never thought he'd strike me. He was pretty. So pretty. I thought – Do you hate me so much, Benvolio?'

'No,' I said softly. My hate was dying with her. 'You are my sister, Veronica.'

'I should not have betrayed your friend,' she whispered, and more tears rolled from the far corners of her eyes, wetting the hair above her ears and the fabric of her headdress, with all its precious pearls. 'I did it for no reason, except to show I could, that I had power over another . . . It was cruel of me . . .'

'Hush. Mercutio is gone. He aches no longer.'

'Then I will meet him soon, and he will accuse me in the eyes of God,' she said, and gripped my hand so fiercely I thought bones would break. 'It feels like a curse on us, don't you think? For what I did. I should have been better, Ben, I should have – Please say you love me, for pity's sake, say—'

'I love you,' I said, but it was too late; her last breath fled, and her face relaxed its tension. Her eyes looked towards heaven, but not with anticipation – rather with dread. Young as she'd been, my sister well knew her sins, and how grievous they were.

Friar Lawrence came with the surgeons, and my sister received last rites dead on the bloody cobbles, twenty steps from the door of the church where her withered old bridegroom waited in vain for his vows and his bridal rights. I could hear his querulous voice raised in protest, demanding satisfaction of my uncle. And my uncle, ever practical, demanding return of the dowry.

I hated Capulets and Montagues alike in that weary moment, and all I could think of was the fevered peace I'd felt in Rosaline's arms, and on her lips.

But if that had been foolish yesterday, today it was impossible.

Capulet had argued that our bravos had started the brawl, and Montague argued otherwise, and my uncle presented his dead niece and grieving sister to the distempered prince of Verona, who levied a harsh fine on both and hanged the Capulet boy who'd delivered the death blow. It was done swiftly before dark in the piazza, so that justice could be seen to be done. I took no pleasure in the death of another child, but my grandmother had bestirred herself for the occasion, and she smiled an awful smile as she watched, and clapped her palsied hands in delight as he danced on the rope. I found myself standing next to my uncle as the old crone was loaded into her litter.

'Malicious old woman,' my uncle said. He sounded as disgusted and weary as I felt, and he leant heavily on the silver-headed cane he carried against the debility of his gout. 'This business is done. Come. We have much to discuss.'

'My mother—'

'Women grieve,' he said, and fixed me with a sharp, dark gaze. 'It is women's work. Men must be about men's business, and now that Romeo has failed us, you must be my strong right hand. You did well, giving up the boy to the prince's justice; a less canny man would have simply killed him, but you showed sense, and cast the blame squarely on Capulet. You're no hot-headed fool, like my son.' He clapped a heavy hand on my shoulder. 'Come, boy. There are plans to be made to take advantage of Capulet disarray. They have bloodied their noses finely today, and their coffers grow empty; Juliet's marriage to Paris in two days will seal their fortunes more securely, but first they must lay on the feast tomorrow for the betrothal. We will need to speak to the greengrocers, the butchers, the spice merchants – any who owe us favours must be made to understand that Capulet should be offered the worst of their wares, at the best of prices.' He smiled and squeezed my shoulder. 'Foolish games, foolish games, but it is the life we lead. Walk with me.'

I would have done, but just then, a fat old woman came huffing through the crowd – a nurse, and one I recognised.

Behind her trailed a tall, mournful beanpole servant. I watched the woman's progress, and realised with a shock, as her gaze fixed upon me, that she meant to upbraid me in the presence of my uncle.

'A moment,' I said quickly, and sketched a quick bow for him. 'I will follow directly.'

He saw the nurse, and his brows drew together, then rose upward. 'Who comes there?'

A lie would be the only course open. 'She is of the Ordelaffi house. A moment, sir?'

'Good Mercutio is not yet decently buried,' he said, and nodded. 'See to her needs, then. I move slowly enough; you may catch up as you wish.'

He limped off, surrounded by his attendants; my mother, Lady Montague, and all of the women were clustered around the cart that now held my sister's body, covered by a blue Montague cloak.

The nurse blinked at all the confusion, as if she'd paid attention to none of it until now. 'Lord preserve, I remember when weddings were joyous things, without all this bloodshed . . . Ah, me, the poor bride, ruined, all ruined, naught to do for it now but pray God forgive the sinners and . . .'

'Madam,' I said, a little too sharply. 'Why do you seek me?' She was Juliet's nurse, and thus no friend of mine. I did not know the girl, nor did I wish to; if she was making some plea and claiming family, I'd walk away quickly. Let Romeo explain this tangle to his father, if he could. I wanted no part in it.

'Oh, young sir, my, how handsome you are. Such eyes, foreign eyes, they seem. Women cast themselves to sea for such handsome—'

'*Madam.*'

She fluttered her fan and cast me a sharp look, much upon her dignity, and leant forward to whisper, 'I have a note for you, a sweetly folded thing that I urge you to keep about your person and your privacy, lest shame fall upon—'

'Oh, give it here.' I sighed, and snatched the small triangle of paper from her fingers. It was sealed with blank wax, and when I broke it and unfolded the shape, I found that there were no names either.

But still, I knew who had written it, and a slow whispering roar filled my ears as I read.

Confession is good for the souls of those who suffer.

That was all. I swallowed hard, one fingertip scraping over the flowing, confident shapes of letters . . . This came from Rosaline's hand, and the scent of her drifted up from the paper, or perhaps that was only my senses and memory playing tricks.

I folded it and hid it away, and bowed to the much-affronted nurse, who fanned herself most rigorously. 'I am grateful,' I told her. 'Do not linger on my account, madam; this place is made unhealthy for those with your . . . political advantages.'

'If you mean Capulets, sir, I will put one of them against six of your Montague buffoons, and take the change in hand,' she shot back, but she had sense enough to keep it a whispered remonstrance. 'Come, Peter, let us home. There is much to do before tomorrow's feast!'

She sailed away, a short and wide ship with much canvas laid on, with poor Peter as a rudder. I reached inside my doublet and felt for the crisp edges of the paper again, and the smooth wax. *Confession.*

Rosaline meant me to see Friar Lawrence, and quickly, or she'd not have risked sending Juliet's nurse with the message. The old woman gossiped far too much for anyone's safety. Rosaline's own servants – as I'd already suspected – were loyal to her aunt, and not to her; she could trust no one else even as far as Juliet's nurse.

If you go, something in me whispered – the rational piece of me that had always guided me towards caution where my cousin rushed headlong – *if you go, you risk your life. Worse, your family's honour.*

I had risked my family's honour nightly for years, crawling the rooftops of Verona. My grandmother had tacitly approved that, because it had pleased her to see me humiliate our enemies. But this was another kind of risk altogether – the risk of alliance with our greatest enemies.

Alliance with the ones who had just killed my sister.

If you go, that part of me continued, *then take your dagger and put it in her breast, for revenge. Your grandmother would smile for that, even if you stretched a rope like that Capulet boy.* And that also was true . . . she would approve of Rosaline's death, and clap, and laugh.

The image sickened me.

I cast a quick look around. My uncle was gone already, limping homeward; his sycophants and favourites were clustered around, and he'd not miss me for some time. He'd assigned me guards, though, four of them, who bracketed me like walking statues as I headed for the cathedral itself. I thought of ordering them away, but my mother's words had proved true: our enemies had no respect for sacred spaces, and now I was virtually alone. If the Capulets had the stomach for a second course, they would find easier meat but a tougher sauce; I was in no mood to dance with them again.

Inside, the hushed vast cathedral held a sense of eternity; overhead, the ceiling vaulted high and clean, and the ever-present grey stone of Verona took the form of rows of huge columns marching into the dimness, while at the end, the curve of the main chapel exploded in colour and light. A child was singing, coached by a patient priest, and his high, sweet voice rang like an angel's from the shining marble floor. The cathedral was filled with penitents on their knees, and I did not know where to look for Rosaline.

The sound of my guards' tread behind me echoed martial and warlike in these holy silences, and I turned to the one at my left – Paolo, a trusted aide of my uncle's, and a fierce mercenary fighter. 'I will go alone,' I said. 'Wait here.'

'Wait?' He peered at me with frank puzzlement. 'We go where you go, young sir. Your uncle takes no chances now with his sole remaining heir.'

'Stay here,' I said. 'I'll not tell you again. My uncle will not be head of the house forever. Think well on whom you would please for your future employment.'

Paolo's eyebrows climbed, and he stared at me with fierce dark eyes a moment before he bowed a little, mockingly. 'As you wish, sir.'

'You can use the time to pray,' I said. 'Surely you all have much to repent.'

'Surely,' he agreed, and stuck his thumbs in his belt. 'But we don't have all year, sir, unless you plan to run off to holy orders.'

'Not likely,' I said. 'I've much to confess, too.'

He laughed, a little too loudly for this place, and waved

his fellows off as I walked on into the church. I was doing exactly what my mother had cautioned against; I had made myself an easy assassin's target, and yet I had no sense of danger here. The cathedral felt cool, calm, and sweetly peaceful. I paused before the beautiful statue of the Madonna, and for a moment, the awful truth crashed upon me, and I staggered and fell to my knees.

Veronica was dead, so pitifully and violently dead, and for nothing. Her killer had died weeping, for nothing.

A plague on both your houses, Mercutio had cried, and he had been right.

I bent my head and prayed, most earnestly, for the soul of my slain sister. I had not loved her as much as a brother should, and she had not been the sister I would have wished, but she had not deserved to die in terror, killed at the hands of a boy barely out of his child's smock. I prayed for it to *stop.*

As if God had answered, a dark-cloaked figure settled next to me on the marble, made the sign of the cross, and bent its hooded head. I recognised the scent of her, warm wax and flowers, and I breathed it in like a drowning man's last gasp of air. I started to turn, but her hand grasped my clasped ones. 'No,' Rosaline whispered. 'For the love of God, stay as you are. We will be seen.'

As quick as that, her touch withdrew. Where her fingers had rested, mine felt seared and aching. 'My sister is dead,' I said. I don't know why; she would have known, of course. But I felt it needed saying. 'I could not stop it.'

'I know.' Her voice was gentle, warm, and sad, all the comfort that I had craved from my own family but would not ever find. 'Benvolio, I am sorry. My young cousin is dead also, justly, for her murder. Tybalt was his idol, and he the willing worshiper. Children killing children, for love of nothing but empty hate.'

I heard the anguish in her, and felt its twin in myself. Why was it only the two of us who seemed to see the uselessness? But I cleared my throat of its sudden tightness, and whispered, 'Why did you send for me?'

The dark hood turned just a fraction towards me, enough that I saw the sliver of a pale cheek, a fine dark eye. 'To tell you that there is something unnatural in this,' she said.

'Hatred is the most natural of things to men.'

'No,' she said. 'Not hatred. There is a terrible thing at work here, and I believe it is hate disguised as love. Juliet is a quiet, biddable child; she is thoughtful and has always done as her parents wished. She made no complaints about the marriage to Paris when her father first approached him months ago; she seemed pleased at her good fortune, to be wedding a fine man such as he.'

'Yet she fell in love with Romeo.'

'It is *not* love,' Rosaline replied, and something dark in her voice struck a chord in me that shivered through my chest. 'She scarce knows your cousin, yet she threw away her birthright, her *life,* for him. She is to marry Paris on Thursday, you know; she begins her married life in terrible sin, or worse – she will flee to join Romeo and throw our family into chaos. There is nothing good to come from this. It is all a ruin.'

I could not but agree; I wanted to think this admirable and fine, this passion of my cousin's, but in truth it had seemed to distress him as much as pleasure him.

'It is something else,' Rosaline said. 'If it did not sound

like a madwoman's rant, I would say that there is some dark sorcery in this.'

It seemed to me as if, in that moment, all sounds stopped in the cathedral, even the soaring song of the child; I heard nothing but the sudden pulse of my heartbeat, loud as a drum in my ears. Mercutio had said as much, in his dying deliriums . . . even the witch had told me he'd sought from her a curse. *Love is the curse, Ben, love is the curse. Do you understand?* He had sought some sign of comprehension in me, but I had not understood him, though I'd pretended.

'Mercutio,' I said. I blurted it out in surprise, and sat back on my heels; Rosaline drew in a startled breath, and made a quick hushing motion with one hand. I assumed a pious position again, fingers folded together. 'Mercutio tried to warn us. "A plague on both your houses",' he said.'

'Capulet and Montague alike,' she said.

It was time to make the confession; it could no longer hurt my sister, who had gone to other judgment. 'You know that he thought what you said caused Tomasso's death.'

'I know, but have always been innocent of that. I knew, of course. But I said nothing.' Her voice dropped even lower, and I had to lean closer, into her intimate perfume, to hear the rest. 'It was your sister. I did not want you to know she had done it from sheer malice. I wanted you to think better of her.'

'I knew already,' I said. 'She told me. And she told me she had put about that you had done it.' I swallowed, choking down my discomfort.

Rosaline shook her head a little, though whether it was denial or sadness I could not tell. 'She was a child,' she said. 'With a child's thoughtless cruelty.'

Veronica had been many things, but thoughtless was not one of them. Still, I saw no reason to confess it. 'How does this help us?'

She thought a moment, and whispered back, 'If someone laid a curse upon the guilty party, but *thought* the guilty party was a Capulet . . . and a Montague was the real villain . . .'

'Then the curse would fall on both houses,' I said. 'Ah, God, Mercutio . . .' He had tried to warn me. With his last breath, he had seen his wrongs, and tried to confess, and I had misunderstood. 'But to make a curse, you need more than malice; you need—'

'You need a witch,' she whispered back, 'and Juliet's nurse babbled today that one makes potions here in Verona, and charms. A young, comely witch, recently come to town. We must seek her out, Benvolio. We must be sure this curse is lifted.'

'I know who she is,' I said. I crossed myself, and rose to my feet. 'If there is a curse, I will see it finished. I promise you that.'

Her hand flashed out to wrap around my calf, and I froze, short of breath, swaying on my feet. Those were idolatrous feelings to have here, under the eyes of the Holy Mother. 'Careful,' she whispered, and let go. 'Be most careful, my Prince of Shadows.'

'And you,' I said, and backed away.

In turning, I narrowly missed a knife aimed for my back. I assume it was a Capulet knife, though the man wielding it had on simple clothes; the knife itself was sharp, double edged, and was of finer stuff than the attacker. He stumbled, off balance and surprised as I dodged away, and fury took me over; I kicked a foot into the bend of his knees and shoved him facedown to the marble floor as the failed dagger skittered from his hand; I knelt on his back and retrieved it, and put it to the base of his skull, preparing to drive it home . . .

. . . and a strong, feminine hand fell upon mine. 'No,' Rosaline said. 'Not here. Not now, I beg you. Not in this place.'

'He was not so delicate of stomach!'

'It is your soul I fear for, not his,' she said, and then she was gone, moving quickly away into the shadows of the Mazzini chapel. The sudden violence had caught the attention of my guards, who shoved the faithful – some of whom had become gawkers – aside to reach me.

I hesitated a long moment, then stood up. I still felt the need to hurt him, badly, but I only flipped the dagger and offered it hilt-first to Paolo, who took it and shoved it in his belt. 'A gift,' I said, and managed a false smile. 'The Capulets send us presents.'

'Aye, they are generous indeed,' he said, and hauled the suddenly chastened assassin to his feet. He was an older man, withered and shaking. Paolo shook him like a terrier with a rat. 'What to do with this one, then?'

'Let him go,' I said.

'Let him go?'

I held Paolo's stare, and he finally grinned, shrugged, and opened his hand. The man stumbled away, clinging to the columns for support, and escaping out into the dusty, dying sunlight.

'I don't know if you're brave or stupid, young sir,' Paolo said, 'but I think I like you.'

'There's no profit in killing a poor farmer underpaid for the privilege of murdering me,' I said. 'Better to set my sights higher.'

His grin widened and became Luciferian, and he clapped a hand on the back of his fellow bravo. 'I'm your man, sir,' he said, and the others echoed him with a gusto ill matched to the cathedral's dusky silence. The priest preparing the altar for the mass turned to give us a disapproving frown, and I quickly led my men out into the falling Veronese twilight.

Locating the witch proved to be no trouble; I had scarce noticed my path carrying Mercutio's dying weight, but Paolo fetched a torch as the stone-faced alleys drowned in shadows, and with that, I was able to track the vivid dark stains that Mercutio had left behind.

The blood led us straight to her door.

It looked the same as any other in the narrow street – made of good stout wood, heavily braced with crude iron. Paolo rained blows upon it, and I did not expect it to open . . . but it did, revealing not the witch at all, but – oh, strange irony – Friar Lawrence.

He seemed as surprised as I, and his fat cheeks pinked as he backed away. 'Young Master Benvolio,' he said, and tucked his hands into his sleeves in an effort to look saintly. 'I thought you would be with your sad family this night.'

'My family can wait,' I said, and shoved past him into the narrow confines. Yes, there was the bed, stripped now of its bloody mattress; there were the dried herbs hanging from lengths of cloth, dangling everywhere and filling the room with a rich, dusty smell. Even so, death was here. Mercutio's pallid ghost haunted the shadows. 'Where is she?'

'Where is who?'

'The witch,' I said, and drew my dagger. I did not menace him, I only held it at my side, but he must have caught the look on my face, well limned by the single burning candle. 'I would have her.'

'Witch, you say? Why, sir, she's no witch, only a woman wise in herbs and medicines, fresh come from the country to see her cousin decently mourned . . .'

I turned the dagger so the edge caught the light in a silvery line; his gaze darted to it nervously, then back. 'Think well on your silence, Friar. There has been too much death today. I would not add more.'

He licked his lips and edged to the door, but Paolo leant in, blocking the way with insolent ease. 'You dare not threaten me, boy.'

'Where is she?'

'"Vengeance is mine, sayeth the Lord . . . "'

'Men do the business of the Lord. Where is she?' I strode forward and took hold of his robe, pulling him towards me. I did not raise the dagger; there was still some chance, however small, that my immortal soul was not completely damned. 'Talk, Friar, or I'll loose your tongue a harder way.'

'Here,' said a voice, and I looked back to see the girl pushing her way out of a small, hidden alcove behind a heap of hanging clothes. 'Here, sir, please, don't hurt him.'

She was smaller than I remembered, and braver; she lifted her pointed chin to hold my gaze with bold resolve. She did not look the part of a witch, I thought, but rather like a saint, ready for her martyrdom.

I let go of the friar, but kept the knife at ready. Witches were unpredictable creatures; if she wished to have me dead, surely she could manage it in an instant, and then escape in a puff of smoke – or so it was said. I did not think she looked quite so fierce.

She raised her empty hands and settled herself on a low stool, then folded her hands in her lap. She looked hardly older than Rosaline, and a good deal more delicately built, as if a stern wind might shatter bones. Still, she'd been strong enough to lift Mercutio's dying weight, and treat his wounds.

There was a focused, intent look upon her face that seemed almost like peace. 'I expected you to return,' she said. 'I thought you knew already.'

'Eventful days,' I said. 'My friend killed, my cousin exiled, my sister murdered in the streets today before she was to wed. I had not spared a thought for you until now. Until I was reminded that "love is the curse."'

She flinched, and her hands tightened together in her lap, but she did not look away. She raised her chin just a little more in defiance. 'It can be, when those around you deem it so,' she said. 'Mercutio saw that as clearly as day. Some loves bring nothing but pain; it is not the love that's at fault, but us. He knew that. He hated you all for it, all of you who stood by, yet he did not mean to curse you. Only the guilty.'

I found I was restlessly turning the dagger in my fingers, and sheathed it, not out of any impulse to mercy but to prevent myself from striking at her. 'Tell me the tale,' I said. There was no other seat in the hovel, save the unmattressed bed with its rope straps, but I perched myself on the frame. She gazed at me, then at Friar Lawrence, and bent her head, finally.

'The friar had no part in it,' she said. 'He came tonight for herbs and tinctures, nothing that might be a sin. May he not depart?'

'No,' I said, when the friar seemed tempted. 'I will need his ears on this. Now, confess, witch. Tell me of this plot between you and Mercutio.'

She licked her lips and began in a soft voice, so soft I strained to hear it. 'My cousin Tomasso's death undid him,' she said. 'He always believed . . . believed that somehow they would be safe together. When it happened, when Tomasso was so foully murdered before his eyes . . . his faith was broken, sir, and rightfully so. He *begged*. He begged his father to spare him, but the rope was thrown up anyway. How should he not feel hate?'

'For his father, yes; for the men who hauled the rope, perhaps. But why *us*?'

'It is a sin to hate your father,' Friar Lawrence said, all unexpected. 'And Mercutio tried to please him, as a son should do. Perhaps he could not curse him.'

'More's the pity,' I shot back, 'since no one bears more of the guilt.' I fixed the girl with my stare. 'Continue.'

'He . . . he thought the Capulets were to blame, sir, and the Capulets were your sworn enemies; he wanted vengeance on them.'

'Then why did he cry "on both your houses"?'

'Because . . .' She hesitated, then shook her head. 'Because the curse we forged named the Capulets, but also said, 'the house who betrayed us.' If that was not the Capulets, but instead someone else . . .'

'Then the curse would fall upon us both,' I said, and squeezed shut my aching eyes. What a tangle of pain this was, so many evil mistakes made, and such mounting consequences. 'How do we remove the curse?'

'Remove it, sir?' She seemed startled at the question, and affrighted.

'Yes, remove it, before more deaths come from it, and for *nothing*!' I took her by the shoulders and forced her to meet my eyes; she flinched, and I remembered how unsettling some found the colour of them. Why, I was but one step removed from sorcery myself. 'How is it to be done?'

'If I tell you, I give you evidence you can use to damn me,' she said, quite sensibly. Friar Lawrence turned pale and crossed himself, no doubt realising that he was guilty indeed of consorting with a witch. 'You must swear I will not be punished for it. I only did as Mercutio asked.' I was well out of patience, and violence was a tool that fit well in my hand; she must have seen it on me, for she flinched and hurried on. 'It was a three-part spell, sir, and all three parts must be destroyed before it can be ended.'

'What three parts?'

'One faith, one mind, one flesh,' she said, and looked away. 'You saw the one in flesh. I drew it there myself.'

The inked inscription, the one I'd glimpsed on Mercutio's breast. 'The letters upon his skin.' She nodded. 'Is his death enough to shatter it?'

'Yes. That link is already broken.'

'And the others?'

'Sir, please—'

This time I drew my dagger. 'One time again I ask you: what of the others? Faith and mind?'

'For the mind, he wrote it down in his own hand,' she said, in a very small voice now. 'The other . . . the other was cast upon rosary beads. Tomasso's rosary, that Mercutio took from his grave.'

'How so?' Friar Lawrence was unexpectedly affronted by this. 'I buried the boy myself, with his rosary in his hands . . .' He paled even more, and crossed himself. 'Merciful God, Mercutio did not desecrate the grave!'

'He unburied Tomasso, and took the beads,' she said. 'And buried him again, with love. If that is desecration, good friar—'

'What else can it be called?' he demanded, but my mind was on Mercutio, digging by the light of the moon, and finding the corrupting body of his lover. No wonder his hatred had turned so poisonous as to infect those around him; I could not imagine the grief and rage that had driven him to it, nor to *this*.

'The rosary,' I said. 'Where is it? And where is the writing of the spell?'

She shook her head now. 'He did not tell me, sir; I only taught him. Where the things are now, I know not . . . but the rosary would have to be in Capulet hands; he meant it to be so.'

In Rosaline's hands, if he believed Veronica's story about Rosaline's betrayal . . . yet it was Juliet who seemed to have given herself over to obsession. Juliet who seemed bent on self-destruction.

'You know nothing more?'

'Nothing.'

'Swear it,' I said, and pointed the dagger an inch from her eye. She did not blink. 'Swear it now, upon your corrupted soul, witch.'

'My soul is not corrupted, but I swear it upon my soul, and upon God and his angels,' she said. 'I know nothing more than I've said. If I could stop this, I would; Mercutio is gone, and vengeance is hollow. His spilt blood told me that, at least.' She smiled a little, through sudden tears. 'He was not a bad man, you know.'

'He was a broken man, and he was my brother, and my friend. You need not tell me he was a good man, for I loved him,' I said. 'And you should never have sent him down this dark path. You imperiled his soul.'

'So does murder,' she replied. 'Yet no one shuns Lord Ordelaffi. Nor you, Benvolio, though you have blood on your hands.'

'Less than you would think,' I said, 'and never but in the thick of a fight that might have cost me my own life. I am not Mercutio's father.'

'You did not stop him,' she said, and met my eyes with level accusation. 'You stood by and watched as Tomasso died, and Mercutio's soul was torn in two.'

I had no answer for that, no clever riposte to give; I lowered the dagger, then sheathed it, and nodded to Paolo.

He drew his rapier. 'I'll kill the witch for you,' he said.

'No.' As he advanced, I backed to stand between them, and drew my own sword and beat his down. It was cramped quarters, between us; the ceiling was so low that my head cracked rafters when I moved unwisely. 'Let the Church deal with her, or the prince, but I'll not have her blood on our hands. Who knows what doom she might lay upon her killer?'

That set him back with a frown, and he nodded and backed from the room. I followed, ducking under the low doorway, and found Friar Lawrence behind me, tugging nervously at his habit. 'That was well-done, young sir, very well-done,' he said. 'I had no notion she was a witch, steeped in the black arts, I came only for her skilled medicaments . . . Yes, yes, most proper you leave punishment to the city's prince and the church elders . . . I can give no evidence of wrongdoing, you understand . . .'

'Why came you here?' I asked him. He seemed so uneasy it screamed of guilt, and fear, rank fear. 'What medicaments did you purchase?'

'Nothing, sir, nothing harmful at all, only a . . . a certain draught, a vial of distilled liquor—'

'Liquor you can purchase anywhere,' I said. 'What effect does this draught hold?'

'Benvolio, I would rather not say . . .' He shook his head, but when pressed by silence, and the closing around of my guards, he said, 'When you drink this liquor off, presently through your veins runs a cold and drowsy humour, and no pulse shall keep native progress . . . no warmth, no breath shall testify that you live. The roses of lips and cheeks fade to ashes, and the eyes' windows fall like death . . .'

'You mean it feigns death,' I said, speaking plainly, and he nodded, ducking his head well into the neck of his robe. 'For how long does this likeness of death last?'

'For two and forty hours,' he said. 'Most precise. And there are no bad effects; you awake as from a pleasant sleep . . .'

He sweated in his guilt, and struggled to think himself innocent, as villains and fools so often do. At least the witch admitted her fault.

'Whom did you mean this draught for, then?'

'Ah, sir, that I cannot confess, for it is a great secret.'

I was all out of patience now. 'Then give the bottle hence, and let it be crushed into the street, where it can do no one any harm!'

That is when he, overcome with pallor, said, 'But I have already given it to she who will drink it, young sir, and for the love of God and your cousin, you must not interfere; you must not—'

I knew, then, what had already happened. It was dark now, full night, and too late, all too late. It was plain from his words that Juliet Capulet's hand had received this dark poison — harmless though he claimed it — and that she would have already quaffed it. Why? To evade her enforced marriage to Count Paris, of course. She meant to feign death, and steal away to my cousin's arms.

It was not a fool's plan, after all. It was dangerous, yes, and it would earn Juliet and Romeo the enmity of both our families, but they might yet escape this curse together, and alive . . .

And yet, if Mercutio was right, if there was a curse at work, surely it would not be so simple as that.

'Too late to prevent the course,' he said, his face round and pale as the moon above the dark cloth. 'The potion is drunk. They will seek to rouse her for tomorrow's solemnities but find her cold in her bed, and will bear her with much lamentation to the family tomb. No sin or blame comes to Count Paris, nor to the Capulets, and the keen lovers will have their happiness despite their quarrelling families.'

'And what of Romeo? What if he hears of her death? I know my cousin's mind in this, and it will not go well, Friar—'

'I have sent to Mantua, sir, with word for Romeo describing the plan. He need only wait a short time to collect his lady from her sleep; I will help him spirit her away before she wakes in the tomb.' He gazed at me with a mournful resignation. 'Sir, I would rather not have done all this, but you know the lengths to which they have already gone; I feared – no, I *knew* – that young Juliet would end her own life, by any means necessary, to avoid Count Paris's bed. What would you have me do, shield my eyes from her intention to self-murder and the gravest of sins? Or help the course of true love—'

'If it is true love,' I said flatly. 'You heard the witch.'

'But, sir, if he thought Rosaline the author of his misery, why then would he send the curse to sting poor, innocent Juliet?'

It was a most excellent question, and it shook my convictions to their dry bones, but I had seen Romeo, seen the torment in him, the unwilling nature of his obsession. I did not believe that Juliet had found her happiness in this so-called love, either; it was a fever that would burn them to bones.

But the friar was not yet finished. He cleared his throat and said, 'It may well be impetuous of me to speak so, but fair Rosaline has also bid me carry notes and arrange assignations, my clever young man. I would well beware that if there is a curse of love, it may seek to fall upon *you*.'

I laughed aloud. I could not help it; the absurdity of it was too great. 'I am no Romeo, to be pushed into the arms of a chance-met girl . . .' But even as I said it, I thought that was exactly what I was. I had chanced into Rosaline's rooms that first evening, when the Prince of Shadows sought his quiet revenge upon Tybalt . . . but no. What there was between me and Rosaline was no curse, and further, it had grown slowly, carefully, and even now, I knew that however it would pain me, I could walk from her, and pretend as if my heart had not turned to ash.

Surely a curse would not *allow* me to walk away.

Friar Lawrence bowed just a little, having well made his point, and said, 'All will be well, young Montague. Only two days more will see the lovers reunited and safely away, and all's well that ends well.'

I felt a deep, terrible disquiet, but I bowed in return, taking a polite leave of him. I cared not about the witch; I knew she had told me all she could, and from the fright in her eyes, she would be off before the morning light. We would, I thought, be well rid of her.

But if there was a curse, as Mercutio had believed . . . if there was, then there were two things I would need to find to end it: a rosary, and something in which he'd written his curse, in secret.

I allowed myself to be speeded home for the gloomy evening, where my mother grieved quietly for her lost daughter, and my uncle for his lost dowry, and I . . . I only grieved, and paced, and slept fitfully until the morning.

All Verona woke to the lamentations of House Capulet, for Juliet was dead.

The morbid details of it came as no shock, and mirrored what Friar Lawrence had predicted . . . the girl had been safely to bed in the night, and in the dawn her fat old nurse had discovered her stiff and cold in her bed, with a bottle of poison close by her side. It was difficult to learn more, since

I was about my uncle's business of the day, which meant making funeral rites for my sister in a suddenly crowded church calendar, as well as dispensing payments to all the necessary guards, bravos, and allies who faithfully served us. Mercutio had been quickly buried, without so much ceremony as might have been honourable; his widow left Verona that morning, sent back to her family with a significant portion of the Ordelaffi fortune packed in her bags.

In the twilight of the evening, as the Capulets mimicked us and hastily changed their day's preparations from wedding to funeral, I walked with the family's procession down the narrow streets and out to where the Montague family tomb was kept, in the care of the monastery. As Veronica's brother, I held pride of place at the front of the bier, shouldering a portion of the weight of her silk-wrapped body; I felt suffocated beneath the traditional black robe and mask that all those who bore her on their shoulders wore, while the men around us carried torches to light our way. Even the prince of Verona was masked and garbed, carrying one side of her slight weight, by which he showed his sorrow for the needless waste of her life.

It was a political gesture, and one that my uncle would have celebrated, had the occasion not been as solemn.

The women of Montague were not allowed to follow, not even at a distance; they stayed within the walls of the palazzo, and grieved in privacy. That, I thought, was a good thing, as well as custom, as we were wary of Capulet anger still.

We settled my sister to rest upon her stone bed within the tomb. In a month or two, once the corruption of her

body had finished, servants would enter and inter her
bones beneath the carved stone lid of her sepulchre, where
she would rest until called to the resurrection. Though the
interior of the tomb was decorated with fine paintings, I
tried to notice little of it; the oppressive sense of death here
seemed suffocating, for all its gold leaf and gentle angels.
Veronica had been wrapped close in grave windings of the
finest silk, leaving only the square of her eyes, nose, and
mouth exposed, and the flesh seen there was as pale as the
grave clothes.

'We all go to our God stripped of our vanities,' said the
prince, standing at my shoulder and looking at Veronica
with me. 'Come, Benvolio; she is in the hands of angels now.'

She seemed very small to me. Death had robbed her of
the vigour and energy with which she had attacked her
future, and however malicious that energy had been, I still
missed its fire. There had been little enough love between
us, but blood knows blood, even so.

And hers was now, forever, cold.

I crossed myself and left the tomb. Outside, I took in a
deep, convulsive breath of the cooling night air, and stripped
away the domino mask as if it burnt me. The smell of the
tomb – old, dusty death – clung to me in the folds of the
robe, and I took it off as well, though custom said I should
wear it hence. I began to hand it absently off to Balthasar,
only to remember that I'd sent him to Mantua, with Romeo.
I wondered whether anyone had told Romeo of the melee,
and Veronica's death. I wondered whether he would even
care, so fixed was he on his love of Juliet.

The prince clapped me on the back. 'That was well-done,
and a credit to your sister's memory,' he said. 'She died

innocent, and God will welcome her soul into paradise.' He moved off quickly, to glad-hand my uncle and other upright, rich town leaders. Capulet was, of course, not among them.

Lord Ordelaffi was.

I made my way to his side. He looked older than I remembered, and more tired, in this unguarded moment; he forced a smile and offered a firm handshake to me. 'Benvolio,' he said. 'My sorrow for your sister.'

'And mine, for your son,' I said. His eyes slid away as he nodded. 'I regret I did not know of his burial before it was done, or I would have gladly borne him to his rest.'

'You had grief enough, with Romeo's exile and your sister's untimely end,' he said, which sounded well enough, but there was falseness behind it. He had not wished to see Mercutio's friends, nor to be reminded of the love that we had borne him. 'It is in God's hands now.'

'I know it is not an auspicious time, sir, but I left with Mercutio a few things that I would like to retrieve,' I said. 'May I come and find them?'

'What, tonight?' he asked, and frowned. 'I suppose there is no reason to wait. I have already given over some of his things to the poor, and to the Church. If what you seek is among them, you must deal with the monsignor.'

I thanked him and drifted to my uncle's side to tell him that I would accompany Lord Ordelaffi home, and thence be escorted by his men to the palazzo; he nodded, much distracted by the hot, whispered argument that was again being offered by Veronica's aged bridegroom over the return of the proffered dowry. Five thousand florins was at stake. My uncle would not care what I did.

The Ordelaffi palace was smaller than the Montague,

but built along similar lines – what windows existed towards the street were high above, and blocked with stout shutters. They were more defensive than decorative; not so long ago, the great houses of Verona had repelled one another's assaults with arrows, spears, and boiling oil. Today we were more gracious, but no less guarded.

The difference truly came inside the Ordelaffi palace. I had been here but rarely, and always with Mercutio. The last time had been more than two years before, and I was surprised to note the barren walls where rich tapestries had once been draped to keep out the night's chills. Portraits still adorned them, but the gold-illuminated icons I remembered were gone, as were the richer candlesticks and plate.

It seemed smaller, and poorer, than ever.

I followed Lord Ordelaffi down a bare hallway to a room set well off from its fellows; it was locked, and he fetched the key from a servant to open it to my gaze.

Mercutio's room had changed, too. It was stripped of its furnishings – gone to the poor, or to the Church, or (more likely) to be sold to cover the cost of his widow's departure. A sad heap of his things lay on a threadbare carpet. My eyes darted to the niche where he had stored away the things I stole on my night-time adventures as the Prince of Shadows. It was still shut tight.

Lord Ordelaffi shut the door behind him, sealing the two of us within. I turned slowly to look at him, and saw a dark glint in his sullen face. 'You knew of his crimes,' he said. 'His dalliances. You lied for him, Benvolio, and you are as guilty as anyone in sealing his fate. You and that cursed thief friend of his, his *Prince of Shadows*,' Ordelaffi's voice was rich with disgust. 'My son consorted with thieves, as well as carried on his . . . his sinful relations with that apostate. Do not try to tell me you were ignorant of all of it. I found the gold, hidden away in a trunk, that my son kept for that criminal!'

That had not been my gold, but Mercutio's; I said nothing in response, preferring to wait. Lord Ordelaffi's eyes were small and reddened with emotion – grief or anger, I could not tell.

'You knew him well,' he said. 'Why did he drive me to such extremes? I beat the boy, as I should have, to drive the folly out of him, but he only became more sullen, and more secretive in his transgressions. Why could he not be . . . be . . .' His hands grasped at a meaning he could not name.

I did it for him. 'Be the son you wished?'

'Yes.'

'Because he was as he was formed, as God made him,' I said. 'All your beating and pushing would not force him into another shape. He loved you, my lord, but you broke his heart with the murder of the one he loved. What he was, after . . . he was neither the boy you wanted, nor the man he wished to be. And much grief has come of his shattering.' I was angry, but in a cold, remote way; Ordelaffi was not the roaring giant he'd been when he'd ordered the execution of Mercutio's lover and set in motion all that followed. 'But rest assured on one account: your son was no thief.'

'He was friend and accomplice to one – a coward, a dog who led my son astray.'

I took a step towards him, holding his gaze, and for all his bluster, all the vicious beatings he had given his son, this time he retreated. 'Careful,' I said, low in my throat.

'Speak ill of your son and it will go just as ill for you.'

He swallowed, looked away, and opened the door behind his back to edge away. 'Take what you like,' he said. 'I care not. Whatever remains may go in the midden, where it belongs.'

The sound of the door closing was a thunderclap of futile rage. I took a deep breath and smelt fear – his, not mine. He would be haunted, I thought; all his days he would be stalked by the ghost of the son he could not love.

The things on the floor were a jumble – broken wooden toys from Mercutio's childhood that I set aside to be mended and given to others; a lute with three loose strings and a cracked neck; a dented goblet I well remembered in his hand. I stirred the pile, and found little else of value, but I bound it all up in the old carpet and made it a bundle to carry. I'd leave nothing for his father's angry hands.

The niche was locked, but I was an expert at such things, and it yielded in only a moment. It seemed empty, but when I felt into its depths, I touched leather, and pulled out a book – a thin volume written in Mercutio's own hand.

I sat down on the sill of the window, where I'd so often entered by climbing the wall, and lit a candle to read.

He had written of me and Romeo, and our adventures together as boys; he'd spoken also of the Prince of Shadows, but never even in the privacy of these pages identified him, only confessed his own involvement in selling on some of the stolen goods. I wondered whether his father had read this, but I doubted he had; he had not the stomach for truth in such searing measures.

Because also, Mercutio spoke of Tomasso. It was tender, and passionate, and equally it was tragic, because my friend had known always that there could be no happiness in his love, only disappointment and grief. Yet he had pursued it to the bitterest end, because it was love.

On the day of Tomasso's murder, he had written only one thing, in writing that seemed jagged and hard.

He died this day. All that is good in me died with him.

From that day forward, the entries were shorter, and there was no hint of happiness in them; on the contrary, as the candle burnt down and my eyes blurred with weariness, I met a Mercutio I hardly knew . . . a boy no longer, but a man forged into a weapon that cut on all sides, like a ball of sharp knives. Love had curdled to a black and furious hatred, and he did not much care where it struck.

I'faith, I almost hate the Montagues as much . . . knowing they saw his death, saw my humiliation, goes hard. Hearing of Capulet guilt makes me think had I not been such fast friends with Montague it would not have happened.

Reading it drew the breath from me, and I felt faint and ill, and for a moment I put down his book, unable to read more. He struck me hard, and from the grave, and I knew it was just.

I read the rest of it quickly, numbed to pain now, and found the entry where he recorded his visit to the witch. On the next leaf he had inscribed what seemed a poem, and well I remembered his half-mad quoting of it . . . and at the end, the simple, dry words etched in the strange colour:

CURSED BE THE CAPULETS.
CURSED BE THE HOUSE WHO BETRAYED US.

This, then, was the second part of what the witch had said we should find . . . the curse, written in his own hand . . . and I realised that the ink, rusted brown rather than black, smelt strange and yet familiar.

Blood.

I flinched back from it, feeling the menace in those sharp strokes of his pen, the slashes of the letters. Here was the doom he had, all unwitting, cast upon not just Capulet, but Montague as well. *A plague upon both your houses.* He had thought to curse Rosaline and all her kin, but instead it had reflected back upon Veronica and Montague.

And Romeo.

I closed the volume, blew out the candle, shouldered the bundle of broken dreams, and carried it all home, where I set a flame to his diary and watched his curse burn to ash. Two-thirds of it was done, then.

But nowhere in the sad collection that remained did I find the third piece . . . the rosary that he had taken from Tomasso's body.

I have given his things to the poor, and to the Church, his father had said.

The rosary would have gone to the Church.

The scribe assigned to Monsignor Pietro was young, and keen; upon forcing the lock on the study door within the monsignor's private residence, I found careful records of all that had been received from House Ordelaffi. It revealed much about the nature of Mercutio's father's penitence; the tapestries I had seen removed were listed, and much of the plate and silver had ledger entries. The records listed a trunk full of Mercutio's precious books he had acquired, and *assorted adornments and religious articles of the young man, now gone to God's keeping.*

But it did not say where such things were stored.

I had resurrected the Prince of Shadows tonight, dressed in dusty grey and black and masked against recognition; the monsignor slept upstairs, in his soft bed, warmed by a woman who slept at his side, against all churchly conventions. His servants drowsed not so comfortably, nor so sweetly attended, but sleep they did, and my job was made easier by it.

I broke the lock on his storehouse deep in the basement with an iron bar, and within found a treasure house . . . gold, silver, precious gems, and jewels of all descriptions. It was a thief's paradise, but I took nothing of it, though it clearly did little for the starving pious poor while languishing here. Another time, I might return and teach a rich man of God to love charity a little better.

I searched until I found a trunk emblazoned with the Ordelaffi symbol, and lifted the latch to find the remnants of Mercutio's life valuable enough to be sold to the Church for his father's indulgence.

It was a pitiful record. His silver comb was there, and a razor too fine to be of daily use; a collection of rings. His books, all valuable, even if venal in nature.

And a rosary.

I seized it, my heart racing, but my relief was short-lived; this was unmistakably the rosary given to Mercutio by his family at his confirmation; it bore the Ordelaffi seal, and was far too fine for a lowborn seminary student like Tomasso.

There was nothing else. Wherever Tomasso's rosary had

gone, it had not been left at Mercutio's house, nor given to the Church. Mercutio's widow, perhaps? No, having read the journal in Mercutio's own hand, I could not see that that unfortunate young girl would wish to keep any mementos of their brief joining.

Then where?

I looked around the glittering storehouse of earthly treasures, and felt a frustration that drove me to kick the wall hard enough to leave a bruise upon my foot. I had no trails left to follow.

I turned incautiously, heading for the door, and a tilting pile of silver plates wavered and crashed loudly to the floor. I sprinted now, because no servant would sleep through such a racket; I just made it out and into the shadows beneath the stairs as a candle's glow appeared, and hushed voices rose with suppressed excitement and fear. Two of the monsignor's servants appeared, bearing cudgels; one had a knife in his belt as well. They examined the door of the strong room and exclaimed when they found the lock shattered; one ran up to alert the household, and the other peered inside, looking for sign of the thief.

I kept to the shadows, hid my face, and stayed as still as flesh might stay. The dull grey of the cloak blended perfectly in the darkness with the stones, and unless they thrust the torch into the space, the illusion would hold. But it would be unhappy hours before it would be safe enough to move, never mind flee, and I knew my muscles would ache first, then cramp in red agony before it was done. I would survive it. I had survived worse, and longer.

But this time . . . this time, luck was not with me.

The servant who peered into the room was not as

dull-witted as he seemed. He backed away from the door, looked around the narrow space, and then thrust his light into the shadows where I hid. Instinct bade me to turn and fight, but I stayed silent, frozen, holding even my breath until the candle retreated. I dared let out a slow, trembling whisper then, but then the cold point of a sword pressed my chest, and a voice in my ear said, 'Hold, villain, or die.'

I was caught.

After all this time, the Prince of Shadows was caught.

I was bound at the hands, and the crowd of murmuring servants placed a rope around my neck that was meant to be a halter but felt uncomfortably like a noose, and I was led upstairs, then pushed down on my knees while the hastily roused monsignor donned robes and slippers to come see this intruder. They had not yet unmasked me when he finally arrived, red faced and furious.

'Call the watch,' he told a servant, who ran off with alacrity. I saw the monsignor's mistress peeping over the banister from upstairs, clearly eager to see the coming events. More eager than I, by far. I calculated my chances; they were not so bad as they appeared, because the servants had been inept at knots, and I had already worked my wrists looser within their bonds. Still, their stoutest man held the rope halter that had been fitted around my neck, and I would need to rise quickly from the ground to deal with him before he could tug me off balance and turn halter to noose, in truth.

The monsignor paced back and forth, staring at my masked face. 'Are you the thief known as the Prince of Shadows?' he demanded. I said nothing. 'Come, lout, speak, or have you no tongue? Has Veronese justice already stripped you of it?'

'Shall we unmask him, Monsignor?' the servant holding the rope asked.

'Yes, yes, of course,' he said, and gestured vaguely towards me as he paced. 'When the watch arrives we will denounce him and turn him to the prince's justice. This villain will hang by the morning! You dare, you cur, you dare to rob God?'

I had two choices, neither attractive . . . first, wait silently to be unmasked, or second, take action – however unpleasant – to ensure I would not be immediately recognised.

I chose the latter, and said, 'I robbed no one, sir. I carry no gold, nor silver, nor precious jewels. You, though . . . you have taken such things from the poor, and hidden them away for yourself in the name of Christ. Is that theft, or blasphemy?'

He interfered with his own servant's unmasking of me to stride forward and give me a blow with his closed fist. Priest or not, he had a powerful arm, and I rocked back on my heels and blinked away painful sparks. I tasted blood, dull on my tongue.

His servants, as expected, took this as a sign, and instead of ripping away my mask they closed in, fists flying as they screamed curses upon me for my insolence. I hunched in to try to ride the blows, but soon I was on my side, and the rope had been pulled tight. Air had become a frantic struggle, and I was all but senseless when I felt fingers tugging at the silk knotted around my face. It was wet with blood, and the knot had been pulled small; I heard them cursing as their fingers slipped from their grip, but finally, one of them managed to peel the cloth away and bunch it on my forehead.

I kept my lids shut. The blood would mask me, and my nose was already swelling; now I looked like a hundred Veronese youths, noble or peasant, save for the striking colour of my eyes.

The monsignor struck me again, a hard blow but an open-handed slap this time. 'What is your name?' he demanded. I lay limp and silent, and judging from his voice he turned away towards his men. 'Do you know him?'

'He looks a bit like one of the Montagues,' someone ventured, but another jeered it down.

'Nothing like him,' that one countered. 'Not with that nose. No, more like one of those Capulet soldiers.'

Another argued that I seemed the son of a barber, another still an apprentice carpenter. I stayed limp and let my mouth gape open to further disguise the shape of my face.

And thus affairs stood when the watch arrived. The monsignor confessed to them that they had apprehended a sneak thief, who might even be the Prince of Shadows; he presented them with the bloody mask to confirm it. The watch captain took hold of the halter rope, frowned down at my battered body, and rightly decided that I was no great immediate threat. He tried to pull me to my feet, but I kept myself slack, despite his kicks and curses, and finally he ordered one of his men to pick me up. The rope was taken off my neck, though my hands remained bound. Loose, but not loose enough.

'Tell the prince that I will be most pleased to attend his

execution and spit on his vile corpse,' said the monsignor, in the true spirit of Christ, and then we were on our way out of his residence, into the quiet night-drenched streets.

I bided my time. The soldier carrying me had tossed me over his shoulder, and as he marched on, I gently slid his dagger from its sheath at his hip, reversed it, and carefully sawed through the bonds holding my wrists. Even then, I did not stir – not until we neared the vast stretch of the Maffei palace. We were close to Lords' Square, and from there it was but a short walk to Prince Escalus's residence at the Palazzo del Podesta, where they would present me and, bloody or not, he would know my face in an instant.

I had lulled my man into false security; his hand was loose upon my back, and he had not felt my hands liberating his dagger. I shifted my weight off balance as he took a step, and he staggered, dropping me to my feet.

I landed running, and made speed across the courtyard and into the nearest alley. I knew it well, and knew also to jump in the dark for handholds near the junction of two walls; I swarmed up quickly, dagger held between my teeth, and pulled myself up to the roof tiles, where I quickly froze flat, listening to the shouts and alarms below. The watch ran past, then stopped a short distance away as they milled about in confusion. Sleepy householders cursed them and slapped closed shutters, but the soldiers began to hammer on doors, seeking me within the walls. 'Go up, you fools!' snapped their commander. 'He likes the roofs!'

There followed confusion, but one of the householders below professed to a ladder, and went to fetch it.

I needed to move, but I knew that if I chanced it, they'd spot me below; the clouds were thin, and moonlight fell hard. This roof was simple and exposed, and the slope of it too sharp for me to stay hidden as I climbed towards the peak. Once they'd caught sight of me, they'd not lose me again so easily.

And that was when an ill-dressed youth slouched in a cloak and an extravagant, though limp, hat appeared at the end of the alley and called out, in a rough and oddly high voice, 'Thief! A thief, running that way!' He pointed down the alley, even as the soldiers were settling the ladder against the roofline. I crawled forward, ready to push it off, but it wasn't needed; the soldiers took to the chase with great enthusiasm, pouring in the direction the boy pointed, though the last of them had presence of mind to grab the young man by the scruff of the neck and shake him hard.

'You'd best be telling the truth, boy!' The soldier cuffed him, shoved him backward, and ran to join his fellows in chase of a phantom.

I made quick use of the ladder – since it was there – and ran towards the boy, who was shaking off the blow and rubbing his chin. Moonlight fell on his face as his ill-fitting hat slipped off and unleashed a tangle of thick, dark hair . . .

And that was no boy at all.

Rosaline.

I did not spare a moment for thought, or for shock; I grasped her arm and propelled her at a run in the opposite direction from where the soldiers had gone. Beneath the cloth, her arm had a different feel from that of a young man – less of muscle, yet somehow still strong. Ahead was the Church of Saint Maria Antica, and I tugged her that direction. My heart was racing with more than the excitement of the chase, and I'd forgotten my bruises and hurts, though they still ached, unremarked.

I pulled her into the shadows and brushed off the ridiculous hat, which drifted down towards the cobbles. Against the rows of white tufa and reddish brick, she seemed taller now, and oddly at home in mannish dress, though her hair tumbled wild over her shoulders. She was breathing quickly, and her eyes caught and held the shimmer of the moon. So did her parted lips.

I was holding her too tight at the shoulders, I thought, and loosened my grip to something gentler. 'What are you doing?' My voice came out low and rough, and I thought the watch would hear the violent pounding of my heart, even as far afield as they'd wandered. 'Don't you know what you risk, stealing out so dressed?'

She plucked at the too-large linen shirt. 'I took them from the laundry,' she said. 'Faith, these hose feel very strange . . .'

What was strange, and dizzying, was seeing a woman's shape so plainly and audaciously displayed, even in the shadows. I struggled to keep my eyes fixed on her face. 'How come you here?'

'I followed you,' she said, with calm assurance. 'Well, to be more fair, I followed your captors when they dragged you from the priest's house. I thought you might go there.'

'You thought – How? Why?'

She smiled a little, but it seemed grim. 'Women are buried in their houses, but we talk; there's little else to do. I asked my maids to tell me gossip of the Ordelaffi, and the fount flowed now that Tybalt is gone and they no longer fear him so . . . I learnt Mercutio's father had already disposed of his son's possessions, and that some had been sent to the monsignor for the Church. I thought Mercutio might have left some clue as to the curse within some writings.'

'And you thought what? That you would try your hand at thieving it?'

'Do you think I would be a bad thief?'

'I think you would be a novice,' I said, 'and novices are caught and hanged every day. If they'd found you to be a girl, it would have gone far worse for you. Women may be buried in their homes, but there is a reason for it: to keep you safe—'

'Safe?' Rosaline raised her chin, and her lips set themselves in a firm, straight line, as did her brows. 'Safe? You know nothing about us, Benvolio Montague. We live our lives in terror, not in safety – terror of our fathers, who may beat or kill us with any reason or none at all . . . Terror of the men we will wed, having scarce set eyes upon them before that moment and yet expected to submit to all they ask . . . terror of other women whispering rumours that destroy us, with no defences possible. You have swords to defend your honour. We have *nothing*. Safety?' She pushed me back, and I stumbled on a loose brick. 'Give *me* a sword, and I will make my own safety.'

'You don't know how to use it,' I said, very reasonably, I thought. But she only glared.

'And if I were taught? Trained? How then?'

'Swords are expensive—'

'Give me a trade and I will earn my own!'

This night had taken on an unreal cast, one that made me think I was dreaming, and the dream had gone very, very wrong.

I heard distant voices ringing out, and stepped forward

again to drive her deeper to the shadows, then snatched up her discarded hat and slapped it down on her head. 'Put up your hair!' I whispered, and she did, twisting it together with quick economy and securing it thus. I stripped off my cloak – even plain as it was, it would be something the watch looked for – and left it discarded on the ground.

Then I drew her behind the church, into a darkened doorway that was little used, and kept barred from within. 'There was nothing at the priest's house we needed.'

'You're bleeding,' she said, and her hand touched my cheek. 'They beat you.'

'A painful disguise, but better than to be recognised.' I did not mean to do it – truly I did not – but somehow my hand touched hers, closed around it, and I lifted her fingers to my lips.

I felt her shiver all the way through.

'I will see you home,' I said. 'Surely they will remark on your absence soon.'

'They will not. All are in mourning for Juliet...' She paused, watching me, and frowned again. 'But Juliet is not dead, is she? I wondered. I saw Friar Lawrence, and he only half listened to my confession today; he is behind this plan, is he not? To sneak Juliet away?'

'If all works,' I said. 'But if there is a curse, and I think there is, then surely this too is doomed to fail. I know not how it can, but perhaps the witch gave the wrong potion, or the friar gave her too much, or she wakes too soon – a thousand things, and none of them we can prevent. But you must go home, Rosaline. With Juliet dead, to their thinking, you are their bargaining chip. They will not waste you on God, but spend you on Paris.' I touched her chin and raised it, very gently. 'You were calling for your own sword a moment ago. Why show fear now?'

'Because I have no sword, nor any weapon at all,' she said, and took in a slow, deep breath that moved parts of her that should have been bound tighter. I was so distracted with this notice that I almost failed to hear the rest, as her voice dropped still lower. 'And because I think I do not love Paris, but . . . another, and if Mercutio's curse has worked so deeply upon our two cousins, if they die, surely it falls upon me next. And upon you.'

I had not thought so far ahead, and I felt an icy shock at her words, as if she had plunged me into a fountain in winter . . . because she was right. Mercutio had cursed our *houses,* and not one person he held guilty. If the curse indeed had struck Romeo and Juliet, and forced them into this ill-considered love, then what would happen next?

Did it account for how I could not forget her, even if I applied myself . . . not her face, nor her voice, nor the way she had looked lit by candles the first night I saw her? That image would not leave me, and it – being honest – was the last thing I saw each night before sleep carried me off, and the first I thought of upon waking. Was it a curse? *If it is a curse, I die cursed, and happy,* I thought, and almost said so. Only the biting of my tongue kept me from it.

'Do nothing to draw attention,' I told her. 'Keep your cloak close about you, and your head down. If anyone calls to us, let me speak; you may pretend to be worse for your cups, if you like, but say nothing. Your voice gives you plain away.'

'I've heard youths with voices higher than mine!'

'Not with your height,' I said. 'Quiet. And keep you close.'

It frightened me, walking with her down the dark streets towards the Capulet palazzo . . . I had ever been with men abroad in the evening, and what few women ventured out were hardened veterans of the streets, well able to care for themselves. She was . . . different. And keenly my responsibility. 'How got you out?' I asked.

She lifted one graceful hand, and I pushed it quickly back into the shadow of her cloak. Those hands, too, would give her away. 'I waited until a group of tradesmen delivered supplies for the kitchen,' she said. 'It was near dark, and the men were milling about readying for Juliet's procession. No one paid me mind.'

'Getting back inside will be different,' I told her. 'You cannot climb that wall, and even if you could, you could not climb to your balcony.'

'I can,' she said. 'I am not weak!'

'Forgive me, but I do not think your needlework has well prepared you for—'

'I ride,' she shot back. 'To the hunt. I have helped spear a boar. My father—'

Such pleasures were normally reserved for men, and I was surprised to hear that the Capulets had allowed a girl so much, but then I remembered that her father was dead, like mine. Unlike me, she had known hers; he must have allowed her beyond what convention and propriety said was right. And she was right: she was no weakling, not if she had faced down a maddened boar bent on escape.

'Well, boar killer,' I said, 'then we will try.'

She was far stronger than I expected, for a housebound young woman; I wondered whether she still, in secret, practised the exercises her father would have made her take to fortify her arms and legs for the hunt, and the weapons she would have to bear. She could not, as I could, climb a wall with a running start, but when I climbed first and gave her the first handholds, she pulled herself up more competently than I expected.

'Careful,' I told her in a whisper, from the top of the Capulets' wall. 'There is—'

'I know,' she huffed back, a bit waspishly, and I smiled down at her and offered her a hand for the rest of the way. Once she was crouched beside me in the single ivy-covered spot of safety – and her balance was only a little unsteady, from effort – I braced myself, took her hands, and lowered her slowly down into the dark corner of the garden.

'Can you make your balcony?' I whispered down, and she looked up, face cool and calm in the moonlight, and nodded. I tried to think of some goodbye, something other than what I ached to say, and I settled for the lukewarm, 'Be most careful.' I think the tone of my voice betrayed me, even so.

'And you,' she said, and her own sounded soft, almost a caress. Then she smiled at me, a full and carefree urchin's grin, and made her way to her safety.

For my part, I waited a bit longer, watched her climb to her balcony and slip inside, and then eased down from the wall and ran back, quickly and quietly, to the monsignor's household. Why would they fear my return, when the city watch had carried me off to meet the prince's justice at the end of a short dangle?

I let myself in as before, made my way down to the still-broken stronghold, and this time I took away as much gold as I could comfortably carry.

Then I piled it in the doorway of the Church of Santa

Maria Antica, with a note scratched into the white stone beside it: *Alms for the poor.*

Then I went home, to an uneasy few hours of sleep.

I slept like the dead until I was roused by impatient servants; my uncle had business for me to do in town, and I received the instructions from him, only barely aware of what I had agreed to do. At least I was dressed and decently barbered, though the steadiest of hands could do nothing for my swelling nose and spectacular bruising, which occasioned much exclamation when I presented myself to my uncle's chambers.

'Well, this won't do,' my uncle said, frowning at my aching face. 'I can scarce recognise the boy myself. Very well, rest, Benvolio, and lay some poultice on those bruises; you'll do me no good bearing my messages out looking so ill used. A Montague is meant to win the fight, you know!'

'But I did,' I said, and bowed respectfully. He waited, head cocked, for more explanation, but I did not give it, and he finally let out a frustrated sigh.

I listened to the man's hasty lecture about how I should comport myself, to reflect honour upon Montague. I suppose he had thought that since Romeo had received these lectures as heir, I had been spared too many of them, but I'd endured hours of sweating, hellish torment in my grandmother's chambers listening to much of the same. I well knew what was expected of me, and in fact, the bruises upon my face were a testament to how much I valued the honour of House Montague, though he could not know it.

It had the fine benefit, though, of freeing me to my own devices for the day – and a portentous day it was. Friar Lawrence's account had claimed that if all went well, Juliet Capulet would wake today in her tomb, and my cousin Romeo would be there to joyfully greet her and see her swept away. A triumph of love and devotion.

Perhaps I was too much of a cynic, but I could not see it happening so. Mercutio's dire words in his journal haunted me, and so did the frantic desperation of the witch who'd crafted the curse on his behalf. If hate could move mountains, then the mountain was still moving, and we could only watch, helpless, as it collapsed upon us.

I had been all but ordered to keep within Montague's walls, but I had never cared for being penned up, and by the time the evening Angelus bell had rung I was moving through the streets. It seemed Verona continued untouched by the upheavals of the past week – all the deaths, the tragedy, the drama had passed by the common folk, whose lives were full of their own troubles. I bought a roasted leg of pork to eat as I walked, and made for Friar Lawrence's cell.

He arrived after the service had finished, out of breath but smiling for all that; he greeted me warmly, clucked over my wounds, and hummed a merry – though scandalous – tune as he ushered me within. 'All's well, all's very well,' he told me. 'Romeo will have received word in Mantua and hastened here, and even now he should have entered the tomb and gathered his love in his arms, to ensure her waking goes from rest to paradise itself.' He seemed so very pleased with himself, I thought. 'And then they will be safely off together.'

'To what?' I asked him. 'Two youths with no funds and no family?'

'Love will sustain them.'

'Hard coin would sustain them better,' I said. In my purse I had some of the monsignor's gold, rescued from his vaults. It was not right to keep it for myself, but a donation to the poor was a just and good use for it. 'You must have been plotting to meet them, Friar.'

'I will see them soon,' he said, and accepted the heavy gift with a smile. 'Your cousin will be most grateful, young master.'

I had no time to question him about the time, though; he poured himself a cup of ale and drank it thirstily, and pressed one upon me that I sipped without savour, though it was the best of the abbey's stock. 'Friar—' I was ready to broach my concerns of Mercutio's curse, but he held up a hand to stop me, one ear cocked towards the hallway.

'Hush, I have a visitor – Here, stay there, and silent!' He pushed me behind the only coverage in the room, a small screen, and I stood there clutching my mug of ale and felt foolish for coming.

Another voice, as hearty as Friar Lawrence's, called out, 'Holy Franciscan friar! Brother, ho!'

'Well, this same should be the voice of Friar John!' my friend boomed, and I heard the two men give fraternal embrace. 'Welcome from Mantua . . . What says Romeo? Or, if his mind be writ, give me his letter.'

I peered around the corner of the screen, and saw a monk as thin as Friar Lawrence was round; he was older, with wisps of white hair circling his tonsured crown. He had a beaming look on his face that clouded over as my friend spoke, and by the end of it, he was as penitent as a tardy schoolboy.

'I went to find a barefoot brother of our order to accompany me to Mantua,' he said. 'And I found him here in the city visiting the sick, but the searchers of the town, suspecting that we were both in a house of infectious pestilence, sealed up the doors and would not let us go forth. So, you see, my passage to Mantua has not yet begun.' He spread his hands in helpless apology.

I watched the hard truth dawn on my friar's face. 'Who bore my letter, then, to Romeo?'

Friar John searched quickly within his robes. 'I could not send it – here it is again.' He handed over the sealed message with an apologetic smile. 'Nor could I get a messenger to deliver it back, so fearful were they of infection.'

'Unhappy fortune,' Friar Lawrence said, and his distress almost crumpled the note in his hand. 'This letter was no simple greeting, but full of import, and neglecting it may do much damage . . . Friar John, find me an iron crowbar and bring it hence.'

'An . . . iron crowbar?' Friar John's mystified face would have been funny to see in any less dire situation.

'Yes, yes, go!'

'I will go and bring it.'

He left, much speeded by the obvious distress of Friar Lawrence, and I came out behind the screen and put the mug aside.

Friar Lawrence met my eyes with mute horror for a moment, and then said, 'I must to the monument alone, then – within three hours will fair Juliet wake. She will be angry that Romeo does not come to greet her, but I will write again to Mantua and keep her here, in my cell, until Romeo comes.'

No more sunny smiles, no more *all will be well* . . . he was afraid now; I could see it in the tight lines of his eyes and mouth, and the wretched washing motions of his hands.

'I will go with you,' I said.

He did not look so much relieved. His thoughts were far from me. 'Poor living corpse,' he said softly. 'Closed in a dead man's tomb.'

I prayed she would not wake to know it, but already I could sense the darkness of the day spinning darker still.

QUARTO

V

It was a cloudy night, with no kindly moon to light the way; out of respect for the friar, I had shouldered the weight of the crowbar and shovel he had demanded of his fellow. The lantern in his hands should have shed enough light for us, but the path was narrow, and the friar's robed bulk blocked out most of the glow.

Yet he was the one who grumbled. 'Saint Francis be my speed! How oft tonight have my old feet stumbled upon graves . . .' He froze suddenly. We were well close now to the graveyard, and to the grand structures of the tombs. 'Who's there?' I prayed it was not the watch; carrying tools of grave robbing was yet another hanging offence in Verona, and here was I, well equipped for a crime I did not intend to commit.

But instead, I heard a familiar voice out of the darkness. 'Here's one, a friend, and one that knows you well.' Balthasar! My servant approached, and I peered around the friar to see the calm set of his face. Friar Lawrence put down the lantern and threw his arms around the man.

'Bliss be upon you!' he cried, and kissed him on both cheeks out of sheer effusion . . . but then, as he pushed Balthasar away to arm's length, his gaze went past, and his face paled. 'Tell me, my good friend, what torch is yonder that vainly lends light to eyeless skulls? It burns in the Capulet monument.'

'It does, holy sir, and with it is my Master Romeo,' Balthasar said, and I closed my eyes for a moment in sheer relief. *All will be well.* Despite the lost letter, despite Mercutio's curse, Romeo had found a way to Juliet. The friar's optimism had been sound, after all.

But Friar Lawrence did not sound reassured. 'How long has he been there?'

'Fully half an hour, sir,' Balthasar said, and I understood that was too long a time.

'Go with me to the vault.' He was speaking to me, but Balthasar had still not glimpsed me behind the friar's bulk, and he stepped quickly back.

'I dare not, sir. Master Romeo thinks I am gone, and he menaced me with death if I stayed.'

'Stay then,' Friar Lawrence said, and pushed past him. 'Fear comes upon me. Oh, much I fear some ill unthrifty thing . . .'

Balthasar called my name in surprise as I came after, carrying the tools, but I had no mind for him in that moment, until he caught my arm and delayed me. 'Master, wait . . . As I slept under this tree, I had a dream – a dream that Romeo and another fought, and Romeo slew him . . .'

I thought he had dreamt of Tybalt, but before I could say so, I heard Friar Lawrence cry out, and none of that mattered any longer. I dropped both crowbar and shovel with a clatter and followed the bobbing light of the friar's lantern down.

I slowed when I saw the blood.

'What is this?' the friar asked, in a trembling voice. 'What is this blood that stains the entrance of this sepulchre?' He was right. The blood was fresh, still red and glistening, and two swords lay entangled together in the dirt, but only one was well smeared with crimson. That sword at least I knew: It was Romeo's. I bent to pick it up, but before I could, Friar Lawrence leant into the tomb, which held its own guttering flame, and cried out in such a voice that I started to my feet again. 'Romeo! O, pale – who else? What, Paris, too, and steeped in blood? Ah, what an unkind hour is guilty of this terrible chance . . .'

Count Paris and Romeo, both dead? But only Paris must have suffered a wound. I tried to force my way past the friar, but he blocked the doorway, and now he said, in a terrible hushed voice, 'The lady stirs.'

I froze, and heard her soft voice, much softened by sleep and the drug, say, 'Friendly friar, where is my lord? I remember where I should be, and there I am, but where is my Romeo?'

There was a noise from behind us, rocks rolling under approaching feet, and I clapped a hand on the friar's shoulder in warning.

'Lady, come you from that nest of death and contagion . . . A greater power than we hold has thwarted our intentions here. Please, come away . . .' He took a great gulp of breath when she did not answer. 'Lady, thy husband lies there dead, and Paris, too. Come to me. I'll get you to the sisterhood of holy nuns. Stay not to question, for soon the watch will patrol – come, come, good Juliet. I dare no longer stay—'

The sound of her movements stopped, and there was a terrible silence, a silence that seemed to me to be filled with unvoiced screams, and then the girl said, in a dreadful soft voice, 'Get thee hence. I will not go away.'

I heard a distant clatter. Men walking on the rocks, armed and armoured. I tugged hard on the friar's shoulder. 'We must go,' I hissed at him. This was a terrible thing, and our presence here would demand questions we could not answer. 'Come away, Friar, quickly! She'll be safe enough; the watch is coming!'

The girl's voice, through some eerie trick of the tomb, followed us as we escaped into the night, with Balthasar quick behind us. 'A cup, closed in my true love's hand? Poison has been his end . . . and no friendly drop to help me after? I will kiss your lips, and hope some poison hangs on them . . .' The frantic anguish in her voice twisted at me, slowed my steps, and I turned back to stop her, but Friar Lawrence's hand grabbed for mine.

'You cannot,' he begged me. 'A Montague, present at such a scene! Come; the watch will save her; they are moments away!'

From behind us, in that torch lit tomb, Juliet whispered, 'Your lips are warm,' and I shuddered as if a ghost had driven straight through me. Now I plainly heard the clatter and calls of the watch as they closed in. 'Noises sound. I must be brief – oh, happy dagger, this is your sheath. There rust, and let me die—'

Romeo's dagger. She hadn't waited for the poison on his lips to finish her.

I heard her cry out, just a little, as the dagger found its place.

Friar Lawrence let out a choked, desperate sound, and now it was my own turn to hold him away, push him forth.

Juliet Capulet was a suicide, and so was my cousin, and Count Paris murdered beside them. Mercutio's curse, made flesh and evil intent.

I felt my body flush suddenly with an unnatural heat, and sweat began to pour from my body, dampening my clothes. I felt as I had always when facing my grandmother – roasting in discomfort, aching to be elsewhere . . . no, not *elsewhere*.

I knew where I needed to be. My body bent that way, like a compass to true north. In the blink of my eyelids I saw Rosaline's face, and I felt the press of her lips on mine like a ghost's promise, and I wanted . . . no, I *needed* her. Fire was a pleasant warmth in a hearth, but it could also burn down a house, and that was what I felt: a fire raging beyond control, beyond sanity.

I breathed, and breathed, and breathed, and behind us I heard the watch coming to discover the dead.

Balthasar hesitated, and then said, 'I will delay them, sir,' and before I could think to stop him, he was scrambling back the way we'd come, and drawing away the pursuit.

'They cannot find you here, young Montague,' Friar Lawrence said. He pushed me on my way. 'I will explain all that occurred here. Go.'

I heard them catch the friar and drag him back, and as I achieved shelter behind another set of tombs – ironically, the graceful marble lines of the Montague death house, where lay my sister only newly arrived – here came a new line of torches and lanterns, and well-dressed nobles roused from their beds to see the horrors that awaited them. Prince Escalus, and with him Capulet and his wife. I was too far now to hear all but the loudest of cries, but Lady Capulet's screams could have sundered a heart of stone.

As I stole away, feeling bruised and broken inside, and drawn like metal to a magnet towards the emptied-out Capulet house, I passed my own uncle hurrying through the streets to join the lamentation. He looked wild-eyed and not himself, and I grasped the arm of his manservant, Gianni. 'Where is my aunt?' I asked. She was too strong-willed; she'd not have allowed herself to be left behind in such extremities.

'Oh, sir, great tragedy tonight – your aunt's breath stopped, and none could rouse her. She died of grief, sir, for your cousin's exile, and now they cry that Romeo is dead, and Juliet, and Count Paris, too; is it true?'

My aunt, dead in her bed. I let go of him, too numbed to feel much. 'It's true,' I said. 'Be careful of him. Too many have died already, and I fear the shock may undo him.'

Gianni nodded and hurried after, anxious for my uncle's health in such disasters.

And I stumbled on, moving in the other direction, through pre-dawn streets boiling with roused, confused citizens all telling dire tales of war, murder, treachery, and assassins.

A plague on both your houses, I heard Mercutio whisper, and give that mad laugh.

'You have your revenge,' I told his shade, which seemed to stalk me in the dark now. I felt dizzy, and there seemed no goodness in the air I gasped in. 'Let it be, my brother; please let it be . . .' But the ghost was not Mercutio, not him in whole; it was made of grief and fury and rage, and it knew no measure or mercy. And so it drove me straight on, through the chattering sleep-dazed crowds gathered by lantern light, through the Piazza delle Erbe and the fountain topped by the serene Madonna, into the streets past and towards the Capulet palace. There was a fell tension in the air, and I saw Capulet adherents fighting Montague on every corner, wildly shouting, 'Murder!' and 'Assassin!' without knowing anything of what had occurred.

Someone ran past me crying that the moon had turned to blood behind the clouds, and another screamed that Lord Ordelaffi had hanged himself from a tree in his orchard, and I stumbled on, anonymous in my grey clothes.

The Prince of Shadows. This was my realm, then, this confusion, for it seemed to me that the sun would never shine again on fair Verona.

The Capulet door was barred, but as I approached it a servant fled through the front, taking with her an apronful of precious silver. Chaos and disaster, and all the world gone to ruin . . .

Turn back, something screamed in me, but the heat inside urged me on, on, into the hall, past Capulet men and women who were too affrighted to challenge my purposeful steps. One man braver than the rest tried to bar my way, but I drew my sword, and he retreated. Juliet's door was open, and her nurse lay senseless on the carpet beside her curtained bed, one hand clutching her prayer beads.

Rosaline's door was shut and locked from within.

I banged my open hand upon it. I did not speak, because I knew she was there, as she would know I was without; I could feel her nearness beyond that barrier, pressed against it. I could almost feel the sweet whisper of her breath upon my face.

'No,' she said. Her voice sounded choked and desperate to my burning ears, and I pounded again, more urgently. 'No, Benvolio, for God's own love, no, you must go; we must be stronger than this; we are the last two of our houses in this generation; if we die—'

If we died, the curse would be satisfied. Perhaps. Or perhaps it would only spin on, seeking ever more distant relations to ruin. But did not all mankind narrow back to a common root, of Adam and Eve? Would Mercutio's curse carry away every living soul, in the end?

'I care not,' I said. My own voice sounded a stranger's to me. 'I care not for death, or doom, or curses; I care only for you, Rosaline, and I know you feel the same; I know—'

'The curse,' she said. I heard tears, and I also heard the key trembling in the lock, as if she had taken hold of it to turn. 'There must be a way to break its hold over us. You *must* know a way!'

She pulled out the key and threw it away; I heard the clatter of metal on stone as it slid over the floor. I put my eye to the keyhole and saw her there, leaning against the door. Only a small, pale portion of her face, and a lock of her hair, but it was enough to drive me to desperation. 'Please,' I said. 'Please open the door, Rosaline. You know you cannot keep me out for long. I can pick the lock. I can climb the wall. I can open the shutters.'

'You won't,' she said. It sounded weary now, and heartsick. 'You won't, because you are not such a man, Benvolio; you are an honourable man, and you will not do it. You need me to let you in, and it rips me in two that I deny you that mercy.'

'They are dead,' I said. 'Romeo and Juliet. Both dead. Count Paris, my aunt, Mercutio's father, all dead this night. Can we not find some comfort in all this?'

'Comfort in each other's bodies, heedless of consequence. And how will it end?' she asked me. 'With poison? Daggers? A rope for you and a cellar-dug grave for me when my uncle rages at my betrayal? There is no peace in it, Ben. Not until the curse is done. It must be broken. *We* must break it.'

'How?' I sank down to my haunches, resting against the solid bulk of the door, and my cheek pillowed against its hard surface as I gazed within at that tiny vision of her face. I felt hot, angry, desperate, and infinitely afraid – afraid of what I might do, equally afraid of not heeding my desires. 'I have no way to find the rosary—'

'What rosary?'

I realised that she had not heard the witch's confession – nor had I told her all of it. I had supposed she knew, since she had been at the priest's house, but she had been looking not for the rosary, but for Mercutio's diary – a diary I had already burnt.

She did not know.

'The curse,' I said. 'It is in three parts. One on Mercutio's flesh, now broken. One in his own hand, in blood, in his diary. And the third placed upon a rosary that he took from his dead lover's grave. I thought it was with the church, but I did not find it there.'

'A rosary,' she repeated, and there was something dull and strange in her voice. 'I had a gift of a rosary, sent here to me. It came to me in secret, the way Romeo once delivered his love notes. I thought it was only another of his gestures.'

'Where is it?' My heart leapt within me, but at the same time, a terrible dark urgency was rising. The curse knew its danger, and the unreasoning fever increased, demanding that I batter down the door, shatter all resistance, do whatever must be done to be with the one I loved . . . if love this was. 'Rosaline! Where is it?'

'I – I gave it away,' she whispered. 'Ah, God, God, I cannot bear this, Ben; my soul cries out for you and I die every minute we are apart . . .' Her voice grew softer, because she had moved. I peered through the keyhole and saw her crawling towards the key.

She would let me in. I had only to wait. Part of me rejoiced in unholy abandon, and part of me despaired, because I would never have the strength to stop. If Rosaline fell, I would fall with her, and we would both burn.

'Rosaline,' I said. Her hand was on it now, trembling with eagerness to pluck it from the stones. 'Rosaline, in God's holy name, *where is it?*'

Her head turned, and she rose on her knees with the key cradled in both hands as tenderly as a nun might cradle a cross. She closed her eyes and swayed, and my whole body took flame at the sight of her barely concealed beneath the linen shift she wore, with the candlelight gliding over her like a lover's hands . . .

'Juliet's nurse,' she said. 'I gave the thing to Juliet's nurse, who had broken her own rosary. I gave it as payment for taking you a message. I meant it a kindness, but what have I done?'

I remembered the old woman, collapsed in Juliet's room, with her hands clasping prayer beads. It was only a few steps away, only a little distance, but I could not move. My flesh was married to this door, and all my will could not force me from it.

She must have known that all my resistance was fled, for Rosaline's eyes opened, and she stared towards the door, towards the keyhole through which I peered.

'Forgive me,' she whispered, 'but I know of no other way to stop myself.'

She took in a single deep breath, and then screamed.

This was no maiden's cry, soft and tentative – it was a full-throated, awful sound that broke through all my drugged, cursed longing and shocked me, just for a moment, back to myself. Back to the Prince of Shadows, who knew that discovery in such circumstances meant death.

As she knew.

I heard the Capulet servants rousing below – even though they had fallen into disarray, her cry had rallied them, and they'd be up in only a few heartbeats to her defence. I would be cut to pieces on the stairs, or in the hall, and the curse would be well satisfied. Rosaline, knowing her cry had brought my death, would find a way to join me.

A plague upon both your houses.

'No,' I said, and forced myself up, back, away. Even then, I could hardly bear to tear my gaze from that keyhole, from the distant view of Rosaline clutching the key to our mutual destruction.

'No!'

Two steps back, then three, and then I broke and ran for Juliet's room.

Her nurse was not sleeping, but dead, eyes wide and staring, mouth agape – like my aunt, her breath had been stopped in the night. Her hand gripped the rosary with pale savagery, and I ripped it free and slammed the door on the startled faces of the arriving armed servants, then turned the key.

I had little time. They would break down the door if needed, and already they shouted for a heavy ram. The rosary felt cold in my hand, ice-cold, and slick as bone; menace clung to it like the miasma of death, and I felt Mercutio's shade again in the room, avid and furious.

'No,' I told him. '*Enough!*'

Juliet's fireplace still held dull red embers. I shoved in more wood, grabbed hold of a lantern, and crashed it into the mess; the oil spewed out, and the wood caught with an eager rustle that quickly became a roar.

The door shivered beneath the hit of something large – a bench, perhaps, carried by willing hands. It would not hold.

'Be at peace, my friend,' I said, and I thought of Mercutio as I had known him best in life – laughing, sharp, brilliant, and tender when no one watched. I thought of the glimpse I had once had of him in embrace with Tomasso, and the purity of the passion in his face. 'What a scourge is laid upon hate, and heaven means to kill our joys with love. Let it be finished.'

I kissed the rosary, and tried to fling it into the fire.

It clung to my hands.

No.

I gave a raw cry of fury, and shook them, but the rosary had wrapped tight and would not loose me. There was a filthy kind of life to it, as if it did not want to perish any more than I.

I heard Rosaline calling my name, chanting it in a wretched, broken voice. I heard the doom in it, the despair.

If I did not give in to this, it would kill her, too. It would take away the only reason I had to draw breath. I knew this as if Mercutio whispered it in my ear, and when I turned my head I saw his shade there, bending close. Bound to this rosary ripped from the hands of the dead.

He was just as I remembered him now. Fire and beauty, passion and wit, love and longing. All his fineness and all his awful tragedy bound up together.

'You are my friend,' I told him, and I felt the grief and heartbreak of it. 'I should have helped you. I should have saved him. You are right to hate me, but for the love of God, for the love of Tomasso, spare her your hate. She deserves none of it.'

His pale shade gazed at me, and just for a moment, I saw a smile curve his lips. He bent forward, and I felt his hand close over mine.

The rosary loosened its grip, but not enough, and I saw the regret and sorrow on his ghostly face. He could not stop it in death any more than he could in life.

There was only one thing I could do, and I did not pause to think. I dared not.

I thrust my whole hand into the flames.

The agony hit in an instant, but I held; I held, though I heard my cry go up to echo from the walls. My sleeve caught fire, and I heard flesh sizzle.

Mercutio's ghost wept.

My whole body shook, and I knew that I would die if I did not pull my hand back.

Better dead, I thought with absolute, cold clarity. *Better it ends here, with me, and she might live.*

Perhaps it was that release of my own selfish desire to

live that caused the rosary to finally let go its grip on my fingers and slip away to drop into the flames.

I drew my poor hand back and batted out the flames on my sleeve as I collapsed to the floor beside Juliet's perished nurse. I felt that same hell-borne heat of my grandmother's rooms pressing on me, through me, as if it meant to ignite me from bones out . . .

And then I felt it turn to ashes and dust, and all the terrible weight of it fled under the press of cool, still air.

The burning in my hand was gone. I turned my head and looked into the fire, and saw the rosary blackening, cracking apart, falling to ruins.

I lifted my hand and slowly clenched and unclenched the unburnt flesh, the unscarred fingers. Then I looked at Mercutio's shade, which still stood looking down on me.

And he smiled. It was the smile of my old friend, the smile of delight and mischief and glory. His lips shaped words, and I read them as if they were written on the air between us.

Love well, if not wisely.

And then he was gone.

I closed my eyes and struggled not to weep: for love of my friend, and for the loss of him, and Romeo, and innocents Juliet and Tomasso, and yes, even my sister, who in no way had been guiltless. For all of them, swept away on a senseless tide of grief.

Then I rose, wiped my face, and reached for the bedroom's locked door.

It shuddered against my hand, leaping against the lock, and I realised that, incredibly, the world in some ways had not changed. I was a Montague, intruding in a Capulet's rooms, with a woman lying dead beside me. There would be no quarter for me here. The door would give in one more blow, and I'd be taken and ripped apart out of their blind fury.

I ran to the balcony. Juliet's balcony, from which she'd listened so ardently to my cousin's declarations of love, and perhaps it had been love after all, true and wrongheaded, at least in the beginning, before the curse took its hold of them. Beneath, the garden was hushed and still, and only the fountain's gentle whisper stirred it.

The door splintered behind me with sudden violence.

I knew I could still win my way free. I jumped up to the balustrade, balancing there; it was an easy jump to soft ground, and a wall I'd climbed more often than I ought to ever confess. An easy escape in the confusion.

But I didn't want to escape.

I jumped for Rosaline's balcony instead.

It was a long way, and a standing jump instead of a running one, and even though I stretched as far as I could, my fingers only grazed the stone railing, and I knew I'd fall . . .

But something bore me up, just for a moment, and carried me those last vital inches, so that my hand wrapped around one of the stone braces beneath and stopped me, and when I looked down, I saw a shade there, limned cold in the moonlight as it broke through the clouds.

My beloved cousin Romeo. Only a last, wavering image of him, shivering like an illusion of heat.

His lips moved, though I heard no voice, and then he smiled, and where he had floated there was only mist rising into the night.

I scrambled up, vaulted over the balcony railing, and found the shutters closed. Shouting from within Juliet's room told me the servants had uncovered the nurse's body, and I quickly slipped my dagger between the wooden leaves of the shutters and raised the latch, and then I was inside Rosaline's apartment.

She was at the door, threading the key into the lock with shaking hands, and she whirled as the fresh breeze blew in to flap the curtains around me. The candle on the table guttered, but did not quite go out.

I stayed where I was, and she where she was, as if we tested ourselves.

'I feel . . .' She swallowed, and hugged herself hard. 'I feel cold. And very . . . very alone.'

I knew that. I felt the desolation, too, the sadness, but I knew that it was only the aftermath of that awful flame that had been lit between us; a passion like that, flaming so fast, could only scorch, not warm.

So I crossed the space between us and put my arms around her, and after a long heartbeat's pause, she sank against me, and rested her head upon my shoulder, and sighed a little in utter relief.

'What do you feel?' she asked me, in a quiet, muffled tone. She did not raise her head to meet my gaze.

'Grief,' I said, and stroked her hair. 'But grief passes.'

'And the two of us, will we also pass?' She was crying, but it was a silent thing; I felt the damp heat of her tears through my shirtsleeve, but she made no sound to betray it.

'No,' I said, and she lifted her head then, eyes shimmering and wet, and lips parted. 'I saw Mercutio's ghost a moment ago. And he spoke to me.'

'What did he say?'

'He said, "Love well, if not wisely",' I said. 'And I love you well, Capulet.'

Then I kissed her, and tasted tears and flowers, fear and hope, dread and dreams. Her lips were as soft and warm as the petals of a sun-heated rose, and something rose within me, a thing of fire and feathers, spreading wide wings. This was not wise, it was not politic, it was not sane, and yet I no longer cared for anything but the way she trembled when I touched her, and pressed so close to me. Not a curse, this feeling. A blessing.

Her lips held the sweetest and most intoxicating brew in the world, and I drank, and drank, and drank until I was dizzy with it, and her.

And so they found us, when they broke down the door, lost in that embrace.

I had been to Castelvecchio only twice in my life – once to be presented to Prince Escalus when I was only six years old, clumsy and fat in my finery, and once when I accompanied my cousin and uncle there for a feast.

This time, I was marched through the long, narrowing series of halls and doors, and the straight line of smaller and smaller arched doorways seemed as if I were being swallowed up by a giant beast of marble, stone, and plaster. Fine works of art glared at me from the walls, as if angered by the clatter of my passing – the jingle of my guards' swords and armour. I walked silently, and unarmed by so much as a dagger. Even my hands were firmly tied.

Following along at a distance came the Capulet family – the great man and his lady, and a heavily veiled and guarded Rosaline behind them. Somewhere in the distance, perhaps, my uncle might arrive, but by the weak, fragile light of this day, I was not sure he had the stomach for more grief.

I resigned myself that this trial would be mine alone. *Oh, Mercutio, is this your last laugh? Am I your final victim?* It might be both.

I felt weary, dirty, and hungry; they'd let me quench my thirst, but I still wore the clothes in which I'd been taken, and the apple I'd downed many hours ago had long since ceased to keep body and soul together. My head ached dully.

And oddly, I had never felt quite so fine in my life. 'I don't understand you,' said the guard at my right elbow; he was a talkative, amusing fellow, while the one at my left was as taciturn as a stone. 'Throwing away your life for a woman. You know the prince will exile you for this, on the Capulets' bitter complaints; he will not be disposed to aggravate their grief just now. And yet you smile!'

'I do,' I agreed.

'Why?'

'Because I am happy.'

He shook his head, and the chain mail lapping his neck made a slithering hiss, like a serpent preparing to strike. 'Fools are happy, young sir. Wise men are always sad.'

'Pray God I am never stricken with wisdom, then,' I said. 'The happiest men I ever knew were followers of folly. It was only when they were stopped from it that their lives turned grim.'

'Men were not made to be happy,' he said, my philosophical guard. 'Men were made to suffer and be made ready for the happiness of heaven.'

'A harsh sentence for the crime of birth.'

He shrugged. 'Life is not fair, young sir; if it were, I'd be swimming in gold and ale.'

'You already swim in ale,' said his less talkative companion, in a repressive rumble of a voice. 'Quiet. I'll not take your lumps for you.'

That must have been an effective warning, because we passed through the last two halls in silence. Servants stood off, watching as they cleaned; courtiers stopped their hushed conversations to turn and watch my progress.

And then we passed the final arched doorway into a large, square room floored in marble, with a single heavily carved chair upon a dais at the end of it. Prince Escalus was not in the chair; instead, he was standing at its foot, listening to an aged priest bending under the weight of his robes, and as we clanked to a halt ten feet from him, he nodded a dismissal to the man and straightened to regard me.

He looked tired, our prince; he'd had little enough sleep, and I could well imagine governing such an unruly city would take its toll on him. He still stood tall and strong, though, and he stared at me a moment before he turned with a swirl of his half cloak, climbed the steps, and settled himself in the throne.

'I will hear the tale,' he said.

It was, it seemed, not my place to tell it, as a smooth-faced courtier all dressed in black robes – a lawyer – stepped forward and bowed. 'My prince, in last evening's late uproar, an alarm was raised within the Capulet household while the lord and lady were absent. When servants answered this call, they found Juliet Capulet's nurse dead upon the floor, and this man – a Montague – in carnal embrace with young Rosaline Capulet, sister to slain Tybalt and cousin to poor Juliet.'

The prince nodded, eyes still fixed upon me. 'And who raised this alarm?'

'Rosaline Capulet, my lord.'

Put in such terms, it *did* sound damning. I looked behind me. The Capulets had formed a knot of red behind me, blocking the doorway, and Rosaline's uncle looked murderous daggers at me. Behind him, the veiled figure of Rosaline stood very still, breath stirring the fabric that shrouded her face.

'And was the nurse murdered, then?'

'Well, my prince, who can say? There were no marks upon her, but a strong young man may kill an old woman by smothering, or by choking—'

'Were there then marks of hands upon her throat?' Prince Escalus asked. He sounded only mildly interested. 'Or did her eyes show red?'

'Red, my prince?'

'A physician from Venezia gave a lecture – perhaps you might have attended it more closely – in which he said that one might tell a smothering by the telltale red stains left upon the eyes, as the veins burst within.'

The lawyer hesitated a moment, then bowed. 'You are most wise, Highness, but there were no such discolorings that I have been told, and no sign of hands upon her throat.'

'Then there is no evidence that the young man smothered or choked the woman, only that she is dead. There has been a plague of death upon this town of recent days, and almost all within three houses: Ordelaffi, Capulet, and Montague.

I understand Benvolio's aunt expired in the night. Shall we suspect him of that murder as well?' The prince waved away the lawyer's response before it was delivered. 'No, the crux of the matter is that Rosaline Capulet raised an alarm. Why?'

'The villain was breaking her door, my prince,' Capulet said, and stepped forward. 'To save her most precious honour, she screamed for aid, and aid was given, but not before this wretch slipped outside, came through her balcony, and began his assault, which was thankfully incomplete.'

The prince's eyebrows rose, though his face showed little else. He turned his attention back to me. 'I do not see your uncle,' he said. 'Is there no one to speak for you, Benvolio?'

'I can speak for myself, my prince.'

'Then do so,' he said, and leant back with his arms on the carved lion's-head armrests of the throne. 'I attend.'

'I must go back, with your patience, to the death of a young man hanged outside these walls . . .'

I told the story, then, of Tomasso and Mercutio. I ignored the cries of protest from those who felt the tale too perverse for the fragile ears of the ladies, and grimly went on with it, to describe the anguish of Mercutio, his fury, and finally, his curse. 'Romeo had never clapped eyes upon the Capulet maiden Juliet until he saw her at the feast where the Capulets would celebrate her betrothal to Count Paris,' I said. 'Is it then sensible that he formed such a close attachment that he would marry her in only days? Or that he would linger in Verona past his exile to stay in her embrace, when he knew well his life was forfeit? Mercutio's lover was ripped from him, and he wished to visit that horror upon those he saw as guilty – to make them feel that love, and that terrible loss.'

'If there is a curse, it follows there must be a witch,' Prince Escalus said. His brows had lowered again, into a frown now, and he rested his chin upon one closed fist. 'Can you produce her?'

I heard a bustle from behind me, and as I turned to look, I spotted the bulk of Friar Lawrence pushing through with whispered apologies. He held up his hand as he came forward. 'Your Highness, the witch is gone, but I can attest that I heard her speak of this curse to young Benvolio,' he said. He had clearly run a long way to be here; his face shone with sweat, and his body trembled as he sucked down whoops of air. I had never been so glad to see his merry face, even if it looked not so merry at this moment. 'Benvolio set out to break the curse; I am sure of it. It is a sad truth that he was too late for his cousin Romeo and the poor child Juliet, who lay together in death, making it a bridal tomb. And too late also for your poor cousin Paris, who did no one any ill in this matter, but only stood between the lovers and so died for it.'

'This curse matters not in what the Capulets charge,' Prince Escalus said, and fixed that broody gaze on me once more. 'Were you then in the Capulets' palace, Benvolio?'

'I was.'

'Came you there upon anyone's invitation?'

'No.'

'Did you knock upon Rosaline's locked door and try to enter?'

There was no help for it. 'Yes.'

'Did you then scale to her balcony and enter in that way?'

'Yes.'

'And did the Capulets truly find you in carnal embrace of this girl?'

'In embrace, yes,' I said. I could not rightly call it wholly carnal. There was too much of heaven in it.

'Then what possible defence do I consider? You agree to the plain facts of the complaint against you. You trespassed, and you compromised the honour of the Capulet girl. You are lucky indeed that the door fell to their servants when it did, or your penalty would be much harsher—'

'Wait!' There was a struggle behind me, surprised and distressed cries, and then a veil settled to the floor like a cloud as Rosaline struggled against her aunt's grasping hands. 'My prince, wait! Let me be heard!'

The lawyer stepped forward, shaking his head, and said, in a low voice, 'My prince, this is not proper. The girl is bound for the convent, and women have no place to speak here!'

'Then there is no harm to her soul in letting her speak, nor to us in lending our ears,' Prince Escalus said, and gestured towards the Capulets. 'Let her come forward.'

I drank in the sight of her as she pulled free of her family's protection and stepped out to walk the distance alone. She was straight-backed and unafraid, head held high, and she exchanged with me a long, warm glance before settling gracefully into a low curtsy before the prince.

He bade her rise, and said, 'What have you to add, then, my lady?'

'Benvolio Montague did not try to force my door,' she said. 'I do not ask you to understand what occurred between us, but there *was* a curse, my prince, and it *was* working upon us both; even so, even with the madness of black magic driving him to me, he did not offer me any violence, nor any insult. I screamed to protect him, sir, and not to damn him.'

'Ho, this is a turn.' The prince sat up straight, and a buzz of whispers ran through the crowd – so many, I had not realised. They'd been slipping in quietly behind me, and now half the notables of Verona were gathered to see. 'How so?'

'To drive him away ere I opened that door myself, so bespelled by the curse was I,' she said. 'And to force him to find the object that fixed the curse upon us. Which he did, in Juliet's rooms, and so shattered the evil.' She took in a slow, steady breath, and said, 'I confess that we did kiss, Your Highness, but there was nothing of violence offered from it, and nothing but sweet comfort, for I love him, sir. I know he is the enemy of my house; I know that rivers of blood lie between our two families. But surely the deaths of our dear cousins must, in shared grief, work to end that anger.' She turned on her uncle and her aunt. 'Did you not say that at the tombs you wept, and so did Montague? That the taste of this feud lay bitter on your tongues?'

'But—'

'She is right.' A new voice, and an oddly frail one; my uncle's normal strength was gone, and he leant heavily upon his cane, and upon the arm of my mother, who stood beside him. 'I have promised to raise a statue to the honour of young Juliet, and so Capulet has also sworn to honour my fallen Romeo. Are we then to deny a living love, whilst honouring a dead one?'

I searched my mother's face for any trace of anger, but she smiled at me, and through her tears I saw a real and genuine happiness.

And then came the dreaded tapping of a cane, and the crowd swirled and parted in frantic haste, for tottering into the room, much supported by her anxious attendants, came the Iron Lady, my grandmother. She wore black, and all the layers of velvet and lace and veils made her look a charred corpse. Her face was eerily white, and her filmed eyes roamed the room, marking enemies, and settled their fiercest gaze upon me.

'Traitor to your blood and your line,' she spat, and raised her cane. 'Half-blooded unnatural thing! My curse upon you, fool boy – look you, my prince, upon the face of that villain you've sought all these years, who foxed your guards and defied your edicts. Look you upon that lawless wretch, the Prince of Shadows!' She stamped the metal-shrouded butt end of the cane upon the marble, with enough force I thought the stone might crack, and the impact rang through the room like the tolling of a death bell. Shock waves went through it, and faces turned towards me, and then towards the prince. Half of those here had been victims of my crimes, and they waited only upon his reaction to cry my neck into a noose.

Prince Escalus, in turn, looked to Montague and my mother. I held out no hopes. For too long, my grandmother had terrorised our house; she had ruled with fear and hatred, and driven us all before her like leaves in a storm.

But now my uncle straightened his back and said, 'My apologies to you, good prince, but my mother is unwell. Her mind has wandered these past few weeks, and she sees threats and phantoms everywhere, as the frail and elderly sometimes do. I beg you, pay no heed to her wild fancies. We will tend to all her needs in our home, and see that she never spreads such wicked lies again.'

Her mouth gaped open, and the dumb surprise on my grandmother's face was so remarkable that I thought I might spoil it with laughter. Had she ever in her life been so directly contradicted? And by *him?*

My mother curtsied to the prince and said, 'My lord, I will take her home, with your kind permission. She is not enough in her wits to be seen here.'

'There's nothing wrong with my mind!' my grandmother spat, and shook her cane hard at the prince. 'You vile English whore, you weak-bellied coward of a son, I tell you my grandnephew is—'

'See she is well cared for,' the prince interrupted. 'And that she is neither seen nor heard from this day forward.'

'My lord,' my mother said. She snapped her fingers at Grandmother's attendants, and they closed around her feebly struggling body, like black-clad ants, and bore her away, still protesting.

My mother followed, and I thought that I could almost see the mantle of leadership settle from the old woman's shoulders to hers as my mother took charge of House Montague.

A new day, indeed.

'My guards swear to me that the Prince of Shadows is dead,' Prince Escalus said. His gaze had fallen back upon me, weighty with significance. 'I think we'll see no more of him now. And with the Lady Rosaline's testimony, I find no weight to a Capulet claim that Benvolio came uninvited to her, nor that her honour was much compromised by it. Now we have funerals, and a glooming peace this morning has brought. The sun, for sorrow, will not show its head today, and so we will go to have more talk of these sad things.' For the first time, then there was a hint of a smile at the corners of his mouth. 'But tomorrow, perhaps, there will be sun, and a lifting of gloom, and a different tale, of two warring houses brought together at last not in grief, but in some measure of joy. Now clasp hands, Benvolio, with your Rosaline. She is not meant for a convent; nor are you meant for a prison house. Go and soothe your family's ills, and tomorrow we will speak of happier things.'

I turned to her, and before I could reach out to her she was reaching to me, both our hands joining and twining, and Prince Escalus was wrong, after all, for just then the sun came spilling in through the window, and in its glow I felt the warmth of a blessing – from Romeo, and Juliet, and Mercutio, and Tomasso, and all the lovers lost.

And in her smile, her glorious and lovely smile, we were lovers found at last.

EXEUNT

TRACK LIST

It was a bit of a struggle to come up with appropriate tracks for *Prince of Shadows* . . . I always turn to music to help set the mood for me in my writing, and I didn't want a completely classical sound, but something edgier and more modern. So I present to you the songs and musicians I chose to help immerse me in the period and the characters, and I hope you enjoy them as much as I have. Please help the musicians continue to produce great and interesting art – buy their work.

'The Mummers' Dance'	Loreena McKennitt
'Warrior'	Wishbone Ash
'Hymn to Pan'	Faun
'Nummus'	Helium Vola
'Star of the Sea'	Mediaeval Baebes
'Man of the Hour'	Falconer
'Mark Hur Var Skagga'	Mediaeval Baebes
'Unda'	Faun
'La Serenissima'	Loreena McKennitt

ACKNOWLEDGMENTS

Besides the props already offered to Seanan McGuire and Tybalt the cat, I have to thank Melissa Marr for listening to this crazy idea and reading the first (very bad) draft of the original chapter . . . and still encouraging me in this risky venture. You're the best, Melissa.

Lucienne Diver and Anne Sowards had so much faith in this project, and so much enthusiasm, and it wouldn't have gotten done without their encouragement and support. And Kami Garcia: Lady, you just rock. Thanks for the love. Sarah Weiss and Janet Cadsawan also gave me much love and support and excitement about this project, as did NiNi Burkart.

Thanks also to the amazing Eloisa James for her recommendation, and to the kick-ass John Ziegler for casting a careful Shakespearean scholarly eye over what I'd done to the Bard, and not weeping (at least, where I could hear him).

And last, thanks to Mr William Shakespeare for making me love the English language even more than I already did.

ALSO BY RACHEL CAINE

The Morganville Vampires series

The **DEAD GIRLS Dance**

Midnight ALLEY

Feast of FOOLS

Lord of MISRULE

Carpe CORPUS

Fade OUT

KISS of DEATH

Ghost TOWN

BITE CLUB

Last BREATH

BLACK DAWN

BITTER Blood

Fall of Night

DAYLIGHTERS